LOST AND PLOOGLITLESS

IAN AISCH

ZYGOL PRESS

LOST AND PLOOGLITLESS

Ian Aisch

ZYGOL PRESS

Lost and Plooglitless by Ian Aisch

Copyright © 2020 Evan Jones

Print ISBN: 978-0-6487008-1-4

Zygol Press

21 Barbara Street Woodend, Victoria, Australia 3442

1

—————

FUGITIVE

ROSS BLAKEY COULD RUN NO MORE. He gasped for breath, and wiped rivulets of sweat from his forehead. He swore. There was a sliver of welcome shade at the foot of a steep, craggy hillock. He sought it, dropping heavily on to the stone-littered ground. The ruddy orange-grey landscape he surveyed was pockmarked by dumps of gravel, rocks and boulders, a dry and shallow gully and low, fractured, rock-strewn hillocks. Rising above was a long irregular plateau, furrowed by vertical fissures, carved by rain or landslides. Shielding his eyes from the alien orange sun, to his right, he could make out the upper portion of the Second Faceless Man, a feature of lighter rock exposed by an avalanche. The larger, First Faceless Man was hidden behind a jagged hill. The two formations looked down on the compound where Earth contractors mined minerals from the sand and gravel-strewn desert of Zygol III and sent the partly refined ore to planet Earth through the Chute. The residue came back the same route.

Blakey figured he was safe. If he wasn't, he'd have to get on his knees and plead for mercy. He had stuffed up bad. He'd drunk way too much of his flask of whisky, all the while breathing the distortive vapours of the Swamp. It had addled his brain.

His wild, panicked dash had begun in speckled light, thrusting out his arms to crash through the encroaching vegetation. He'd disturbed a perched pair of vulture-like chageen with their large, blood-red eyes; they'd hissed at him as they slowly flapped away. Twice he'd leapt across narrow creeks. The lush vegetation had quickly given way to chest-high, blue-tinged, gnarly plants and bushes, and the sandy puddles of a stream bed.

Panting, snatching frantic glances behind him, Blakey plunged through thigh-high coarse bushes that cut at his legs. He clawed his way up from gullies and dry, stony creek beds, cursing, until he bent over, exhausted, at the edge of the desert.

At twenty-nine, Ross Blakey was tall and lean with thick, dark hair that touched the nape of his neck. He wore the uniform of the mining company: a brown cotton, short-sleeved shirt with its prominent green-and-red logo; loose, dark-brown pants; ankle-high boots.

His still-whirling mind managed to tick over a cog. The compound was on the opposite side of Channen village. Awkward. Getting to his sanctuary through the village came with a major risk. He'd have to pass close to Zglta's hut. When Zglta went ballistic, Blakey had stuttered, palms out. "Let me explain..." But she was in no mood to listen. He would only have blustered, anyway. He'd been a bastard. Simple as that. Never had he seen such fury. He turned to run; she blocked his path. Blakey took off the opposite direction. One problem averted… a great big, new one now confronted him.

In the desert, Blakey managed to disentangle two options: either wait until dark and sneak past Zglta's hut, or take the rougher, more time-consuming route, following the plateau to the compound's rarely used north entrance.

Either way, if all went well, he'd be tucked in his bed before midnight. He'd get on the next Chute jump back to Earth.

The afternoon was cloudless. Good. For, later, the Zygol night sky would hold twice as many stars as the Earth sky. Also, Zygol III had two moons. He would most likely find some water at the base of the plateau to quench his raging thirst.

But his luck ended there.

The mining company forbade taking any device outside its gates.

Not even a watch. Or a torch. That left him with no communicator and no stun gun. The communicator would have been useless anyway; rescue was impossible. No vehicle was permitted beyond the fenced perimeter, and a search party on foot was equally forbidden. Not having a stun gun was a huge drawback; ravenous predators lurked in the rocky desert. These predators generally steered clear of the villages, which were guarded by outposts of armed aktel. Guards. Yet the animals sometimes encroached. Worse, he now sat beyond any guarded outpost. There would be embarrassing questions to answer back at the compound, but that was the least of Blakey's worries. Besides, he would be sacked regardless.

To think that the day had begun so very pleasantly. Attached to the mining compound is a self-contained fenced-off area, the size of a tennis court, located a forty-minute walk from Channen village. This area is dubbed the Airlock. The Zygols and mining employees meet there to sort out any issues that arise. But, mostly, it was where the mining company paid the Zygols their (absurdly cheap) monthly dues for rental of a segment of barren, stony desert. Payment is mostly by Earth-manufactured goods such as simple farming and kitchen implements or ornaments. But no devices. The goods are transported to one of the Three Villages, or beyond, on the broad backs of beasts that have the bulk, but are longer than a bull, called uckliablahts. These beasts have six legs (the upper two being shorter, thinner, and more dexterous—more like claws—than the other four). Uckliablahts are short-haired animals, brown or black in colour, and somewhat resembled a camel, hippopotamus, gorilla and a hyena—only totally different.

The delivery of goods to the Zygols is presided over by one of the compound's senior managers, in the company of an interpreter. The latter was usually the geologist, Ross Blakey. Blakey had been keenly anticipating the morning's meeting; Zglta would be coming. Zglta, as with all Zygols, could be mistaken for someone of mixed Asian heritage. She and her male companion wore typical Zygol garb: knee-length tunics (in their case, orange; his was plain; hers had a green triangular pattern at the front) and uckliablaht-hide sandals.

'Would you like me to take you to the Swamp after we finish our transaction?' Zglta had a glint in her eye. 'You enjoy being there a lot, I believe.' The Swamp is where low-lying, sodden and rotting vegetation gives off vapours that bring about a pleasant lightness of mind.

'I would love to come. Thank you for your invitation. I have a flask of Earth whisky in my pocket, which you enjoyed last time. I was hoping you'd invite me.'

'What is she saying?' pressed the mining manager.

There was a reason why Blakey did not offer language lessons to his fellow miners. 'She is asking me if I want to check out a new farm located between two of the Three Villages. We might be able to get some useful produce if the farm does well, especially if we get more of the leaves the Zygols use as medicinal bandages. I said I'd go. I wouldn't like to risk insulting her by saying no.'

The manager stroked his chin. 'I'm uncomfortable about you going off compound again, Ross. But we don't want to be rude after you've been given an invitation. The farm sounds interesting. Ask her if I can come, too.'

Blakey nodded. 'Zglta; look at my companion. Make a serious face and shake your head.'

She did so. Her male companion smiled. Hopefully, the mining manager was oblivious to why.

'As you can see, sir, the answer is no. Sorry.' Blakey shrugged. 'Zygols get nervous about Earth people being away from the compound. They even get nervous about me, whom they know better than anyone.'

The last thing Blakey wanted was anyone else getting out of the compound. Someone might work out what he got up to on his visits to Channen village.

A few hours later, Ross Blakey's pleasant little existence caved in.

IT WAS PAST MID-AFTERNOON. No time to dwell on the perils he faced if he opted for the desert route. Zygol III's predators—the most dangerous being the large ravenous cfaldi—did most of their hunting after sundown. When he'd fled Zglta, the risk of getting devoured hadn't registered in Blakey's heaving mind. But with the fog beginning to lift from his head, anxiety began seeping through the crevices. With some trepidation, he stood and made his way with soft tread, through the rugged landscape, following the line of the plateau, his ears alert for any sign of danger. The air was still. His breath was heavier than he wished it to be.

After perhaps fifteen minutes of hesitant progress, Blakey stopped.

Many large boulders and hillocks stood in his path—too many places for predators to lie in ambush. He delved into his swirling mind. No. He'd hide near Channen village and wait until dark.

After backtracking a few steps, he froze. Heavy, hoofed steps were approaching. Blakey gasped. He conjured a chilling vision of huge, dagger-like teeth tearing apart his chest, with blood, flesh and bones exploding everywhere. A cfaldi. Sucking quick, gulping breaths, his spine quivering, skin tingling, Blakey scrambled to huddle behind a low curtain of rock, his hand clasped over his mouth. If cfaldi had a keen sense of smell or hearing, then... Cfaldi are black and big—at times two metres tall—and somewhat resemble a werewolf. Their wolf-like heads are filled with long, very sharp teeth. Cfaldi usually walk on their massive hind legs but are equally adept when on all four. They also have two, short upper arms that sport massive claws. Truly nasty, very nasty animals.

Blakey silently cursed he hadn't taken his chances with Zglta. She had much smaller teeth. Heck. Zygols are usually easy-going. Not if you behaved like a bastard, obviously.

Something swift bounded above his refuge, clawing at the rock. Blakey dropped onto his backside in shock. Then he tapped his forehead against the rock-face. It was only a lemur-like plooglit, the size of a young greyhound with the same speed and agility. Its claws made it adept at climbing and digging. More importantly, the animal was harmless. Not only that, out in these desolate parts, a plooglit would almost invariably be in the company of an uckliablaht. And uckliablahts are also harmless unless one of the hulking beasts stepped on your foot. For an uckliablaht to be this far from vegetation, there was a good chance it had a rider—an armed rider. As long as it wasn't Zglta…

Trembling, Blakey peered out. Realising he faced no danger, he took a breath and stepped boldly from his hiding spot to gaze at a puzzled rotund Zygol male atop an uckliablaht. The startled Zygol pulled up his steed and examined Blakey, then rode cautiously up to him. Behind the long saddle were two large, bulging sacks tied on opposite sides on the beast's flanks. The immature green-brown plooglit cavorted around the uckliablaht, dashing hither and thither seemingly without purpose, as plooglits do. Blakey felt mightily relieved. Much-needed help might be in the offing.

'Who are you?' the Zygol demanded, eyeing Blakey closely. In Earth terms, he looked to be in his mid-fifties with his creased, leathery face and thinning black hair liberally sprinkled with streaks of grey. He wore the grey smock of a servant.

'I'm an Earthman heading back to my compound.'

The man leaned forward and spoke rapidly. 'Then you are taking a difficult route. It is best reached by going through the village. The path is to your right.'

'Thank you for the bearings.'

The Zygol leaned his head to the right with an almost imperceptible nod. The action was a Zygol sign of understanding or agreement, often given when a person did not wish to be heard. 'It is strange that you are in a place where cfaldi are known to dwell. But that is incidental now. How can it be that an Earthman is not in his fenced village?'

'I have permission.'

'Your presence here is permitted? I thought otherwise. Why have you come to this place?' The Zygol sounded impatient.

'What are *you* doing here?' Blakey countered, irritated by the Zygol's tone. Surprisingly, the rider appeared to be unarmed should a cfaldi attack.

'It is no business of yours,' the Zygol growled. 'You display poor manners. And you... you are but a visitor, in a place where it is not wise to be.' Then the Zygol did something strange. He turned away and although he couldn't tell for sure, Blakey had a definite feeling the Zygol was directing hand signals towards some boulders. He faced Blakey once more. 'You speak Zygol.'

'Fairly well. I'm good at picking up languages. Some of your people gave me lessons. Even when I hear words I don't understand, I can usually make out what is being said.'

'I have heard talk of an Earthman who speaks Zygol a little. You must be him. Do you understand Zygol hand signals?'

'Hardly any. But I'd very much like to—'

'Good.' Blakey's admission brought a broad smile to the rider's face. So skilled are Zygols that they can hold two entirely different lines of conversation—one using hand signals—at the same time.

Observing the Zygol's apparent communication with a boulder, Blakey rolled his eyes.

'Are you running away from aktel?' The rider peered nervously in the direction from which Blakey had come.

'Guards? No, I'm not running from aktel.' The Zygol's abruptness was annoying him. 'Are you running away from anyone? You look worried.'

The Zygol glowered, then smirked. 'Oho, Earthman. You are here, unarmed, where cfaldi may lurk. Either you are a fool, and I can readily believe that, or you have done something wrong. Very likely both. Tell me if you are a fugitive. You *must.*' His sour face reflected his derision.

Blakey shrugged. 'I have not done anything violent. What about you?'

The Zygol muttered something under his breath. 'If I had committed a violent act, I would have told you immediately! Why are you in this place, Earthman? I do not wish to dwell.'

Blakey thought to fess up. Maybe the Zygol could offer him some advice, or better, guide him to safety. 'I did something stupid, and I made a very nice Zygol woman very angry with me. I tried to apologise. But she—'

The briefest smile spread across the Zygol's face. 'Does this woman feel the cold for you?'

'No. She doesn't love me. We are alien to one another in too many ways, and besides, we have few opportunities to spend time together.'

The Zygol grunted. 'How badly did you anger this woman? Did she threaten to cut off your balls and feed them to a cfaldi?'

Blakey stiffened in surprise. 'Close. She yelled that she was going to feed my bones to a cfaldi. She had something metallic in her hand. I wasn't about to find out what it was.'

'Oho. You *are* in trouble, Earthman.' The Zygol sat up. 'If it's any consolation, a very sincere apology, perhaps brokered by a mediator, usually sets things right. Usually. Importantly, you must promise never to do whatever you did again. Besides, it would be apparent to your lady friend that you are liable to do foolish things. I knew that the instant you uttered your first words. But it is vital you make your apology as soon as possible. You must endure the harsh words she will say, which is what her threat really conveys. Usually. Any delay would seriously compound your mistake. Take too long and she might well become much angrier.'

'Thanks. I'll try to find a mediator. And, hopefully, put things right. Are you going to Channen village? Anywhere in the Three Villages will do.'

The Zygol spoke gruffly. 'Your manners are... It is no business of yours where I am going. Answer this: how strong is your commitment to the six elements?'

'The six elements. Let me think... From memory, there are some fine qualities there.' Zglta had explained them to him. He had probably jotted down those he remembered afterwards, but at the time, he was preoccupied.

The rotund Zygol looked upon Blakey with disdain. 'If you are not bound by them, you will journey with me until I allow otherwise.'

Blakey stood with his hands on his hips and laughed. '*You* are commanding me? Is this some sort of a joke? Why should I comply?'

'Earthman; you must have seen us. And we cannot take the chance of you telling others that you saw us. That means you must journey with me until I say you can go. We leave now.'

Us? Him and his boulder? This haywire day was lurching towards the weird. 'Oh, you think so, do you? Well... I'm not coming with you. I need to go and apologise to my lady friend, like you said.'

'Earthman, there will be dire consequences if you do not come with me.'

Ross Blakey figured that the rotund man could not beat him in a fight. And, should Blakey flee, it would be easy to clamber over rocks that the uckliablaht could not negotiate. 'I'm leaving now, but not with you. Happy travels.' Blakey gave a wry smile.

He turned to leave and found the point of a kraxl-da—a short, broad sword—uncomfortably close to his nose. At the other end of the blade were two intense green eyes that belonged to a woman, the likes of which he had never seen before. She was lithe but strong, perfectly proportioned and as tall as he was. Her brown hair hung loosely over her bare shoulders. This apparition of an Amazon was clothed in a green tank-top-style garment and green shorts that extended half-way down her thighs, with both garments partly covered by a gossamer wrap of the same colour. From her belt hung a kraxl—a dagger with a thin blade. Blakey had seen off-duty aktel dressed in their crimson tunics before; some sported weapons. There was no way this Zygol was merely an aktel. This had to be a fully fledged warrior.

'Who is she?' Blakey asked the rotund rider as he raised his hands in surrender.

'If you don't know, it is none of your business. We must—'

'But I—'

'We go now! If you refuse, you die. Here.'

Blakey's jaw dropped. 'How about if I promise not to tell anyone that I've seen you? I don't even know who you are.'

The Zygol glared at Blakey with cold eyes. 'No! We cannot trust someone who has no commitment to the six elements. Come or die!' The female's snarl behind the pointed kraxl-da made Blakey flinch. The Zygols' threat clear, he had no choice.

'Okay. Okay. Which way?' Blakey sensed he was in big trouble. 'But promise you'll let me go soon. You'll do that, won't you?'

He received no reply. The rider prodded the uckliablaht into movement. His tall and lithe companion waved her kraxl-da, her steely gaze as intimidating as her weapon.

Blakey was led diagonally up the plateau. He trailed along, shaking his head in bewilderment. Forlornly, he kept glancing behind him. He could only sigh. Dotted about were a few narrow pathways up the plateau; the Zygols ignored these. Instead, they chose a boulder-and scree-strewn route through a long-ago avalanche.

From time to time, the rider shared hand signals with his companion who took the lead, though she kept to one side and often disappeared. She moved up the uneven ground with breathtaking ease. The energetic plooglit dashed about hither and thither. The rider turned to Blakey. 'Realise that you have no status with us. That may be to your benefit.'

'How is it to my benefit?'

'I will tell you nothing.' He sighed. 'You are rude and ill-disciplined! You have no status. Be satisfied with that.'

Blakey was miffed. 'No, I refuse. I demand to know what you intend to do with me. Are you going to let me loose in cfaldi country?' He received only a withering look. 'Will you give me food and water? Can I ask that?'

'Yes, I will,' sneered the rider. 'But no more questions. You annoy me greatly. For now; keep up.'

'What? You force me to come with you on the threat of death and won't tell me why. And you say that it's *me* who's annoying *you.*'

The Zygol twirled his raised index finger above his head. 'Dze... dze... dze.' The sign for "I don't give a damn." 'Why didn't she kill you, Earthman? You will only slow us down. Unfortunately, she dislikes killing, she does. Even when she is attacked by a cfaldi, she scares it away by injuring it. I acknowledge that it is the Zygol way to care for all creatures. And it is right that it is so. But there are times... when we come across a creature that is so obviously... damaged beyond help… that it is surely kindness to put it out of its misery.' He looked at Blakey with contempt. 'And here you are; insufferable. I say this to you again: I have no obligation to tell you anything. You have no status.'

A puffing Ross Blakey whistled. 'This is madness. Let me go. I'll go straight to my compound, the dangerous way. I'll take my chances with the cfaldi.'

'I wish with all my being for you to be gone. But no. You must come with us.' The two men glared at one another.

On they pressed, up the plateau with Blakey often having to run or clamber to keep up. He envied the plooglit, which dashed about with seemingly endless energy. To his frustration, when the trekkers came across a pathway or an uncluttered slope, the Zygols veered in the opposite direction. From time to time, the rider sent hand signals to nowhere in particular—no doubt to where the warrior was.

Three-quarters of the way to the top of the plateau, Blakey was parched and struggling to keep up. 'I'm really thirsty. Can we stop for a short drink break?'

To Blakey's astonishment, the Zygol didn't admonish him. Instead, he sent another hand signal, grimaced, and dismounted. Also, to Blakey's surprise, the warrior appeared some fifty metres away and came bounding towards them, moving with easy grace. She leaped effortlessly over fissures and clambered over boulders and steep ridges, as if she were a panther in human form.

The rider brought out an ahk (a human-torso-sized container of uckliablaht hide) from a saddle pack as well as three clundrns to drink from. As the three slaked their thirst, Blakey sat to examine the woman's face. She glared back at him. Rather than being a great beauty, it was her easy confidence and dignity that struck him.

'I'm just fetching water.' He backed away. He seriously didn't want to anger a woman that fought off cfaldi.

'We go now,' the Zygol male pronounced. The look on the warrior's face made it clear that, yes, it was indeed time to go. As the rider hastily packed away the ahk and clundrns, the warrior bounded off and vanished. Blakey figured it wise to do as he was told. She didn't believe in killing. That made his strategy simple: stay alive. Get to the compound. Somehow. Zygols are hospitable; they wouldn't dump him in the middle of nowhere when they were done with him. If he was set free above the Second Faceless Man, he could climb down to the compound under starlight. For the Zygols would surely head towards the distant verdant hills and not into the harsh desert plain.

In the meantime, Blakey would seek to improve his now-obvious, horribly inadequate knowledge of Zygols. *If* he could. Sure, the first arrivals from Earth encountered problems with these seemingly relaxed locals, but he figured those disagreements were caused by an ignorance of the local language. Now he wasn't sure. All things considered, though, he was in reasonably good hands with what had to be a capable protector and a supply of food and water.

The Zygol steered his uckliablaht with what appeared to be a system of hand and foot coordination directed at the great beast's shoulders and flank. While the animal had a thick rope tied around its neck, this seemed to be used more for the rider to keep balance. When heading in the desired direction, the Zygol grasped one of the saddle's two short horns and gave the steed its head. To Blakey's surprise, although the uckliablaht protested from time to time as it encountered a tricky obstacle, it showed itself to be surprisingly adept at traversing through the rugged countryside, moving steadily even through rough parts—sometimes using its front claws. Ross Blakey, however, struggled to keep up. Eliciting the considerable chagrin of the rider.

TWILIGHT WAS FAST APPROACHING. Even though Blakey, as a geologist, was no stranger to climbing up hills, the relentless pace had his legs protesting, and he sported grazes on both knees. The laden uckliablaht was also visibly tiring. Still the traverse continued. At times, the Zygol rider dismounted to clamber awkwardly for a short distance, holding the steed's tether. The energetic plooglit continued to dash about haphazardly, sometimes leaping on the back of the uckliablaht.

Hmmmmmmmmmm it cooed, seemingly in contentment. Then it bounded off again.

The Zygols were in a hurry and wanted to stay out of sight. They had to be on the run.

At last, the group reached—with Blakey stumbling—the top of the plateau, which extended out in the shape of a wide, crooked Y. One fork stretched past the Faceless Men and into the distance to meld into a mountain range flanked by expanses of greenery. The other sloped downwards past bare, isolated hills and dry gullies, and closer to the horizon, out to a vast orange desert.

To Ross Blakey's consternation, the Zygols turned towards the desert.

'You can't be going that way,' Blakey wailed as he sank to his knees.

No answer. But the warrior drifted before him and lifted the hilt of her kraxl.

'What if I...' Blakey pointed feebly in the direction of the Faceless Men. The look on her face was a clear answer. Hungry and annoyed, Ross Blakey dragged himself onto his feet and trudged behind them. Again, the Zygols chose the most rugged route they could possibly plot. At least they were going downhill. A warm desert breeze blew into his face—a harbinger of what was to come. Not long after, the breeze picked up. Soon, the three were pushing hard into a howling wind that flung stinging grit into their faces and onto exposed arms and legs. Blakey's protestations, as did those of the uckliablaht, were drowned in the roaring onslaught.

With her hair billowing, the warrior bounded over to the rider. The two donned bandana-like face coverings and eye hoods. The warrior also wrapped a heavy shawl across her bare shoulders. Rystyn threw a set of face coverings at the trailing, muttering Blakey. After fumbling about, he worked out how to put them on, despite the buffeting. Hand signals followed, but the three pressed on, the female staying close.

Dusk transformed the sky into an orange-purple haze. Blakey threw a stone against a rock-face in front of the rotund Zygol to get his attention; his captor took no notice. Not long after, they reached a wedge-shaped vertical fissure in a twin-peaked, rocky hillock that offered protection from the wind and swirling grit. The two Zygols paused; exchanged hand signals.

'We will camp here,' the rider called out to Blakey. The Earthman sank to his knees in relief.

'How do you expect me to get back to my compound now?' They had to be close to the desert plain. He was ignored.

Their rough and upwardly sloping wedge-shaped sanctuary of bare rock was no more than fifteen metres long, and at its entrance, about five metres wide. High above them, the air was turbulent, tossed about by the hill's wind shadow. In gloomy contemplation, Blakey dropped onto the stony ground. The warrior sat beside an outcrop of rock at a vantage point above the encampment. There, she had to be exposed to some of the swirling grit. The other Zygol untied his sacks from the back of the uckliablaht and prepared a fire by rubbing together two fire sticks beside some thin logs.

Blakey slammed his fist painfully against a boulder beside him. 'Tell me! How do you expect me to get back to my compound?'

The Zygol sighed. 'Be quiet! You have no status.'

'Then give me status and tell me what's happening.'

'No! You will not be given status.'

'Why not?' Blakey stood up, furious.

The two men glowered at one another, their fists clenched. 'Because you have no status!' The Zygol stormed off. Muttering, he took a large pot and some small pouches out of one of his sacks. 'Sit over that way,' he growled with a flick of his hand. 'Your presence is intolerable.'

Blakey examined the entrance to their sanctuary. Beyond was dark, swirling dust. 'No way. I've been told that the further someone sits from a fire at night, the greater the chance of being taken by a cfaldi.'

'You've been told that?'

'Yes, I have. So I'm staying right here.'

'Please yourself,' the Zygol said, sighing. 'But consider that a plooglit has an excellent sense of smell. It will most likely alert its companion uckliablaht, and us, if a cfaldi approaches. If it does not, it is far more likely to become a meal for a cfaldi because of how it wanders as it does.'

The Zygol began cooking. He tossed handfuls of grain into a pot of steaming water. Although the fire was fed only by two small and thin logs, the flames gave off surprising heat. A short time later, he approached the warrior in her small cavity in the rock-face. Her indifference infuriated Blakey as much as the cook's rudeness.

This time, she actually spoke in whispers with the cook, who returned to battle with the stubborn uckliablaht for prime position in their protected space. He managed to push the protesting animal roughly aside. The beast then settled down uncomfortably close to Blakey, who felt it wise to move across a few paces as the uckliablaht spread itself. When the Zygol offered a pail of water and a pile of vines and green branches, the beast seemed to relax. The plooglit did as plooglits do; it leaped up and down the rocks and jumped on (Hmmmmmmmmmm) and off the uckliablaht. Once, it leapt over a cursing Blakey's lap.

Blakey found himself in the least-desirable, rock-strewn and uncomfortable spot near the edge of the sanctuary. Yet he managed a smile. 'So; Rystyn,' he announced as the Zygol stirred the contents of the pot.

The Zygol froze, then looked up, stunned.

'You thought the wind would drown out your little discussion but, at times, your voices were amplified. Your name is Rystyn. And you're a cook. Also a guide I think.' Blakey grinned. He basked in his delicious crumb of knowledge.

Rystyn simmered but was silent. He abruptly turned his back on Blakey and tended to the evening meal.

Blakey savoured his tasty little victory. 'She's too good to sit with the likes of us, eh?'

Rystyn bristled. 'You are the most ignorant fool I have ever had the displeasure to meet. It is impossible to attempt elapelc with you.'

'Ah yes, elapelc,' Blakey mused. 'Even though it's a fundamental part of Zygol culture and psyche, my Zygol friend, Zglta, found it difficult to explain the concept to me. I've written a report on it. It goes like this: elapelc deals with how two or more people consciously or unconsciously come to agreement, compromise or acceptance, even if it takes time. Zglta believes people are born innately with elapelc. On

Earth, it would explain how people, for instance, adopt the accent of a particular culture. I don't know the Zygol term for accents.'

'You are boring me. What I do know is that elapelc is beyond your capabilities.'

'But... if elapelc is such a vital part of Zygol culture, shouldn't you try and establish it with me? And why doesn't she... up there... try as well? Tell me that.'

'Why don't you go and ask her?' Rystyn's wicked look was a warning.

'Consider, Earthman,' Rystyn continued. 'Grains of sand in the desert and drops of water in a forest stream do not have to seek elapelc, and even if the two come into contact, the grains of sand still remain grains of sand and water is still water. That is why I will not seek elapelc with the likes of you.'

'That sure explains how things get muddied on your planet.'

'Enough. I remind you yet again, you have no status.'

Rystyn hastily took a plate of food and a ladle to the female who, Blakey guessed, was on watch duty. The cook returned and roughly dropped a plate and ladle at Blakey's feet and stormed off.

The food, which had the consistency of porridge, tasted quite good, much like a basic risotto.

As they ate, the plooglit continued to cavort, but it spent a great deal of time near the prone uckliablaht, which seemed to tolerate the energetic animal.

'Shall I tell you what happened with me and Zglta? Maybe then you'll see that I'm harmless, and you can let me go.'

'No!'

'We're good friends. Well... we were. Lovely woman. I like her a lot. There are thirty-three men in our compound and only five women. Zglta thought the imbalance to be unnatural, an affront to elapelc. A while back, she invited me to the Swamp with her. I made some excuse to my boss and went along. We were at the Swamp again today, enjoying ourselves when I stuffed up. I'd drunk too much Earth alcohol.'

'I'm not interested.'

'This man came along, and she went off with him. She told me she wouldn't be long. But she was gone a long time. Well... at least I think it was a long time. But... the vapours from the Swamp and my Earth alcohol might have played tricks on my mind. Then a woman who I met the previous time began talking to me and—'

'You are wasting your time. I am not listening!'

'This woman was friendly. Real friendly. We were in the Swamp, after all. We started off debating about the tall fence around the mining compound. A lot of Zygols are not happy that they can't access the area. While I'm talking, I'm getting angrier with Zglta. Anyway, me and this woman, who had a bit of whisky by that time, start to get to know each other. Closely. Not sexually. Just becoming... very familiar with each other. That's when Zglta found us. She'd drunk a fair bit of whisky as well, of course. And Zygols aren't used to the stuff. Well, Zglta just lost it. I can't blame her. I behaved like a—' He stopped short. For there are no pigs on Zygol III. 'So you have to see? My problem is personal. I'm no threat to you. Please let me go and apologise to her. I want to. She can yell at me all she likes; I deserve it. And I promise I'll never leave my compound again.'

Rystyn turned away from him. Blakey became reflective as his emotions ebbed from anger to despair. When Rystyn later threw a sleeping sheet at him, Blakey tried to snatch some restless sleep on the uneven, rocky ground.

<hr>

AT DAWN, the grit-laden wind was blowing harder. Amid the near-deafening roar, Rystyn prepared the morning meal. He tended to the warrior before dropping Blakey's meal and a clundrn of water beside the Earthman without uttering a word, to return some minutes later to pick up the items. The grumpy Zygol had to yell to be heard above the din. 'We leave now.'

Ross Blakey, still huddled in his sleeping sheet, was stunned. 'We can't go out into that. It's wild out there. We'll die.'

'Get up, or you die here,' Rystyn said matter-of-factly, then strode away and put on his face coverings.

Sore and angry, Ross Blakey dragged himself out of his sleeping sheet and hurled the bedding at the Zygol. 'Bastard.'

'Dze... dze... dze,' went the Zygol cook, gauging that the Earth word was not complimentary.

Keeping close, the small group set off into the roaring wind, protected only by their face coverings and the shawl the warrior wore. Hunched over, and yelping from the stinging grit, Blakey struggled to keep his feet, let along walk. The uckliablaht bleated its discomfort almost constantly as Rystyn clung low to the beast's neck. The plooglit seemed the least unperturbed, disappearing into the haze and reappearing, but it took to spending extra time on the great beast's back. Hmmmmmmmmmm. The fluctuating dust reduced visibility at times to less than ten metres; the warrior moved in and out of sight, like an apparition. Onwards they pressed onto the desert plain.

'Are you this desperate to get away from whoever's chasing you?' Blakey called out to Rystyn when a rock ridge gave them a brief but welcome protection from the stinging wind.

'Tsalc chooses to be harsh to us.'

Tsalc. Chance. Fortune. The unforeseen. Blakey recalled how Zglta described it. The mysterious 'sixth element' of Zygol philosophy.

The flat, sandy plain was made up of a smattering of stones, gravel, dry creek beds and occasional clumps of knee-high hardy and wind-blown vegetation. Rystyn dismounted and walked alongside the uckliablaht for a time, his face wreaked by worry.

Perhaps an hour later, the roaring wind, thankfully, eased. Blakey was exhausted. His exposed skin was aflame.

The day's second meal was prepared in a dry creek bed, where the three dusted themselves down. As Rystyn bent over his pot, with the female nowhere in sight, Blakey needed to talk. His voice was hoarse, even while sipping water. 'How can I stay alive? This is crazy. Even if you are running away from someone.'

No response.

'I'm not a bad person. Let me tell you more about myself.'

'I do not want to know about you at all.'

'I want to tell you.'

The Zygol sighed, leaned against a rock and shut his eyes.

'Every thirty-three days, we workers can return to Earth using the Chute for a seven-day break. For me—'

'I do not care to hear your ramblings,' Rystyn moaned.

'You need to understand. Using the Chute causes many people to vomit. It affects me badly. I can't stop vomiting for days each time I come out from it. It drains me. I go back to Earth because I have two small children there. I don't see much of them. Their mother doesn't like me anymore.'

'Ah. A very sensible woman.'

'When the teacher of my eldest asked her what her daddy did, she said that he vomits. How sad is that? What I'm getting at is that I spend little quality time with my kids. And I don't have the time or energy for companionship. I send money back for my kids, Rystyn. I love them. But I am on my own here. And I'm mostly on my own when I'm back on Earth. Zglta sympathised with me, being the lovely, caring woman she is. Spending time with her at the Swamp became the highlight of my time on your planet. Then I stupidly went and made her furious.'

'You most definitely are a fool. Enough! You bore me,' the Zygol snapped. 'Eat quickly. Never have I known a wind as this. It has eased now. It might stop. But it might become strong again. We must make haste while we are able.'

'But I have to rest. It's okay for you; you're not the one walking all the time.'

Rystyn grunted. He took a plate of food to the out-of-sight female. When he returned, he looked as if he'd swallowed vinegar.

He dropped food and some water at Blakey's feet, as had become his custom.

When the saddle bags were packed, Rystyn was soon atop the beast, ready to leave.

Stiff, his skin stinging, Blakey struggled to his feet. It was going to be one tough afternoon. The wind might have eased, but that only brought into focus the early afternoon desert sun.

Rystyn glared at where his companion seemed to be, then he surprised Blakey. 'You can ride with me for a short time. Or until the wind blows strong once more. Know that our uckliablaht is suffering. I can offer only a brief respite.' He gave Blakey a withering look. 'But do not annoy me!' He looked away.

Blakey smiled. 'Thank you for your gracious offer, lady,' he shouted towards the bend in the creek bed.

Reluctantly, Rystyn yanked Blakey up behind him. The uckliablaht bleated its protest.

Blakey kept balance using two small horns on the back of the saddle. Riding brought him a bizarre sense of pleasure. The gesture showed that maybe the warrior cared. A little. Blakey took great pleasure in being close to Rystyn, which no doubt annoyed the hell out of the cook. More importantly, riding gave Blakey a rest, though one disturbed each time the hyperactive plooglit leaped onto his lap with its claws only partially retracted and jumped onto the hind quarters of the uckliablaht (Hmmmmmmmmmm) before it dashed off. When the wind stopped and the residual dust in the air mostly settled, Blakey took in the desert landscape from his relaxed vantage point, ever the geologist. He whistled in admiration at the fantastic wind- and dust-sculptured formations about him.

Blakey straightened. 'Wait on! You see that long formation of lighter-coloured rock over there, Rystyn? Just there. There!'

The Zygol responded to his eager pointing with a sigh.

'Very porous rock, that is. Very old rock too, It's almost guaranteed to have underground caverns. If there's a stream nearby, even if it rains only rarely, you'll probably find some water under that rock. Must be. Look; there are gullies and shapes formed by rainwater. Perhaps millions of years ago, this area must have been under water.'

The Zygol responded to Blakey's enthusiastic explanations by gazing back at him. 'I care not for your teaching or your questions, Earthman. I particularly do not care how what we see came to be.'

Blakey found Rystyn's attitude peculiar. He wore a seemingly constant frown, unusual for a Zygol. Other Zygols seemed keen to learn and talk. They'd been sympathetic when he spoke of his ordeals when taking the Chute. That was the art of elapelc.

But Rystyn seemed irritated by anything he said. Yet, as he described the landscape, Blakey noticed the aloof female had drifted a little closer, perhaps to listen. He couldn't help but notice her exposed skin. Her legs and arms were red from the stinging dust.

Ross Blakey would not be deterred. 'But Rystyn, if you knew why things came to be as they are, you would understand what you see that much better.'

Rystyn became exasperated. 'Earthman; I have told you what I think about your explanations and questions. Yet you refuse to heed me. Never have I come across...'

Just then, the wind sprang up.

'Off,' Rystyn bellowed triumphantly as it became fierce. 'For the sake of the uckliablaht,' he added with a grin.

Damned Tsalc. 'But Rystyn, if I—'

Without warning, the Zygol made the uckliablaht rear. Blakey slipped off the back of the steed and crashed onto the sand. The fall hurt. As he picked himself up, the warrior silently chuckled.

'Bitch!' Blakey murmured in his Earth language as he rubbed his backside. If the wind didn't ease... 'Why don't we travel only when the wind drops?' he demanded.

Rystyn replied. 'Perhaps the wind will blow for days. We only have so much food and water. We must go on. Tsalc will surely look upon us with favour soon.' The three hastily donned their face coverings.

Blakey winced. 'Your uckliablaht is losing its fur,' he called out as he brushed clumps off his pants.

'I know,' Rystyn replied, looking concerned. 'That is a bad sign.' Blakey didn't ask why; the situation was desperate enough. In the harsh wind, he battled to keep up. Some gusts were so fierce that, twice, he fell to his knees. Loose sand dragged at his feet like tubs of molasses.

The uckliablaht loudly bleated its discomfort and tried to throw Rystyn off its back. The Zygol clung grimly onto the beast's tether and neck. He soothed the animal by patting its neck. The plooglit took to spending more time either directly in front of the uckliablaht or on its rump. The Zygols shared hand signals, their heads often leaning to the right, indicating yes. But yes to what?

'I'm really struggling here,' Blakey pleaded with the warrior through the howling wind and grit.

She ignored him. 'Heartless bitch!' No reaction. 'Bastard!' he spat at a smirking Rystyn.

Blakey trudged onwards—ever onwards. The sun was obscured by clouds of dust. Finding some relief from the wind behind a large outcropping of shattered rock, the group halted.

'We will stop for an early evening meal,' Rystyn announced. 'And rest a while. Perhaps the wind will ease again.' The Zygols and the plooglit crowded around the uckliablaht, showing concern for its wellbeing.

None showed concern for Blakey, who slumped against a rock, hovering on the edge of collapse. His inner thighs and backside had become itchy after he'd gotten off the uckliablaht. And the itch was getting worse. Realisation dawned on him. The first arrivals from Earth had mentioned the rash. One time when he was walking with Zglta to the Swamp, he had contracted a small dose of the affliction on his forearm. Dousing the itch in water and soap had minimal effect. Lotion worked, but he had no lotion. At the compound, they had dubbed the itch "plooglit-piss rash." Blakey uttered an oath. Yet more misery.

Ross Blakey knew that plooglit piss was not urine. The creatures secrete a substance from glands near their backsides, which they deposit on their companion uckliablahts and on vegetation uckliablahts may graze upon or brush against. No one knew why.

Zygols suffer no effects from the substance, but from the earliest days, the mining company had taken precautions to counter it. Plooglits were banned from the compound; they climbed and scratched about the Airlock fence with its coils of barbed wire strewn atop, when their companion uckliablahts were ushered inside. And no employee was permitted to touch an uckliablaht. Blakey hadn't considered the substance when he was offered a ride. He was in no shape to turn it down.

Blakey had been lucky during his forays into Channen village, apart from his one mild dose. Sturdy fences kept uckliablahts from getting inside the Swamp to prevent the beasts from devouring the lush and rotting plants that fed the vapours. The vapours seemed to deter plooglits, anyway. When Blakey had begun his wild dash through the initial band of vegetation, he must have, thankfully, dodged the stuff.

Blakey squatted on his aching haunches; sitting was painful; the itching was getting worse. As he squirmed, a scowling Rystyn brought him his meal. 'We will continue after eating. But we will stop for the night after a short time.'

Blakey replied with a few words of his Earth language.

'Keep quiet!' Rystyn hissed. 'In the desert, only a cfaldi can hear you scream. Also, it is known that disturbed people dwell in these parts.'

'Disturbed people like you and her, for instance?'

'Ha, Earthman.' Rystyn put his hands on his hips. 'Your tongue is so clever that she will gladly free it from the constraints of your mouth if you continue to annoy me.'

'Tell me something, Rystyn: are we lost?'

To Blakey's amazement, Rystyn answered. 'We are not... lost. But it is better when we see certain landmarks. We can never be lost when we have a plooglit—our uckliablaht's companion plooglit at that. Plooglits may be the stupidest beings on the planet... though you are challenging that notion... but they can find their fellow plooglits whenever they so desire. And plooglits live where there is vegetation.'

Blakey instantly changed his mind about longing to strangle the plooglit (and every other plooglit on the planet).

The uckliablaht took, with relish, to patches of metre-high, withered and blackened plants scattered amid a pile of rocks.

'Now watch,' Rystyn said brightly as the plooglit approached the nearby plants.

It sniffed a couple, 'Hmmmmmmmmmmm,' then it nibbled at them. 'See, Earthman. The plooglit knows what desert food is good to eat and what water is good to drink. It avoids plants that would make it and us ill. I will collect some of the plants it nibbles. They are not tasty, but they are food. And our stocks are low with you and the tiring uckliablaht needing extra rations.'

Rystyn was pleased with his explanation, Blakey less so; he needed the plooglit to be in the mood to be sociable with its fellow creatures.

Rystyn fetched two food pouches from the saddle bags.

'Does the uckliablaht know the difference between good food and bad as well?'

'With an uckliablaht, it doesn't matter.'

'Really! But this animal looks like it is getting sick.'

Rystyn took a breath. 'Yes, it is. But not from the food. It does not like the desert wind.'

Too soon, the group resumed their journey. Rystyn sent hand signals to the warrior and received a short, sharp reply. Blakey knew the reply. No. He also knew the question. At the Swamp one time, Zglta had sent him the same hand signals. When Blakey had stared at her dumbfounded, she giggled. 'I forgot. You don't understand me. I was telling you to leave now.'

You should go. No, the warrior had replied.

The three pressed slowly through the relentless, gritty air. Though he was bone weary, Blakey was able to draw alongside Rystyn and his ailing uckliablaht, whenever the animal suddenly halted, prompting the Zygol to feel compelled to rub its neck. Even when it was in motion, the uckliablaht moved only with a slow shuffle.

'Rystyn; I can't keep going. I need to stop.' Even the warrior's head was bowed.

'We have to find a suitable place away from the wind.' On they pressed.

The plooglit continued to flitter about but didn't wander far. One time, it stopped directly in front of Blakey and gazed at him with its large, vacuous eyes. Blakey shook his fists at it. 'Just don't sit there! Go and find some $%#@&^ plooglits.'

'You are talking a great deal in your Earth language,' Rystyn remarked.

Blakey replied with some different... some repeated... choice Earth words.

On they trekked with Rystyn and the warrior peering anxiously through the savage, swirling haze.

As the sand grasped at his feet like fingers of death, Ross Blakey contemplated the frightening likelihood that he would die in this desert. If he did, what would become of his children? What if no one ever found out what happened to him?

One foot in front of the other. Then the other. Then the other...

He lost the will to cover his ears from the relentless, howling wind.

Twice, Blakey lost sight of Rystyn and the uckliablaht in the haze. He cried out. Soon after, there was the plooglit, Rystyn and the uckliablaht in sight again.

Battered, near senseless, his mind was shutting down, his body collapsing. One foot in front of the other. Then the other. So much stinging grit and soft, grasping sand. Stones kept tripping him.

The group came to a halt before a gaping dusty gorge, its bottom concealed by a gloomy haze of dust. As Blakey swayed, the warrior indicated a way down. Rystyn, who leaned back on the protesting uckliablaht, went down first. Blakey followed—he had no choice—stumbling on loose stones and crashing hard against boulders he hadn't the energy to dodge.

The others were gone again. Before him was the downslope of a sand dune. With legs wobbling like jelly, Blakey couldn't backtrack, so he plunged onto the dune. The sand shifted. He stumbled, fell over, rolled. He dragged himself to his feet only to lose balance again. He rose unsteadily and found himself surfing down the shifting slope, whooping, arms flailing. Miraculously, he was still on his feet when he reached level ground. He thrust out a leg to stop, but it buckled like paper. The ground crashed hard into his face.

Blackness.

WHEN ROSS BLAKEY pried open his stinging, gritty eyes, he found himself draped in a sleeping sheet, lying on soft sand beside a scatter of large rocks. He made out the shape of the sun through the haze and guessed it was late morning, or maybe early afternoon, given the heat. At least he was in the shade, and the wind had eased. Small mercies. His legs were knotted with pain; his head was throbbing. His lungs ached. He felt as if a blowtorch was spouting fire into his throat. And the itch from the plooglit piss rash on his bum and thighs was near unbearable. Blakey trembled, for the scene he gazed at—barren, jagged rock and dumps of windswept sand—had to be his final resting place.

The uckliablaht and the plooglit were nowhere to be seen.

A distance away, Rystyn and the warrior were engaged in an earnest discussion. Perhaps over what to do with Blakey's corpse. A cfaldi would fix that problem. One word was spoken by the warrior. *No*. Twice. Emphatically.

When Blakey reached to scratch his itches, his legs seized.

Rystyn heard him moan, and ran over. The warrior disappeared. 'Leave me here,' Blakey groaned as he massaged his legs, then coughed. 'I'm finished. You get your wish to be rid of me.'

'Speak to me again when it is time to leave,' Rystyn replied. 'You have slept a long time. You are fortunate; our uckliablaht has also needed a long rest. I have given it extra food and water to help it recover as much as it can. Even the lady took a much-earned nap. But we must leave soon. Tsalc now decides our uckliablaht's fate. We need to get as far as we can before it can do no more for us.'

'Is it dying? Like me.'

'No. It will not die. But we need to keep it functioning as an uckliablaht.'

Rystyn's words made no sense. Perhaps Blakey hadn't heard right. But there were far more urgent matters.

'You wouldn't stop for me back there when I was begging you to. You wanted me to fall down and die.'

Rystyn puffed out his chest. 'We are Zygols. The... lady... especially values the preservation of life. Even of a worthless one such as yours.'

'You're lying! You both want to get rid of me. Her especially.'

Rystyn's lips curled into a snarl. 'Never! She is a...' He stopped short, his mouth forming an O.

'She is a what? I deserve to know if I'm about to die.'

'Nearly, Earthman. I nearly fell for your trap. You display your ignorance once more. The lady has honoured you. She has tested your strength and resolve to its limits. Also understand that we could not camp exposed to the wind and dust out on the desert plains. And consider. How do you think you came to this sheltered place, lying in your sleeping sheet?'

'It doesn't matter. It's only delayed the inevitable.'

Rystyn glowered at Blakey. 'We will leave soon. We may continue into the night if Tsalc blesses us with stars. You can ride the uckliablaht with me,' the Zygol frowned, 'for it will make no difference to the fate of the uckliablaht. It is in pain. Nothing can heal it in the short term.'

'Are we still... almost... lost?'

'There is still haze about. But the wind has dropped. Tsalc must surely take pity on us soon. And we can never be—'

'Lost when we have a plooglit. Oh, I can't believe how lucky I am!'

Rystyn turned on his heel. 'I will make food. There is little left of our original supplies. The uckliablaht needs to eat a great deal because of its suffering.'

Blakey lowered his head. 'Then save your food. I'm finished.' Rystyn twirled his finger above his head as he walked away. 'Dze... dze... dze…' But the Zygol brought Blakey some water.

Blakey's raw-red eyes were leaden. His stomach was rumbling; his mouth parched. He ached. He itched. But the alluring smell of the cooking food wafting towards him was too tempting. After Rystyn had served the warrior her meal, Blakey gestured wildly for Rystyn to serve him his share. He tossed down many clundrns of water. Maybe... if he could build up a little strength… And he would be riding on the uckliablaht.

'I assume you now wish to continue?' Rystyn growled with arms crossed as Blakey wolfed his meal.

'Maybe. So I can annoy both of you.'

Rystyn glared at him then walked away, muttering. In a matter of minutes, Blakey was asleep. Or unconscious.

2

——

LOST

ROSS BLAKEY PUSHED ASIDE a sheet of woven fibres that served as a doorway and followed the smiling Zglta into her bedroom. Her inviting eyes were bright with alcohol and the vapours of the Swamp. Blakey's body was warm from the whisky, his mind floating pleasantly. Zglta's bedroom was simple, small and windowless, shaped in a quarter-dome. At its highest point near the entrance, the ceiling was two hand spans above him. The room was barely large enough to accommodate a smallish, low double bed of hide and soft leaves. On a segment of the wall, clothes hung on twigs. Other items were stacked on a narrow, raised plank.

The room was in semi-darkness, lit only by a small, smouldering, resin-covered fire stick at the side of the bed. The ceiling and walls were lined by living bluish-green branches and stiff vines sporting leaves the size of small door mats, teased together to form a reasonably waterproof living space. Patches of animal hide or flattened bark dyed a dark orange filled the gaps. All this was held together by vines or patches of stretchable resin. It was amazing to think that most of what Blakey gazed at was living vegetation. Blakey turned to take his companion by the waist.

The room was gone. He was at the Swamp. Before him, Zglta's face was livid with rage.

'I'm going to feed your bones to a cfaldi!' she screamed.

He sucked in a breath.

Blakey awoke to a world that was no less a nightmare. He was enveloped in a dust-filled haze. He struggled, coughing, onto all fours, heaving for breath.

He flicked up his face covering and dropped his hood over his eyes as he should have done before he fell asleep. Whatever flimsy scraps of energy he'd built up during his long sleep, were sucked from his body. He moaned and collapsed on his side.

He was kicked on his backside. Rystyn handed him a clundrn of water, which Blakey drained in one gulp.

'We leave as soon as I have packed up. We have rested too long. Do you prefer to stay here and die?'

'I...' Blakey spluttered hoarsely.

'We will leave you then. Earthmen give up so easily.' Rystyn began walking away.

'More water,' Blakey gasped. Through the haze, he made out the faint outline of the sun. It was past mid-afternoon.

Rystyn grunted but he returned with an ahk across his shoulder and filled Blakey's clundrn three more times. Blakey had neither the will nor the energy to lift himself from his sleeping sheet let alone scratch at his plooglit piss. Yet, unbeknown to him, he would soon become remarkably energised.

Rystyn hastily stowed the ahk and clundrn away, then lifted the large saddle sacks onto his shoulders and hauled them behind a boulder. His cry of alarm echoed through the chasm. The Zygol backed into view, stumbling in his haste; his face aghast. A cfaldi? But wouldn't Rystyn have called out to the woman who fights cfaldi? Instead, the cook stood stock still, gaping at Blakey.

As the warrior poked her head from behind a rock, Rystyn approached the Earthman. Two steps. Very hesitantly. He fidgeted with his hands.

'Let me guess,' Blakey inquired sourly, 'the plooglit is feeling unsociable.'

Rystyn tilted his head to the left. No. His mouth flapped.

Blakey shrugged as a quivering Rystyn floundered. Whatever it was the cook was struggling to say had to be very bad news. Blakey had the decidedly strong feeling that, after the last couple of bummer days, things were about to get even worse.

'We're lost, aren't we?'

The Zygol cook fidgeted even more and took a step back.

'I'm ready for the truth, Rystyn. Tell me what's wrong. Whatever it is.'

In the tradition of Zygols, when he could get the words out, Rystyn was straight to the point. 'The uckliablaht has eaten our plooglit.' He then cowered in fear.

Blakey didn't respond with the uncontrollable rage Rystyn obviously anticipated. Instead, he merely nodded. This had to be the last straw.

The Zygol backed away when Blakey somehow found the energy to stand up and approach him.

'So, our plooglit is dead,' Blakey rasped. 'Our main hope of finding our way out of this desert is dead and gone. Great!' Blakey felt remarkably calm. He even smiled.

The Zygol cowered more. Perhaps he saw the look in Blakey's eyes. 'That sort of makes being "practically" lost more definite, doesn't it, Rystyn?'

The Zygol leaned his head to the right. Blakey exhaled loudly, spat out some grit and took a couple of menacing steps towards the cook. 'But... wait a moment,' he mused, stopping in his tracks. 'Uckliablahts are plant-eaters.'

Rystyn apparently mistakenly believed that Blakey might be appeased by an explanation. 'Almost invariably,' he replied. 'However, uckliablahts aren't used to enduring such prolonged harsh conditions. And it has done so carrying a heavy burden. It has suffered a great deal. The poor creature feels awful about eating the plooglit. It is a catastrophe for him, given the strong bond formed with its companion plooglit. You can tell by looking at him. For—'

'Great! That's really great!' Blakey sneered. 'The uckliablaht is so very sad. We are doomed, and the uckliablaht is unhappy. How tragic. My heart is breaking.' Blakey toyed with the idea of punching the Zygol's lights out, but instead, he brushed past him and headed for the cause of their dire predicament—the hulking beast that had sealed Blakey's fate.

'Don't do anything silly,' Rystyn pleaded as he trotted after Blakey, keeping his distance. 'We still need him for transportation, for as long as possible. And he didn't mean what he did. He was just so terribly depressed. He—'

'Well I'm getting mighty depressed myself!' boomed Blakey.

Rystyn gestured frantically for Blakey to calm down.

Blakey had reluctantly come to regard plooglits—or this particular one, for the time being, anyway—with some... affection. Of sorts. With the plooglit dead and eaten, Blakey's mind teemed with dark thoughts of revenge on its behalf.

He stepped between the boulders to where the hulking uckliablaht rested. The great beast was, unusually, sitting upright like a human, its broad, hunched back partly resting on a boulder. Its massive, tree-like hind legs lay flat on the ground, while its longer, thinner, but still formidable middle legs held it upright. Its smaller set of upper legs grasped these forelegs for added support. Lying beside one of the animal's large paws were two small, grey front claws from the unfortunate plooglit. The uckliablaht's great back, as well as its floppy ears and long, broad head were bent over; its lips were puckered, and its large yellow eyes glazed.

Blakey paced before the beast, mumbling in rage. He yearned to extract revenge yet keep the animal functioning. Damn it! It was needed to carry their food and water. And, hopefully, he and Rystyn as well. As his mind teemed with dark urgings, Blakey burst into a coughing fit. This did not improve his mood. He stopped before the uckliablaht, which looked up at him with its large and sad, yellow eyes.

Its black, leathery lower lip drooped. But sympathy wasn't on Blakey's mind.

'You useless #@#&%!' he yelled hoarsely.

Keeping his distance, Rystyn begged Blakey in a whisper to lower his voice. Blakey glared at him and resumed his verbal abuse of the uckliablaht.

The animal reacted to Blakey's agitation by bowing its head lower as if to acknowledge its misdeed and to seek pity.

The sight of the massive but pathetic animal, combined with Blakey's strong desire to scream at it and beat it to death, only served to infuriate him more. In frustration, Blakey took a wild kick at the uckliablaht, grazing the animal's hind flank. Dissatisfied with his poor contact, Blakey steadied himself for another, better directed blow.

Before he could, the uckliablaht hissed a warning and bared its massive (and bloodied) yellow teeth. This was the first time Blakey had caught a glimpse of an uckliablaht's formidable teeth, but awestruck as he was, he didn't take a backward step. The great beast swung at him with one of its clawed front paws. Had it connected with Blakey's head, it would have crushed his skull as if it were an eggshell. Blakey dodged the blow, tripping over a rock. Fuming with rage and impotence, he figured that Rystyn would be a better target.

'Damn it! You must have had some idea the uckliablaht would do what it did,' Blakey rasped as he advanced on the retreating cook, his throat aflame like the catacombs of hell.

'There is no safer place for a plooglit to be than with its companion uckliablaht. Neither I nor the plooglit expected it. And there was no noise that could be heard over the sound of the wind. The realisation of what he has done will devastate the uckliablaht for many, many days. It is already suffering a great deal.'

Facing a rapidly impending and miserable death, Blakey was poised to explode at the cringing Zygol.

Before he could, the warrior was at Rystyn's side, her hand hovering over her kraxl-da. The malice of her penetrating green eyes dissipated almost every vengeful thought from Blakey's mind. Almost...

Blakey raised his arms in supplication. 'Okay. I'll behave. But remember, I'm about to die. For what? I have no idea.'

The warrior turned to Rystyn. 'It appears our situation is now desperate.' Her voice was clear and resonant. 'Without the plooglit, we now risk being poisoned from the food and water we gather.'

Ross Blakey moaned in despair.

'The timing is unfortunate,' Rystyn replied. 'The loss of our plooglit—'

'Can we still find our way out of this murderous desert?' Blakey chimed in.

A deflated Rystyn ignored Blakey. 'What shall we do?' he whined.

Blakey butted in again. 'Hope the food or water will kill us quickly, that's what.'

The female lifted the hilt of her kraxl a few centimetres, and Blakey prudently opted to mumble to himself.

'We have to hope that Tsalc will provide us with good food and water,' the warrior said. 'Given the harsh conditions, we must continue to drink but we should eat only whenever it is imperative to do so. The position of the sun suggests we are heading towards our destination. So, we travel in the same direction.'

'But we must eat to keep up our strength,' Rystyn protested weakly. He looked as disconsolate as the uckliablaht.

'We will try,' she replied calmly. 'It is all we can do. We need to go.'

Rystyn leaned his head to the right. He drifted over to the uckliablaht and cooed to it as he stroked it. The beast staggered to its feet. It shuddered as the Zygol cook loaded the sacks onto its broad back.

'We will walk for a while,' Rystyn informed the gloomy Blakey. 'It will give the uckliablaht time to deal with its loss. Then we can both ride.' Blakey grimaced; just standing had his legs protesting.

The warrior took the lead. Blakey's choice was to walk or lie down and die. He nearly laid down.

The despondent trio of beings followed the warrior slowly. Their route was regrettably, yet somehow inevitably, uphill. Blakey winced in pain with each step. One foot in front of the other. Then the other. Then the other. At least the wind and dust were bearable, but the haze lingered.

The Zygols looked about them. Only distant vague shapes could be made out.

Blakey snarled. 'Don't eat or drink. Great thinking. And, of course, ignore the Earthman. Always ignore the Earthman.' He addressed his complaints to the warrior when she came within earshot.

'Earthman, you have no status,' Rystyn said wearily. 'If you were a Zygol, you would know what that entails. But being the ignorant fool you are, you do not.'

'I can't stand it,' Blakey pressed. 'It might be one of your quaint Zygol customs. But it really annoys me.'

Rystyn sighed. 'Ignorant Earthman.'

'But, hey,' Blakey rasped. 'You need to keep me alive so I can be the one who tests the food and water. I'm expendable. And I'm doomed to die soon anyway.'

Rystyn sighed. 'If you knew hand signals, you would know that I am to be the food tester. Even though, as you correctly remarked, you are the expendable... totally useless... one.'

Blakey opened his mouth to speak, then changed his mind. He trudged on, grumbling.

Rystyn lifted himself onto the back of the suffering uckliablaht. 'Will it try and eat us?' Blakey asked before joining him a short distance later. It meant a new dose of plooglit-piss rash, but it was ride or perish. His legs were finished.

The Zygol rolled his eyes and leaned his head to the left.

The ride was an ordeal. Several times, Rystyn had to cajole the massive beast into movement. Without the plooglit, he struggled to steer; the hulking animal did not care for commands. At times, the uckliablaht shuddered in pain. Then Rystyn and Blakey would dismount and shuffle beside it for a while as Rystyn stroked the animal's neck. The warrior's head became more and more bowed.

When the group came across a dozen blackened plants in a dry creek bed, the uckliablaht attacked them with a desperate relish.

Rystyn hurried to pick some small, dark-purple berries before the uckliablaht demolished every bush. He examined the withered berries with suspicion before placing those from one bush in a food sack and others from a distant plant in a separate sack.

Blakey didn't give a damn. He hoped only for delirium to take hold before he perished.

'You say words I don't understand, Earthman.'

Blakey snapped hoarsely. 'Earth words let me express how I feel right now. You said before that there may be disturbed people nearby. If I could possibly manage it, I'd yell and alert them. *Anything* rather than die in misery. *Anything*. Who knows, they might rescue us.'

'Your death at the hands of the desert dwellers would both be certain and very unpleasant.'

'Oh, why doesn't that surprise me?' Rysten looked at Blakey strangely.

Blakey's rock-bottom morale took another massive nosedive when the wind and dust picked up, forcing the group to huddle close as they fought their way forward. Dusk was falling. One foot in front of the other. Then the other. Why he kept going, how he kept on going, Blakey had no idea. Perhaps delirium had set in.

Thankfully, the trekkers found a sheltered place behind a low rocky hill. Blakey sat down heavily with his back against the hill and closed his eyes. He burst into another coughing fit as he scratched at a fresh dose of plooglit piss. Fortunately, this dose was milder than his other doses. A small blessing. Or maybe he was losing feeling.

'I will cook now.'

'No need. I'm not hungry.'

'That cannot be after the energy we spent getting here.'

'I'm not hungry.' Blakey lied.

Rystyn gave him the faintest, briefest smile. 'The lady will not eat, either. So, we rest for a time, drink water, and continue on. But we must eat later. Do not think that elapelc is happening, Earthman. I still think of you badly.'

Despite the exhaustion and pain wreaking his entire body, Blakey had to smile.

When they headed off once more, Rystyn and Blakey rode atop the uckliablaht. Both were physically spent. The wind had eased but they journeyed in near darkness, with the starlight often hidden behind a veil of dust.

Before long, the uckliablaht staggered twice for no apparent reason and it came to a stubborn halt so often, they covered little distance. When they came across a string of boulders, Rystyn signalled the warrior, who reluctantly leaned her head to the right.

He turned to Blakey. 'We will rest and eat here. We must allow our uckliablaht to deal with its suffering. I should let it go. But we are in no state to walk. If Tsalc is kind, it will give us stars to travel by later.'

Blakey sighed. Oblivion was beckoning, with cooing promises to free him from his suffering.

Rystyn gave the uckliablaht almost all their water, leaving only enough for a single clundrn for each trekker and a little for the pot. 'I won't get out of the desert riding on your back, Earthman,' he growled as if he read Blakey's mind.

The female disappeared. Rystyn made a campfire. He produced the small sacks containing the dry berries. 'See; I have taken the berries from this sack.' He placed the other sack beside Blakey.

Blakey watched keenly. The smell from the food as it cooked was making him salivate. Rystyn's moment of truth was near at hand. But Blakey could forego food no longer.

The warrior, her legs and clothes wet and glistening, appeared shouldering a half-full ahk. She deposited it on one of the large saddle sacks and disappeared. She could not possibly have found the water from above ground.

'I will test the water,' Rystyn said. First, he gave a generous serving to the uckliablaht then he poured some into a clundrn.

Blakey watched eagerly with parched lips. If the water killed Rystyn but the death was not agonising, he would gladly drink some himself. He felt more dead than alive already, anyway.

The Zygol quaffed the water then looked at the sky in contemplation. He sighed, poured more into the clundrn and drank.

Blakey pressed forward and drank greedily of the water Rystyn offered. 'Thanks.'

'Water is a small risk,' Rystyn said nonchalantly. 'It is only poisonous when it is contaminated badly by poisonous plants.'

'She should be here for a time like this,' Blakey rasped. 'You might die for her benefit.'

Rystyn looked at him in surprise, then anger. 'You are an unbelievably ignorant fool. The lady would defend us both to her last breath if we were in danger. Even you. Who else fetches our water from dangerous places? Who is it who keeps watch over us? She goes where she risks being ambushed by a cfaldi. Fool. Why didn't you stay in your compound?'

'Believe me, Rystyn, I wish that I had done just that.' He needed to stop talking. It was destroying his throat.

'Idiot!' Rystyn spat.

Blakey shrugged. If they ever met, Rystyn and Blakey's ex-wife would have the most enjoyable conversation.

The two sat in gloomy silence as Rystyn stirred the contents of the pot. Even Blakey knew with his limited knowledge of Zygol cooking that Rystyn was stirring the pot long after the food was thoroughly cooked. The flames became embers. Blakey felt guilty, but he longed for the Zygol to sample the damned food.

At last, Rystyn took up a ladle and poured the steaming gluggy, grey contents onto a bowl. He looked up at Blakey, who watched him intently.

Rystyn spoke calmly. 'Observe that I have taken the food from this pot with the wave design on its side,' he remarked. 'If the food is poisonous, I will likely be in agony for a time before I become paralysed and unable to speak.' He paused. 'I might be paralysed for a short time, but I might be paralysed for much longer. If that should happen, or I should die because of this food, you must give the remaining food to the uckliablaht, then throw the pot away. Understand?'

Blakey nodded solemnly. He was thinking, shut up and eat!

Rystyn continued gravely. 'Don't be alarmed if I collapse in total agony. It is important that you act immediately and responsibly. Place my face covering in my mouth so my screaming won't alert cfaldi to our location. Hopefully, I will die quickly. Understand?'

Blakey nodded. Then he leaned his head to the right. *Eat!* he longed to cry out. The steaming food was making him salivate. Its smell was overpowering.

'Realise, too, that you can do nothing for me, no matter how much I will be in unbearable pain.'

Blakey waved the comment away in irritation.

'But more important,' Rystyn continued, 'listen to me! If the worst happens, then you must be the one to test the berries from the other food sack, using a new pot. If, after trying this food, your body feels that it is about to turn into fire, then as your last act before you become paralysed or die, tip the pot over so that my companion knows the food in it is also bad. You *must* try to do this. Understand? Even though you may be experiencing unbearable agony. Even if the pain is so indescribably—'

'I get the idea,' Blakey interrupted gruffly. 'Err. How long before we know if you, err...?'

'If I am dying or becoming paralysed?' Rystyn took a deep breath. 'You will know very soon. If all goes badly, I hope I will not display too much of my horrible agony,' he said with disarming calm. 'But don't be overly alarmed. Most food is good to eat. Tsalc surely must now look kindly upon me.'

He took a deeper breath. It was time. Rystyn looked around, muttered something (seemingly derogatory) to the darkness about him and shrugged his shoulders. He drew the ladle of food towards his lips.

'Err... Rystyn,' Blakey said as a whisper. The Zygol scowled at him.

'Good luck. And, if it goes badly, then I'll be truly sorry, despite everything that's happened between us.'

'Thank you, Earthman. And let me say in return that I am sorry to have come across the likes of you. You have slowed us down. You are disagreeable, aggressive and you have asked far too many annoying questions. Yet it is you... you who may witness my dying breath.'

Blakey had to chuckle at the man's frankness. 'I understand.'

'You! Understand? Humph!' Rystyn sneered. He made a hand gesture—a semi-circular sweep of his index finger—which Blakey guessed to be a request for silence. Illuminated by the orange-white glow of embers, and after a final furtive glance at his surroundings, Rystyn lifted the steaming glutinous concoction uncertainly towards his mouth and shut his eyes.

3

A TASTE OF THINGS TO COME

ROSS BLAKEY BLINKED. He blinked again. Shadows were moving.

The cold, sharp kraxl at his throat was definitely not a figment of his deteriorating mind.

A male voice hissed in his ear. 'Stay quiet, and don't move. Or you die!' Blakey thought the request reasonable. He even had the wherewithal to lean his head to the right.

The kraxl-brandishing intruders, who had soundlessly surrounded Rystyn and Blakey, numbered three: two Zygol men and one Zygol woman in crimson tunics under reinforced, brown-black uckliablaht-hide battle armour, segmented from shoulder to knee. They wore rounded helmets with chin guards. On their thick belts dangled kraxl-das and dart shooters. Aktel.

Whoever was chasing Blakey's captors had found them. One intruder gestured urgently.

Rystyn responded with a brief nod and leaned his head to the right.

To Blakey's surprise, Rystyn looked at ease after his initial shock. He gleefully tossed the ladle of steaming food back into its pot and tapped the bridge of his nose to acknowledge that he was fine.

Blakey imitated Rystyn's action and the kraxl at his throat was withdrawn. Blakey relaxed. Could this be a rescue? For him and seemingly Rystyn anyway.

If the raid sought to capture the warrior, then, well, he owed her nothing. Sure; she'd allowed him time on the back of the ailing uckliablaht and had taken risks to fetch water from what had to be dark and slippery underground passages. Okay, she'd also kept guard during the nights. But, damn it, most times, her heart had been uncompromisingly cold as he sank ever-nearer to death. She refused to talk or listen to him. Yes, throwing her in jail was fine by him. Hell... might the aktel escort him to his compound? Not that he had the energy to do anything to help the warrior, even if he could. Or wanted to. Which he didn't.

From behind her boulder emerged a very contrite-looking warrior, flanked by four armed aktel. One pointed a kraxl-da at her back, while three others moved crablike a distance to her side, their reed-like dart shooters drawn and poised. The aktel moved fluidly, yet they possessed little of the easy, powerful grace of this Amazon-like Zygol.

The three aktel, who had surrounded Blakey and Rystyn, stood guard, kraxls drawn. Rystyn gestured for Blakey to remain calm. He seemed relaxed. Surely he would have alerted the warrior if her life had been in peril. Zygols have a strong sense of honour.

'Put your weapons away,' demanded the warrior. 'I am your Spmite.' She stood, proud and defiant before her captors, who looked ill at ease. Blakey had the feeling that, should she so much as blow on these aktel, they would topple over.

The three aktel with dart shooters remained crouched, ready to fire. The one with the kraxl-da fronted her. This aktel was shorter than the others and had a gold streak across the chest of her armour. Blakey guessed her to be the leader of the group.

She sighed loudly, her shoulders slumped. 'How can you claim to still be the joint chief protector of the six elements when you fled your judgement? It was the action of a renegade.'

'I fled judgement, yes, to escape a blatantly contrived injustice. I seek a place where I can face an independent judgement. If I receive such a hearing, it will be the Zookspmate who you will be accusing of failing *his* duty as a joint chief protector of the six elements.'

The aktel took a breath. 'My orders leave me greatly conflicted, for I have admired you for many years and welcomed with enthusiasm your recent elevation as Spmite. I believed then that the protection of the six elements could not be in safer hands.'

'Safi, it is vital that you believe me,' the warrior, who wished to be called a Spmite, pressed. 'The charges against me of plotting to kill the Zookspmate are trumped up. For the past two years, the Zookspmate has increasingly surrounded himself with his cronies, and it is they who will be called upon to be witnesses against me. Those who will preside over the judgement are also cronies of the Zookspmate— stooges who he has elevated to the rank of Grycyryn, our wise ones. He parades these pretenders as being the finest in their ranks— Grycyryn-da. But they are unworthy of that esteemed title.'

'I know of a fine Grycyryn-da who was demoted. I don't know why.'

'You know full well that appointments require my consent after a full assessment of those seeking promotion. Yet the Zookspmate acted without consulting me, ignoring my protests and the protests of fine Grycyryn whom he deposed. It was when I sought to reverse his most appalling actions that the charges against me were made—charges fabricated up by the very undeserving people he has promoted. At a judgement, under his direction, I stand no chance. And my deep fear is that the ruling will end in my execution.'

The Safi's shoulders slumped even further. 'I hear you. Thank you for telling me your side of the story.'

'If you believe me, Safi, then recognise me as your Spmite. Escort me to a village where I can receive the independent judgement I fully deserve. If that is not acceptable, then set me free, and we will go our separate ways.'

The Safi and the other aktel stole glances at one another. 'I am deeply conflicted by your words,' she said as a sigh. The others seemed equally conflicted. 'But I am only a Safi, and I am required to obey orders. Because you fled judgement, you surely relinquished your right to truly be called a Spmite, even though you carry a Spmite's talisman. Your actions have rendered the Zookspmate to be the highest authority in the lands of the Three Villages. I must defer to his orders. I have given my solemn oath to do so.'

'No, you must defer to the six elements,' demanded the warrior. 'They are the higher authority.'

The young Safi cringed. 'But I cannot defy orders that I have sworn to uphold.'

'Yes, you can. You must. If you defer to him, realise that you will be condemning me.'

The Safi took a deep breath. 'By fleeing, you must now be treated as a renegade. It allows me to call you by your name, Alena.'

Alena bristled. 'Safi; you *must* understand. Do the Zookspmate's bidding, and his power will be unchallenged. With me removed, he will surely seek to appoint a Spmite of his own choosing, though the six elements demand that he not do so. That is what is at stake here. You *must* listen to me.'

The Safi and her fellow aktel communicated in a flurry of hand signals. Yet their weapons remained drawn. Blakey was familiar with one signal. *No.* But there were shrugs and looks of doubt amid the no's. Then the Safi replied, 'Call it injustice, and I feel that it is, but I was given direct orders from the Zookspmate to execute you without mercy. I have already defied him by not having executed you immediately when we ambushed you.'

'What you say is an outrage!'

The young Safi cringed. 'In deference to you and the doubts I now have about you being branded a renegade, I am prepared to allow you to live on the condition that you return with me, bound, to the Three Villages. But I must insist on you doing so demoted to your previous rank of Dsolcspmite. That requires you to hand me your talisman. I realise what I ask must greatly anger you, but I cannot compromise further. By offering you this option, I will be punished. But be aware that we aktel face banishment if we allow you to retain your talisman or aid you in your quest. So, I beg you, drop your weapons and hand over your talisman.'

Blakey's chief kidnapper simmered as she placed her hand on her kraxl-da. 'I would die rather than hand over my talisman. Regard me as a tainted Spmite if that is your wish. But I cannot accept the humiliation you propose.'

The Safi sighed. 'I feared you would react this way... but I will return to the Three Villages with your talisman. Either with you alive, or as my orders demand, with you dead. I cannot negotiate further. Return with me, and I will bring my mentor to you to negotiate your hearing.'

The woman who claimed to be a Spmite, and whose name was Alena, leaned her head to the left. 'I fear you are not aware of what is at stake here. Your mentor would only place herself in danger if she sought to assist me. She would be accused as a co-conspirator. As would you. No. I will not bow to your request. You know full well that only at a formal hearing may a Spmite be asked to hand over her talisman.'

'In that case, what I must do now grieves me,' said the Safi as a sigh. 'For I have no choice but to declare you as the most dangerous of renegades. Although it pains me, I must fulfil my orders to execute you.'

'No! Do not do this! Executing me without recourse to judgement, even a grossly unfair judgement, defies everything the six elements stand for. You must realise that.'

The Safi swooned. 'Please, Alena. This tragic situation is very difficult for me. We were sent to this place because it was felt you would not be found here.'

Alena raised her hands, almost as an act of surrender. 'Safi; if you try to fulfil your unjust orders, I will have to fight. But I do not wish to kill anyone. I beg you to desist. I repeat, kill me and you do an undeserving Zookspmate a huge favour.'

'But, Alena, I must obey my sworn orders. As must my aktel.'

'Why don't they throw her in jail instead?' Blakey asked Rystyn as the conversation was taking place.

To his inquiry, the smug-looking Zygol cook merely shrugged. Blakey was shocked. While he harboured a deep resentment against this woman called Alena, Rystyn's derision made him seethe. 'You two-faced bastard,' he growled in his native language.

Although he did not understand Blakey's words, the Zygol squirmed. 'I gave her two chances to escape,' he retorted. 'For it was clear Tsalc had abandoned her. Yes, her motives remaining with us were noble; for she wished to lead us to safety. But be aware, she led us on a roundabout route to escape capture. She made her choices and Tsalc chose to punish her.'

Rystyn's dismissive attitude and the possibility this Alena faced an immediate execution rankled Blakey. A little. Was what she claimed the truth? The one who was called a Safi seemed to sympathise. Okay, he didn't like Alena one little bit. Her arrogance towards him had grated since their first encounter. But...

Without thinking, Blakey stood unsteadily.

'Sit down!' Rystyn hissed and grasped at Blakey's hand. 'Don't get in the way. It may cost you your life.'

Ross Blakey pulled his hand free. He was not so foolish as to get involved. He was too weary. He was... curious; that's all.

The aktel ignored him when Blakey shuffled near enough to better take in what was taking place. The three aktel who had been guarding him followed.

All aktel appeared hesitant. 'Please do not fight us... Alena,' continued the Safi. 'I have no doubt you could kill or disable a few of us if it came to a fight, for we are an inexperienced team.'

'I regret our situation, but I warn you, I will not apologise for resisting.' Then Alena noticed Blakey a short distance away. 'Be aware, aktel. This is an Earthman with no status here.'

The Safi turned towards Blakey. 'I don't know how you came to be here, stranger. But because you have no status, rest assured you will be taken safely to any place you nominate when we are done.'

Blakey's eyes bulged. 'Anywhere? Safely? Even if a Zygol back there might want to... harm me?'

'I have guaranteed your safety until you reach your chosen destination. What happens after that becomes your concern.'

Blakey punched the air. Safe! 'Yes! Will I get to ride an uckliablaht to my mining compound?'

'Yes.'

Blakey turned to Rystyn. 'I finally get this no-status thing,' he said with a wide grin. 'Great! Can I rest first and eat some fine Zygol food? I'm very hungry.'

'Of course,' the Safi replied, a little testily.

'Oh, wow! Where have you guys been until now?'

Alena gave him a look of sheer poison. Rystyn and even the Safi gave a slight lean to the left. The unspoken no.

Blakey turned sheepishly to Alena. 'Look, Alena,' The Zygol fumed, wide-eyed. 'I don't want to seem ungrateful but—'

Alena exploded. 'Only my friends and those of appropriate rank may call me by my name. You have no status. So you will not!'

'Okay... whatever you are. I'm sorry. I'm being thoughtless. I didn't appreciate what having no status meant until now. You were looking after my welfare. Thank you. That was very generous of you.'

Alena was expressionless, but the Safi leaned her head slightly to the right.

'Alena,' said the Safi, taking a nervous breath, 'I beg you one last time. Drop your weapons and hand me your talisman. Accept being recast as a Dsolcspmite and face your judgement. That way you, and we aktel, will live. And your account of why you fled will be heard.' The Safi gulped and steeled herself. The other aktel surrounding Alena resumed their fighting stances.

'I will not do what you ask! You are acting on trumped-up orders. I am only prepared to face an independent judgement *with* my talisman, as I am entitled. I am sorry but persist, and I will choose to fight to the death.'

The Safi's chest heaved. 'I cannot delay any longer. The dart shooters are set to paralyse you. After that, you will be executed. I have no choice.' The Safi couldn't look Alena in the face. 'But I promise to inform some respected Grycyryn-da of your claim.'

'Does the truth... justice... mean nothing to you?'

The aktel looked at one another, doubt etched across all their faces.

'Alena, your fate was sealed when you fled. Please, you cannot defeat us all.'

Alena jutted her chin and drew her kraxl part-way from its hilt. 'I apologise to those who I may kill or injure, but you give me no choice.'

The... Dsolcspmite... Spmite... renegade... whatever she was... had been taking tiny steps to drift close to two dart-shooter-bearing aktel. They had been too captivated by the discussion to notice.

Before she finished speaking, Alena sprang into action, moving with incredible speed. The hilt of her kraxl sent the two shooters into unconsciousness. One managed to fire off a hasty shot; the hissing barb flew wide.

Alena took a step towards the third dart-shooter aktel. She froze. She was in this aktel's sights, too far away to launch an attack.

The instant the shooter fired a barb, a clenched fist crashed into his jaw. The shocked aktel turned to face his assailant and was surprised to see Ross Blakey. The aktel smiled approvingly at a well-executed blow before collapsing.

Blakey swallowed. Up until he'd delivered the punch, he'd been resolutely determined not to get involved. His safety had been guaranteed. *If* he didn't interfere. He stood, staring at his fist in disbelief of his act of inexplicable stupidity.

Alena took up a stance, with both kraxl and kraxl-da in hand. The four conscious but stunned aktel hastily dropped their blades. Four aktel against a human fighting machine weren't enough. Alena gave a hand signal and the aktel leaned their heads to the right and retrieved and sheathed their weapons. It was to Ross Blakey they glared.

Satisfied, Alena turned to face Blakey, perplexed. 'By your act, Earthman, you now have full status. And by breaking your word not to get involved, you can be executed on the spot, without judgement, by anyone who captures us. Even I, as a joint chief defender of the six elements, should inflict some sort of punishment for what you did.' But her eyes, reflected by the campfire, held a trace of admiration.

Blakey, still stunned by his actions, spread out his arms and shook his head. 'I... don't know why I...'

'I choose to not punish you,' Alena pronounced. 'I believe that you, like the Safi, were conflicted by how to apply the six elements in this clearly unjust situation. You wished to secure justice for me, though you had given a solemn promise to not get involved. I believe you chose incorrectly, but I acknowledge the dilemma you faced.'

'Well, thank you... err.' Thinking back, justice could well be one of the six elements Zglta had explained to him. However, apart from Tsalc —chance, luck or the unforseen—he was pretty well clueless. On some inexplicable impulse, he'd saved the life of this Alena. The act done, his only chance of ever returning to his compound alive rested with the warrior. He cringed at the realisation.

'All of you, be aware,' Alena said calmly. 'Should you choose to help me seek independent judgement, you will be regarded as renegades in the eyes of the Zookspmate and by those who have sworn allegiance to him.'

The aktel and Rystyn leaned their heads to the right. 'Rystyn, fetch me two clundrns of water.'

The frowning cook hastily did as he was told. Alena tossed the water onto the faces of the three unconscious aktel who woke looking wildly about them. There were hand signals. One incredulous aktel uttered a cuss that Blakey knew. *Zeeplat!*

'I will not be offended if any or all of you opt to return to your villages.' Alena then turned to the Safi. 'I see in you a strong desire to be true to the six elements. If you choose to come with me, you can remain as Safi.'

'I am honoured to be able to serve you... but forgive me. I struggle to know what to call you. Perhaps a hybrid term: Dsolcspmite-Spmite,' replied the Safi. 'I fully commit myself to helping you with your quest for justice. I am greatly relieved I did not execute you.' A couple of aktel leant their heads to the right.

'I ask that I be addressed as Spmite. But if doing so conflicts you, then I accept your label of Dsolcspmite-Spmite. You have much to be proud of, Safi. You showed me compassion and some semblance of justice by allowing me to explain why I fled. I can understand... but cannot agree... why, as an aktel, you bowed to the Zookspmate's command rather than defer to the six elements. Rest assured, however, I will be honoured to have a Safi such as you as part of my troop.'

The Safi turned to her aktel. 'Do you wish to leave or join us, aktel? As renegades, we would stand to possibly be executed if we are captured. You know full well there are many aktel who will be hunting us. Even after the Dsolcspmite-Spmite receives her independent judgement, we may not be exempt from some form of punishment. Come forward if you wish to join us.'

Three aktel approached the Safi; the other three looked embarrassed. One spoke on behalf of the latter three. 'We are sorry, but we deem the risk of continuing with you too great. We pledge we will not betray you or the Dsolcspmite-Spmite, even if we are faced with the threat of death.'

'You need feel no shame,' the Safi replied. 'Perhaps the three of you will wait here until the morning sun so the rest of us can be a distance away. You may face some form of punishment when you join your fellow aktel, even though I take the blame for the failed mission. My advice is to seek judgement organised by a trusted Grycyryn in the Three Villages. The Zookspmate is gathering an increasing reputation for harshness, as we can now attest to.'

The three smiled in relief. 'We can manage with two uckliablahts. You may keep the other five. That way you can travel faster.'

The Safi turned to Alena. 'It is best we seek sanctuary as soon as possible, Dsolcspmite-Spmite.' They both gazed at the sky. A soft starlight filtered through the evening haze. 'It is light enough to guide our immediate route, yet the haze will help conceal us from hostile eyes.'

'We leave once we have eaten. But our uckliablaht can go no further,' Alena said.

'Our uckliablahts and plooglits are tethered close by,' the Safi remarked. 'Your companions can share a ride with my aktel.' Apart from the Safi, the aktel slipped into the night at her words. 'But eat hastily. Others will soon work out that something has gone amiss. And they will investigate.'

'I guessed as much.'

The Safi turned to Blakey and punched him hard in the stomach. He doubled over, sank to the ground, and groaned.

'That is for breaking your promise to not get involved,' she spat. 'Your punishment would have been more severe if I hadn't pledged my support to the Dsolcspmite-Spmite. Yet I am grateful that you prevented me from committing an act that would have haunted me for the rest of my life.'

'You have a strange way of showing your gratitude,' Blakey moaned. His stomach now hurt, just like the rest of him.

'Earthman, you have demonstrated that promises mean little to you. Yet I ask you nevertheless to pledge total loyalty to the Dsolcspmite-Spmite. Keep in mind, should you show any inclination to break that promise, all of us are pledged to kill you without warning. Do you pledge total loyalty to her?'

Blakey looked up at the Safi as he regained his breath. 'Can I leave with the aktel who are going back to the Three Villages?'

'No!' Alena growled. 'We cannot take the chance of you betraying us. My lack of trust in you is why Rystyn and I forced you to come with us.'

'If you don't pledge unconditional loyalty, we will kill you,' said the Safi. 'That is the alternative we offer.'

Some decisions are very easy. 'Then I pledge my complete and total loyalty to... her.' He indicated Alena with a wave of his hand.

'Good.' The Safi turned to an anxious Rystyn.

'Do you pledge total loyalty to the Dsolcspmite-Spmite?'

Rystyn examined his sandals.

'Why are you asking this of Rystyn?' a surprised Alena asked.

'It is necessary,' the Safi replied.

Alena studied the fidgeting Rystyn. 'Were you part of the plot against me?'

Rystyn sighed. 'That is so. I was forced to comply, under threat of banishment. My role was to inform the Zookspmate's aktel of our escape route and leave behind pointers to our location. But the sandstorms put paid to most of that plan.' Rystyn glared at Blakey. 'From the start, I had the feeling that the Earthman would be a problem. But I promise you, sincerely, Dsolcspmite-Spmite, I had no idea the Zookspmate wanted you executed without even a hearing. Had I'd known I would never have agreed to the plot.'

Alena gazed sourly at the uncomfortable cook. 'If I hadn't heard those words from your lips, I would never have believed them.'

'I am deeply sorry, Dsolcspmite-Spmite. Now I pledge total loyalty to you.' Rystyn dared not look at Alena.

The aktel returned, leading the uckliablahts and plooglits, which were tethered to the beasts. Two aktel fetched an ahk, cooking implements and a food bag from one of their sacks. They deposited the contents of Rystyn's pot before the ailing uckliablaht, and began cooking.

After contemplating his new circumstances, Ross Blakey put his hand up. 'If I now have status, I want to be treated like a person. For starters, call me by my name, Ross Blakey.'

'If that is what you prefer,' replied the Safi, 'Rossblakey.'

'I still choose to call you Earthman,' growled Alena.

'And I too,' snarled Rystyn.

Blakey wasn't about to insist. Not to a fully armed warrior.

'Can I ask a question... err, Safi?' he continued. 'What is a spumite and a dsol... whatever it is you said?'

The Safi rolled her eyes. 'Rossblakey; a Spmite is the highest-ranked female defender of the six elements. She achieves her rank after contests every two years among the female Dsolcspmites and wisest female Grycyryn-das of the region. The contests involve proven commitment to the six elements by skill, brave deeds and wisdom. The talisman that a Spmite carries is a symbol of her rank, power and esteem. She cannot be Spmite without it. Only in rare circumstances can she be challenged for it.'

'And a dsolc...' Blakey mused out loud. 'Whatever you call her.'

'I need to prepare for our departure,' said the Safi, a little annoyed. 'Whichever aktel you ride with will explain these matters to you. Your food is almost ready. Eat and drink quickly so we can leave.'

Blakey was all for leaving quickly. He was still grappling with utter disbelief for what he'd just done. *Moron!* If only he was sitting in the

Chute, seat-belt on, bucket at his feet, his mouth hovering over the intercom to say, 'Yes, I'm ready.'

Alena, Rystyn and Blakey ate and drank swiftly as the others made preparations to depart. An uckliablaht, with its tethered companion plooglit, passed by (Hmmmmmmmmmm) the new pot of food. However, the plooglit huddled close to its uckliablaht when it came across the sad, hulking form of the plooglitless uckliablaht, which gave a strangled moan.

The Safi approached Alena as preparations were made. 'Do you approve of our tactics to capture you, Dsolcspmite-Spmite? We hid ourselves downwind and muzzled our uckliablahts while you searched for water.'

'Your tactics were indeed well implemented. I was low on energy and morale and came back from an urgent task I had to attend to. You caught me off-guard.'

The Safi smiled, then approached Blakey. 'Rossblakey, we must do something about your cough. It may reveal our whereabouts.' She handed him a small, earthen vial and a clundrn of water. 'Take one small sip.'

Blakey did. So foul was the taste that he almost spat it out. He drowned it with water. Yet shortly afterward, his rasping cough had eased. *Stuff the minerals we mine*, Blakey thought. *If I sold that elixir on Earth, I'd be filthy rich.*

'You did not bring medicine with you?' the Safi addressed Rystyn. 'We departed in a hurry,' the evasive Zygol cook replied.

One of the aktel approached. 'It is best your uckliablaht is let go to follow us to the Three Villages. He is beyond journeying further carrying any burden.'

'I know,' Rystyn replied. 'I will set it free. Three short, sharp whistles will get him to follow you.'

After hugs and words of farewell with those remaining in the camp, the Safi organised who would ride the five uckliablahts. 'Both the Dsolcspmite-Spmite and I and one aktel will have their own uckliablahts,' she explained. 'I am not being selfish. It is because we face the harshest punishments, along with Rossblakey. But he does not know how to ride an uckliablaht. It will allow our Dsolcspmite-Spmite to have the fullest possible freedom to defend herself and us.'

'It is best if I continue to ride my uckliablaht by myself,' said a male aktel. This aktel was the tallest and most strongly built of the group. 'She is showing some signs of suffering in the harsh conditions.'

'I agree, Gentok,' the Safi said. 'And you are also a highly capable fighter.'

As the renegade aktel mounted their uckliablahts, they seemed cheerful, given their dire circumstances. Blakey and Rystyn, though, were miserable. Alena and the Safi set off at the front with Blakey and Rystyn and their riding partners positioned behind and Gentok at the rear. The plooglits were kept tethered to their companion uckliablahts. These plooglits were remarkably languid.

With his chances of surviving resting with Alena, Blakey practised pronouncing her rank over and over with coaching from his accompanying aktel, Trimff. Trimff was thin and short; with a youthful face beneath his helmet. *Dsolc... spmite. Dsolcspmite... Spmite. Whatever the hell she was.*

'You betrayed your... err... Dsolcspmite-Spmite,' Blakey teased.

Rystyn, who was sharing the uckliablaht in front of him, lowered his head.

The renegades headed into low-lying hills under a hazy night sky. They trekked slowly through rough country. As they journeyed, Trimff answered the Earthman's questions in whispers.

'I guess having her own uckliablaht means she has a better chance of being able to escape,' Blakey whispered.

Trimff gave the Earthman a withering look. 'You cannot be referring to the Dsolcspmite-Spmite.'

A big oops moment. 'I didn't explain that well,' Blakey back-tracked. 'I still struggle with your language. And being out in the harsh desert has affected my thinking. She will defend all of us, won't she?'

Trimff seemed satisfied. 'She will defend us all to the death.'

'Right. Now... if the people chasing us catch up with us, is there anything I can do or say to stop them from killing me? An apology... perhaps made on my knees?'

'By saving the life of the Dsolcspmite-Spmite and breaking your promise to not get involved, you frustrated the orders of the Zookspmate. And this is a Zookspmate who has become harsh of late. Anything you say at a hearing will be of no use. You will most certainly die. Perhaps a long, lingering death.'

'Thank you Trimff.' Blakey swore.

'Not only that, we aktel cannot intervene if you are condemned to be executed. Even the Dsolcspmite-Spmite cannot save you.'

'What else could I expect?'

'Although your judgement will certainly result in your death, many will debate whether your actions were correct or noble. But your fate is sealed, regardless.'

Blakey shook his head. 'I can't believe what I did back there. But I wish you well, whatever happens.'

Trimff turned and smiled. 'Thank you for your kind wishes. It is my belief that what you did for the Dsolcspmite-Spmite was very noble.' Then another expression etched across his face. 'Incredibly stupid. But very noble. I fear the Dsolcspmite-Spmite is doomed, regardless of whether she receives a proper judgement. Even if she is found innocent. The Zookspmate has set the tumbling rock into motion and he will surely pursue it until it comes to rest. Her only hope of staying alive is to be rid of him. But I cannot see how that can happen. So, unfortunately, your noble effort was almost certainly in vain.'

'But, if the Dsolcspmite-Spmite is cleared of her charges, is there a chance I will be spared?'

Trimff considered the question. 'No. You are doomed whatever happens. I say it again: you frustrated the orders of a Zookspmate, breaking a pledge. The Zookspmate will demand your death. His grounds are sound.'

'Oh,' was all Blakey could respond. He slammed his thigh. To think that he had been offered safe passage to the compound. Pensive, he needed to talk more.

'Okay then. What is a... Dsolcspmite?'

'The high rank of Dsolcspmite emphasises physical or fighting abilities. A Spmite, who came from the rank of Dsolcspmite, is clothed as you see in front of you. It is both practical and acts to warn others that she is not someone to trifle with. Had she achieved her rank of Spmite after being a Grycyryn instead, she would wear a tunic but it would be both orange—signifying a wise one—and, mostly, green. The Zookspmate was a Grycyryn, so he wears a blue and orange tunic.'

'What's this guy like anyway? He and the Dsolcspmite-Spmite obviously don't like each other.'

Trimff thought for a few moments. 'There are people who will tell you he has made many welcome changes, yet there is a growing feeling that he is becoming increasingly selfish and shows little tolerance to those who don't agree with him. It defies elapelc. Also, there are those who accuse him of diverging from the ideals of the six elements. Earlier, the Dsolcspmite-Spmite alluded to whispers that he has organised people loyal to him to preside over disputes that involve him, rather than using more-respected Grycyryn-da.'

'You believe the charges against the Dsolcspmite-Spmite are fabricated?'

'I do not know. I know little of the manoeuvrings of the highest ranks. But I am now convinced that the Dsolcspmite-Spmite has more integrity than the Zookspmate.'

'That put you in a tricky position, didn't it, being sent on this mission when you aren't sure about the integrity of the man who gives the orders?'

Trimff took a breath. 'We all held some doubts certainly. But with the Dsolcspmite-Spmite being declared a renegade, and with no Grycyryn-da or respected Dsolcspmite publicly disputing that claim, we had no choice but to obey. Has the Zookspmate become unworthy? I cannot say for certain. It is not unknown for unworthy people to be stripped of their rank before the next round of Succession Games selects a Zookspmate for the next term. The problem with this Zookspmate is that there are those who will tell you one thing and those who say the opposite. It is difficult to know the truth. It is why I firmly believe that the Dsolcspmite-Spmite deserves the right to be given a proper judgement.'

'If there are doubts about this Zookspmate, why is he able to wield so much power?'

'This Zookspmate is sharp in mind. Of that there can be no doubt. He has done great things. But the doubters are becoming more numerous, though many have chosen to be silent, which is not the Zygol way.'

'He sounds like a bastard to me.'

'I do not know of this rank, Ross Blakey.'

'It's an Earth term for someone who is not worthy.'

Trimff leant his head to the right.

Blakey took a deep breath. That unworthy man, who dispatched power that seemed unchallenged, would be demanding he die if he were captured. And there was nothing Blakey could do about it.

4

____

RACE TO MKELDI VILLAGE

THE RENEGADES RODE through the night. A frustrated Ross Blakey became convinced that the route chosen by Alena and the Safi invariably involved taking the most unlikely, indirect and rugged option. At times, the airborne dust blocked out the stars and Zygol III's smaller, dull moon, bringing the group to a halt.

During a break, the Safi sat beside Blakey, cradling a fire stick. 'I am curious, Rossblakey. How did you apply the six elements when you decided to save the Dsolcspmite-Spmite?'

Blakey shrugged. 'I didn't think. It just seemed the right thing to do. By her. But, for me...' He shook his head.

The Safi looked at him as if he were an alien. Which he was.

He had an idea. 'While you're here, Safi, maybe you can help me.' He took a small notebook and pen from his back pocket. 'Can you tell me what the six elements are? I think I've got them written them down back at the compound, but I want to make sure. Tsalc is one. I'm guessing another is about justice. But tell me what they are.'

The Safi recoiled. Gaping, she moved a few steps away from him. 'Zeeplat!' came her stunned reply. She struggled to speak. 'You speak our language, yet you know nothing about five of the six elements? That is opitek of the worst kind! Knowledge without wisdom.'

'Well... I...'

'You did not ask such a vital question when you first came to our planet?' The Safi swooned. 'There can be no excuses. You need to be applying them. Constantly. Your ignorance explains why you act without reason and why no one trusts you.'

Blakey sighed. 'Okay. I have been badly negligent. But let me set this matter right. Tell me, please? I will write them down. Maybe knowing them will help me somehow. Otherwise, if I can get this notebook to my compound, maybe my fellow Earth people won't make the same mistakes I have made.' Hopefully, he'd hand them the notebook in person.

The Safi turned her back on him. 'Your words devastate me.'

'Please tell me. I will be deeply appreciative.'

The Safi faced Blakey and spoke with a voice tinged by a quiver. 'The six elements are the guiding principles we carry throughout our lives, no matter what individual path we follow. They are intertwined with the notion of elapelc, which is—'

'Elapelc I know about. Maybe I'm bad at it... well, obviously... but I know what it means. Go on.'

The Safi looked at Blakey strangely. 'The first element is justice and integrity.'

'I figured justice was there somewhere.' Blakey nodded and whispered the words to himself as he jotted them down.

The Safi examined his jottings blankly. 'With this element—'

'Just list them for now. You can explain them more if we have time.'

The Safi frowned. 'The second element is compassion and caring for all forms of life. The third element, the one that I have chosen to guide me more than any other element, is learning and teaching, which can never be separated. Then comes the fourth element: strength and agility of mind and body. The fifth element—'

Blakey was jotting furiously. 'Slow down a bit.'

The Safi paused until Blakey nodded. 'The fifth element is courage and application. I don't need to remind you of the sixth element, Tsalc. It is the sole element that directs your existence.'

Blakey thought for a few moments. 'But wait. There's nothing about knowledge, logic and wisdom in the six elements. Aren't those qualities vital?'

The Safi leaned her head to the right and smiled weakly. 'An important question, Rossblakey. Those attributes are indeed vital. As with elapelc, they are intertwined with each of the six elements. Think. How can there be justice if we do not know what is just and what is not?' Then she added, as a growl, 'Otherwise, we would act merely out of reflex. As you do.'

'Another question,' Blakey said. 'You say your guiding element is learning and teaching, yet you are a guard, a warrior. And you have a higher rank than the other aktel with you. Why is that?'

The Safi was confused. 'Why you are perplexed, Rossblakey? An aktel is primarily a defender of the six elements. Defenders come in different forms. I became a Safi at the last Succession Games, selected by my fellow aktel because of my knowledge and ability to teach and learn. Of course, to attain my rank, I had to also show leadership and a capability to protect my people.'

'Yet you obey orders without question.'

The Safi made a double take. Her head dropped. 'You raise a dilemma. It is one that I had not encountered before. Rest assured that I will be more questioning when such a problem arises again. I will demand to know all the facts. And consult respected Grycyryn-da for advice.' She gave the faintest smile. 'I hope, one day, to become a Grycyryn and to devote more time to my chosen element.'

Some starlight broke through the haze. Others were already mounting their steeds. 'We must go now.' As the Safi and Blakey returned to their uckliablahts, she took him by the shoulder. 'I don't know what to make of you, Rossblakey. In some ways, you are a fool and yet, in other ways, you are not.'

'My people have similar fine principles to yours. They are not laid out like yours are. But we are not so different.' As he walked over to his uckliablaht, he muttered to himself, 'It's just we often ignore our principles when they get in the way.'

The renegades rode on.

An apprehensive Ross Blakey kept pressing Trimff. 'How much further do you think?'

'I do not know,' Trimff replied each time. 'We are taking a roundabout route to try and avoid detection. You need to be patient.'

'Be patient! If I get captured, I get executed. And you ask me to be patient.' Twice Blakey fell asleep on Trimff's shoulder only to be jolted awake when the uckliablaht stepped awkwardly. He hoped to be asleep if a kraxl-da was plunged into his neck. He dreamed of his ex-wife and children. He almost fell when he reached out to pick up his youngest.

The first faint orange rays of dawn emerged. Ross Blakey blinked to wake himself, but he kept nodding off. His head was low when a thick branch brushed past his head. A branch in a desert of rock and sand? Instinctively, he bent beneath it.

Trimff was gone. The young Zygol never saw what struck him. The uckliablaht bucked and Blakey gripped the saddle desperately, somehow managing to hold on. The uckliablaht in front tried to bolt with Rystyn and his companion pulling hard on its rope.

Blakey caught a glimpse a large, dark shape on two massive hind legs disappearing into the shadows, A limp Trimff was draped across its shoulder. Gentok, who was riding at the rear of the group, gave a cry of alarm and drew his kraxl-da to no avail. The dark shape clambered where his uckliablaht could not follow. The attack was over in seconds.

As Blakey stared in shock, Alena and the Safi ran over, kraxl-das drawn.

'What happened?'

All a shaken Blakey could do was shrug. It was Gentok who spoke. 'A cfaldi took Trimff. It went that way.' He pointed the way.

'I'll bring him back,' Alena vowed.

'Don't go,' pleaded the Safi, gripping Alena's arm. 'Trimff is dead. If you go after him, you will have to fight a ravenous cfaldi in terrain it thrives in. In near darkness. It isn't worth the risk. Not to retrieve a body. We are close to our sanctuary. That must remain our priority. I know this is hard for you to accept, as it is for me. Trimff was a fine young man, but listen to me. Don't chase the cfaldi.'

Alena stared at where the cfaldi had vanished. 'But Trimff is my responsibility. If I'd been on foot, and on lookout, I would have—'

'No one could have prevented this. The cfaldi chose its spot well.'

'The Safi is correct, Dsolcspmite-Spmite,' chimed in the female aktel who was riding with Rystyn. 'As fine an aktel, and a person, as Trimff was, he would not want you to risk fetching his body. If you are injured, what then? And besides, what would we do with his body?' She bowed her head, embarrassed.

Alena slumped. She looked at the sky. But she tilted her head ever so slightly to the right. 'As much as it pains me to admit it, you are both correct. There is no point. We will continue, and I will speak to Trimff's parents if I am able. Though I feel I have failed in my duty to defend a brave aktel who chose to support my quest.' She sighed; with head low, she returned to her uckliablaht.

The trek continued in solemn silence with the female aktel sharing the uckliablaht with Blakey and all but him riding with kraxls or kraxldas drawn.

'What if the cfaldi comes back?' Blakey asked in a quivering voice, his eyes darting.

'That cfaldi will not attack us,' she said. 'Trimff will last it many days. Then it will rest. But other cfaldi may lurk nearby.'

'Poor Trimff. He could have chosen to go home back at the camp. But he chose not to go.'

'He was a very wonderful, principled guy. He was destined to become a Safi,' the female aktel said with a voice that faltered. 'My name is Kasmin.'

'Ross Blakey.'

Kasmin leaned her head to the right.

'Tell me something. Rystyn told me that a plooglit can detect when cfaldi are nearby. Why didn't that happen?'

'It is normally so, yes. But look at these plooglits. When they are subdued by tethers, they drift into a dream-like state. It is not their nature to be constrained. Their senses become much diminished, as they are now.'

The fugitives continued in silence, following in the steps of Alena's uckliablaht. She brought her uckliablaht to a halt and looked about. Before them was a wide, dry riverbed. On both sides were steep rising cliffs and treacherous, loose, orange-black rocks.

'Be silent,' Kasmin whispered as the riders exchanged hand signals. 'We must go this way. We cannot afford the delay of finding an alternate route with daylight so near. We fear that our trail has been detected. If you listen carefully, you can sometimes hear echoes of others not far away. But going this way carries with it a risk of ambush.'

Ross Blakey cursed the rising sun under his breath, then shut his eyes. Perhaps twenty minutes later, after moving steadily up through the narrowing dry riverbed, the riders reached a small gap between two steep outcrops. Beyond was a mostly flat mesa about the size of a suburban block. Alena was reluctant to proceed. To their immediate right and left were intimidating masses of shattered large boulders and steep rises. At the end of the mesa, a long, thin, perpendicular rock faced a wide rounded, low hill beside it. Beyond the perpendicular rock, the land seemed to fall away.

'This is a very dangerous place,' Kasmin whispered. 'That distinctive rock marks the boundary of the valley that belongs to Mkeldi village. If we pass it, we will receive genuine, independent judgement.'

'But isn't that way much closer?' Blakey said anxiously pointing to his right where the land also seemed to dip away.

'Yes, it is closer. But I know this place. It is a cliff. We must pass close to that rock.'

Blakey calculated the rock could be reached in about ten minutes on the back of an uckliablaht moving briskly. Less if the uckliablaht had one rider. Yet Alena was hesitant.

'The authority of the Zookspmate isn't recognised in Mkeldi. His forces cannot detain us if we enter its territory. But we *must* get there first.'

Blakey, exhausted and fearful, couldn't bear the tension. He was impatient to take off on a wild, desperate dash. But Alena dismounted from her uckliablaht and clambered silently up one of the outcroppings. Near the top, she lay flat, checking for signs of danger. Then she clambered down and leaped on her uckliablaht.

Kasmin interpreted the hand signals. They would make a dash for safety, though the open territory left them vulnerable to attack. There was little residual dust in the air and they no longer enjoyed the concealment of darkness.

'We have no choice,' Kasmin muttered. 'The Zookspmate's aktel are closing in behind us at speed.'

Blakey sucked a breath. Alena and the aktel brandished their kraxl-das. Then Alena cajoled her uckliablaht forward.

Boom! Boom! Two loud explosions shook the ground, spewing two large puffs of brown grit. Alena cried out; enveloped by two huge, heavy nets. As she fought to claw herself clear, her panicked uckliablaht fell, causing beast and rider to crash to the ground. Alena drew her kraxl and furiously began cutting at the nets. Somehow, the uckliablaht dragged itself free.

The Safi, following behind, escaped the nets when her uckliablaht had reared. She leaped off her startled steed, kraxl in hand. As she reached the nets, with Gentok and Kasmin trailing, about twenty aktel in full armour rounded both rocky outcrops, some brandishing kraxl-das, many others sporting dart shooters. Half of them rode uckliablahts; their plooglits tethered close.

'Drop your weapons!' commanded a male in Safi uniform. 'All of you.'

Reluctantly, Alena's Safi signalled Gentok and Kasmin to comply. Resistance was pointless.

'You others, dismount,' the man ordered.

Blakey, who couldn't run or ride an uckliablaht even if escape was possible, swallowed, his fate sealed.

Alena let loose a stream of invectives as their captors tightened the nets around her, dragging her forcibly to the ground, face down. 'I am your Spmite. I demand to be taken to Mkeldi village and receive independent judgement!'

Some aktel laughed. When Alena was pinned, one pushed her head into the dirt while another threw her weapons clear. The aktel hammered wooden stakes into the ground to tighten the nets around her.

Alena's Safi spoke. 'Listen to what the Dsolcspmite-Spmite has to say before you act in haste.'

An aktel fired a barb into the Safi's chest. She buckled and collapsed.

'Jkilm!' Alena shouted. 'How dare you? She had surrendered.'

'Curse me all you want,' sneered the male Safi as he dismounted. He was tall, with broad shoulders, and he walked with a swagger.

'Don't grieve for her. Yet. The dart has only rendered her unconscious. My Zookspmate wishes to be present when renegades are punished.' He smirked. 'But should any of you offer resistance, I won't hesitate to act.'

He turned to Kasmin. 'You. Explain to me why the renegade Alena is alive and how you came to ride with her. And explain who this Earthman is.'

Kasmin answered, 'You have an unpleasant manner, Safi. We surrendered, yet—'

'I do not tolerate insolence,' he snapped and stepped across to tower over the young renegade. 'Understand who is in charge here.'

'Certainly.' Kasmin fired off a hand signal as she spoke. Her captor didn't like the message but two aktel behind him leaned their heads slightly, but briefly, to their right. Then Kasmin gave a quick recount of events.

Alena watched, impotent. Barely able to move.

Ross Blakey cringed when the Zookspmate's Safi glowered at him.

At times, Alena chimed in with some Zygol words Blakey did not know.

After Kasmin finished, the male Safi, scowling, turned to face the renegades.

'You will all be punished for your acts. Especially your Safi, who has acted with incompetence and a lack of judgement. Never give a Dsolcspmite or Spmite even the smallest leeway. The traitor should have been executed immediately when you ambushed her, as you were ordered. You say you wished her to die with dignity? Weaklings, all of you. Watch how I enact my orders. The renegade Alena will die where she lies like a trapped cfaldi.' He swaggered over to Blakey.

'Earthman, you acted dishonourably when you frustrated the Zookspmate's orders. You condemn yourself by that deed. Although I could kill you now, the Zookspmate will gain particular satisfaction being present at your execution. Take note, aktel. This man is untrustworthy. Treat him accordingly. Should he make any false move, be aware that he can't run far if his feet are removed.'

The Safi stepped back. 'Do you renegades promise not to interfere with the execution of the renegade, Alena? If you don't promise this, you die now.'

Some of his aktel raised their dart shooters. He paced triumphantly before a furious Alena.

The renegades complied silently as Rystyn had done the previous day; their faces crestfallen. Ross Blakey feigned ignorance and did not comply. Not with Alena being his only chance of escape.

Kasmin spoke. 'We have done as you have demanded, Safi, but we wish it known that we consider executing the Dsolcspmite-Spmite without judgement to be highly improper.' Kasmin looked forlornly at Alena. 'I am sorry, Dsolcspmite-Spmite.'

'You bring yourself no dishonour,' Alena replied. 'There is no need to die fighting for a cause that is lost.'

'Obviously your Safi is in no position to comply,' the male Safi boasted. 'It will give me considerable pleasure when she wakes to find your dead body beside her, Alena. Ah, such a waste of your training. All that dedication. And you will die with your precious talisman in my warm hand. Oh, the look on your face! Such anger. Yes, I will have it in my hand as you take your final breath. What humiliation. Without your talisman, you lose whatever vestiges you have of ever having been a Spmite, dying as a mere renegade.'

Alena remained silent. Her eyes burned.

The male Safi turned to four of his aktel. 'Fetch the talisman for me. It is in her zain.' The four recoiled, mouths agape.

'Aktel, I have issued an order. She is a renegade who is in possession of a Spmite's talisman. Fetch it!'

The aktel hesitated before cautiously sidling to Alena.

'No!' pleaded Alena. 'Execute me if that is what you want but I insist on keeping my talisman. Do not dishonour me and the six elements in this vengeful way.'

'I obey only my Zookspmate,' growled the Safi. 'His instructions are for you to die humiliated. Protest all you like. It will do you no good. Indeed, your cowering brings me pleasure. Do it,' he commanded the four aktel, who descended on the prone Alena.

'The day will come when you pay for your dishonourable act, Safi, and your Zookspmate will not be able to protect you,' Alena growled. She struggled in vain to free her arms and reach her zain.

'You do not frighten me,' scowled the male Safi.

As the aktel held Alena still, one reached down into a side pouch of her zain and removed a round, flat and flexible disc, slightly smaller than an Earth DVD. The sight of the talisman brought about a collective breath of awe from those gathered. Their task achieved, the four aktel moved clear of Alena, who let loose another stream of invectives.

'With your humiliation complete, I will now perform your execution.' Grinning, the Safi drew his kraxl-da and strode to the helpless Dsolcspmite-Spmite as an aktel approached him, holding out the talisman.

'Jkilm!' Alena spat. The renegades echoed her words. Did a couple of the male Safi's aktel whisper the same word? Some hand signals passed around; a couple of the guarding aktel seemed uneasy.

Kasmin leaped forward and snatched the talisman as the aktel placed it in the male Safi's hand. 'You cannot do this!' she yelled. She only managed a few steps towards Alena before she was tackled to the ground by two aktel. The talisman tumbled to the ground and stopped at the feet of Ross Blakey, a man with nothing to lose.

'You will die for that act of insolence!' the Safi spat as he dug his knees into Kasmin's chest and readied to plunge his kraxl-da into the helpless young aktel. Those looking on took a collective breath.

Gentok sprang forward but was halted by the points of three kraxl-das.

'I really think you should look my way before you do anything,' Blakey called out.

All eyes turned to him as he knelt beside a fissure in the rocks, the size of his forearm, the talisman in his hand. The green-brown disc felt like nothing he had ever touched. It felt like an odd mixture of velvet and soft wood. It was flexible but not soft. Even in the dull morning light, the talisman sparkled softly.

'You want to kill me, and I haven't the energy to run. So, how much do you want this thing?'

'Give me that talisman! Now!' thundered the male Safi, rising to his feet. Eight aktel came at Blakey, brandishing kraxl-das.

'Drop your weapons. Now!' Blakey hovered the talisman over the fissure. 'Try anything and I drop the talisman. And this fissure looks deep. Really deep.' In truth, he had no idea. It was worth the gamble. The aktel hesitated. But none dropped their weapons.

'Earthman,' called out Alena. 'If you are able, bring the talisman and place it in my hand so I can die with dignity. They will never be able to remove it from my grasp while I live. I beg this of you!'

Blakey wasn't at all keen. He faced a wide semi-circle of armed aktel, a murderous intent in their eyes. He was a dead man if he so much as stood up. And Alena wouldn't get the talisman back unless his throw was absolutely perfect.

Gentok called out. 'Throw it to me. I'll give it to the Dsolcspmite-Spmite.' But that was also a death sentence. The talisman was his only leverage. Three aktel immediately tackled Gentok to the ground with a kraxl resting against his throat. That put paid to that idea anyway.

'Kill the Earthman now!' screamed the male Safi. So much for Blakey's bargaining chip.

Yet the aktel stood their ground, uncertain. 'I won't warn you again. Try anything and I'll drop it.'

'Drop it and we will retrieve it,' said an aktel nearby. 'Even if we have to dig through rock to get it.' But no aktel stepped closer, transfixed by the talisman in Blakey's hand. Kasmin and Gentok looked on, mouths agape.

The stand-off had its benefits for one person. Perhaps two. Out of sight, Rystyn had picked up a kraxl that the surrendering renegades had tossed aside. He quietly cut at the nets closest to Alena's arms. Soon the Dsolcspmite-Spmite had her forearms free and Rystyn quickly passed her a kraxl and kraxl-da. They both cut feverishly at the nets.

If Blakey could keep the attention of their captors for long enough, there may yet be a faint hope for him. 'This fissure is very, very deep. If I drop the talisman, there is no way you will be able to retrieve it.'

'Remember, Earthmen tell nontruths. They have no honour,' commanded the male Safi. But his voice was tinged with doubt. As with all those gathered, his eyes were fixed on the talisman.

To Blakey's surprise it was Alena who spoke. 'Earthman. Do not drop the talisman down the fissure. Not under any circumstances.' She, with the aid of Rystyn, was close to freeing herself from the nets. 'I would much rather die than have my talisman lost to the world.'

Blakey blinked. Big help she was. Not!

The male Safi became infused with a new confidence. 'Don't stand about, aktel. Kill him. Now! He will not drop the talisman.'

As Alena pulled herself free from the nets, Rystyn silently mounted an uckliablaht and slowly rode away. The aktel surrounding Blakey raised their kraxl-das, ready to strike. One aktel launched a surprise attack, lunging at the talisman. With his hands trembling, Blakey's grip was loose. He fumbled the disc. For a split-second, it hovered on the edge of the fissure, then slid silently out of sight. Just beyond two pairs of desperately grasping hands.

There was a brief sliding sound, then a faint but dull thud as the talisman hit rock. The aktel, now pressed around the fissure, gave a collective gasp. In the brief silence that followed, they turned as one towards Blakey with kraxl-das raised. The talisman below bounced dully off more rock. This elicited a louder collective gasp and furtive glances. Far below, it hit another rock, followed instantly by a faint splash.

An eerie silence followed. Many shoulders slumped. Someone muttered a zeeplat, which was echoed by others.

'Jkilm!' uttered the male Safi as he glared at Blakey.

To Ross Blakey's amazement, he was still alive. Everyone—

including the now-free Alena and Kasmin and Gentok—gathered around to gaze at what was definitely a very deep fissure.

Rystyn kept riding, glancing back anxiously.

All eyes turned to the cringing Blakey. 'I... err... didn't mean...'

The unbridled fury in Alena's eyes made Blakey shudder. 'Do you know what you have done?' she thundered, her voice trailing into a strangled scream.

Blakey felt a little miffed. From his perspective, Alena would be gurgling blood if it hadn't been for him. He, with Rystyn's help, had given her a chance to flee or fight. But she wasn't even the remotest bit grateful.

'No. What have I done?' Blakey volunteered tentatively. He tried to back away. But, behind him was only rock. Armed aktel and a furious Alena blocked all the other avenues of escape. He hadn't the strength to run, anyway.

Alena sucked in a breath. 'What manner of being are you? You have shamed me. Please, Safi, for the sake of the six elements, grant me time to search for the talisman. I promise I will hand it to you if I find it. And you alone. And will then willingly accept my execution.'

The male Safi was shaken into a reply. 'The Zookspmate would forbid it,' he said as a whisper. 'Even though every female in our region will now blame me for the loss of the talisman.'

Alena shook with fury. 'Earthman; you have destroyed me. And sowed chaos on our entire region. Now, no one can call herself Spmite until the talisman is retrieved or a new talisman is made and verified. That will take...' Her voice faltered. 'Only Tsalc knows what will happen until then. Our entire system of justice is now in total ruin. Because of you, some good people will likely die or be banished, or demoted at the unchallenged whim of a Zookspmate who is obsessed with power. You have made death a welcome release for me.'

'Sorry,' Blakey mumbled sheepishly.

'Sorry!' boomed Alena. 'You say... sorry. No! You must pay for your despicable deed. I will feed your broken bones to a cfaldi.' She raised her kraxl-da and shoved aside a couple of aktel to get to the cowering Earthman.

'Umm... I'll go look for it,' stammered Blakey. He needed a deep fissure to drop into.

'Stand aside renegade,' commanded the male Safi. 'It is I who must execute him!'

'No!' scowled Alena. 'It is against me that he has committed the greatest harm.'

'Look, I can help you,' Blakey pleaded. 'I'm very familiar with the structure of caves. Also, I can return to my compound and bring back a tool that will show the exact spot directly below where we are now. Honest.'

'And give you a chance to escape?' the male Safi boomed. That idea had occurred to him. Yes.

'You die now!' Alena spat. Her eyes were aflame as she raised her kraxl-da.

'You can't,' blurted Blakey. 'I was the last person to touch the talisman. That must count for something.' This had to be grasping at the thinnest of straws.

'That counts for nothing!' snapped Alena.

Blakey figured as much. As Alena readied herself for the blow, he pressed back against the rock-face.

'Wait, Dsolcspmite-Spmite,' called out a female aktel.

'She is Alena. A renegade,' scowled the male Safi.

'But the Earthman has a point; though not the one he makes. In my opinion, his offence is unheard of. I believe it might be wrong to execute him at this time.'

Ross Blakey's mood lifted.

Alena hesitated, fuming. 'What point do you wish to make, aktel?'

'Earthman, are you happy for me to speak on your behalf?'

'Very happy,' Blakey blurted. Maybe a miraculous salvation might yet present itself.

'I believe a serious and unpresented offence as this requires formal judgement.'

'Yes, I demand independent judgement,' stammered Blakey. Hell, everyone else was asking for it.

The aktel continued, 'With such a judgement, the punishment...

invariably very painful execution… would be formalised and carried out in a public space as a warning to anyone foolish enough to contemplate taking such a despicable action.'

'Hang on. I thought you—' But the cold blade of Alena's kraxl-da against his throat encouraged his silence.

'You have a point, aktel. But I prefer to enact the punishment immediately.' The look on her face was sheer poison. 'That too will serve as a warning.'

'May I interrupt here, renegade,' barked the male Safi, regaining his composure. 'You have no authority here. You are my prisoner… nothing more than a common criminal about to be executed. It will be me who executes the Earthman. And your death will follow.'

Alena looked bemused. 'Safi. Observe. I stand before you. I did not promise I would not escape. How can it be that I am your prisoner?'

The male Safi's mouth flapped before twisting in anger. 'Disable her. Kill her if you must,' he commanded his aktel.

Two aktel reached for their dart shooters. But Alena, moving with amazing speed, effortlessly took out both shooters with the hilt of her kraxl-da. She leapt onto a boulder and brandished her weapon at those courageous enough to edge towards her.

'Do you wish to die, aktel?' mocked Alena 'for events over which you bear no blame?'

The male Safi looked pained. 'There are many of us, Alena. You cannot defeat us. Kill her,' he commanded again. Most of his aktel didn't seem at all enthusiastic.

'You should have paralysed me when I was caught in your nets, Safi,' Alena smirked. The male Safi tapped his forehead. When her words brought out dart shooters from three of the aktel's belts, Alena's look of triumph collapsed. She spun on her heel and dived out of sight as two barbs whistled and crashed on to rocks above the boulder where she had stood an instant before.

The male Safi and his aktel gave chase. Seven mounted their uckliablahts. 'She must not escape,' the Safi yelled. 'Even if it means your death!'

Two aktel sporting kraxl-das, and another poised with a dart shooter, remained to defend the two prone aktel, and guard Kasmin, Gentok and Blakey. 'Try and arm yourselves, renegades, and you die!' growled one of the three.

The two prone aktel began to stir.

'Err... aktel,' Blakey ventured. 'Won't your Zookspmate be pleased with me for getting rid of the talisman? If that's the case, he'll let me go back to my compound, won't he?' Worth a try.

'The Zookspmate will certainly heap praise on you, Earthman,' a strongly built female aktel replied, smiling. 'But after doing so, he will have you executed.'

'But... if I've helped him...'

'No, Earthman. You frustrated his orders to kill Alena. Even disposing of a Spmite's talisman is a major crime that demands your death. There can be no other outcome.'

Blakey closed his eyes. There were sounds of thuds, in a very brief sequence.

Blakey opened his eyes. All of the male Safi's guarding aktel were prone on the ground. Instead, a bristling Alena stood before him. After glaring at the Earthman, she picked up her unconscious Safi and lifted her, sack-like across the saddle of an uckliablaht. She removed the barb from the Safi's chest, snapped it angrily in two, and flung it away. Kasmin and Gentok retrieved and sheathed their weapons, and those of the Safi. They leaped on uckliablahts with Gentok choosing the beast that carried the Safi.

Blakey made a bee-line towards Kasmin, his only hope of a ride to safety. Alena was triumphant. 'I choose to punish you here and now, Earthman.'

There was a cry from behind her. She'd been spotted.

'You better run for it,' Blakey suggested in hope. Hurrying hoofs sped their way.

'No! I must do this!' Alena was hunched over in rage.

Blakey dived behind the uckliablaht supporting the unconscious Safi as Gentok prodded the great beast into motion. He clasped the back of the saddle, moving astride it, practically being dragged along. Alena baulked, concerned not to dislodge the Safi.

'You *must* run, Dsolcspmite-Spmite,' urged Kasmin. 'We will protect the Safi. Go!'

Alena gave a cry of frustration. She fumed at Blakey. 'Jkilm! See to it that the Safi lives.' She ran off. 'But you will not escape me, Earthman. That I vow.'

As the aktel closed in, yelling and readying their dart shooters, Alena clambered onto a rocky outcropping and dashed away, keeping low. She zig-zagged as barbs whistled past her.

'Get behind me,' Kasmin urged Blakey. She pulled him onto the back of her uckliablaht and the two set off at speed after Gentok. Though Alena wished him dead, Blakey felt admiration for the warrior. She had chosen to lead her pursuers from her fellow renegades.

For the briefest time as the four fled, the Zookspmate's aktel were intent on Alena. Then, to their left, a call split the air. Three riders split off from the pursuit of Alena to give chase. Being one to an uckliablaht, they closed in fast.

Kasmin's uckliablaht drew level with Gentok, who was holding on grimly to the unconscious, flopping Safi. The chasing aktel came up beside them. Safety was an agonising few minutes away.

Thwack! Gentok's uckliablaht collapsed, a barb protruding from its neck. Its two riders crashed hard onto the ground. Gentok staggered to his feet, nursing his knee with one hand while unsheathing his kraxl-da with the other. The tethered plooglit sat up stunned. Gentok urgently waved Kasmin on. But, in seconds, a chasing aktel drew along-side her and fired his dart shooter. Kasmin instinctively draped herself over her uckliablaht's vulnerable neck. The barb struck her on the shoulder. She slid to the ground.

Blakey was mortified as the huge beast came to an abrupt halt. Even more so when the beast trotted towards Gentok's prone uckliablaht. The pursuing female aktel laughed as Blakey struggled to urge his confused steed to go the other way. The aktel reloaded.

Realising the futility of his urgings, Blakey leapt off his uckliablaht as a barb whistled past his ear. The aktel cursed and reloaded. Gentok stood over the prone Safi, wielding his kraxl-da with such force that the two other aktel's uckliablahts baulked.

Desperate, Blakey flung a stone at the female aktel. It struck her uckliablaht's nose. The beast bellowed, bucked. The rider dropped her dart shooter. She dismounted and ran at Blakey, drawing her kraxl-da.

Gentok leaped behind Blakey's uckliablaht, to keep the attacking aktel at bay.

To Blakey's amazement, Alena's Safi was on her feet. 'Tend to Kasmin,' she called groggily to Gentok. Fumbling with her kraxl-da, she stepped unsteadily between Blakey and the charging female aktel. Gentok ran to the unconscious Kasmin, whistling for the renegades' uckliablaht to keep abreast.

The staggering, grim-faced Safi and the female aktel took fighting stances. Emboldened, Blakey threw a torrent of stones at the two riders chasing Gentok.

Gentok practically threw Kasmin across his uckliablaht and mounted the beast. 'I'll come back!' He sped off.

'No chance,' Blakey sighed in his native language.

The two aktel riders rode swiftly to block Gentok's passage. Gentok veered suddenly and rushed headlong at one of them, flaying his kraxl-da wildly while keeping his grasp on Kasmin. His ploy worked; there was a clash of kraxl-das but Gentok's momentum broke through. The other aktel drew a dart shooter. Figuring he was a dead man walking, Blakey flung stones at the shooter. The fired dart missed its mark.

Behind Ross Blakey, there was the clash of two blades. The Safi, screaming with the exertion, was tackling the female aktel with energy reserves she surely could not have.

Blakey kept flinging stones at the two aktel chasing Gentok. When the renegade pulled up his uckliablaht; his chasers did the same, in a spray of grit and invective. Gentok and Kasmin must have passed into Mkeldi territory. Blakey gave a very brief fist pump.

The two mounted aktel did not dwell; they rode to surround Blakey and the now staggering, cursing, but still battling Safi, dart shooters in hand. The Safi's desperate defensive parries were wilting, her screams louder. 'Keep throwing stones,' she gasped, as if in a trance. 'Don't let them drive us back.' With their lives depending on it, Blakey did just that. One stone hit a rider in the face, winning a momentary reprieve. But he and the Safi were almost done.

Then, the weirdest thing happened...

The renegades' stunned plooglit had somehow broken free from the tether that bound it to the unconscious uckliablaht. For some reason, the drowsy plooglit leapt onto the lap of an aktel who had steadied his beast to fire a barb. Hmmm—

The plooglit tethered to the rider's uckliablaht suddenly roused from its stupor and attacked and clawed at the invasive plooglit, which clawed back. The rider wailed in pain, a cut across his thigh. He dropped his dart shooter as he shoved the invasive plooglit off. The confused plooglit then bounded to leap onto the lap of the other rider. Hmmmmmm— Again plooglits clashed and the rider baulked, cursing. Blakey and the Safi edged a few steps forward.

Then, there was Gentok beside them, atop his uckliablaht. He thrust with his kraxl-da and cut the female aktel's arm. She dropped her kraxl-da and fled, nursing her wound, whistling to her uckliablaht. The two aktel riders veered toward Gentok; one now armed with a kraxl-da, while the other sought a clear shot with a dart shooter. Blakey hit this aktel with a stone.

The stumbling Safi seized on an escape route with Blakey in tow. Five steps later, she gave a loud sigh and collapsed into Blakey's arms. Groaning with the weight of the Safi draped across him, Blakey tottered, staggering towards sanctuary.

Gentok clashed blades with one of the chasing aktel. He broke free and drew up beside Blakey. Together, they hoisted the Safi roughly onto the front of the saddle. Blakey gripped the back of the saddle, in desperation.

Gentok wielded his kraxl-da at the two aktel before riding off, dragging Blakey along. But his grip on the saddle was loose. Cursing, he slid off. Tsalc had to be smiling for, that same instant, a dart bounced off the saddle, right where he'd clung.

In agony, Blakey shuffled forward. When he felt the hot breath of an uckliablaht on his neck, he braced for the pain of a kraxl-da or the sting of a dart. Nothing. Only two very angry jkilms.

'You are safe!' a dismounted Gentok exclaimed, into whose arms Blakey fell. 'You crossed the border!'

Gentok laid the disbelieving and groaning Earthman on the ground. Lying beside Blakey were the prone Safi and Kasmin. Their pursuers were left as fuming statues, no more than a metre away. 'Zeeplat!' But they would not move one centimetre closer. And Blakey could not move one centimetre further.

Rystyn appeared and passed a vial beneath the noses of the two unconscious renegades. They began to stir. 'You're safe,' Rystyn assured them. Their wide-eyed alarm transformed into weary smiles.

Blakey noticed a line of interspersed welcome-mat-sized, grey, smooth and slightly rounded stones, part covered by dust, immediately behind him. The stones stretched between the distinctive perpendicular rock and a cliff. He would not die yet. At least he'd die knowing he had helped save the life of some fine, brave aktel.

The Safi tried to rise, but Rystyn eased her gently down. 'Not yet. You're still weak. You'll only collapse and risk more harm. You are safe. Relax.'

She looked up. 'Rossblakey. Gentok. You saved my life. Thank you.'

'And you and Gentok saved mine,' Blakey responded, between heaving breaths.

Gentok smiled shyly. 'Both of you fought well.'

The Safi smiled. 'How I found the strength I do not know. I suspect my assailant was a novice.'

'How is Kasmin?' Gentok asked as Rystyn finished testing her arms and legs.

'She's groggy. But no broken bones from what I can determine. Slight concussion most likely.' Rystyn smiled. 'Tsalc has been kind to us.'

'About time,' growled Blakey.

Kasmin spoke as if waking from a deep sleep. 'You broke your promise to that rude male Safi, Rystyn. You promised you wouldn't get involved. By cutting free the Dsolcspmite-Spmite, you did get involved. Was that not a dishonourable act?'

Rystyn smiled. 'I only promised not to interfere in her execution, young aktel. I did not break my word at all.'

'You might need to clear that statement with a couple of lawyers,' Blakey said, grinning.

'Law... yers. What are they?'

Blakey recalled his messy divorce. His wife's lawyer had been ruthless. Stripped to near destitution, the divorce had driven him to sign up for Zygol III. 'There are some things we do on Earth that are so horrible, Zygols are better off not knowing.'

Rystyn looked perplexed but leaned his head to the right.

Back at their battleground, the fallen uckliablaht rose unsteadily to its feet. Kasmin whistled to it and the great beast trotted over slowly, its unlikely heroic companion plooglit at its side.

There came much yelling from an incline near the top of the rounded hill. Eyes turned to see Alena running, zig-zagging, with both kraxl-da and kraxl in her hands, fighting her way forward. The male Safi and his aktel, some on foot, others riding uckliablahts, had her surrounded. Some aktel readied dart shooters, seeking a clear shot. Even if, miraculously, she broke through, two aktel with dart shooters waited at the bottom of the hill. They were joined by the three aktel who had chased the fleeing renegades.

'She is doomed,' moaned the Safi. 'She could kill some of them, but she won't. I know it.'

Alena dodged darts and the kraxl-das that slashed at her legs and arms. With the circle about her constricting, suddenly Alena rushed, full pace, at two aktel armed with kraxl-das. There were sharp clangs of blades. She broke through, aided by a dart that thudded into an aktel who stepped into the dart's path. But Alena's escape route was to a sheer cliff that faced the perpendicular rock. She flung her kraxl-da and kraxl towards that rock without breaking stride.

Rystyn gasped. 'Not even she can survive that jump.'

Blakey took in the cliff-face. 'She can't possibly be—'

Alena picked up speed and leapt off the cliff, as barbs hissed about her. She soared into the air, arms and legs flailing. The aktel, waiting at the base of the hill, had to be gaping as she passed above them. The renegades gave a collective gasp. Before crashing heavily, Alena tucked herself into a tight ball. She landed with a thud, in a spray of dust, and rolled, coming to rest, arms sprawled, face down.

'Can she possibly be alive?' fretted the Safi, struggling to her feet. Gentok was already running towards Alena. Rystyn followed, leading an uckliablaht with packs on it. The other three staggered as best as they could.

Rystyn called out, 'She is not in Mkeldi territory.' The mounted aktel at the base of the hill also figured it out. They spun their uckliablahts around and rushed towards Alena. But Gentok was quicker. He grasped her under the arms and dragged her towards safety.

With the line of stones within touching distance, a mounted aktel fired a barb into Gentok's back. Groaning as he fell to his knees, Gentok summoned the strength to tumble Alena forwards, down a slope. She rolled far enough for Rystyn to reach over and drag her across the line of stones.

The mounted aktel stopped with the hooves of their uckliablahts beside Alena's head. She was safe if she wasn't dead. The aktel let out a torrent of abuse at Gentok, who'd fallen forward; his eyes rolling. An aktel stabbed him in his side with a kraxl-da.

'Jkilm!' screamed both the Safi and Kasmin.

The Zookspmate's aktel roughly bundled Gentok in front of one of their riders who rode off with him, a kraxl held against his throat.

'I must rescue him,' Kasmin pronounced.

The Safi restrained her. 'There is a kraxl against his throat. Chase after them and both he and you will be killed.'

'Oh, brave Gentok,' whispered Kasmin as she watched, with her shoulders slumped. The aktel rode away at speed.

Rystyn bent over to examine Alena. She was covered in dust and by blotches of seeping blood. 'She lives,' he gushed in disbelief. He began testing her neck and back.

'By the grace of Tsalc and Gentok's bravery,' Kasmin added, her gaze wistfully fixed on the aktel riding away.

The male Safi straddled the top of the cliff, and looked down on the renegades, flanked by four aktel. 'You have failed, Safi,' Kasmin shouted at him. 'Tsalc looks upon you with the contempt you deserve. What excuse can you possibly make to appease the Zookspmate?'

'How dare you!' he growled as the aktel beside him walked away. 'I would not be gloating yet renegade. Our aktel have you and Mkeldi village surrounded. And Tsalc has a big surprise awaiting you.' He spun on his heel and disappeared.

Rystyn urgently applied ointment and then hastily bandaged Alena's more serious wounds. The Safi fetched water and began gently cleaning Alena with a large, damp leaf. When they were done, the warrior looked more like a greased mummy than a Spmite. Only then did Rystyn place the open vial beneath Alena's nose.

Alena came to, dazed and recoiling. She tried getting to her feet. 'Do not get up, Dsolcspmite-Spmite,' commanded Rystyn. 'You must be concussed, and I still have not assessed all of your injuries.'

'Address her as a Spmite,' the Safi insisted. 'Her deeds demand it. You know full well that the Zookspmate's charges have no substance. And no one possesses her talisman. So it is hers.'

Rystyn pursed his lips. 'Raise your arguments with a Grycyryn-da.' He turned to Alena. 'You are alive and don't seem to have broken any bones... Dsolcspmite-Spmite.' The Safi snorted. 'How, I will never know. But I believe you have damaged a couple of ribs and a shoulder. Tell me, is there anywhere where it especially hurts?'

Alena grimaced as she swooned. 'Everywhere. My head feels like it is being slammed by mallets.' Then she caught sight of Blakey and smiled. 'You are still alive, Earthman. I am so very pleased.'

Blakey smiled in response. Here was reconciliation.

Alena raised an arm. 'Rystyn, help me stand. I need to kill him. His mere presence humiliates and angers me. Let me do this and after I will rest as long as you wish me to. I promise.' She looked about for her weapons. They were on the side of a sand dune nearby; Blakey wasn't about to fetch them.

Rystyn was adamant. 'Not yet, Dsolcspmite-Spmite. I am still examining your injuries.'

Alena brushed Rystyn aside and tried to stand. Her legs collapsed beneath her and, with a howl, she flopped down on her back, grasping at her head, muttering.

'Take heed of me! Rest!' Rystyn scowled. 'You have so many bruises people will think your skin is purple. Let me test that shoulder.'

Alena cried out in pain and frustration.

'I will prepare a sling. You can have full treatment when we reach Mkeldi village.' He stepped over to rummage through a pack on the uckliablaht beside him.

Kasmin related to Alena how they had all escaped.

'I am told that life in Mkeldi is harsh,' said the Safi. 'Yet it is there where we may have to remain until you are acknowledged by your rightful rank, my Spmite.'

'Yes, it is a very impoverished village,' Kasmin chimed in. 'But, if I am banished, I will choose Mkeldi. I know some of the villagers.'

'Kasmin; As ruthless as the Zookspmate is, he would never win an independent judgement to punish you for your minor role,' said Alena grimacing. 'You might be assigned a few unpleasant extra duties. Nothing more. And I will do everything I can for Gentok. But that task is problematic; he is the prisoner of a tyrant.'

'If he is alive.'

'Gentok's armour should have blunted the full thrust of the blade. And he is strong in body and spirit,' Rystyn assured Kasmin. But his face expressed doubt.

'I hope so,' Kasmin whispered. 'Dsolcspmite-Spmite, might they execute Gentok as a renegade?'

Perhaps it was her wounds that caused Alena's face to look pained. 'I can't answer that question, aktel. I am sorry.'

Kasmin looked hurt.

'Banishment seems a more logical outcome. He was bound to act as he did by his pledge,' chimed in the Safi.

'But understand, Kasmin and Safi,' Alena chimed in, 'Gentok faces an angry Zookspmate who has lost all regard for justice. I will send communications to the Zookspmate appealing for leniency. I owe Gentok so much. He was captured saving me.'

Then Alena arched her back in pain and buried her head in her hands. Ross Blakey thought it prudent to slink slowly away.

———

OUT OF SIGHT, behind a sand dune, the Safi approached Blakey and sat beside him.

'I owe you my life, Rossblakey. You risked your own to help me. For that I will always be grateful.'

'And you risked yours to save me. You must be the only person on this planet who doesn't want me dead.'

The Safi was adamant. 'That is not so, Rossblakey. Of course, you must die. You disposed of your Dsolcspmite-Spmite's talisman. Such a heinous act deserves no mercy. Do you not realise that? Tell me, why did you do such a despicable thing?'

Blakey spread his arms in an appeal. 'I wanted her to stay alive.'

The Safi gaped at Blakey with distain. 'You disposed of her talisman. You did that and you wished for her to stay alive! What did she do for you to despise her as much as that?'

Blakey blinked. 'I thought I was doing a good deed—'

The Safi recoiled. 'You thought... How...!?' She shook her head. 'You cannot be serious. What you did completely crushed your Dsolcspmite-Spmite. Only her sense of obligation matter to her now, helping those who pledged loyalty to her, perhaps somehow weakening the influence of the Zookspmate. And your fully deserved punishment.'

'How is she my Dsolcspmite-Spmite?'

The Safi glared at him. 'Of course, she is. You pledged loyalty to her. But to my thinking, she is my Spmite. I don't need a Grycyryn-da to decide on her rank. After all, the six elements demand we exercise flexibility of thought. Surely her brave deeds over-ride her not having her talisman, which no one possesses?'

'But the talisman might be found. I believe we are very likely sitting above a cave complex. I know caves. I can look for it.'

'Fine sentiments, Rossblakey. But you do not seem to

comprehend the gravity of what you have done. It is said that, when Alena was three years old, she ran around in her underwear calling herself Spmite. That's how much her rank meant to her. She applied herself so hard to achieving her goal. Then you do your heinous deed. Not to mention plunging our region into chaos as we now have no sanctioned Spmite. You have boosted the power of your Dsolcspmite-Spmite's unworthy enemy. Yet you claim you were trying to do a good deed?'

Blakey sighed. 'I honestly thought I was helping. I didn't intend things to turn out badly.'

The Safi leaned her head to the left. 'You anger me! Yet as hard as it is for me to comprehend what you say, Rossblakey, the look on your face tells me you are not lying. You saved my Spmite from being executed by me. You showed then you can be noble. And I am alive because of you. So I must concede that you are actually so incredibly ignorant that you thought you were helping. It adds to the tragedy. But...' She became lost for words.

Blakey was downcast. 'If you want me dead, why did you save my life?'

The Safi smiled faintly. 'Your Dsolcspmite-Spmite deserves to be your executioner. Not the Zookspmate.'

'How considerate of you. Thank you for believing me. I am glad I helped rescue you. Perhaps you can convince your Spmite that I was trying to help. Maybe if I offered a very sincere apology...'

The Safi pursed her lips. 'You ask the impossible, Rossblakey. You cannot expect my Spmite to offer you the slightest semblance of compassion. I can tell her you acted as you did because you are a total buffoon, if you wish. And despite how absurd it sounds, you did not intend any malice. But the only chance for you to explain yourself is if you are granted a judgement. At a judgement, your Dsolcspmite-Spmite will be compelled against her will to listen. Then you can tell her you didn't act out of malice. That won't help you. But you may feel better by saying it. But, under no circumstances, tell her you were trying to help.'

'Right.' Blakey stood, shaking his head.

'Seek to have a judgement at Mkeldi. Having your dead body left to a cfaldi here offers you no dignity.'

Blakey became despondent. 'But I can't run any further, Safi.' He took a few steps away from the Safi and sat down heavily in the dirt. 'Earth people think differently to you, Zygols. To us, the saving of a life is more important than saving an object.'

The Safi also stood up, not pleased. 'A talisman is not a simple object, Rossblakey. It is a symbol of authority, a reward for outstanding achievement, and a solemn promise to defend the six elements. This is not your planet. You are not in your compound. Your action was a violation of my people. Not merely of my Spmite. Yet, despite this, I make a promise to you, Rossblakey. Because you saved my life, I will seek to have you face judgement in Mkeldi village.'

'Why bother. What good will a judgement do me?'

The Safi became indignant. 'It does matter! After judgement, you will be given a more dignified death. At a judgement, you will get the opportunity to say your piece. But...' She trailed off when she saw that Blakey, head low, was not listening. The Safi sighed and wandered back to join the other renegades.

A short time later, an anxious Safi, riding atop an uckliablaht, returned to where Blakey was sitting. 'Quick. Get behind me. We must go to Mkeldi village now. My Spmite is up and about and looking for you.'

Blakey paused but nodded. The Safi helped lift Blakey behind her, and they headed off, moving cautiously. 'I told her to go in the direction you first wandered off. I didn't tell her you weren't to be found that way any longer.'

'Why do this, Safi?'

'I wish you to enjoy having the privilege of being sentenced to death at an independent hearing,' said the Safi brightly. 'Isn't that something to aspire for?'

'I should feel so incredibly privileged,' Blakey muttered sourly in his native language. 'By taking me to the village, won't Alena—'

'Don't insult her name! Especially you,' the Safi hissed. 'She is your Dsolcspmite-Spmite.'

He clicked his tongue. 'Sorry. Like I was asking, won't she be angry with you for taking me to the village?'

'Of course, she will. But I owe you this gesture. One of my aktel was killed earlier. Another aktel may also be dead. I am not ready right now for the death of another who has acted nobly.'

'You don't have to do this.' Yet he was grateful. Fleeing would buy him precious time to, hopefully, make written arrangements for the care of his children.

The two made their way around the side of a ridge, along a rough, dusty and stone-strewn, switchback trail. The uckliablaht's plooglit, which the Safi had released, cavorted with joyful zest. They turned right onto a narrow ledge that ran the length of a cliff-face above and beneath them. On the cliff-side, the wide, mostly dry, valley came fully into view, maybe sixty metres below. Three sides of the valley were orange-brown hills. On the far side, the hills became increasingly higher and verdant. The valley was split by a long, snaking green oasis, wider in the middle and flanked on both sides by bands of what appeared to be orange-brown fields in the shape of an inverted tear. Amidst the trees were glimpses of a glistening, meandering stream and, to the right, what might be a small lake. The stream passed by an uckliablaht pen and seemed to disappear directly below them. Some five figures in grey tunics moved slowly about the fields.

The cliff-side ledge ended with a series of switchbacks, passing craggy rock and tall boulders. On top of the boulders were perched numerous vulture-like chageen.

'There are so many. Strange,' the Safi muttered. Instantly, she jolted to a stop. A stone tumbled from above. They heard hoof steps, moving at speed. 'An uckliablaht. It is most likely my Spmite. Only she would give chase.' She urged her uckliablaht on.

'Will we make it in time?' Blakey pressed. 'I'm safe if we get to the village, yes?'

'Yes. Mkeldi village has a Dsolcspmite, and it has its own head of the village, a Sklim. Because her rank of Spmite is disputed, she can't kill you there without consulting the Sklim and the Dsolcspmite. For you, it means you are certain to secure a judgement, though the hearing will be brief.'

Two plooglits dashed into view, cavorting on a boulder beside them. Annoyed chageen were cast into flight. The Safi gasped. 'My Spmite is getting close.'

The plooglits cooed. Blakey, being ignorant of their habits, believed the plooglits were somehow in the barren, rocky desert, finding food that was good to eat.

He sighed, closed his eyes. The rough, switch-backed trail made progress frustratingly slow. The sound of dislodged stones behind them became louder. Blakey kept glancing back; Alena had to be closing in fast.

They both let out a cry of relief when they rounded another outcrop. Before them, a short unobstructed path led to a crude wooden bridge over a sluggish narrow stream. As Blakey had surmised, the stream flowed to the bottom of the dry, rocky ridge and then simply cascaded out of sight, most likely to a cave system. The talisman may yet be found.

On the other side of the rustic bridge, to the left, was a large, dust-strewn uckliablaht pen with perhaps twenty grit-covered beasts separated into two fenced-off areas. Three calves in the pen huddled close to adults, seeking protection from the beating sun. A short and narrow dug-out channel diverted water into two large troughs at the edge of the pen.

'When we reach that pen, your judgement is assured.' The Safi smiled.

Immediately beyond the uckliablaht pen was a narrow band of low, dusty and scraggly vegetation. On either side of that vegetation were patches of even scragglier plants and bushes. Undulating dry fields, seemingly harvested, spread out to the left and right. Deeper into the oasis, the expanse of vegetation became increasingly taller and more verdant.

There were no dwellings visible—not surprising given they would be exposed to the desert winds. High in the trees, Blakey caught glimpses of chageen... lots of chageen... and some plooglits. These plooglits were motionless, as if tethered.

The pen reeked terribly, but to Blakey, it was the smell of a temporary sanctuary.

'Thank you, Safi.' *Maybe*. His mind drifted to composing his last will and testament. And how to get his notebook back to the mining compound.

There was an emphatic "zeeplat!" from behind them, confirming the Safi's assurance. Riding towards them, the furious, bandaged, bloodied and dust-covered Dsolcspmite-Spmite, with one arm in a sling and the other arm brandishing a kraxl-da, was a vision from a horror movie.

The Safi slowed their uckliablaht to allow Alena to come alongside.

Ross Blakey was not enamoured by her gesture.

'So, Earthman,' Alena growled, an uncomfortable arm's span from him. 'You will live a little longer. But it will be me who administers your punishment. Of that, you can have no doubt.' Glaring at the Safi, to Blakey's great relief, she sheathed her kraxl-da.

'Damn it! If it wasn't for me, you'd be dead,' Blakey snapped. The Safi gave a cry of despair and placed her hands over her eyes.

'Yes, I am alive,' fumed Alena. 'Rejoice in the shame you have cast upon me. And gloat at my humiliation. Mock me for how you enhanced the power of a Zookspmate who needs to be stripped of his rank.'

'What about those aktel who stuck by you up there?' Blakey retorted. 'If it wasn't for what I did, the Safi, Kasmin and Rystyn would be in big trouble now. You risked your life to allow us to escape. You did that because you knew that your zooky guy would have shown us little mercy.'

'That is no excuse,' snapped the Safi. 'We joined my Spmite's quest fully accepting the risk, Rossblakey.'

But did Alena's anger subside the very tiniest bit?

'Spmite,' interrupted the Safi. 'Do not be intimidated by this embodiment of opitek. Remain resolute. You will now face independent judgement. There you will surely expose the lies of the Zookspmate and his cronies. Even with your rank disputed.'

'I can only hope, Safi. Though my task is more difficult because of my disputed rank. It is as if the Earthman was sent to destroy me.'

'That's not so,' Blakey snarled. 'Never heard of him, never seen him. Never heard of you, either.' He wished he still hadn't.

'But it is said the Zookspmate spends time observing your compound.'

'Don't believe me then. But I mistakenly believed I was helping you up there.'

The Safi cringed as Alena erupted. 'Helping me!? How?' Alena lifted the hilt of her kraxl-da.

'Spmite,' implored the Safi, 'remember your training. And the six elements. Be resolute.'

Alena reluctantly released the kraxl-da. 'This Earthman pushes me beyond the boundaries of provocation, Safi.'

'I know. Think of the Earthman as a plooglit, my Spmite. He acts without thinking. But I believe he did not act out of malice.'

'You believe that?' There were a few moments of cold silence. But Alena's hand moved a little further from her kraxl-da. Blakey thought it best to let the Safi's insult go.

'There must be subterranean passageways back there,' Blakey ventured. 'It might be possible to find your talisman. We only need to follow the water. If someone dropped stones through that fissure up there, we'd have an even better idea where to look. I'll be happy to help.'

'No! I want no assistance from you.' Blakey and Alena shared icy glances.

'I must search for my talisman before facing judgement.' Alena's chest heaved. 'But I fear that Tsalc has abandoned me.' Then she half-smiled, a smile of triumph. 'Only your impending judgement gladdens me, Earthman. And, if I am somehow able to, I must do whatever it takes to weaken the power of the Zookspmate. Jkilm! I must not fail.'

Blakey couldn't suppress his urge to speak. 'Maybe if—' The Safi dug her fingernails hard into his thigh.

'Ow!' With the Safi's fingernails still resting on his leg, Blakey had second thoughts. 'I was out in your harsh Zygol sun and wind for too long. Why else would I have done anything so stupid as to try and help you live?' Blakey sneered at the warrior.

'Your excuse counts for nothing, Earthman,' the Safi stormed.

Blakey was about to snap at the Zygols. But he sighed, then nodded.

The Safi had been good to him; he held back. 'I apologise for what I did. And yes... Dsolcspmite-Spmite, I acknowledge your incredibly brave deeds. Even before today. You have done the six elements proud.'

Alena's mood may have softened the tiniest bit more. Maybe.

'I cannot forgive you, Earthman. Not after what you have done.' Blakey averted his eyes in anger.

Alena cleared her throat and whispered, 'Thank you, Earthman, for helping to save the life of my Safi and aktel.'

Blakey spun around, wide-eyed. 'I'm sorry. You spoke so softly that I didn't hear exactly what you said.' He looked over to Alena, who glanced at the Safi who, in turn, rolled her eyes.

Alena glowered. 'Thank you for helping to save the life of my Safi and aktel. If you are still not satisfied, I will gladly carve it on your chest with my kraxl.'

'That's not necessary,' said the now-grinning Blakey. 'But it is so nice to be told that I have done something right.'

Alena grunted. Annoyed, her attention shifted to the uckliablaht pen.

'She doesn't seem to be angry with you,' Blakey whispered in the Safi's ear.

'You do not understand hand signals. She suggested I do something very unpleasant and anatomically impossible.'

The Safi also turned her attention to the uckliablaht pen. The two compartments of the pen contained only a few scraggly bushes that had been nibbled to their stems. The chewed-back, dusty bushes on the village-side of the fenced area would provide limited shade but only probably after mid-afternoon. The rest of the pen was bare, churned dirt, sand and stones, and fresh and broken-down uckliablaht poo. Grey dirt was piled up against the fence posts. A low pile of cuttings lay in both enclosures. Most of the uckliablahts had gathered to feed on the offerings while three drank from the water troughs. The beasts were languid; their heads low. There were a few equally languid plooglits in the pen, a couple perched on the backs of uckliablahts. They did not coo.

'Where are the rest of their companion plooglits?' Alena shook her head. 'Their uckliablahts are suffering. Even our plooglits won't go inside. It is a sad place.'

'Many plooglits are perched in the nearby trees,' the Safi remarked. 'Barely moving. I can also see many chageen.' She looked puzzled. 'So many. The trees are swarming with them. There are no happy animals in this village.'

'Never have I seen uckliablahts kept so badly,' remarked Alena, tilting her head to the right. 'This must be remedied. I will have some harsh words to say when I meet the village Sklim.'

The riders made their way to where the vegetation began before bringing their uckliablahts to a halt in the shade.

Alena briefly doubled up in pain. Blood showed through her bandages and her torn gossamer covering.

Blakey took the opportunity to check the hurried annotations he had jotted in his notebook the previous night and elaborated on some of his comments. The notes needed to be useful. 'Safi, what is the fourth element again? What I wrote isn't clear. I was writing in near darkness. And you were talking quickly.'

Alena glared at him. The Safi rolled her eyes.

'Strength and agility of mind and body,' the Safi repeated through gritted teeth.

'Thanks.' He wrote, avoiding the Zygols' disparaging looks. Flicking to a fresh page, he scribbled "Last Will and Testament of Ross Blakey, Mining Contractor." And he began the gut-wrenching task of bequeathing everything he had to his children, fearful that they may forget him; hoping they would remember him with fondness.

One by one, the village plooglits descended cautiously from the nearby trees until many were level with the heads of the riders. The renegades' animals were examined closely. There may yet be some happiness to be found in the village this day. The uckliablahts in the pen could only bleat their displeasure.

The three were joined by Rystyn and Kasmin, who came beside them, sharing the back of an uckliablaht. Rystyn would not look at Blakey. He and Kasmin were also shocked by the poor conditions in the pen. They dismounted, so Blakey did the same, wincing as he stretched his legs. He scratched impotently at his multiple plooglit-piss doses, and then he grimly wrote words of farewell to his children and added more instructions for his fellow Earth humans.

'Dsolcspmite-Spmite,' Rystyn began. 'If you allow me, I will speak of what I know of the plot against you at your judgement. I only know a little, but I believe I can assist you.'

'That will be appreciated, Rystyn.'

'Strange,' Rystyn whispered as he gazed into the trees at the jet-black chageen perched there, staring at the visitors with their huge red eyes. Their stares seemed malevolent. 'There are so many chageen. It disturbs me. Aren't there stories—'

'It must be their time for breeding,' interrupted Kasmin.

'That is unlikely,' the Safi said. 'When they are breeding, there is much flapping of wings. Sometimes they battle. Even so, it doesn't explain why so many chageen would want to congregate in the same place, in a village where food stocks are said to be low. It makes me uncomfortable, too.'

The Zygols looked pensively at one another.

Ross Blakey shook his head. *As if the chageen mattered.*

5

___

A PROMISE OF DEATH

FOUR VILLAGERS CAME into sight along a path that meandered through the trees. Two walked slowly in front. One was a thin old man, who moved bow-legged with the aid of a walking stick. He wore a tatty brown smock with a wide orange stripe. A woman beside him, aged in her forties, wore the plain orange smock of a Grycyryn, a wise one. Behind them were another man and woman aged perhaps in their late twenties, both also in orange smocks.

'They don't look particularly glad to see us,' Rystyn remarked as the greeting party neared. 'Odd, considering they must think their Spmite is visiting them.'

'Don't jump to conclusions,' Alena replied, but she looked uneasy. 'Maybe it's an inconvenient time. Keep in mind this is a poor village experiencing a major drought. Providing for our stay may involve hardships for them.'

'But as Zygols, it is expected—'

'Don't judge, Rystyn,' hissed Alena. 'We will dwell only long enough to arrange the necessary judgements.' She turned to Blakey and broke into a grin. 'Earthman,' she said matter-of-factly, 'it is in this place you will die. Very shortly.'

Blakey looked away.

'Until your judgement, you will be under constant watch,' she tormented him. 'Go beyond the perimeter of this village and you will be stopped with whatever force is necessary, short of killing you.'

Rystyn chuckled.

Escape? Blakey had no strength to run. There was nowhere to run. 'I thought that Zygols hated inflicting suffering. Even on animals. It's one of your six elements, isn't it?'

'That is true, Earthman. Compassion is an essential tenet of the six elements. But your crime is not deserving of a semblance of compassion. It is justice that requires to be served.'

Miffed, Ross Blakey wandered off to write more, stretch his aching legs, and to scratch at the more awkward parts. Alena cringed with pain. Rystyn and the Safi looked at one another, anxious. But Alena was upright in the saddle when the villagers stopped before her.

Those in the greeting party were thinner and shorter than most people in Channen village. Their faces were sun-drenched, and their clothes looked a little frayed. Blakey recognised the younger female Grycyryn, who was an occasional visitor to the Airlock, back at the all-too-distant compound.

'Welcome, Alena,' the old man said solemnly. His voice was clear and dulcet. 'Mkeldi village is honoured by a visit from our Spmite at a desperate time such as this.'

The Zygol renegades became puzzled.

'Thank you, Sklim. I am honoured to be here. However, while I am dressed as a Spmite, the Zookspmate of the Three Villages has issued trumped-up charges against me and declared me to be a renegade. Also, earlier, this Earthman disposed of my talisman.' She glanced, simmering, at Ross Blakey. 'So my rank may be disputed.'

The Sklim gasped in indignation. 'I readily believe that your Zookspmate is capable of treachery. When he was our Zookspmate, he treated our village with contempt. That is why we now recognise another as our Zookspmate. As for disposing of your talisman; I am filled with contempt. What manner of barbarian would do such a thing?' The Sklim puffed his cheeks and glared at Ross Blakey.

'I am told I have the mind of a plooglit,' Blakey shrugged.

'Ignore his annoying presence. The matter is simple: the Earthman requires immediate judgement for his act. In order to establish a legal precedent, I seek his execution. Please arrange the hearing as early as possible.'

'Of course, Alena. It is an urgent matter. If I had been in your place, I'd have cut the barbarian down where he stood.'

'I wished to Sklim. But my Safi felt the Earthman should face a judgement. She brought him here while I was being treated for my injuries.' She glared at the Safi, who turned to look up at the chageen.

'What impudence,' said the eldest Grycyryn.

'As you acknowledge that my Zookspmate is devious, I request that I be addressed as a Spmite even though I do not possess my talisman. The talisman was taken from me without authority and disposed of improperly. What say you as the village's lead Grycyryn, Abrik?'

'Her deeds this day were those of a great Spmite,' the Safi chimed in.

The eldest Grycyryn glared at the Safi before addressing Alena. 'Your appearance seems to bear testimony to what your Safi claims. The circumstances are unique. I readily accept that you should not be regarded by the reduced rank of a Dsolcspmite. Yet I cannot bring myself to call you a Spmite.'

'Let me tell you of her bravery,' the Safi responded sourly.

Abrik was insistent. 'Hold your tongue, Safi. No! Regardless of any bravery, I cannot call her Spmite without her talisman.'

'Is she less of a Spmite when she bathes?'

Abrik, fuming, sent a hand signal to Alena.

'My other companions have chosen to call me Dsolcspmite-Spmite. I will accept nothing less than that.'

Abrik nodded. 'That seems a reasonable request. You have my assent.'

The Safi sucked in a breath. Alena sent her some firm hand signals. The Safi held her tongue but stayed sour-faced.

Abrik glared at the Safi. 'My decision is final, precocious Safi.'

Abrik sent more hand signals to Alena, who surprised the Grycyryn by responding with a smile.

'My Safi and one of her aktel, who was captured in the hills, will also require a judgement, summoned by our Zookspmate.'

The villagers seemed dumbfounded by the request.

Alena recoiled. She spoke hesitantly. 'Because of the false charges against me, I too require a judgement, for which I call upon your Zookspmate and you, Sklim, to act as judges on my behalf. The Zookspmate of the Three Villages seeks my death.'

The surprised Sklim blinked and pursed his lips. 'That is a serious matter, Alena. I understand why you would wish to begin this action.' By the reaction of the renegades, the Sklim's choice of words seemed odd.

The Sklim continued. 'I was disappointed when I heard that your Zookspmate's rank wasn't revoked at the recent Succession Games. We lodged many objections to his behaviour. But we are a poor and isolated village, and no one cared to act on our concerns.'

'Believe me, Sklim,' Alena answered. 'I, and some respected Grycyryn-da, tried to act on your allegations. We were thwarted because this Zookspmate has installed many of his cronies into positions of power. They frustrate every complaint about him. It is why I seek to strip the man, and his cronies, of their rank. He has responded by wishing to be rid of me. I acknowledge that my judgement will take a few days to organise as witnesses will need to be called. But I need the process to begin as early as possible. Despite what the Zookspmate claims, I refuse to be judged as a renegade.'

'Rest assured, you will face judgement as Dsolcspmite-Spmite,' said the Sklim. 'We will communicate with the Zookspmate's signaller in the mountains.' He looked pained. 'For now, you may tether your uckliablahts outside the uckliablaht pen. As you can see, our pen is in dreadful condition. The drought we have experienced for a number of years, combined with the incredibly fierce winds from the desert over the past six days, have regrettably taken a heavy toll on our animals. It is calm now, but it is likely that the wind will blow strong again later.'

'You should not have allowed their suffering to deteriorate to this extent,' Alena added testily.

The Safi grunted her agreement.

'When I visited you some... sixteen days ago, I made an offer for your villagers and uckliablahts to stay in the Three Villages on a rotation basis. I also offered to return with food stores. But you insisted you did not need any assistance. No representation has been made to me since. This is unacceptable. If my rank of Spmite wasn't disputed, I would be seeking the appointment of a new Sklim.' Alena's stare made each of the greeting party wince.

The Sklim's shoulders slumped. He would not meet Alena's eyes. 'I freely acknowledge my incompetence, Alena. I put pride before the welfare of the village and our animals. We will now pay a high price.'

Abrik spoke. 'As the village's head Grycyryn, I have arranged lodgings and food for you all, Dsolcspmite-Spmite. And you obviously need ongoing medical attention.'

'My Spmite risked her life to save ours,' the Safi said proudly. 'Her injuries were caused by her great deeds.'

Kasmin and Rystyn murmured agreement.

'I believe you,' said Abrik. But her tone was grave. 'After treatment, Dsolcspmite-Spmite, it is best if you change into the attire of a Dsolcspmite. Our own Dsolcspmite, Brlma, can loan you some clothes.'

'Ah, Brlma.' Alena brightened. 'During our contests, she caused me considerable anxiety. It took days for the bruising to heal. She is truly a worthy competitor. I look forward to seeing her again.'

Abrik's mood remained solemn. 'She wished to be here to greet you, but she is resting. She stopped a dangerous stampeding uckliablaht two days ago. While restraining it, the animal trod on her foot, damaging it badly.'

'That is unfortunate. I will see her as soon as possible.'

For some seconds there was an awkward silence.

'Sklim. Abrik,' Alena said. 'Why are you being evasive? You keep ignoring my hand signals. Something is badly wrong. And it is not merely your shame. You must tell me. All of us.'

Abrik sighed. 'Only now do we realise that you are not aware of our plight. We will talk as we escort you to the village square.'

Alena was irritated but dismounted, wincing with pain.

The renegades tethered their uckliablahts to trees with low branches that were dust-free. The group then strolled along the meandering earthen path. Alena limped beside the Safi along with the Sklim and Abrik at the front.

The renegades' energetic plooglits climbed up and down trees, disturbing some of the numerous chageen. The chageen hissed and flew off, wings flapping. The village's plooglits huddled against the tree trunks.

'Here and there you will see that we have stripped some trees of a few of their branches to feed the uckliablahts. With the long drought, our crops have been poor again and the harsh desert winds these last six days have damaged what remains of our unharvested crops. But our plight is far, far worse.' Abrik bowed her head and fell silent.

The path brought the group to the first of Mkeldi's villagers and their homes. As in Channen village, the homes were created mostly using living vegetation. These homes were, on the whole, rudimentary compared to those in Channen. Whether walking or sitting, the villagers seemed as languid as their animals. Most showed no interest in their visitors. A number of languid plooglits, of varying sizes, were visible in the more luxuriant vegetation to their right, looking on.

'Those plooglits are a long way from the uckliablahts,' Blakey inquired of Kasmin. Keen to take his mind from his impending fate.

Kasmin answered with enthusiasm. 'These plooglits seek better food for themselves and their young,' she explained. 'Are you aware that there are many more plooglits than uckliablahts? An uckliablaht can have several companion plooglits; but usually accepts only one at a time. Sometimes the plooglits squabble for attention but most times they accept the need to be patient. Particularly when they are looking after their young. Or breeding. At times, they simply need to rest.'

'Seems logical.'

Through gaps in the verdant vegetation, the small lake Blakey had spotted when traversing the cliff-face became visible. In the shallows of that lake were what appeared to be crude wooden structures.

Alena simmered; the Sklim was hesitant.

At last he spoke. 'Do not think we hold ill-will towards any of you. Indeed, Alena, you are much admired in our village. But, regrettably, I must advise you that, apart from a select group of twelve, of which you qualify because of you have the highest rank in our village, your visiting party and our villagers are doomed to die at the teeth and claws of the chageen the coming morning.'

The renegades gasped. They stared at one another in disbelief. The old man continued. 'The fortunate twelve will have sanctuary in a cavern where a stone barrier built across the cave entrance will prevent the chageen from entering.'

The Sklim and Abrik gazed at their feet. 'If what has been described in the distant past happens again, and we are certain it will, the village will be over-run by an enormous swarm of rampant chageen. You see that they are everywhere, and none are eating. They are starving themselves for their feast. Everyone remaining in the village will be eaten alive. With their excellent vision and sense of smell, the chageen will rip apart any structure people hide behind. Only rocks can stop them.'

Ross Blakey broke into uncontrolled, hysterical laughter. Alena glared at the Sklim.

The old man spoke. 'Our signaller warned the Zookspmate's aktel in the hills to stay clear, but you obviously received no such alert. If we had detected your entourage approaching Mkeldi, we would have warned you. But you caught us unawares. Hardly anyone visits us from the desert hills. And we did not have aktel at their post today for fear they would be attacked by the chageen.'

'Is there no chance of escape?' Rystyn pressed, fear etched on his face. 'Maybe if we leave now.'

'Impossible,' said Abrik, grim-faced. 'You will be consumed if you flee. Even if you sneak out during a starless night, they will detect you. They surround the entire village. No one can escape.'

'I don't believe this,' Blakey rambled wild-eyed. 'This whole planet is insane.'

The Sklim and Abrik scowled at him.

'Sklim, your pride... your trust in Tsalc has doomed everyone,' Kasmin snapped.

The Sklim bowed his head. 'Yes. I have brought great shame on myself.'

'This news comes as a cruel blow,' Alena said wearily. 'It seems Tsalc is determined to be rid of me. And I have doomed those who have journeyed with me. I am sorry for you all.'

'It is no fault of yours,' said a downcast Safi. From the look on his face, Rystyn held blame for another.

'Well, this disaster isn't my fault,' Blakey mocked him.

'But if you had not disposed of the talisman...'

'As is obvious, Alena,' continued the Sklim with irritation, 'it is impossible for our villagers to send a negotiation team to your Zookspmate until after the chageen have departed. Those in the Survival Party will have to organise a judgement for you.'

'Are you absolutely certain about tomorrow?' Rystyn pressed.

'Yes,' replied the Sklim with a deep sigh. 'We know this from what has happened before. And from tales of other villages in the desert. We have written accounts. Perhaps you do not in the Three Villages.'

'I have been told stories of attacks that happened many years ago,' said a downcast Alena.

'I saw it unfold in this very village when I was fourteen,' the Sklim said, solemnly. 'After the Survival Games back then, I was granted sanctuary in our cavern, which can only hold twelve, including room for sanitation and to store enough provisions for perhaps thirty days. Unfortunately, the cavern and stream cannot be navigated beyond that space. Some say that even twelve is too many. I remember the horror of that attack, as clearly as if it happened yesterday. The chageen flung themselves at the rock barrier for many, many days. Night and day. The screaming of the villagers and the scratching and screeching outside the cave will haunt me until my final breath. Such rage. The chageen took so long to give up. The group nearly starved all those years ago. When we emerged, it was to witness a scene of utter carnage.'

'Why is it happening in this village?' demanded the Safi. 'There are chageen everywhere on our planet.'

'We do not know, but it is most likely that the harsh conditions have contributed to it. Regrettably, it is too late to prevent the disaster now.'

'If only twelve can live, how many children will die?' Alena seethed.

'All of them,' replied Abrik gravely. 'The youngest in the Survival Party this time is fifteen. The next youngest seventeen. Those who will survive must not be burdened by children. Or by the old and infirm. We are presently performing the heartbreaking task of having to tell the children their fate. It is a tragedy. I cannot begin to describe how heavily it weighs upon me.' Her chest heaved. The Sklim and Abrik walked on, their heads bowed.

'What are you telling them? That your precious six elements... or whatever... are demanding that they lie down and die.' To everyone's surprise, it was Ross Blakey who spoke. 'Is that what you're doing?'

'The Earthman has opitek,' the Sklim said gravely. 'Knowledge without wisdom.'

'You think so. What about your fourth and fifth elements?' Blakey growled. 'If I remember them, one is agility in mind, yes? The other courage, yes? Well... don't you need to show those qualities now?'

'Opitek!' the Sklim bellowed.

'As annoying as the Earthman is, I agree with him,' Alena remarked icily. 'It is not the Zygol way to accept such a terrible fate without resisting to the very end. We must do everything possible to try and avert this tragedy.'

'If anything could be done, it would be tried!' The Sklim folded his arms, affronted. 'Do you expect the drought to disappear by morning? The skies are clear. They will also be clear in the morning.'

The Safi took a stance in front of the Sklim, halting the group. 'The six elements are not merely fine words to teach young children, Sklim.

They demand that we be dynamic. Not sit around in despair. To do so is an affront to our teachings.'

Alena leaned her head to the right. She turned her attention to the two silent villagers dressed in orange. 'What say you, Grycyryn?'

'We agree with the Sklim and Abrik,' the man said, cringing. The woman seemed embarrassed. Alena and the Safi glared at the two Grycyryn with distain.

'What do you suggest we do, young Safi?' Abrik fumed, her arms crossed.

'The chageen are most likely responding to the suffering of your animals. Animals, as do humans, seek elapelc.'

'It is a reasonable assumption, Safi,' replied the Sklim. 'But the last time this disaster struck, the animals were suffering nowhere near as much.'

'Tell me,' the Safi responded, 'is it only humans the chageen will kill?'

'Only humans, yes. But, before you leap to conclusions,' countered the Sklim, 'be aware that the pen has been in its present location since the village has existed and only once has this disaster befallen us as far as we know. And that was sixty years ago. Mkeldi village has experienced harsh conditions many times during those years.'

'Were your uckliablahts kept in their pen all the time when the harsh winds were blowing?' the Safi demanded.

Abrik answered icily. 'Unfortunately, with the wild winds and dust, there was little opportunity for our uckliablahts to be let out the last five days. Sandstorms panic them. Brlma's injury testifies to this. But we have always had harsh winds. Where your argument is leading to doesn't hold, Safi.'

'But, during harsh conditions, couldn't you set up a temporary pen away from the sandstorms?'

The Sklim looked sourly at the Safi. 'Understand that our village is located on a small oasis. We do not have the luxury of being able to locate our pen amongst lush vegetation as occurs in many villages. The pen, of course, must be located downstream of the water we drink and bathe in. So, we have no option but to leave it where it is.'

I understand that,' Alena countered. 'But why didn't you tether your uckliablahts to lush trees away from the harsh winds?'

'We tried,' the Sklim said testily. 'But uckliablahts chew through their tethers, even double tethers, when they are panicked. They break free and cause havoc. Again I say, ask Brlma of this. They foul the water. They eat homes. They sometimes fight and might stampede. We expect the strong winds to return.'

'But they will not cause as much havoc as the chageen will tomorrow,' the Safi said with irritation. 'It is clear that the chageen are angry. If angry is the right word.'

Both the Sklim and Abrik bristled. 'The Survival Party will consider all possibilities,' Abrik growled. 'Perhaps we should have tethered our uckliablahts longer during the strong winds. Triple tethered them perhaps. Hindsight is easy. Don't think of us as being complacent fools.'

The Safi gripped Abrik by the shoulder. 'You make that claim yet you choose to do nothing.' Abrik angrily brushed away her hand. She, the Sklim and the Safi stared hard at one another.

'Enough squabbling!' Alena cried out. 'We should devote our energy to averting this looming catastrophe. Why not set your uckliablahts free now for the sake of perhaps restoring some elapelc? It is surely worth trying, even if the winds return.'

'Dsolcspmite-Spmite, let the villagers spend their final night alive in peace. We will open the gates of the pen at first light, so the beasts will not starve.'

'Set them free now,' the Safi implored, her eyes set on the two younger Grycyryn. 'Surely the villagers will try anything to save the lives of their children.'

'I hate to disappoint you, Safi,' said Abrik, raising her voice in irritation, 'but the decision is ours to make, particularly as we no longer have a Spmite. The villagers have voted how they desire to spend this final day. Respect their wishes.'

It was the turn of the Safi and Alena to bristle. 'The six elements require us to seek answers to what baffles us,' the Safi retorted. 'To adapt... to learn... we must always strive for answers.'

'Think what you will,' growled the Sklim. 'You are young and full of youthful idealism. Life offers many questions that have no answers.'

'I guess Earthmen and plooglits are not the only ignorant beings on this planet.' It was Blakey who spoke.

The Sklim and Abrik averted their eyes. The younger Grycyryn gazed at their feet. 'Opitek,' spat the Sklim. 'Perhaps, Safi, you have spent too much time in the company of this Earthman. I suggest finding elapelc with him has diminished your ability to think clearly.'

'To my way of thinking, the Safi is making more sense than anyone here,' Alena countered.

Seething, the Sklim and Abrik brushed past the Safi.

'We have little time left,' Abrik ventured as she strode on ahead. 'This discussion needs to end. Let us quickly arrange a judgement on the Earthman.'

The Safi grasped Abrik by the arm. 'The Earthman cannot face his judgement in his poor physical state,' she spat. 'He needs to rest and bathe.'

Alena glared at her Safi and shot off some quick, animated hand signals.

The Sklim responded with a dismissive flick of his hand. 'You cannot be serious. The Earthman cannot possibly defend his barbaric actions, rest or no rest. We merely waste precious time by delaying the judgement.'

The Safi gritted her teeth. 'Rossblakey, may I speak on your behalf?'

Blakey shrugged. 'If you want to.' Alena was visibly unimpressed.

'Sklim, Abrik. I agree that the Earthman must be punished,' insisted the Safi. 'But it is the Zygol way to allow people to retain their dignity. You cannot dispute that.'

The Sklim glanced at a fuming Alena. Reluctantly, he spoke, 'Fine then! To preserve the reputation of our village, I will defer to your request Safi. Besides, the delay will allow us to re-convene the Survival Games. This we now must do with Alena having to be included in the Survival Party, as she is the highest-ranked person amongst us. As a consequence, one of our villagers must now lose their position.' He smiled faintly. 'The Earthman will face judgement after the completion of the contest.'

'I find that reasonable. Thank you.' The Safi forced a smile. She avoided the burning eyes of Alena.

'There is no reason for a delay, Sklim,' Alena spoke. 'I choose not to depose one of your villagers from the Survival Party.'

'You do not have that option, Alena. The Survival Games will be re-convened in accordance with our practices. I will discuss the matter no further.'

Alena leaned her head to the left. The Sklim and Abrik walked on. Alena followed, bristling. The Safi chose to trail behind.

The group came to a three-way fork in the path. The main, short path led to what was apparently the village square, flanked on its far side by a long, rough building. The path to the right headed towards the stream in which a water wheel groaned, feeding water into a narrow aqueduct. The fork to the left led to an area where several dwellings stood among the vegetation. The few villagers visible were as languid as the others they had passed.

'Our Grycyryn will show you to your quarters,' the Sklim announced. 'We need to advise our last-placed qualifier and Dsolcspmite Brlma that they will now need to compete for the last position in the Survival Party. Alena, if you follow Abrik, you will get the treatment you need and be shown our guest room and library in our communal hut.'

Alena looked as if she had been hit by a club. She grasped Abrik's arm. 'Are you saying that Brlma risks losing her position, even with her considerable attributes?'

Abrik looked grave. 'Brlma could only qualify as the highest-ranked defender of the six elements because of her damaged foot. That exemption no longer stands. Her fate will now rest with Tsalc.'

'That is... a tragedy,' Alena replied with a deep sigh. 'The survivors need such a capable person to re-establish the village.'

The Sklim did not reply. He gravely touched his cheek and nose to signal the end of a formal conversation and took the path leading to the village square, with Alena limping, looking forlorn, at his side. Abrik followed behind.

With their spirits low, the other renegades silently followed the two Grycyryn along the path to the left, where they were ushered before two very rustic, partly dilapidated dwellings.

'I will not share a hut with the Earthman,' Rystyn insisted.

Kasmin leant her head to the left.

'Then that leaves me,' the Safi said with reluctance.

'It will only be for a short time, Safi. The Earthman will be executed soon,' Kasmin said with a disarming cheerfulness. A quick glance at Blakey and she lost her smile.

'Rest now,' their female escort said. 'When you are ready to bathe, go to the lake. We passed it earlier. You will find bathing spots there. We will provide you with clean clothes soon. Your current clothing will be returned to you washed and dried.' The Grycyryn gazed at Blakey. 'Unless there is no need to do so.'

'You're not worried I'll corrupt your mind even more?' Blakey asked as he and the Safi stepped into their cramped dwelling. It had two rooms barely large enough to accommodate a rough bed of leaves and hide, in each. Branches had pierced the inside of the walls and there were gaps in the roof. Luckily it didn't look like rain.

The Safi smirked. 'Before I met you, many people told me I am... difficult. It is my nature. Though... perhaps your presence brings out the worst in me.'

'I enjoyed the interesting discussion you had,' said the female Grycyryn. 'Your words will be considered by those who live after the chageen have gone. We will leave you now. The Survival Games will resume soon.'

'What are the Survival Games?' Blakey asked.

The Grycyryn hesitated at the door. 'In normal circumstances, they are called Succession Games and involve a series of physical and mental tests to help select people of rank. But, faced with this tragedy, a combination of differing tests decides who shall live and who shall die. It is hoped the contests will select a range of people with different skills. But there will be no children, as the Sklim explained. Though I understand the reasoning.' The Grycyryn departed.

'What a awful decision to have to make.' Blakey's chest heaved. The Safi bit her lip and she slumped against a wall. 'As for now, can I rest before... you know…?'

'You can rest for a short time,' the Safi replied.

'Good. I'm about to collapse. As long as I'm resting, they can't make a judgement on me, can they?' He tried to smile. Then he yawned.

'The judgement will take place immediately after the Survival Games. So your rest must be brief if you also wish to bathe.'

Blakey swore. He slipped into the second room. The bed of large leaves and hide did not look particularly comfortable. He flopped down on it. Sleep came surprisingly easily.

6

____

THE SURVIVAL GAMES

ROSS BLAKEY WAS JOLTED awake by the babble of people outside the hut. A stream of villagers were strolling towards the village square.

With the whole of eternity to rest, Blakey stretched, scratched at his plooglit-piss rashes, slapped his aching legs and went to investigate. There was a large bowl of water and two clundrns beside the door of the hut; he drank deeply before stepping outside.

Directly opposite the entrance, Blakey found a freckle-faced young woman, sitting cross-legged against a tree trunk, facing him. The young woman was short and thin for a Zygol and had flowing, red hair. Her crimson aktel tunic, uckliablaht belt, and her kraxl and kraxl-da seemed out of place on her young body. There was a gold streak across her tunic. 'Safi?' Blakey asked, not entirely sure of who the woman was.

'Yes. It is me Rossblakey.' Her eyes drifted to some villagers strolling past, grim-faced. 'Do you wish to witness the Survival Games?' There was a look of expectation in her eyes.

'You look different without your armour and helmet. And you have obviously had a bath.'

The Safi snorted, impatient. 'I had a quick bath. I have been assigned to guard you, Rossblakey, until your execution. It is my punishment for delaying your judgement. Answer me. Do you wish to watch the Survival Games? Decide now as there will only be one event and that will be over quickly.'

Blakey pursed his lips. 'But won't the Dsolcspmite-Spmite have me executed?'

'Not yet. Your judgement will take place after the Survival Games. And after you bathe. Come. If you are hungry, there is food in my room.'

Blakey shrugged. 'Not hungry,' he lied. 'Okay; let's see what's happening.'

The Safi stood. 'You are such a filthy mess. Your change of clothes is inside the door. Bring them. You must bathe immediately after the Games. Immediately after. Hurry.' Blakey ducked inside and tucked the grey Zygol clothes and sandals under his arm, and the two joined the rear of the passing villagers.

At the square, about two hundred men, women and children were gathered. Most communicated with hand signals; some spoke in soft whispers. The children were urged to be silent. Along the path to the stream, a water wheel was grinding slowly.

'There's only going to be one event?' Blakey whispered in the Safi's ear as they sought a vantage point nearest the lake. 'Just having one seems harsh when the loser is condemned to die.'

'It is indeed very harsh,' the Safi whispered. 'But allowing Tsalc to preside reminds us of the importance of the sixth element. And how fragile life is.' The Safi looked Blakey in the eye. 'I find your concern interesting. Although it is happening late, I feel that elapelc may, at last, be beginning within you.'

'Perhaps I'm not a bad person,' Blakey smiled weakly. 'But it doesn't matter anymore, does it?'

'It always matters,' she lectured with the tone of a primary school teacher. 'We must always strive to improve. To our dying breath.'

Blakey raised his arms as if to surrender.

'Did that strong burst of wind wake you earlier?'

'What do you mean?' Blakey examined at the gently swaying trees. 'Was the wind stronger earlier?'

'It became fierce while I was bathing. It blew dust, leaves and branches everywhere.'

'Didn't notice. I wouldn't have noticed if our hut had been blown away.'

'Why am I not surprised? You never notice what is evident.'

Blakey looked at her sourly. 'I...' Then he noticed the curling smile on the Safi and he let his pique pass. 'Anyway. Tell me, what is this one event going to be?'

'It is yet to be decided. Now speak softly.' The Safi took Blakey by the hand and eased into a small gap in the crowd, dragging him with her.

The village square was an irregular-shaped earthen open space, sheltered amidst tall trees. The villagers sat or stood around its perimeter, many with children. Interspersed through the crowd were the occasional crimson tunics of aktel, none wearing armour. The wearers were mostly aged in their late teens. One was probably Kasmin. On the far side of the square was the solid, long communal building, with a canopied roof of poles and vines, thatched with large leaves and uckliablaht hide. The hut stretched between two large trees.

As Blakey and the Safi reached their vantage point, the crowd murmured. A few restless children were bade to sit still.

Blakey couldn't help but stare at the young children with their raggedy clothes and hair. All of them were doomed to die a horrendous, brutal death. They, like the adults, seemed calm, perhaps blissfully ignorant of the carnage awaiting them.

Blakey gasped as Alena emerged from the communal hut, flanked by the Sklim, who was wearing what appeared to be an apron, and the three Grycyryn, including Abrik. All were stony-faced. Alena, obviously washed, groomed and patched up, was clothed in a mid-thigh-length green tunic, with a crimson streak in the shape of lightning. The tunic, which appeared oversized, hid most of her bandages and bruises, and her shoulder was no longer in a sling. The five dignitaries took up a stance a few steps into the open area of the square.

The Sklim stepped purposely forward. The crowd hushed and those at the back of the crowd craned their heads for a better view. 'Villagers of Mkeldi,' the Sklim announced. 'The arrival of a visitor whose status lies between Dsolcspmite and Spmite demands that the village includes her in the Survival Party.'

Alena's gaze fell to her feet as a wave of whispers passed through the crowd. The Sklim waved his arms for silence. 'Accordingly, Dsolcspmite Brlma must now take part in a contest with the last-placed successful contestant, for the final position in the Survival Party. It is what Tsalc has deemed. Tsalc will also be the arbitrator of the event to take place. As such, there can be no complaint from anyone. Will the two contestants come forward?'

Two dark-haired women stepped uneasily from the front of the communal building and into the open space. One combatant, aged in her mid-twenties, was dressed in a simple brown tunic. She was tall by the standards of this village and had a wiry figure. The other, who was clothed in the same coloured tunic as Alena, was a few years older than her competitor and looked stronger than Alena, though less athletic. Blakey's attention, as was that of many gathered, was transfixed on this woman's left foot, which was splinted and heavily bandaged. Dark traces of blood seeped through the bandage. Though this Dsolcspmite tried not to show it, she grimaced as she walked.

A softly whispered cry of anguish passed through the crowd as she reached the Sklim's side. She obviously commanded great respect. Even her competitor seemed in awe of her.

'Brlma is one of the few Dsolcspmites ever to emerge in Mkeldi village,' the Safi explained to Blakey. 'Without her injury, she would have by far the best chance of qualifying. But now, she is at the mercy of Tsalc.'

'But how will—?'

'Watch.'

The Sklim lifted two carved fist-sized wooden shapes, painted with elaborate designs, from a pouch. He held one aloft in each upturned hand and the crowd became deathly silent. With their own hopes of survival gone, the villagers now pressed forward, seemingly pinning their hopes on their favourite. 'Each face of the cube in my left hand represents one of the six elements,' began the Sklim. 'The octagon in my right hand will decide which event within that element will be selected. We use the random toss of both shapes to decide the event because Tsalc is the intangible element of life, which is largely beyond all learning and application.' He looked around the faces in the crowd. 'And, without which, elapelc and life can never be complete. Indeed, should Tsalc be the selected element, the face of the octagon alone will decide who survives and who will not.'

The Sklim glanced at the two contestants, who leaned their heads to the right, then he spun the wooden shapes high into the air. All eyes followed the shapes as they clattered onto the ground out of Blakey's sight. The reaction of the crowd, which leaned forward, and the two contestants, made the winner clear. While Brlma's head and shoulders slumped, the other woman clasped her own shoulders in muted triumph before stealing a guilty glance at her competitor. Many in the crowd mirrored their reactions.

Alena shut her eyes and heaved a sigh. The Sklim made the grave announcement. 'The deciding element is agility of mind and body. The event will be the juchublid.'

'What's that?' Blakey asked.

'Watch. But it is all over for Dsolcspmite Brlma. Tsalc has chosen an event that she would excel in, if not for her injury. It is a great tragedy for the re-establishment of the village.'

'The whole contest is cruel,' Blakey whispered. He couldn't take his eyes off the children who would perish the next day.

'Yes, sad and cruel.' The Safi again gazed at Blakey strangely. They, and the villagers, watched silently as the event was set up. The two combatants tapped one another on the shoulder with the back of their hands as a sign of deep respect.

A section of the crowd on one side of the open space parted, leaving a long strip of earth clear. Two thin and straight wooden poles were brought in and laid out at one end of the strip, between two and three metres apart. 'Each can have two attempts,' the Safi explained.

The contestant wearing the brown tunic went first. She strode confidently, took a deep breath and then ran, full pace, towards the sticks. She leaped as she reached the first stick and cleared the second. The woman showed not a semblance of joy; instead, she looked sadly across to Brlma. A murmur passed through the crowd.

'It's like a long jump,' Blakey remarked in his native language. He watched Brlma limp to the run-up area. 'She doesn't stand a chance.'

The Safi and a couple of Zygols nearby leaned their heads to the right.

Clearly in pain, Brlma took up her position and tried to run as best as she could to the take-off stick. She leaped but landed hard on the second stick and crumpled to the ground screaming in pain and disappointment. Her leap was remarkable, given her injury.

The crowd groaned. Her competitor and Alena stared at the ground. Brlma, now hobbling badly, her face wracked by agony, dusted herself off and dragged herself back to the run-off point as the pole was put back in place. Fresh blood was now liberally seeping through her bandage. Some people in the crowd were in tears. Others walked away.

'It's not worth it,' whispered Blakey. As Brlma began her run-up, screaming in pain, he could barely look. She could only hobble, and her jump fell well short of her previous mark. She cried out in agony and despair as she sank to the ground. The grim-faced Sklim and the successful combatant rushed over to tap Brlma on the shoulder with the back of their hands as they helped the Dsolcspmite struggle to her feet.

A sadness descended on the gathered villagers.

'It is not the triumph or failure that is most important,' said the Safi to no one in particular, 'it is the attempt.' But she became embarrassed at her words. Some nearby leaned their heads half-heartedly to the right. Most took no notice.

'Sometimes you need to act with compassion and not always seek to dispense wisdom,' said Blakey. A couple of the villagers filing away leaned their heads a little to the right.

'You are right. I still have much to learn.'

As Brlma limped towards the communal hut supported by her competitor and another villager, many people she passed gave her a respectful tap on her shoulder. One was a tearful Alena.

'Observe,' the Safi remarked. 'My Spmite is a fine and

compassionate person. It is unfortunate you have only known her at a time when she has been hardened by being subjected to a vicious injustice. Not to mention having to endure the unconscionable act of an ignorant Earthman. Someone she admires will die to allow her to live to face judgement. Tsalc is indeed a harsh master.'

'Have you forgotten that you almost executed her in the desert?'

The Safi closed her eyes. 'That is so. I acted against someone I admired at the behest of a man whose deviousness has since become apparent. I am deeply ashamed of what I nearly did.' Then the Safi started. Although the crowd was dispersing, Alena had approached the Sklim and the gathered Grycyryn, including Abrik, and was engaged in an earnest discussion.

The Safi took an involuntary breath. 'Come with me.' She took Blakey by the arm and dragged him away from the village square. Her grip was surprisingly strong.

'What's happening? Are they about to make a judgement on me?' He sucked a breath.

'It's better we don't wait to find out. You should bathe and change clothes now.'

The Safi increased her pace, dodging around the trudging villagers. 'Besides, I have a plan. You, having no scruples; you make the perfect accomplice. With our questioning tongues, we are the most unpopular people in the village.'

'You want me to help you do what?'

'I will tell you later. But, despite my harsh words to you, I am beginning... to believe that you are not a total barbarian. In time, if not for our fate, I believe you could eventually... yes... it would take a long, long time... achieve elapelc and loosen your enchantment with Tsalc.'

Blakey turned to her. 'You think that?'

'Yes, I am beginning to believe that, despite your incredibly foolish, amazingly ignorant and clumsy ways... behaving in a manner that defies all reason, you show a glimmer of promise. You can be noble. But it is abundantly clear you are seriously misguided.' She gave Blakey a half-smile.

'Thanks,' Blakey said doubtfully.

With their progress slowed by the listless villagers before them, the Safi grabbed Blakey's arm more firmly and pulled him into the vegetation.

'I could teach you Zygols a few things,' Blakey said as he dodged plants and trees, aware of the plooglits in the trees about him. Another dose of plooglit piss was the last thing he needed. Well... the second-last thing. 'For instance. I could teach you a great deal about the composition of your hills and mountains.'

The Safi looked doubtful. 'That knowledge has interest for some people. Not many.'

Okay... if you're looking for something more useful. Fine... I would be making the cave larger to hold more people. I'd find ways to make strong shelters with large storage areas that could house many people until the chageen gave up. I'd be doing *something*.'

The Safi, who kept glancing nervously behind her, scowled. 'You are wrong. Zygols do not choose to accept death so easily. As much as I sympathise with your intentions, Rossblakey, almost all Grycyryn would tell you that we cannot deny the chageen the flesh they now crave. Making strong shelters would be no use. The chageen would stay until they were able to satisfy what elapelc demands of them. Only a few people can be allowed to escape.'

Blakey shook his head. 'What else could I expect from your crazy planet?'

'Think what you will. But perhaps the chageen's need for elapelc can be satisfied in other ways. I hope so. I have convinced some in the Survival Party that more water needs to be diverted to allow shade trees to grow around the uckliablaht pen. Doing so might reduce the risk of a collapse of elapelc.'

'That makes sense.'

'It is not a new idea. But the work has been overlooked because it involves moving a great deal of solid rock. But it is now deemed to be imperative.'

'Good thinking. Even if it's a bit late.'

After another nervous glance behind her, the Safi sped up. 'I believe they are searching for us.'

Blakey did not dare look behind. Nor was it advisable. They were plunging through dense vegetation. 'You have to slow down!' He tucked his change of clothes under his shirt as best as he could as he was dragged through branches and fronds he could not dodge. He felt about his clothes and face, and groaned. 'Look, Safi. I'm getting plooglit piss all over me. I'm going to be one huge ball of pain soon. So slow down!' He swore. Loudly.

'Just a few steps more.'

The determined Safi tugged Blakey, halting only when they reached the banks of the lake. The lake was the size of a small, oval sports ground, and surrounded by the tallest and broadest trees in the village. Leaves, some the size of doormats, hung from their broad branches. Watermarks showed the water level to be low. To their left a crude wooden water wheel ground as it diverted water through a low sluice to inside the village. Some children were swimming and laughing nearby. To their right were five small, three-sided, wooden enclosures, built into the shallows. The enclosures were formed by tightly knit, thin and upright branches, that rose out of the lake by about two metres. To the right of these, the stream reformed and meandered sharply to the right, towards the uckliablaht pen.

7

____

THE SAFI'S RUSE

AGHAST, Ross Blakey surveyed the plooglit piss on his arms and seeping through much of his clothes. He winced at the wetness on his face. The thought of a kraxl-da being thrust with venom through his torso no longer seemed so horrid. Oblivious, the Safi took him by the hand, and led him towards the wooden enclosures.

'Wash,' she pronounced. 'The villagers will not disturb you if you are bathing. For a short while.' Then she shuddered at the rows of red-eyed chageen perched in the trees.

Blakey tossed his change of clothes on the ground, and hastily took off his wet shirt, pulled off his boots and socks, and his pants in the hope of lessening the coming pain. If only a bit.

'Go to the last bathing spot,' the Safi gestured with a sweep of her arm. 'It is the most convenient.'

Ross Blakey waded into the lake, feverishly washing off as much of the plooglit piss as he could, uttering Earth profundities. The reflected face was filthy; his jowls and the stubble of a beard were grizzled, and his unkempt hair was grey with dust.

Two teenagers approached. 'Do you need those clothes washed, Safi?' one spoke.

'If you wish to help,' the Safi replied, smiling.

The teenagers smiled and picked up Blakey's clothes, examining them with mirth. 'Artra, fetch some soap leaves. I will wet the clothes.'

Blakey remembered his precious notes. 'There are a couple of items in the... pouches,' he called out. 'Please put them inside my shoes. Don't let them get wet.'

'Don't wash his clothes yet. There is one item still to come.' The Safi stared hard at him, arms crossed.

Self-conscious, Blakey stepped into the enclosure the Safi had indicated. Its size would perhaps allow room for four people, sitting together in comfort. Inside, a rough bench protruded above the level of the water, and above it was a bulging pouch. Blakey hid behind a wooden wall, and reluctantly threw his underpants onto the shore. A child scooped them up and, laughing, showed them to the other child. Giggling, they ran off. Blakey did not expect to see his clothes again.

The Safi moved to have a clear view of the naked Earthman. He turned his back on her.

'You are so in desperate need of a thorough wash.'

Blakey craned his head to look at her. 'Are you going to sit there and watch the whole time I'm washing?'

'Of course. I have been ordered to not let you out of my sight. Ignore me. Wash yourself... thoroughly. There are soap leaves in the pouch.'

Ross Blakey began to rinse his hair with his back to her.

The Safi chuckled. 'Are you uncomfortable with me watching you?'

'Well... Yes, I am.'

'Would you be more relaxed if I bathed with you?'

Blakey nearly choked on the water running down his face. 'If you want...'

'Okay then. But I have not told you my name.' Blakey looked at her blankly. 'Not knowing my name means I do not wish you to touch me as man to woman. Is that understood?'

'I understand. But you know my name.'

'That is so, Rossblakey,' she said with an off-handed shrug. The

Safi undid her belt. Then she removed her tunic and undergarment and waded casually into the wooden enclosure.

Ross Blakey's eyes dwelt briefly on the lithe young body before him. Maybe she was a little thin, but she was very easy on the eyes. 'Look. I'm grateful for what you've done for me. I really am.'

The Safi curled up on the opposite side of the enclosure to Blakey. 'Now bathe. No touching.'

'Relax; I won't. I'm not going to risk getting myself into even more trouble.'

The Safi smiled. 'You will most certainly try nothing. Realise though, that because I follow the element of learning and teaching, I am likely to be more tolerant of your bizarre behaviour than most Zygols. Realise that I do not shiver for you. Ha! The mere thought evokes terror in me.'

Blakey certainly needed this wash. Not as much as a few double whiskies. A helicopter and pilot would be better still. He fetched some silky soap leaves from the pouch and, by rubbing them together, generated a thin lather, which he applied to his arms.

'You are not doing it properly,' the Safi admonished him. 'I'll show you.' She fetched two handfuls of soap leaves and waded to him. Her youthful, smiling face and her clear, bright eyes, and lithe body, made Blakey sigh.

'You scrunch up the leaves like this. See the extra lather I'm getting?' Then, with unhurried and sweeping movements, she applied the lather to his shoulders and chest. Blakey basked in the Safi's touch. And, with her being so pleasingly close, he couldn't help but be mesmerised by her beautiful, laughing and alive, green eyes. It was such a pleasurable way to spend perhaps his last hour. His nether region was making an admirable effort—given his exhaustion and anxiety—to make a final gesture.

Laughing, the Safi fetched some more leaves. Blakey now had a good idea of how to scrunch them up but figured he'd leave the task to the Safi. She brushed his arms aside and kept applying more lather until she covered all of his body. 'Now stand close to the sluice and rinse.' Blakey longed to be washed lots more. But the Safi lifted the sluice. Not ready to leave, Blakey rested on his side, letting the gentle warm current of the stream run across his body.

'Ibatra,' she leaned over and whispered in his ear—*wait here*. The Safi stood and strode up the bank of the lake. She reached down, then returned, smiling, with something hidden behind her back. She sat beside Blakey and leaned towards him.

Suddenly, the Safi produced a kraxl. Blakey tried to yell, but the sight of the glinting metal froze his throat. He tried weakly to ward her off, but his muscles were paralysed by fear.

'Ooooh, shit!' he blurted as the naked Safi knelt beside him and drew the knife towards his throat. 'Oh my God!' So, this was how it ends. Executed by a beautiful young, naked woman who he believed to be the only Zygol who cared about him. *This* was her secret plan? How had offended her so badly?

The Safi scowled. Then to Blakey's surprise, she smiled. A sadistic psychopath.

'Are all Earthmen such cowards as you?' she asked. 'I have done this before. It is easy.'

Blakey swallowed. He closed his eyes and waited to die.

'Stay still,' she commanded. 'I promise you will feel no pain.' She took Blakey's chin and then he felt the kraxl's cold blade against his throat. He began choking in sheer terror. To mock him, she drew the kraxl up from his throat to his chin. Then she took the blade away, dipped it in water, only to repeat the act. She did the same again. It then dawned on Blakey, like awakening to the most brilliant of sunrises, that the Safi was giving him a shave. He opened one eye, took a deep breath in relief and chuckled.

'Am I tickling you? Stay still or I will cut you.'

Blakey opened his other eye and looked at her puzzled face. 'I just thought... never mind.'

'You are truly strange.' She shook her head and deftly completed the job. When she was done, she rinsed her kraxl carefully and tossed it on to the bank of the lake. Blakey laughed. The Safi backed away, confused. But her eyes were sparkling.

Blakey suddenly became thoughtful.

'What are you thinking?' the Safi asked. Blakey mused that this had to be a question that unites women across the universe.

'It's weird. I'm not breaking into a new plooglit-piss rash.' The Safi blinked. 'But I should be about to roll around in agony right now. Why isn't it happening?' He searched her face.

'That is what you are thinking?' The Safi looked decidedly unimpressed. 'Perhaps the lather from the replti bush has washed it away.'

Blakey shook his head. 'It can't be that. We use the replti lather in the compound. It does little to stop the itching. We get leaves from this village. And others. Besides, you didn't soap me all over. You went over a couple of parts twice. But you missed some bits.' The Safi raised an eyebrow. 'There's no new plooglit-piss rash forming on the spots you missed. This has never happened to an Earthman before. Never.'

'The things you think about,' the Safi said, perplexed.

'Oh, don't get me wrong. I am so very glad that you joined me for my bath.' He figured he'd not mention he would have been even happier if a helicopter and pilot came to fetch him. Only just. 'Okay. Forget about the rash. Safi, why are you so relaxed? You're going to be eaten alive by chageen tomorrow.'

'How would being sad change anything? Besides, you will die before I do.'

'Ah, yes. The... Dsolcspmite-Spmite.' With his bath done, Blakey's judgement was uncomfortably imminent. Despite it all, and although the Safi's clear, bright eyes were enchanting, a chunk of his mind was fixated with plooglit piss.

'Rossblakey,' the Safi remarked. 'You have an expression on your face that puzzles me.'

'I think I've worked it out. Plooglit piss has no potency in this village. Why is that?' He stared at the Safi.

She broke into a half-smile. 'I can't be definite. But you have given me even more reason to implement my plan. And you are going to help me. But we must move quickly.'

Blakey was drawn by her mischievous grin.

'Squeeze through the sluice. Keep out of sight. Wait for me behind the tree with the small yellow flowers by the bend. I will bring your change of clothes.'

As the Safi emerged from the lake, splashing water as if to draw attention to herself, Blakey squeezed through the sluice, slunk to the shore and dried himself with the large, velvety leaves behind the tree she had indicated.

When the Safi had dressed, she ran over with Blakey's fresh Zygol clothing, his boots and notebook. He checked them out. They had small traces of plooglit piss on them. But what choice did he have?

'Hurry!' The Safi looked nervous as she poked her head around the tree.

Blakey got into the tatty grey tunic. 'They could have given me the tunic of a taller man.' The Safi looked at him and giggled.

Blakey tried to tug the tunic lower. 'Where are we going?'

'The uckliablaht pen. Follow me and keep low. But understand; I must take you to my Spmite after we do this. She will be furious with me for delaying your judgement again. She longs to search for her talisman.' The Safi touched the hilt of her kraxl-da.

Blakey shrugged. She'd done him a massive favour, so what she asked was reasonable.

The two waded along the stream towards the uckliablaht pen, footwear in their hands, with Blakey at the rear. 'Tell me something. But don't ask me why I need to know. What is the significance of a person wearing an orange tunic but with three green shapes on it that make up a sort of triangle?'

'You've seen this tunic on a villager?' inquired the Safi.

'No. Elsewhere.'

'The design you describe signifies a Grycyryn who mixes herbs and minerals to make potions.'

'Yes. I remember now.' The Safi looked at Blakey for an explanation but he didn't reply. He'd recalled Zglta's tunic. She would never know how deeply he regretted upsetting her.

The two emerged beside the rough bridge they had crossed that morning. Inside the pen, many uckliablahts and a few plooglits pressed against one part of the fence where the shade had reached.

The Safi moved briskly to the wide gate of the pen. 'Zeeplat!' The gate was tied to the gate post by a thick rope tied in a large, elaborate knot. 'Why is it so tight?' she grunted as she struggled to undo the binding, even prying at it with the point of her kraxl. But the tight knot held firm.

Blakey tried to help to no avail.

'I will have to cut it,' the Safi said.

'Step away from that gate!' a voice boomed from their right. Blakey and the Safi spun around. She slumped and Blakey groaned.

Alena strode towards them brandishing a kraxl-da, her limp a little less pronounced than before.

Ross Blakey muttered under his breath. 'My Spmite,' begged the Safi, 'Allow me to set the uckliablahts free. I must try something... anything... to try and avoid the chageen attack.'

The Safi swallowed. Alena pointed her kraxl-da at Blakey's chest. 'I expected you to bring the Earthman to me earlier. You knew I wish to search for my talisman.'

'I reasoned I had more chance implementing my plan if I had an excuse to come this way, with the villagers preoccupied.'

Alana glared hard at the Safi. 'Your plan defies the expressed will of the Sklim. Stand to the side. Both of you. I will do what I must do,' The Safi looked disconsolate as she and Blakey took a step away.

Alena raised her kraxl-da high. Blakey gave a cry and fell to his knees, his hands covering his head—his pitiful attempt to ward off the savage blow.

Alena brought her kraxl-da down hard, and sliced, not Blakey's head, but the knot.

Blakey and the Safi gaped.

'My Spmite,' the Safi said, bursting into a grin. 'I am shocked. You have acted dishonourably.'

'Did you consider whether the uckliablahts may now cause havoc?' Alena asked as she casually tossed the rope aside and swung the large gate open.

'Yes. Uckliablahts prefer fresh leaves and branches and will avoid the staler fare homes are made from. Many will graze near the lake. As there is no wind to whip up the dust, they should remain calm. But even if these things weren't so, I would have let the animals loose. I had to try *something*.'

Alena leaned her head to the right and smiled. 'Your reasoning is sound. Come. Let's get these miserable animals out of this horrible place. Avoid their huge feet.'

The Safi was rapturous as the three herded the uckliablahts towards the open gate. Some animals needed a slap on their backsides to get them to move.

'Our actions will make the Sklim and Abrik furious,' the Safi remarked with glee.

'I know,' Alena grinned. 'But the six elements demand we act. Protocols are a secondary concern.'

The animals spread out, some heading to the greener vegetation, while others trotted to the fields to partake of the stubble there. Their appearance sent the village plooglits moving slowly but purposely about the trees. Annoyed chageen hissed and scattered.

With their task done, Alena and the Safi leaned against a railing and smiled at their handiwork.

A worried Ross Blakey kept his distance.

'Don't look so satisfied, Safi. You have delayed the Earthman's judgement. He should be dead,' Alena mocked.

'I know,' said the Safi. 'I was about to bring him to you. He had his bath. And I wanted his help to—'

'And when he bathed, you kept him under close... supervision.' Alena's lips curled into a smile.

The Safi reddened.

'Tell me, do you shiver for... him?' Alena spoke with distain.

The Safi bristled. 'For *him?* You insult me! To suggest that... I... would shiver for someone so ignorant. He needed to bathe. I used him to implement my plan. That is all. Though... he did save my life.'

'You delayed me getting justice,' Alena frowned. The Safi looked at her feet. 'As for now, take the Earthman back to your hut and keep him there until I return. Do anything you need to do to prevent him from escaping short of killing him. When I return, he will face an immediate judgement. Delay me further and you will both face my wrath. Understand?' She gave Blakey a triumphant smile then turned to leave.

'Where are you going?'

'I have delayed the search for my talisman too long. There are fire sticks and some rope in the cave. A few in the Survival Party have volunteered to help. The Sklim believes the talisman may be at the bottom of a shaft in what is called the chimneys, because smoke from fires lit in the habitable part of the cave follow drafts that reach the surface. I am told that reaching that place might not be possible. But I must try. Though I long...' Alena glared at Blakey as she tapped the blade of her kraxl-da. 'No. The Earthman's judgement will need to wait. Besides, with the talisman back in my possession, his punishment will be doubly pleasurable.'

'I will not disappoint you, my Spmite,' the Safi said, her stern eyes fixed on Blakey.

'I believe you. Guard the Earthman. But there will be no more... bathing.'

The Safi looked sheepish.

'I hope you find your talisman,' Blakey ventured as Alena turned to leave.

Alena looked at him oddly. 'For my sake, or for yours?'

'For your sake. Obviously finding it won't do me any good.'

Alena looked at him intently, yet her expression revealed nothing. 'True. Finding it won't save you, Earthman. Go,' she said to the Safi.

Alena signalled the end of formal discussion by touching her cheek and the bridge of her nose then she ran off, with her faint limp, towards the cave.

'May Tsalc smile on you,' the Safi called after her.

She faced Blakey. 'Yet again, Tsalc has spared its most ardent disciple, Rossblakey. It is now possible you will remain alive until dark. But Tsalc must surely be tiring of you.'

Would Tsalc abandon its favourite plaything? 'Is there still food in the hut?' Blakey asked wearily. 'I'm really hungry.'

'There will be food in the square. Some villagers were planning a feast.'

As they wandered along the path, they untethered the restless uckliablahts the renegades had ridden into the village. 'Gentok's steed nearly chewed through its tether,' the Safi remarked.

The release of the uckliablahts caused their companion plooglits in the trees above to scurry about with frantic zest. Even the Safi was taken aback by their joy. More chageen scattered, hissing.

Walking on, the two passed groups of villagers in small open areas. Many sat around looking solemn as a few emptied satchels of grain or edible stalks into sacks. A couple of toddlers crawled from adult to adult, who picked up the youngsters and hugged them, often breaking into sobs. One woman filling a sack was heavily pregnant.

To Blakey's unanswered question, the Safi sadly leaned her head to the left. Blakey whispered an oath.

When each sack was filled, it was sealed by needle and thread and deposited by the side of the path. 'Some sacks are for the Survival Party,' explained the Safi. 'Others will be stored in the communal hut. The villagers will keep all the doors of the hut open. That way the chageen will discover there are no humans there. And so will not damage the food stocks.'

Blakey and the Safi came across seven villagers, wearing an array of tunics, heading in the opposite direction, including the young female Grycyryn. The seven moved slowly, carrying sacks of food, bound to their shoulders and backs. Their fellow villagers approached to hug them. Limping badly and aided by a walking cane, Dsolcspmite Brlma brought up the rear of the group. Her foot and ankle were newly splinted.

Brlma looked crestfallen. 'Have you heard, Safi? Alena has given me her place in the Survival Party.' Blakey and the Safi recoiled. 'Of course, I refused her offer, which defies the first rule of the Survival Games. But she refuses to be part of the Survival Party. If I chose to not go, my place would be taken up by Abrik, as our Sklim is deemed too old. How would that truly benefit the re-establishment of Mkeldi village?'

'My Spmite must take her place,' the Safi moaned. 'How else can the duplicity of the Zookspmate be exposed?'

Brlma's chest heaved. 'I told Alena this over and over. But she is resolute. Perhaps you can convince her not to make such a tragic sacrifice.'

The Safi struggled to gather her composure. 'I won't be able to change her mind. It is how she is.'

'I have no choice then.' Brlma bowed her head. 'But I will not rest until I find her talisman. Or die trying. And, if I emerge from the cave, I will get the justice Alena is to be denied.'

'Oh, what a Spmite she could have been. I grieve for her,' the Safi said, downcast.

'I will grieve as well. I will do my very best to do her proud.' The Safi gave Brlma an affectionate tap on the shoulder. Distraught, Brlma shuffled on.

The Safi trudged along the path. Ross Blakey left her to her thoughts. When the two reached the village square, they found many villagers crowded around three fires. The inviting smell of food wafted from many pots. Near one of the fires stood the familiar rotund form of Rystyn, who was talking animatedly with Abrik. The two were drinking from clundrns. By the way they swayed, the liquid was not water.

Though the Safi held back, Blakey approached this fire. Rystyn smiled only a greeting to the Safi. 'So, Earthman. I will have to wait longer for you to be punished.'

'How disappointing for you.' Blakey smiled.

'Sometimes having to wait longer can make an outcome even more pleasurable. Have you been told of the Dsolcspmite-Spmite's decision?' The crestfallen Safi leaned her head to the right.

'Do you have any food to spare?' Blakey asked a villager.

'Help yourselves,' Abrik replied. The shared glare between her and the Safi dripped with venom. Then Abrik stormed off with the hint of a stagger.

Blakey and the Safi took up clean plates and ladles and took samples from a couple of pots.

'Have you seen Kasmin?' the Safi asked Rystyn as she ate.

'I believe she is with friends, which is a good thing. She has taken her impending death very hard.'

'I guessed as much.' The Safi sighed. 'She would have far more courage if Gentok were here.'

'I, too, am struggling with my fate,' Rystyn added gravely. 'But you, Safi, seem to be coping well.'

'Is that how I appear? It is not how I feel.'

When Blakey and an introspective Safi finished eating, a villager handed them clundrns filled with a green liquid that had an odour that reminded the Earthman of the Swamp. Both Blakey and the Safi took a sip. It was *definitely* alcoholic, though the taste was not particularly agreeable. But taste didn't matter.

The Safi caught sight of the Sklim striding purposely towards them, gesticulating wildly with his walking stick. His face was red with anger.

'I am in more trouble,' she muttered.

'Do you know how the uckliablahts came to be freed?' the Sklim demanded of the Safi.

The Safi bade Blakey to be silent and looked the Sklim in the eye. 'It was my idea. I could not sit idle in the face of our impending fate.'

The Sklim shook in rage, his eyes burning. 'I knew it was you! You act like a Grycyryn-da. But you are nothing but a young, overly headstrong and irresponsible aktel. Opitek! Do you realise how long it will take to round the beasts up? This is supposed to be a day for farewells. Now you have burdened us with a major task.'

'Then let them roam free,' the Safi replied. 'They may... yet repair the village's elapelc. It is worth the chance.'

'Opitek again! Opitek! Who gave you permission to act?'

'No one.' The Safi jutted her chin.

'I think it is not opitek,' a middle-aged man, who was listening, remarked. 'The young Safi has spirit. I applaud her. And why round the animals up? Many villagers will not sleep this night, anyway.' A couple of others leaned their heads to the right.

'Then you are also irresponsible,' the Sklim growled. He looked at the faces of other villagers, including a couple of aktel, who were standing nearby. None spoke. He threw his hands in the air. 'If that's what you all think. Anyway, I need to find Abrik. Does anyone know where she is?'

'She went in the direction of her hut, perhaps to sleep off the effects of the alcohol,' a swaying old woman with a much-creased face said, her words a little slurred.

'No!' wailed the Sklim. 'With Brlma and a Grycyryn gone to the cavern, Abrik and I are the ones who should make a judgement on the Earthman. I will summon Palin only as a last resort. He is too filled with bitterness for not being selected in the Survival Party. The judgement does not need Alena to be present; the matter is straightforward. We have witness accounts. Then Alena can punish the Earthman whenever she desires. But Abrik needs to be sober.'

Ross Blakey smirked.

The Sklim fumed. 'But first I must find some responsible villagers to round up our uckliablahts.' He glared at those nearby.

'Good luck finding anyone,' said the tipsy villager. The Sklim glared at her and stormed off.

'Rossblakey, we will go back to the hut now, as my Spmite ordered.'

'Umm. Just a little longer. I think this green stuff will put me in a better frame of mind for my judgement.'

'We will leave...' She touched the hilt of her kraxl. But the tipsy old woman began to fill Blakey's clundrn. The Safi rolled her eyes. 'Okay. One final drink.'

Blakey turned to the Zygol cook. 'Rystyn, shall we have a toast together for what we've been through?'

'I will toast only the outcome of your judgement, Earthman.'

Blakey shrugged and checked the contents of the pottery bottles nearby as he drank his newly filled clundrn. He gave a cry of triumph when he found one that was almost full. 'I'll take this one with me. By the way, can you point the way to Abrik's hut?'

'What are you thinking, Rossblakey? Are you about to try my patience again?' the Safi snarled.

'I will show you,' the tipsy villager said. She, the muttering Safi and Blakey, who cradled the jug of alcohol, walked along a narrow path leading from the village square.

The Safi placed a hand on Blakey's shoulder. 'If I am guessing your intentions correctly, be aware that you are definitely and improperly embracing Tsalc and blatantly snubbing the other five elements. All of them. Does that mean nothing to you?'

'Relax, Safi. And what do you do in the village?' he asked the villager, as he sidled beside the old woman.

'I am a weaver,' the woman replied proudly. 'My specialty is to weave the vines, branches, leaves and uckliablaht hide into dwellings. It is a task that requires more skill than most people believe.'

'Ah, a truly worthy craft. I imagine that being a weaver of homes in this village would be particularly difficult given the harsh winds you get. How do you deal with very strong winds and heavy rain?'

'We get wet, Earthman,' said the villager, looking puzzled. 'Is it not the same on your planet?'

'Well...' It would take too long to explain. 'Of course.' The old woman gave him a strange look. Blakey quarter-filled the woman's clundrn.

'Rossblakey!'

'Here is Abrik's hut,' the villager announced. The dwelling was quite small.

'I forbid you to do what I believe you intend to do!' hissed the Safi, touching the hilt of her kraxl-da.

Blakey stood by the front door flap. 'Abrik! Do you mind if we come in?'

'Go away!' Abrik boomed. She sounded drunk.

'I have a bottle of your finest alcohol.'

The Safi leapt in front of him, kraxl-da drawn. 'No! You will not do this!'

'Is that your disagreeable Safi with you? You can come in. But send her away.'

When the Safi rolled her eyes, Blakey brushed past her extended arm and dove into the hut.

He found Abrik slouched on a wide stool, her back pressed against a wall. 'I need to sober up,' she said in a slurred voice. 'I must be ready for your judgement. Soon I will take the antidote. Soon. But I am greatly pained. When I am sober, I become confronted with the consequences of my inaction.'

Blakey held up the flask of alcohol. 'Surely the antidote can wait a little longer.'

An impatient gasp came from outside. Abrik gazed up at him for a few seconds. Then the Grycyryn leaned her head to the right. 'Okay, Earthman. One more drink. Just one. It is a terrible day.' She sobbed. But Abrik reached for two clundrns.

Blakey grinned. 'It certainly is.' Outside, the Safi was making slashing movements with her kraxl-da.

The bottle of alcohol was emptied. Remarkably quickly. By this time Abrik was staring vacantly at the roof. As Blakey reached the door flap, she slowly slid down on her side and passed out. After a nod of satisfaction, he stepped outside.

The Safi glowered at him. 'We go now. Or you part ways with one of your feet! And I will drag you back to the hut.' Kraxl drawn, she shook with anger. 'You have behaved dishonourably. My Spmite and I extended your life to seek a greater purpose. But you... you act only out of selfishness.'

Blakey nodded. 'Yes. I admit it. Can't you grant a condemned man his last act of defiance to a hostile world?'

'What! You think that—'

'I promise I won't disappoint you again. Let's go.' As they strode away, the Sklim approached Abrik's hut from the opposite direction. They heard him wail.

When Blakey and the still-furious Safi reached their hut, Blakey yawned and flopped heavily on his bed. 'Stay here until your judgement,' she pronounced. He thought it best to comply; she gripped her kraxl with purpose. Besides, his body needed sleep. And sleep he did.

Sometime afterwards, Blakey was vaguely aware that the Safi had cautiously entered his bedroom. For a while she stood in the doorway watching him. Then she dropped her belt and snuggled next to him and draped his arm around her. He had to be dreaming.

'I have not come for affection,' she whispered. 'I must guard you. But, outside, I have only plooglits for company.' When Blakey didn't reply, she relaxed. She need not have spoken. Ross Blakey's snatches of consciousness were brief. Beside the hut, an uckliablaht crashed through the underbrush as plooglits climbed up and down trees. Seemingly, the Sklim hadn't been able to get them rounded up. That brought a smile to his face.

8

AN EARTHMAN FACES JUDGEMENT

SOMEONE WAS TUGGING Blakey's arm. The Safi. It was night. From the expression on her face, Ross Blakey knew why she had woken him.

'Drink this.' She handed him a clundrn.

Blakey tossed it down without thinking. His throat was parched.

'It is time for your judgement. My Spmite has returned from the cave. The Sklim and... possibly Abrik, possibly another Grycyryn, are ready for you. I can mention your part in saving my life if you wish. You can then say the words you need to say to my Spmite.'

Blakey flopped back on the bed. 'So Tsalc is done with me.'

'That is the whim of Tsalc. Get up. It is best we deal with this matter quickly.' She gazed into his eyes. 'Be brave, Rossblakey. You will be regarded better... even by my Spmite... if you are. Emphasise that you meant no malice. That you are merely an imbecile. Those present will readily accept that.'

Blakey made no move to get out of bed. 'You've given me the antidote, haven't you?'

'You must face your judgement with a clear mind.'

'You didn't have to. I wasn't drunk. Abrik guzzled nearly all of it.

Even if I was, what difference would it make? Everyone in the village is going to die in the morning.'

The Safi scowled. 'You need to show courage. Pretend if you have to. If not for your sake, then for the sake of those who need to summon courage for the fate that awaits them in the morning. Whatever you think of us Zygols, your punishment, as deserved as it is, will not be a time of joy.'

Blakey swallowed. 'It will be for the... Dsolcspmite-Spmite... and Rystyn.'

'No! It is a punishment she must do.'

Blakey yawned. 'Tell them I'll come soon. Promise.'

'If I tell them that, my Spmite will punish you without ceremony in your bed. You will be remembered badly as a criminal and a coward, rather than the fool you truly are. You will not be able to say any final words.'

Blakey pursed his lips and looked around the room. 'Yes, I was a fool. To think I had the offer of safe passage to my compound. I guess it doesn't matter, but did... she... find her talisman?'

The Safi clicked her tongue. 'She so much deserved to. But no. Tsalc has remained harsh with her. Getting to where the talisman lies is extremely difficult. Parts of the cave are narrow. Parts are submerged. She has bouts of dizziness from her fall. And her shoulder is too badly damaged to manoeuvre far through the passages. Others are trying to retrieve it. It is a pity. She was optimistic when we saw her by the uckliablaht pen. Did you sense her improved mood?'

'Her improved mood? Oh, definitely. She told me there how much she was looking forward to killing me. Before that moment, she wanted to obliterate every atom of my body from the entire universe.'

The Safi smiled. 'Do not look upon my Spmite as harshly as Tsalc has done. What she has had to endure is so undeserved. Allow her to gain satisfaction from your punishment. How she will administer the blow, I do not know. My guess is that you will die swiftly with minimal pain. For she is a compassionate person.'

'How very kind of her,' Blakey said with a strong hint of irony.

The Safi sighed. He reached out and gently stroked her chin. She did not pull away. 'It looks like the mystery of the non-potent plooglit piss in this village is about to die with me.'

The Safi looked oddly at him. 'You still think about such things. If you want an explanation, perhaps my Spmite may help you. Since I have known her, I have found her to be not only an expert protector but also a capable thinker.'

Blakey snorted. 'She do something for me? Won't happen. She hates me too much.'

'She will give you an answer if she is able,' the Safi retorted, miffed. 'A Spmite or a Dsolcspmite cannot refuse a genuine request for help. Not under the most trying of circumstances. It is fundamental to her training.'

He smirked. 'Ha! Let's find out then.'

Grunting, Blakey lifted himself to his feet and slapped his knee. Inside the entrance to the hut he found his boots and Earth clothes. They were clean and dry, though poorly stacked and folded.

'I want to change into my Earth clothes.'

The Safi huffed but, reluctantly, leaned her head to the right. She waited outside while Blakey changed.

The two set off wordlessly for the village square. The Safi had to keep pausing for him to catch up. 'Move faster. You make my Spmite angrier.' He was definitely making the Safi angrier.

Blakey shrugged. 'I can't. I'm aching all over. Anyway... how much angrier can she get?' The Safi snorted.

As they meandered towards the village square, Blakey spotted a Zygol toilet amongst the greenery to his left. 'I'm sorry, but I need to go there, Safi. Honest, I do.'

'No! We are already late. Your execution will be swift. So there is no need.'

'If I don't do what I must do, I risk embarrassing myself at the judgement.'

'No!' He dived towards the toilet as the Safi uttered some choice Zygol words. Blakey bumped into a man rushing out as he entered the toilet. It was the Grycyryn who had been part of the greeting party. The two men were startled at the sight of one another. Then the Grycyryn disappeared into the vegetation.

'If the Dsolcspmite-Spmite thinks I'm being too slow, she can have me executed, can't she?' Blakey teased from inside.

'Any more delays,' she thundered, 'and I will do much of her task for her!'

Blakey did what he needed to do. And the small steent, which congregate in numbers around Zygol toilets and uckliablaht pens, took to Blakey's droppings with gusto. Although the experience for non-Zygols takes a bit of getting used to (Blakey hadn't reached that stage; he needed to grip the trees on either side very tightly), the steent ensured toilet paper is not required on Zygol III. Fortunately, only very occasionally do the steent "bite the hand that feeds them."

When he was done (after cleaning his hands with some soap leaves), Blakey shuffled along while the Safi, with many cold stares, was compelled to slow to his pace. She breathed deeply with relief when they reached the communal building. Villagers were still congregated around the three fires. The Safi led Blakey roughly by the arm to the door flap of the building and poked her head inside. Blakey quivered uncomfortably behind her.

An admonishing exclamation came from inside the hut. A highly impatient Alena was not in a jovial mood.

Blakey shuddered as the Safi dragged him inside. But, while he felt sorry for himself, he also felt sympathy for everyone left in the village, including babies and the young woman with sparkling eyes he had bathed with at the lake. They would die the most horrific death the coming morning. He had to be the fortunate one.

The communal hut was built around two stout trees, their trunks visible. While some branches had been trimmed to make space inside, others had been twisted and bound to form the uneven supports for the walls and ceiling. The Zygols had manoeuvred living vines and large leaves as well as large, supporting branches and beams, with copious quantities of uckliablaht hide, to enclose the building. The roof was well thatched.

The meeting room was furnished simply with raised sitting mats, and some low rough benches. At the far end of the room were two flap doors. One was tied partly open, revealing many stacked sacks. The hut was lit by candle-like fire sticks around the walls and on the benches in the middle of the room.

Everyone was standing. Alena approached him, furious, her arm back in a sling, and with both a kraxl and kraxl-da hanging from her belt. Her eyes were aflame. Behind her stood the Sklim and two armed aktel.

Alena fumed at the Safi. 'Why did you take so long? The remaining time for the villagers is short.' She then glared at Blakey. 'This delay is unpardonable.'

'The blame rests entirely with me,' Blakey volunteered. 'Go easy on your Safi. She showed me compassion even though I was slow.'

Alena stepped unnervingly close to Blakey, her nose almost pressing against his. 'Safi, you should have inflicted an injury for his tardiness. I would have approved. Anyway, let us begin. But where is Abrik's replacement? He was here before.'

'He needed to go to the toilet,' said the Sklim. 'But that was some time ago. I sent an aktel to fetch him. We can't proceed without him. Abrik is in no fit state.' The Safi glared at Blakey.

An aktel burst into the room, breathless. 'Sklim! Sklim! Palin has been spotted making a run for it into the desert hills. The fool.'

'How can that be?' the Sklim gaped. 'Escape is impossible.'

'I must stop him. Guard the Earthman,' Alena blurted as she dashed out the door.

'It's too late,' the aktel called after her. But Alena was gone.

The Sklim, moving with surprising speed with his walking cane, headed towards the village's drinking water wheel. The others followed. Blakey, with the Safi beside him, kept pace. She, and the aktel had their kraxls drawn.

Many villagers also ran towards the water wheel. 'Who is fleeing?'

'Palin?'

'Are you sure?'

'Yes.'

'Surely not Palin.'

'He is the last person I thought would panic so.'

'He is doomed.'

'Oh Palin.'

Blakey and his minders mingled with grim-faced villagers who jostled at the banks of the stream, seeking vantage points looking across to the desert hills. Two were unintentionally shoved into the shallows. A few pointed. 'There he is.'

Blakey could not spot him.

'Turn back!' someone yelled.

'Hush. Don't alert the chageen.'

'They will already know. He is doomed if he does not turn back.'

'Where is he?' Blakey asked the Safi as they scanned the scene. 'I can't see him.'

'He goes speedily from behind one boulder to the other. He is hoping the darkness will hide him.'

'But it's not that dark.' Although neither of Zygol III's two moons had risen, the hills were lit up by the planet's innumerable stars, which shone as effective as a full moon on Earth. Still Blakey could not see the man. But should this Palin succeed...

Blakey froze when he first heard the dull flapping, and then the sight of dozens of flying black shapes, converging in the sky above them. Other chageen descended from the desert hills. The chageen moved slowly but inexorably. As the villagers held their collective breaths (some couldn't look), the swarm swooped behind a table-sized boulder below the cliff-face with the ear-shattering sound of screeching and beating wings. Blakey fought the urge to vomit.

'No,' came the soft chorus from the bank of the stream.

For some minutes, everyone stood about in stunned silence.

'We need to return to the communal hut,' the Sklim said, 'and await Alena. Abrik will be forced to take the antidote, regardless of how much she resists. Only she can take part in the judgement now. Our potion-maker is only a Safi.'

'I'm in no hurry,' Blakey replied, trying to collect himself.

The Safi prodded him with the point of a kraxl. He yelped. Behind him, the chageen continued to screech.

After the Sklim dispatched two nearby aktel to run to Abrik's hut, the dejected group returned to the communal hut. In the room, the Sklim, Blakey, the Safi and two aktel were sullen. Even Blakey was shaken by the frenzy of the attack.

Presently Alena returned, shaking her head. 'I couldn't reach him in time.'

'Don't despair, Alena,' the Sklim said. 'No one could have saved him.'

Alena closed her eyes for a few seconds. 'As tragic as this event is, I need to proceed with the judgement of the Earthman. It grieves me that you are being delayed from spending your final night with those you love. The outcome of the judgement is straightforward. Surely Abrik only needs to be awake.'

'I'm sorry. Alena, but Abrik must be partly lucid,' the Sklim said gravely. 'The reputation of Mkeldi village is at stake.'

'But if we are all to die in the morning...' Alena pleaded.

The Sklim jutted his chin. 'I wish to face death knowing my final allegiance is to the six elements.'

Alena stared at Blakey.

Blakey would sooner look at Medusa. The Safi shut her eyes.

'The Earthman is but a criminal,' stormed Alena. 'Aktel, lead him to a place where he will be bound, ready for me to inflict punishment on him. Don't let him out of your sight.'

'I have no objection,' the Sklim replied.

'I need to end this,' bemoaned Alena, flinging her hands into the air. She then clutched her damaged shoulder. 'I wish to search longer for my talisman.'

'Of course. We will revive Abrik.' Alena prowled around the room.

'Can I say something?' Blakey asked meekly as the aktel prodded him with their kraxls. 'Seeing we have some time, I'd like to offer an apology.' The Safi would surely approve.

Alena stared, open-mouthed. 'Any apology from you is worthless,' she thundered.

'An apology would grant the Earthman a chance to repent,' the Safi said. She sent off some hand signals.

'Safi,' Alena snapped, 'I have earned the title of Dsolcspmite twice and, for all too brief a time, I was an undisputed Spmite. Don't suggest that my reasoning is affected. This is possibly to be my last act—'

'What a heap of shit!' Blakey blurted. What happened next was the last thing he expected. In an instant, the Safi had him pinned against a tree trunk with the point of her kraxl thrust against his Adam's apple.

'What is the meaning of that Earth word you spoke?' she spat through clenched teeth. 'If it is a slur on my Spmite, I will remove your tongue here and now. Without ceremony. And don't think you can speak untruths because I will know. Believe me, Earthman. Now, tell me!' Her furious face pressed close to his as she stared hard into Blakey's eyes.

Alena stood beside the Safi, her kraxl drawn.

Blakey took a breath. Was the Safi the same woman with the laughing green eyes that had enchanted him at the lake? 'Err... shit... on Earth... refers to... something previously hidden from view,' he stuttered. 'That needs to come out.' And he clenched his jaw in a valiant attempt to briefly delay what was surely inevitable.

The eyes of Alena and the Safi bored into his. The sharp edge of the Safi's kraxl moved across his bare throat. Then she turned uneasily to Alena. 'I am not certain, my Spmite, but I do not think he is lying.'

Alena looked doubtful. 'I too am not certain.' She glared first at the Sklim and then at Blakey. 'Aktel, take him from my sight. You have your orders. Tie him up. We will await Abrik.'

The Safi stepped clear of him. As the two aktel in the room drew their kraxls, Blakey pulled his notebook from his back pocket. 'Can I make a request? I need someone to make sure this gets to the mining compound. It contains important knowledge. It may stop my fellow Earth people from making the same mistakes as I did.'

'I will issue instructions to those who will return from the cave.' The Sklim took the notebook and pen.

The Safi also spoke, 'Before he is taken away, there is one matter I have promised the Earthman I would raise with you my Spmite.' She jutted her chin at Alena defiantly.

Alena looked about to explode.

'I promised he could ask you a question—a question that may help explain why the village is to be beset upon by the chageen.'

'Hmm,' Alena answered testily. 'I will try my best.' She turned disinterestedly to the cringing Blakey. 'What is your question?' Each word was like a stab from a kraxl.

'In the circumstances, it doesn't really matter,' Blakey quipped.

The Safi's eyes transformed into green ice. She prodded Blakey, not too gently, with her kraxl.

'Excellent,' Alena said with a sardonic smile. 'Safi, help tie the Earthman outside.'

Alena and Blakey exchanged glares.

The Safi and the two aktel surrounded Blakey. 'Don't resist,' the Safi said. 'If you do, your remaining time alive will be spent in considerable pain.'

Ross Blakey stood his ground. 'Wait!' he said tersely. 'I've changed my mind. I *do* want an answer to my question. Tell me, Dsolcspmite-Spmite, who judges so impartially, tell me why I haven't broken out into a massive rash after being covered by plooglit piss during my time here in this village? Do you know how it effects Earth humans?'

Alena leaned her head to the right.

'Of all the Earth people who have been in contact with it, including me, it is in this village... and only in this village... I mean... I am the only one who hasn't been affected... by the plooglit piss in *this* village. The Safi will tell you I had plooglit piss all over me when we were at the lake. Tell me why I'm not in unbearable pain right now.'

Alena stood immobile for three or four seconds, gazing at Blakey. She then looked at the Safi who leaned her head to the right. A flurry of hand signals followed.

'Earthman,' Alena said at last, 'it could be many things. Too many to make guesses. Any speculation on my part is close to worthless. Safi, take him outside and tie him up. Tightly.'

Blakey gaped, enraged. 'That's it? Not even a discussion? That's the height of Zygol wisdom?'

Alena bristled.

'Come,' the Safi said, touching him tenderly on the arm. 'Think of the unfortunate villager who will have to clean up the floor, and the walls, if you are injured horribly here by saying something stupid.'

The Safi's words, and the look of sheer hatred on the face of Alena, made Blakey stiffen. He remained silent, his jaw twitching from his restraint.

The Safi prodded Blakey with her kraxl again. Then she and Blakey, flanked by the aktel, walked out of the communal hut followed by a muttering Alena and the Sklim.

Outside, the Safi and one of the aktel pinned Blakey hard against a tree trunk while the other aktel bound him. Blakey could barely move his legs; his forearms a little bit more, though the knots were out of reach. But, in one way, the aktel were considerate; he was partly able to sit on a low branch.

'We need Abrik,' growled Alena. The Sklim looked sheepish.

The Safi approached Blakey. 'Are the bindings too tight?'

'I'm okay. Besides, I won't be here long.'

Suddenly, Alena's eyes drilled through his from no more than a handspan away. 'Earthman, I was once an undisputed Spmite and I wish to die worthy of being a Spmite. So I will consider your question further. It is perhaps a coincidence that the only place where you have not experienced your rash is a village where the chageen are about to attack. But it may be another clue to solving the mystery that baffles us. It may point to finding a way to identify danger signs before the same tragic situation arises again.'

'At the compound we could analyse the substance for you and find out how it is different here.' Blakey was still the scientist. One hoping for a late, even temporary, reprieve.

Thankfully, Alena stepped away from him. 'We have ways to determine the make-up of substances,' she said, deep in thought.

'Does anyone have any questions to ask the Earthman?' She looked at the others.

Everyone standing around shrugged. 'You have to ask why would the plooglit piss... I mean...' Blakey began, but stopped.

The Safi had placed her hand around Blakey's forearm, then dug her fingernails in. It was a sort of you're-doing-okay-so-don't-stuff-it-up-now-and-shut-up gesture.

'I understand what you are saying, Earthman,' Alena answered coldly. She could not look at him. 'It confirms to me that the problem is most likely with the location of the uckliablaht pen. The pens leave the uckliablahts at the mercy of the wind, sun and dust. The Sklim has said it has been an unusually harsh period of late.'

The Sklim shrugged.

'So perhaps the substance emitted by the plooglits changes composition in response to the suffering. Perhaps this change is a signal to the chageen of a major break in the fabric of elapelc in the village. Chageen have an excellent sense of smell. If that is so, in future we may be able to anticipate a chageen attack by checking the composition of what the Earthman refers to as plooglit piss when animals... and people... are subject to harsh conditions. I am probably wrong, but it is a possibility worth investigating.'

'Also,' the Safi chimed in, 'the plooglits in this village are not as carefree as they are elsewhere. They do not coo and hum and run around. Instead, they spend more time high in the trees. The change in the substance may explain why so many plooglits avoid the uckliablahts here.'

The aktel and Alena leaned their heads to the right.

'I had thought they acted so because of the threatening presence of the chageen, but maybe their behaviour began before most of the chageen came.'

'As you said before you are only guessing,' the Sklim ventured.

'That is true but ideas such as these are all we have. I will document it so those in the Survival Party can be alerted to this interesting possibility,' the Safi said. 'I will see to it that samples of the substance will be taken.'

The Sklim shrugged. 'Zhezhanifd village was attacked many years ago. But its uckliablaht pens are well positioned.'

'Ah. You seek a single cause, Sklim,' Alena countered. 'The reasons for attacks may vary. Regardless, my Safi and I suspect a breakdown in elapelc between species, and between animals with humans, could be the reason for a chageen attack. How strange it would be if we Zygols were to discover that the solution to this baffling mystery rests with, of all animals, plooglits.'

For the first time in the company of these Zygols, Blakey felt he was an equal. He leapt in, a contributor. 'You might be on to something.'

'Guesses, Alena. I would not get your hopes high,' the Sklim said but he too was listening intently. There was even a glimmer of hope in his eyes.

'Perhaps the act of setting the uckliablahts free might set things right, though in a way we hadn't anticipated,' the Safi ventured.

'It was worth trying,' Alena said as she smiled at the Safi. 'But, even *if* it is the correct solution, there probably isn't enough time to make a difference.' Then Alena turned to Blakey, her face contorted by some inner turmoil. 'I thank you deeply for your contribution, Earthman.' Yet she couldn't conceal her iciness. 'But it changes nothing between us.'

He longed to say something derogatory. Instead, he looked towards the sky.

'Don't be dismayed, Earthman. If what you have suggested proves true, the inhabitants of my planet will mourn your death and remember you fondly. Sklim; alert me when Abrik is ready to participate with the judgement.'

'I will go to her hut now,' the old man said.

Alena signalled the end of formal discussion and strode towards the communal hut.

The Safi looked at Blakey with admiration. 'Did I not tell you my Spmite would give you the answer you seek? Can you now see how she devotes herself to the betterment of all living beings?'

'She still wants me dead.'

'Well... ignoring that exception, what I said about her is true.'

'She is smart. You're right about that.'

'But, Rossblakey, you can now face your death with the satisfaction of knowing you may be remembered with considerable fondness if your contribution proves correct.'

'Pity that I'll be dead when you Zygols find out.'

'Rossblakey; any Zygol would gladly die leaving a legacy such as the one you may make. And did not my Spmite act like a true Spmite? Even towards someone who cast shame on her. Yet her training was not from the stream of Grycyryn.'

'So now I wait.'

'Yes. It is best that your judgement takes places soon. It will relieve you from your anxiety. And Alena wants to search for her talisman. For now, I must find the potion-maker and take samples left by the plooglits.' She gave Blakey a look of sympathy.

'Don't take too long,' Blakey called out as the Safi walked away briskly. He was left tied up with only two uncommunicative aktel companions. Who did not want to be there.

Trying to make sense of the past few days only hurt his brain. He burst into palpitations each time he heard footsteps or chatter heading his way. But no judgement party emerged. He heard uckliablahts roaming about. Plooglits cautiously climbed down trees.

Early in the night, the tipsy weaver appeared before him and thrust a clundrn in his hand. She filled it with a liquid, then disappeared into the night. By leaning over, Blakey was able to bring his forearm up just far enough to partake. Later, after the bored guarding aktel had silently wandered off, the same tottering woman came and refilled his clundrn and mumbled something incomprehensible. It made a brief, welcome interlude.

When Blakey became stiff, sore and beyond fretting anymore, he drifted in and out of sleep. Once, he woke to find the Sklim yabbering before him. But Abrik wasn't with him. 'It is my fault that our children are going to die. It is me who should face judgement.' He sobbed and disappeared. An indeterminable time afterwards, Blakey heard the despairing cry of a woman.

The uncomfortable night became one of fleeting sounds and images, and exhaustion-bouts of unconsciousness.

A hungry uckliablaht brushed Blakey's arm.

One of his more potent images of the night was Alena's hand cupping his chin, her gaze, thankfully hidden by darkness, boring into his face. He caught only snatches of what she said. She was scary. Something was kicked and clattered against a distant tree. When the staggering old woman with the alcohol next came around, she could not find Blakey's clundrn.

The Safi appeared. 'Still we wait! It is agony not knowing when this will end.' By then he may have been hallucinating.

Later, Alena returned with two aktel. 'Take him to his hut!' Incredibly, she was even angrier than earlier. Blakey felt hands untie him. The aktel frog-marched him to his hut.

He was laid on his bed, and his hands and legs were bound. Arms tugged at his jaw as the aktel tried to force Blakey to drink. But he was too tired, and too belligerent, to imbibe. Most of the liquid spilt. A man swore.

He woke to hear mournful singing accompanied by musical instruments that seemed to play a tune discordant to that sung by the female singer.

When he awoke again, surprisingly, all instruments and voices were performing a mournful song in a pleasant but bizarre harmony.

9

MORNING OF THE CHAGEEN

ROSS BLAKEY OPENED his leaden eyes. The faint light of dawn filtered into his room. To his amazement, he was alive. But, he felt like shit, so not being dead wasn't such a blessing. His pathological companion, Tsalc, was obviously not done with inflicting torment on him. His nemesis was most likely sitting comfortably, cradling a bag of popcorn and an ice-cream treat, salivating at the pleasure of watching Blakey being ripped to shreds by blood-crazed chageen.

Blakey smiled; *no chance Tsalc.* He would go to Alena. She'd get the satisfaction of executing him. He would get a far less-horrible death. Blakey stood up, blinked and absently scratched at the latest—albeit mild—itch on his forearm.

He heard urgent voices outside the hut. A single word resonated: chageen. A chill ran up his spine. Could Tsalc be one step ahead of him?

His mind's eye pictured the frenzied killers smashing through the hut's fragile walls, screeching, wild-eyed, claws bared, beaks stabbing. Would he reach Alena in time? If he didn't, he'd face his killers outside, on his feet. Unsteady with his bindings, he shuffled into the morning air.

Villagers, some sporting clubs; others sporting farming

implements, were walking past, heading towards the village square. Even children barely old enough to walk carried sticks.

He found the Safi, wearing full armour, leaning against a tree trunk. 'I was about to wake you, Rossblakey. Again, Tsalc has shown its contempt for the worthy. Jkilm! Abrik was pronounced unfit to preside over your judgement. She refused to drink the antidote. You share the blame for her state. This morning she is too overcome with grief for the children who will die. By avoiding your punishment, you left my Spmite greatly frustrated. Why couldn't you embrace elapelc for just one time?' The Safi would not look at him as she untied his bindings.

'I'm sorry. I wasn't ready to die then. But I am now. I'll go to her. She can execute me without needing a judgement. I gather the chageen are coming. The villagers are all heading the same way.'

'Unfortunately, what you ask, cannot happen. Tsalc has deemed that you shall die at the hands of the chageen Rossblakey. It is the punishment you deserve. We will go with the villagers to the fields. Look all about you. There are no chageen anywhere. They all flew off in the middle of the night. Now they are returning in huge swarms. My Spmite is busy organising the village's defences.' Frowning, she thrust a filled clundrn into Blakey's hand.

Her words made Blakey simmer. 'I can't even begin to tell you how much I've come to despise Tsalc.' He took a sip of the liquid. Then he quaffed it in one gulp. It was water. 'You didn't put in the antidote this time.'

'Did I need to?'

'No. More importantly, it seems your plan for appeasing the chageen didn't work.'

Blakey and the Safi joined the line of villagers, her head bowed. 'I still believe it was the right plan. If it had been implemented earlier, we would have known for certain. As for now, Rossblakey, we need to take up our positions in the village's defences.'

'Defences?'

'You are to be placed directly behind my Spmite and the Sklim. In front of the rest of the village. But keep your distance from her. Be aware that she is about to die without her talisman. And you caused her shame.'

'Why am I being put at the front?'

'It is not an honour. The Sklim and Abrik believe you should be amongst the first to die because of your heinous act against my Spmite. May Tsalc allow Alena to see you die.'

Ross Blakey swallowed. At least he would be spared the sight of most of the carnage. 'Right.'

'There will be no delay along the way,' she growled. 'Do not defy me. I have no patience left for you.'

He complied. Ignoring his urge to pee. He would not let down this delightful young woman again. Tsalc had to be truly evil to seek to switch off the brightness that shone from her stunning, alert eyes.

Many villagers congregated in the village square, to tap one another on the shoulder, or to share emotional hugs. There were some tears. Then they headed silently towards the stream.

Blakey absently scratched his arm. 'Isn't defence against the chageen hopeless?'

'It is the Zygol way to face death bravely. The chageen expect us to do so.'

Blakey grimaced. 'Many Earth people would do the same.' But not him; he'd opt for fleeing. Taking the Safi with him.

Curious plooglits moved about the nearby trees. Uckliablahts drifted through the vegetation in no particular direction, seeking fresh greenery.

'Are you prepared for this?'

'No.'

Two aktel in front wore full battle armour and sported kraxl-das and kraxls. Along with many of the villagers before him, Blakey stopped to take a few hand-cupped gulps of water from a narrow wooden aqueduct. Up ahead he heard the wailing of young children.

The two waited their turn behind a bottleneck of villagers before a rustic narrow bridge that spanned the stream. On the other side, to their left, and behind a long tree-covered mound, the village children came into view, calling out desperately as their tearful relatives moved on. A few older villagers stayed behind, trying to calm them and to stop them from running to their parents.

Seeing and hearing these distraught children cut at Blakey's heartstrings. The Safi's face fell. She moved on briskly when the path was free. 'The children will stay behind the line of the trees,' she explained, suppressing a sob. 'They are to be spared the carnage that will befall those gathered in the fields.'

'But they'll hear what's happening. How can that be comforting? They'll soon realise what's about to happen to them.'

'That is so,' the Safi replied and sighed. 'But if the children came to the fields, their parents would desert the defences to be with them.' Blakey thought the strategy futile, if not heartless.

The two emerged from the line of trees onto gently undulating fields of mostly ankle-high stubble of harvested crops interspersed by occasional small bunches of waist-high bushes and a few shallow, dry channels. Aktel were directing dour-faced villagers into three semi-circles; one behind the other. From what Blakey could make out, young teenagers stood in the semi-circle nearest the stream. In front of them was a smaller semi-circle of aged or disabled villagers. The outermost, and largest, semi-circle was composed of more 'able' adults, including aktel. Some villagers argued about which semi-circle they belonged to and their wishes were usually accommodated.

As the villagers moved to their allocated positions, they hugged or tapped the shoulders of their fellows and whispered their farewells. *Die well.* The Safi handed a young man her kraxl, and the young man responded by thrusting the club he was holding into Blakey's hand.

'Die well,' the young man said stoically.

'Die well,' the Safi answered.

Blakey passed a miserable-looking Abrik at the edge of the front semi-circle. She cringed whenever a child cried out. The Grycyryn stood a distance from Alena, who stood defiant at the apex of all those gathered. She wore full battle armour. Her injured shoulder was strapped and not in a sling. Alena was placing able adults about two metres apart with help from the Sklim. Although she did not look his way, the expression on her face hardened at Blakey's approach.

Ross Blakey assessed the lay of the land ahead. The narrow stream cascaded from the barren hills to their left onto the gently undulating fields, to disappear into the verdant vegetation. At the foot of the hills, a few man-made channels (devoid of water) forked out from where an unmoving water wheel and some large sluices stood.

Blakey's gaze took in the sky above the barren hills. He gasped at the vast, hovering, swirling black cloud. Chageen.

The Safi led him beyond the front semi-circle, close to Alena. 'Die well, Rossblakey.'

Blakey gnashed his teeth. 'Die well, Safi.'

The Safi abruptly turned away before he could hug her. After offering Tsalc some choice Earth words, Blakey's gaze was drawn again to the chageen. Much of the desert hills to his right was hidden by a tongue of trees beside the lake. Those trees partly hid another large, dark and swirling cloud. He shuddered. He should have gone for a pee.

Averting his eyes from the approaching horror, Blakey spotted Rystyn standing alone, looking forlorn, near the edge of the older villagers. He was sporting a roughly cut branch. To the Safi's consternation, Blakey diverted towards the Zygol cook. 'I want to say I'm sorry for all the trouble I've caused you, Rystyn. I really am.'

'Hmph... fine,' Rystyn said grumpily. 'I have accepted my fate. Now leave me be.'

'Okay. Goodbye, Rystyn.' Blakey turned away.

'Die well, Earthman,' Rystyn called gruffly after him.

Blakey halted momentarily. 'Die well, Rystyn.'

The Safi sent Blakey some hand signals, delivered with a grimace. 'I'm going to my place now.'

'Time is short,' the Safi said grimly, glancing towards the barren hills. 'See. The chageen are coming ever closer.' Ross Blakey examined the dark cloud. Chillingly, she was definitely right. 'Delay any more, and I will injure you. I say it again, die well, Rossblakey.'

'Die well, Safi. I owe you a lot,' Blakey said with a sigh. 'Thanks for sticking up for me. I'm sorry I let you down so many times.' He almost thanked her for bathing with him. It was very likely the wrong time.

The Safi smiled fleetingly and stepped back to join her fellow aktel. Blakey stiffened and swallowed. Then he nervously approached... but did not get too close to... Alena. She may well beat the chageen to parts of his anatomy.

Alena greeted Blakey with a scowl. 'Stand beside the bush to your right, Earthman,' she commanded. 'You will not try to run or back away or I will drag what parts of you that I leave intact to the same place. Understood?'

Blakey understood perfectly, took a breath and gazed at both swirling dark masses, which were drifting steadily closer. With visions of snapping jaws tearing at his flesh, he steeled himself as best he could. Much like a piece of paper would in a hurricane.

Figuring it was the protocol, he blurted, 'Die well... Dsolcspmite-Spmite.'

Alena spun around, surprised. 'Die well, Earthman.' She resumed her discussion with the Sklim about the possibility of a few more sympathetic adults being assigned to protect and comfort the children once the front line was breached. 'They should die knowing that we cared and are fighting to the death for them.'

'I agree,' replied the Sklim and he passed some hand signals to the aktel behind them, who began communicating with hand signals to those standing further behind.

Blakey waited beside the bush assigned to him, fighting an urge to run in sheer panic. There was a constant murmur behind him. People kept pointing. *They are coming closer. So many of them.* Some villagers were frightened. Others sought to comfort their fellows. He didn't make out Kasmin amongst the aktel.

Blakey forced his gaze towards the huge black masses, which had come close enough to discern as teeming chageen. They emitted a high-pitched shrill that was beginning to hurt his ears. There were many thousands of them. A living, sharp-clawed and sharp-beaked nightmare. Wide-eyed, Blakey began muttering between shallow gasps, 'Oh shit! Oh shit!'

The villagers kept repeating, 'They are getting closer.'

Chunks of the sky became blocked out as the two masses were converging, seeking to form one gigantic, elongated swarm. The shadows they cast, were enveloping their prey. Their shrills became ever more intense. And more chilling. The water wheel behind them was stilled. Blakey could only stare ahead and block his ears.

A man carrying two narrow poles almost as tall as he, stepped up a flat, table-sized rock to Blakey's right. The top sections of the poles were covered with thick and bound, cloth-like leaves. The man removed the covers then he wrapped his arms around the bottom half of the poles. He rubbed the tops of the poles together causing those sections to burst into a bright red-white light. The man manoeuvred the poles with surprising dexterity tracing lingering pink-silver lines in the air. Then he rested both poles vertically beside him. Two lines of similar light burst into view on the desert hills and danced in the air.

'The Zookspmate bids us to die well,' announced the Sklim. His comments drew a few "jkilms."

Alena uttered something under her breath.

'He will certainly welcome having my Spmite perish,' the Safi growled.

'Has their signaller informed you of the fate of Gentok?' Alena called out to the Sklim.

'No, Alena, despite our request being acknowledged late yesterday.'

'Jkilm! He is cruel to us to the very end.'

Ross Blakey was transfixed on the swarming chageen. He could now make out individual animals, flying in and out of the swarm, their eyes being so many red dots amid the swirling blackness. He regretted looking. He was finding it hard to breathe.

Alena was seemingly calm and poised for battle, with kraxl-da and kraxl drawn.

Glancing to his right, Blakey saw the Safi with her long red hair and laughing green eyes hidden behind her helmet. She, who lived life with an insatiable curiosity, was doomed. As was everyone.

A female aktel mocked the Safi. 'Your idea to save us has come to nothing.'

'Did you really expect otherwise?' a male aktel beside her sneered.

The Safi puffed her chest. 'Didn't you notice how the uckliablahts and plooglits have begun to behave more normally? If there was more time, maybe our fate would be different. Perhaps the chageen have not sensed that elapelc is being re-established.' She shook her head. 'It is a pity the wind is not blowing from the desert. If it were, then maybe... just maybe, the essence of the emerging elapelc might somehow drift over the fields and reassure the chageen.'

'Your mind is cluttered with fantasy,' scoffed the male aktel. 'Admit that you were wrong.'

'What was your contribution to save the village, aktel?' Alena snapped. 'At least she tried something.' The chatter ceased.

Only then did Ross Blakey become aware that the wind, which had brought him such misery from the day his ordeal began, was still. On this of all days. Perhaps the Safi was a hopeless optimist but surely the wind carrying any so-called essence of increasingly contented animals had to be their only escape from disaster.

Blakey was already a coiled spring of terror and frustration. As the Safi stared at her feet, he exploded. 'I don't believe this,' he screamed in his Earth language. He threw down his club in disgust before the astonished villagers. Alena, her kraxl-da at the ready, took a few steps towards him, as did some aktel, while keeping a discrete distance from what must have seemed a crazed Earthman.

Blakey's face contorted in rage as he glared at the desert hills. 'You stinking shit-heap of a wind!' he bellowed, speaking in a mixture of Zygol and his native language. 'All that crap you put me through. You did your damnedest to break me. All the pain you caused. But where the hell are you, now that I need you? You useless great big fart! I've had a gutful. Come and blow on me one last #@*^# time. Come on. Or are you done with your best shot?' Blakey shook in anger. The trees behind him were still. 'Well... blow. You useless waste of air! Damn you!' Blakey snorted.

A sea of puzzled and baffled faces gazed at him. Feeling like a colossal fool, he slunk sheepishly back to his designated spot. Heck. Even if a hurricane had been blowing, it surely would not make a skerrick of difference.

The Safi approached him. 'What did you say, Rossblakey? I couldn't make most of it out through the hissing of the chageen. And you used many strange words. Wait, the signaller is sending another message... It is about you.'

Blakey blinked. 'Why? I was just babbling.'

The Safi wasn't listening. She was captivated, as were many villagers, as the signaller began throwing his poles of light backwards, forwards and sideways with great gusto. Even Alena was watching.

'It is rare to be in the presence of such courage,' gushed an aktel behind Blakey. 'I consider myself privileged to stand behind the Earthman. He has made facing death easier for me.'

Others nearby leaned their heads to the right. Many aktel smiled at a dumbfounded Ross Blakey.

'Outstanding courage,' an old villager behind the aktel called out.

Other villagers leaned their heads to the right.

The aktel who had criticised the Safi earlier spoke. 'I am in awe of you, Earthman. I, too, will face death with courage because of your words.'

'What are you talking about?' Blakey blurted.

'Such modesty!'

The Safi grinned. 'Very few would summon the courage to say what you did about the Zookspmate, Rossblakey. I, too, stand in awe of you. I am glad you had this opportunity to demonstrate what noble spirit truly lies behind that deeply flawed mind of yours.'

'Huh. What do you think I said?'

'I won't repeat it. There isn't time. But you called the Zookspmate things a Zookspmate should never be called. Never. He is a man so filled with pride that he will be greatly insulted. Our signaller has let those in the Zookspmate's camp know exactly how you feel about the man. Your insult has truly honoured my Spmite and, by the reaction of those here, you have honoured Mkeldi village as well.'

Indeed, Alena was looking at Blakey with her head tilted to the right.

Blakey shook his head and gave a nervous chuckle. 'Let me guess. After getting the signal, the Zookspmate will demand what's left of me to be totally destroyed.'

'Oh, most definitely. If you somehow, miraculously, survive the chageen attack,' the Safi answered, 'you would be executed in the most horrid... but honourable way to appease the Zookspmate. Of course, you would be executed anyway for letting my Spmite escape. But now, with those words, your death would be made as excruciating and prolonged as possible.' She smiled at him. 'It would be such a fine and deserved way to die for your bold and defiant stance. But, sadly, the chageen will deny you that fate.'

'Oh what a shame. And what a surprise. Another... but even more horrible... way of dying. What else could I expect from your planet? But, Safi, I have to say, the signaller wasn't accurate in translating what I actually said.' Blakey had become pale.

However, the Safi's attention had turned to the chageen. 'Let us not discuss trivialities at a time such as this.'

'Trivialities! Perhaps I should get the signaller to send a clarifying message. I'll stand beside him so I can dictate carefully.'

The Safi placed a restraining hand on his arm. 'It can't be done. Look at the chageen. We can no longer see the desert hills for our killers have almost converged. Besides, the signaller has placed his poles in their covers. Die well, Rossblakey knowing you have given my Spmite some satisfaction after what you did to her. She may even believe, as I have begun to believe, that elapelc would indeed be possible with you under different circumstances. Eventually... She may even deem to be so kind as to put you out of your misery after the chageen have devoured chunks of your body.'

As Blakey's eyes bulged, the Safi returned to her semi-circle, kraxl-da in her hand.

'Why the hell did I come to this totally insane planet.' Blakey slapped his head.

The Sklim took him by the arm. 'Earthman. My villagers and I were inspired by your words. Come with me. You have earned the privilege to stand beside me and Alena at the front of the defences.' With his chest puffed with pride, he led a reluctant Blakey, placing him between Alena and himself.

At least no one would notice when he pissed his pants.

The chageen now hovered close enough for Blakey to feel the draught of their wingbeats against his face. Amongst the thousands of fiery red eyes, too many had set their sights on him, their necks craning in gleeful anticipation, beaks snapping. He almost choked in terror. 'Screw you, Tsalc,' he whimpered as he scratched absently at the rash on his arm.

The chageen descended slowly until they hovered perhaps a dozen steps away. Death had to be... maybe seconds... away. His killers only needed to swoop.

The villagers stood resolute.

'Stop this torture,' Blakey whined. 'Do it!' He spread his arms in welcome. 'Come on...' He almost choked once more. Dust and sand had blown into his eyes and mouth. The desert wind had sprung up, but the innumerable beating wings of the chageen fanned the airborne grit into his face. Blakey swore as he wiped his stinging eyes.

Three eager chageen broke formation and swooped at Alena. With remarkable dexterity, she cut down the overeager, but not particularly agile, feasters. Another chageen screeched as it swooped to take a chunk out of the Sklim's left arm. He screamed in pain, but cut his assailant in two as it returned for a second bite. Bleeding, the Sklim crushed its head with his foot in anger.

Behind the Sklim, hidden by trees and barely discernible over the screeching of chageen, the children called out desperately to their loved ones. As Blakey spat grit, a chageen attacked him. He swung out of the way of its snapping beak, which tore a hole in his shirt sleeve, drawing a trickle of blood. As the chageen steadied itself for another attack, Alena deftly stepped over and sliced off its head with her kraxl-da. There was no time to thank her. Nor did she pause.

Perhaps wary after the tragic fate that befell their overeager fellows, the chageen seemed to hold back, an intimidating two arm's reach away. They had to be readying themselves for an irresistible, all-out attack.

Ross Blakey stood, his weapon impotent beside him. He watched Alena, ready to avert his eyes the instant she perished in an explosion of blood.

Seconds passed. Some more seconds passed. Then Blakey exclaimed in shock. He watched, dumbfounded as Alena lowered both her kraxl and kraxl-da and rested them along-side her legs. Their chief protector had given up. The villagers gave a collective gasp. The Sklim, with blood flowing down his arm, also lowered his kraxl-da to his side. Seconds later, the aktel behind them did likewise.

With this, the villagers let out muted cries of joy, which turned to cheering. Villagers dropped their weapons and began hugging each other. Blakey looked at them, stupefied.

With an almighty effort of will, he dared to look at the chageen. Were his eyes deceiving him or were they further away than before? If only a bit. He saw few red eyes. As he watched, the chageen seemed to drift further away still. Blakey realised what the Zygols knew. The chageen were retreating.

'Well, I'll be...' he whispered. With his mouth agape, the wind blew grit into his mouth and eyes. He swore. But managed a brief, choking chuckle.

People ran around laughing, hugging and falling over one another. Some dashed off to their children. The aktel, Sklim and Alena sheathed their weapons, grinning and joined the rejoicing.

Blakey stood stock still. 'I don't believe it. Her crazy plan worked.' Rystyn also stood immobile, stunned.

Abrik dropped to her knees in relief. Others did as well.

A beaming old woman gave Blakey an almighty hug. 'Celebrate with us, Earthman. You are a hero of Mkeldi village. No. You are a hero of our planet. I can hardly believe it. We are all saved.'

Ross Blakey could only shake his head. He watched disbelieving as the celebrations raged. People were falling over and colliding with one another in their excitement.

Blakey spun around as a hand touched his arm. The Safi had

thrown off her helmet. Her smile would melt an icecap. They clasped one another.

'Your plan worked.' Blakey was in a state of disbelief.

'Our plan. You inspired me to be more determined. This is the proudest moment of my life. If I never accomplish anything again, I will remember...' But, before she could say more, she was swept away by celebrating aktel.

Blakey's long-depleted reserves of emotional and physical strength deserted him. He slumped down on a step of the signaler's rock.

Immediately, he was lifted to his feet by a remarkably thin but very feisty old woman. Cheering villager after villager lined up to stop and hug him or tap him on the shoulder.

'Imagine the looks on the faces of the ones in the cave when we fetch them,' a laughing male yelled in Blakey's ear.

'The children have been saved.' A teary Abrik sobbed as she clung to Blakey. 'I can look them in the eye again.'

Blakey yanked himself free from Abrik's firm grip and bumped into someone as he stepped back. He turned, and found himself looking into Alena's beaming face. Her smile disintegrated when she recognised who she was about to grasp. She stepped back and gave Blakey a formal tap on his shoulder.

'The villagers have been saved, Earthman. Elapelc is being restored. It is an incredible... heroic... achievement you and the Safi can justifiably be proud of.'

'You played your part.'

'Hmm.' Alena became thoughtful. 'Now I am left with a dilemma. I... and my fellow Zygols demand... that I punish you for disposing of my talisman. But, with you being feted as hero of the village... that task is now problematic.'

She turned abruptly and resumed celebrating with the wildly animated villagers.

Blakey thought that smiling suited her. Executing people did not. But his execution was obviously still very much on her mind.

10

____

EVERY GOOD DEED

'WHAT HAPPENED IS... SO... SO... INCREDIBLE,' the Sklim enthused, bobbing about, choked with emotion. He touched Blakey's shoulder with the back of his hand as a sign of respect. 'I have been yelling so much that I can barely speak.' As he spoke, a villager was valiantly bandaging his ointment-covered arm. Another villager cleansed Blakey's superficial wound. 'Your solution worked Earthman! Thank you! Oh, thank you!' The old man gazed at Blakey as if he was a demigod.

'I didn't do much. You should be thanking our Safi. It was her plan.'

The Sklim tilted his head to the right and smiled coyly. 'I will thank your Safi deeply when the time is right. For now, be aware that she and Abrik had many rows yesterday, and this morning. Things were said that were best left unsaid. So I need to be diplomatic for a while. Later. Oh, what a remarkable day!' His rapturous gaze drifted to the children squealing and dancing as adults looked on, laughing, clasping one another. 'Join in the festivities, Earthman. Tsalc has been appeased. And Tsalc has not always been a friend of my village.'

Some chageen were settling in the nearby trees. Blakey started.

The Sklim smiled. 'Don't be alarmed Earthman. What you see is normal. Those chageen mean us no harm. Look; they are seeking seeds. They must be very hungry.'

The Safi came striding towards Blakey, politely brushing past villagers wishing to hug her or dance with her. Her expression was grim.

The Sklim signalled the Safi to be silent. 'It is only right I tell him, Safi.' He turned to Blakey, beaming. 'Earthman, I will summon the signaller to let the Zookspmate know we can proceed with his desired judgement of you. I believe you are fully aware of the inevitable outcome. Take considerable satisfaction that the very slow and terribly excruciating death you will face for your bold insult will be a truly fitting death for a hero of Mkeldi village.'

Blakey winced. 'Ah yes, the signaller. Where is he? I need him to send a clarifying message for me. This time I will stand beside him and dictate.'

The Sklim lost his smile. 'Did the signaller not convey the meaning of your message to the Zookspmate correctly? Perhaps he did not use your exact words, but the meaning was correct, wasn't it? This is vital to establish.'

'Before you answer that question, Rossblakey,' interrupted the Safi, 'be aware that the signaller will face the death reserved for you by insulting a Zookspmate so awfully. *If* he was badly mistaken with his message.'

'And the signaller is a poor widower with three young children,' added the Sklim, his brow furrowed. 'The incredible joy he and his family are feeling at this moment will end in despair. This is a poor village, facing constant hardships. Life without a parent will mean a hard existence for his children.'

'But what about...? Err...' Blakey spread his arms as an appeal. The Sklim and the Safi looked at him, pleading.

The Safi gazed intently into his face. 'Consider this Rossblakey. You will die in considerable pain at the hands of the Zookspmate regardless, given how you frustrated his desire to execute Alena... twice. The Zookspmate will be especially angry that someone who frustrated his will is now being hailed as a hero in a village that has rejected him. Rossblakey, you cannot avoid being executed in great pain. Please don't cause the needless death of another.'

'But I...' Blakey's mouth flapped.

'If it gives you comfort, I expect the Zookspmate to press for me to receive a harsh punishment at my judgement. While I expect banishment, I may also be tortured. I beseech you to choose the honourable course and not bring about the shocking death of the signaller as well as your own. Be the hero you have become.'

'I also beseech you to heed the Safi's words,' the Sklim pleaded.

Blakey sighed deeply. 'I accept that I'm doomed. But... err... won't the Dsolcspmite-Spmite... execute me first?' Fingers crossed.

'Alena is impeccably generous in spirit,' answered the Sklim with pride. 'Rest assured, she will defer your punishment to the Zookspmate.'

'But she needs to execute me.'

'Alena will undoubtably recognise how much your long and painful dissection will greatly honour my village as well as being an appropriately heroic death for you.' The expression on his face was sheer rapture. 'Besides, killing another does not reflect her true nature.'

Blakey was disbelieving. 'You think that?'

'She wishes to execute you, because it is a punishment that must be enacted,' added the Safi.

'I will talk to her,' said the Sklim. 'Do not be concerned, Earthman. She will readily grant your wish for a slow and agonising execution. She may settle for causing you a significant injury at the beginning of your punishment. The Zookspmate must concede that gesture.'

Blakey forced a wide-eyed smile. 'Right. I'm about to face a very slow and unbelievably agonising death, eh? But that's the *best* option. Oh, but it will be so honourable.'

Was the rustling he could hear the sound of Tsalc taking up a front row seat, with a new supply of popcorn and an ice cream?

'I knew our hero would respond with such bravery.' The Sklim, oblivious to sarcasm, puffed out his chest and again tapped Blakey on the shoulder with the back of his hand. 'When the pain becomes unbearable, you can surely seek comfort recalling your great deeds. It is said that the inner strength of true heroes is such that they are able to rise above any agony inflicted on them.' The Sklim could barely whisper these last words, he was so emotional.

Blakey was also emotional. For an entirely different reason. He took a deep breath, miserable, amid a scene of sheer, unrestrained joy. 'So... when will this judgement take place?'

The Sklim composed himself. 'It must happen this day. But it need not happen immediately. You should participate in the festivities. You deserve to be thanked. Unless, of course, you wish to begin your punishment immediately. As an inspiration to us all.'

'Oh... why do all of my inspiring at once, eh?' If he could swing it, somehow, his judgement could wait until he'd vomited taking his first step from the Chute back on Earth. Hell... didn't a hero of Mkeldi village deserve the privilege of making his farewells to his fellow Earth people? Bugger the dishonour that came by escaping.

'Fine: we will arrange the judgement for when the shadows are long. One thing; protocol requires us to guard you until we set off to the Zookspmate's camp. You must not leave the village. Do not feel insulted, Earthman. I know you, as a true hero, would never consider fleeing.'

There it was; fleeing was impossible. He had hours left before the dissection. Blakey turned to the Safi. Hug her? No. This incredible—stunning—young woman belonged with those who were celebrating. Not with a miserable, doomed man. He would get drunk instead.

The Sklim smiled. 'I will deeply regret your passing, Earthman, despite the pride you will leave us as your legacy. The Zookspmate's Arak-zook, who will carry out the execution, is a healer with an extensive knowledge of the body. She is known to keep offenders alive over many days as she inflicts horrific pain upon them. Such is her skill that she will string your organs and veins over poles for you to view. But, rest assured, that when you eventually die, I will personally see to it that no piece of you... not the tiniest scrap... will be left to the cfaldi. We have some fine weavers in our village. They will piece you together again as best as they can, though I will insist on a memento or two of you being displayed prominently in our communal hut. Maybe a bone from your forearm or leg. The rest of you will be buried in a prominent place in our village.'

Blakey's face was in shadow. Otherwise the enthusiastic Sklim and the Safi may have noticed its loss of colour.

'I must seek Alena,' the Sklim enthused. 'She, too, faces a judgement.' He paused. 'That is, unless... she issues a challenge. There is a possibility she may do that with her talisman lost. She most likely won't wish to prolong her life with the deep shame of her status being greatly diminished.'

The Safi spoke. 'You could be right, Sklim. That may suit her best.'

'Yes, Safi, she would die knowing she leaves the magnificent legacy of her deeds these past two days. Besides, she may yet fare badly in a judgement. The Zookspmate will use all of his cunning to gain the outcome he seeks.'

'What happens with a challenge?' Blakey inquired.

'It usually involves weapons,' replied the Safi. 'With my Spmite and the Zookspmate, death is the likely outcome. But the conditions need to be agreed to by both combatants before a challenge can take place.'

'So Al... the Dsolcspmite-Spmite might fight this Zookspmate? Right. I get it. Is he any good at fighting?'

'Compared to my Spmite, he is but a novice,' the Safi huffed dismissively.

'So, she should win.' Blakey broke into a smile. If she won before his dissection began... Okay, that would only bring him a swifter and less painful death. But Blakey would gladly take it.

'As a full Spmite, she would win easily,' said the Sklim, measuring his words, 'because the two of them would fight as equals. But the Zookspmate would not be so foolish to accept a challenge if she were an undisputed Spmite. Because he would be fighting a person whose rank is diminished, he will be given many advantages, giving him the upper hand.'

'Why wouldn't she go for a judgement then? It's why we came here, isn't it?'

'Alena does not have her talisman,' the Sklim replied. 'Her

diminished status means the Zookspmate would have the larger say with how a hearing will be held. If what Alena believes proves to be correct, the judges appointed by the Zookspmate would be hostile to her. The truth may never emerge. But if she issues a challenge instead, she will cause the Zookspmate considerable embarrassment. A challenge would prove that she is not a coward who fled. But someone prepared to die for what she believes. So, even if he kills her, it will surely herald the end of his rule. For his reputation will be considerably diminished. Many will seek justice for Alena. Mkeldi village, as well as some respected Grycyryn-da in the Three Villages will demand it.'

'The Zookspmate will be removed,' growled the Safi. 'I will battle Tsalc itself if it gets in my way. And my Spmite will be exonerated. This I pledge.' By the determined look on her face, Blakey figured that the Zookspmate would be advised not to resist.

'So, why would he accept the challenge?'

'With Alena killed in a challenge, he will have time to secure the terms of how he will be removed from his rank. But should one of his cronies falter at a judgement for Alena, the Zookspmate risks losing everything with immediate effect. Even if it he gets the outcome he seeks, his duplicity will certainly be exposed shortly after.'

Blakey's head was spinning.

'All is not lost,' the Safi said. 'A Dsolcspmite has been known to win even when the conditions of the challenge had been heavily negotiated in favour of a Zookspmate.'

'Jsete, the Great,' chimed in the Sklim. 'Yes, there is that possibility. Though...' The two Zygols looked at one another.

'Though?' Blakey enquired. 'Explain "though" to me.'

'Well,' began the Safi, 'Jsete believed the Zookspmate of the time was actively preventing her from becoming Spmite. Which is dishonourable. Her claim was later proven to be true. She challenged him, wishing to bring the Zookspmate to submission and have him banished. She figured she had nothing to lose. He sought her banishment in return. In the ensuing battle, there was controversy as to whether Jsete knew the cliff was where it was, or not.'

'A cliff? What's a cliff got to do with the challenge?'

'The Zookspmate fell down a cliff after he broke free of Jsete's grip and died soon after.'

'He broke free and fell down a cliff? That sounds very coincidental.'

'That is the account of the events passed down to us,' the Safi insisted. 'We have no reason to doubt what we have been told. There were witnesses. Although... their view was obscured to a large extent by some boulders.'

'Jsete then became a great Spmite,' the Sklim added quickly.

'Are there any other instances of a Dsolcspmite winning without there being a convenient cliff nearby?'

The Safi and the Sklim leaned their heads to the left.

'So, you are telling me that... the Dsolcspmite-Spmite... has almost no chance if there isn't a cliff nearby?'

'There is always a possibility,' the Safi replied. 'My Spmite is skilled both in body and mind. But, regardless, she will be prepared to die if it means bringing down the Zookspmate.'

'That is so,' the Sklim said. 'She will get her desired outcome in due time. Most likely at the cost of her life.'

Ross Blakey formed an idea. 'Wait here, both of you. I'll only be gone a short while.' Blakey turned and double-backed through the fields, moving as swiftly as his weary legs could carry him, ignoring those who wished to hug him. Before him, the two swarms of chageen were drifting away slowly and dispersing. Blakey took a breath and set off after them towards the low, dry hills. He cursed as his aching legs fought with him.

Blakey ran through the fields. He could jump the smaller irrigation ditches with little difficulty, but the larger ones caused him to clamber. His legs knotted in pain, his breath came in rasping gasps, yet he forced himself on. To his utter dismay, the chageen kept drifting further away, dispersing. When he reached the low foothills, the upward slope brought him to a cursing halt, hunched over, hands on his knees; the chageen well beyond reach.

'Come back and eat me, you bastards,' he yelled between heaving gulps of air, reduced to a stagger. 'Look at all this nice meat. Fresh

Earthman. Yum yum. Get back here! Bastards!' But he was spent. Blakey plumped down heavily on a boulder and, between gasps, he swore hard and often. When he stood, he saw the villagers watching from the fields. He was greeted by an almighty cheer as they raised their clubs and implements as one.

Blakey's mind hatched a desperate, hasty plan. A simple one. Keep going. There was no way he was going to be dissected alive. Even ending up as a meal for a cfaldi beat that. And he longed to never set eyes on another Zygol again. Well... except for the Safi.

After only no more than a dozen steps, his newly hatched plan disintegrated before his eyes.

Running from where the chageen were dispersing came three aktel: two females and one male, in full battle armour. They were beaming, breathless with excitement.

Blakey murmured an Earth word he believed appropriate.

The three aktel came to an excited stop before him and peered towards the village.

'It is true, isn't it stranger? All the people in our village have been spared?' Did they not believe their eyes?

'Yes, they have been spared. You are from Mkeldi village?'

'Yes. Mkeldi village,' chirped one excitedly. 'This is our territory up to the top of the hills you can see from here. We were returning from a neighbouring village a day ago when aktel from the Three Villages warned us what the chageen were about to do. So we stayed in the hills. The chageen swarmed above us. Twice. Once going to the village and then when they returned. We felt so helpless. And had such terrible thoughts. Then we saw you. Alive. And we heard the villagers cheering.'

'It was agony for us. Waiting. While the chageen...' The aktel choked up.

'There were so *many* of them.'

'But everyone lives. Tsalc has been kind.'

'It's true,' Blakey smiled broadly, his plan still intact. He did not venture how Tsalc had been helped out; he couldn't afford the delay in explaining. 'Quick; go and join in the celebrations. Oh... as a matter of interest, which way is the nearest village?'

'That way,' pointed one aktel. 'See the path? You can be there by the time the shadows begin to lengthen if you do not dwell. You have no weapon. So be particularly alert for cfaldi.' The three aktel dashed off, waving to the villagers who were watching on.

'I will.' Blakey took a breath. 'Okay, Ross. Your plan is clear... And you have nothing to lose.' He rubbed his hands.

He had taken no more than six steps when a familiar voice boomed behind him, 'That is not the way to Mkeldi village.'

Blakey spun around. 'Dsolcspmite-Spmite.' He winced.

Still fully armed, Alena stepped atop a boulder no more than ten metres from him. 'I came to make sure that you do not fall into the hands of the Zookspmate's aktel. The boundary of Mkeldi village ends close to here. You would face exactly the same death after your capture, which is a certainty, but your death would come with no honour for Mkeldi village. It would be a coward's death. Or one reserved for the worst of criminals.' She sat down.

'What if I choose to keep going and take my chances?' Blakey sneered. 'Remember, I'm a hero of Mkeldi village.'

Alena grimaced and was silent for a while. 'Yes, you are a hero of Mkeldi. Despite everything that happened before, on this day, you have proved yourself worthy. I am still incredulous of the wondrous salvation that has just taken place. Despite of your fine deed, I still must punish you for disposing of my talisman. To do that, I need to rescue you from being captured by the Zookspmate's aktel. His aktel surround the village. And he wants you dead almost as badly as he seeks my death. It is a Zygol saying that the true test is not in becoming a hero, but in passing the perhaps greater test of having to live up to being one.'

'But all I want to do is to go home,' Blakey said sullenly. 'The Safi can claim credit for all this hero stuff. She deserves it. It was her plan. And what if I didn't say the words that were—'

'You are about to throw up matters of great complexity at an inopportune time,' Alena interrupted him. 'I don't wish to discuss these matters. It is up to you to decide what to tell the villagers. But, before you do, a Zygol hero should first consider the effect of their words and actions on those who look up to them, before speaking. Particularly as your doom is sealed, regardless. You are destined to die in great pain. You will never see your compound again.'

'But what I'm supposed to—'

'Use your words wisely when you return with me,' Alena said firmly. 'Very carefully. Choose to die with honour. Die a hero. The villagers expect you to.'

'Ha! Tell me, why didn't anyone else tell the signaller to send the same message as I was supposed to have said?'

Alena grinned. 'They had no need. After your words, someone in the village, particularly the Sklim, should have immediately renounced the words attributed to you. But no one did. No one. The Zookspmate will be deeply insulted over that slight. And his aktel will be well aware that there was no retraction. Mkeldi village has caused him to lose face. Even better, because the chageen hid the hills, the Zookspmate cannot bring anyone to judgement for the implied insult. There, it is made clear to you. You have done the village proud. And you have restored... a little... of the pride you destroyed when you lost my talisman.' She gnashed her teeth with these last words.

'How nice of you to say so.'

'Come.' Alena became insistent. 'We have talked enough. Otherwise, should you continue, you will return to the village in a condition that needs me to carry you there. I do not wish you to have an unfortunate fall out of view of the villagers. Return there as a hero. Then die as the hero you have become. As for your execution, Abrik will give you hints so you can manoeuvre your body in a way that a cut becomes fatal faster than it normally would. If that is what you desire.'

He glared at her. 'Oh thank you for always thinking about my welfare.'

'I understand it is difficult for you. But the six elements are a greater force than any individual. So, join in the village's rejoicing, Earthman. You have earned the right to be part of it. The villagers want you there.'

Blakey sighed and bowed his head in defeat. Without speaking a word, the two trudged back to the village. The crowd cheered them all the way. His somber mood did nothing to lessen their joy. He would die. Horribly. They would live. Watching on, Tsalc had to be doubled over in unrestrained laughter.

As Alena and Blakey re-joined the villagers, the Sklim raised Blakey's arm. 'Behold, citizens of Mkeldi village. I present to you, your hero.' The villagers cheered.

'No. No,' protested Blakey. 'Wait. There are two others who are more worthy of your praise. They are the Dsolcspmite-Spmite here who could have prevented the release of the uckliablahts but came and helped.' The crowd cheered, and Alena may have blushed.

'And there is the person who did more than anyone to save your village. Our Safi. It was her plan. She implemented it and deserves the highest praise of all.'

Blakey looked about but could not see her until some aktel pushed her out from behind them. A cheer rose up for her, although Abrik, at the front of the crowd, looked miffed. The Safi's embarrassment gradually transformed into a shy smile.

'That was noble of you,' Alena whispered in his ear.

After escaping the many hugs from the villagers, the Safi strode over to him. 'Rossblakey, if you embarrass me like that again, I will cut off your balls and feed them to a cfaldi before my Spmite or the Zookspmate have their way with you.'

When Blakey's face fell, she broke into a huge grin.

'That's not funny.'

The Safi chuckled. She looked at Blakey. 'I wish to tell you my name. You may call me Jsete if you desire to.'

'Jsete. As in Jsete the Great.'

The Safi grimaced. 'My mother named me. For much of my life the name has been a burden. Perhaps after the events of this day, I might cringe less when my name is spoken.'

'You must never cringe again.'

'A little, perhaps.' Safi Jsete smiled shyly.

Should a living corpse hug her? As he hesitated, squeals of joy rang out. The Survival Party came sprinting to join the villagers with Dsolcspmite Brlma trailing behind, leaning on her walking stick. The story of how the village came to be saved was recounted with gusto; each villager eagerly butting in with their own particular slant. *"There were so many chageen!" "They covered the sky!" "I couldn't look." "That vomit over there is from me."*

Brlma hugged Jsete, then Blakey (nearly breaking his spine), and lastly, she had a drawn-out hug with Alena causing the Dsolcspmite-Spmite to yelp. Brlma whispered in Alena's ear. Alena laughed. Yes, laughing definitely suited her.

Those gathered drifted towards the village square. Eating implements, food and an assortment of liquids were being brought out. Villagers began singing and dancing to some crude musical instruments. Blakey and the Safi were engulfed. The enthusiasm with which clundrns were taken up, suggested that many containers were filled with alcohol. A suspicion confirmed when a clundrn of familiar green, foul-smelling liquid was thrust into his grasp.

Looking on, Blakey's mood sank ever deeper. His coming death was looming. He toasted his life before quaffing the liquid in two gulps. His clundrn was refilled. But, as he brought the clundrn to his lips, he was swept away to dance by Brlma's competitor at the Survival Games. The precious liquid spilled. He cursed.

His dancing partner either didn't notice or didn't care. 'No one is happier than me.' Many seemed to be challenging her claim. 'I would be honoured to receive your seed.'

Blakey only wanted a filled clundrn. Jsete, who was dancing with Kasmin, drew close, tapped him on the shoulder, and butted in. She laughed as she spun around. 'It is a Zygol saying that learning comes in myriad ways. Who would have believed a deeply flawed being such as you could contribute so?'

'But when I get things wrong, I lose my balls. Or die.'

'Ah, Rossblakey,' she said smiling, 'do not think such things. Believe me, if you were to pull up the tunics of all of the male villagers here, you would discover—almost with certainty—that all of them still have their balls.' She drifted into thought for a moment before grabbing Blakey by the arm as his dancing companion tried to whisk him away. 'But I am not suggesting that you go and check. It would not be wise.'

He and Jsete were swept away by their dancing partners.

Blakey passed next to the Sklim, who was talking to Alena and the signaller. The old man seemed troubled. The Earthman pulled clear of his dancing partner so he could overhear. 'The Zookspmate's signaller has sent the terms of the challenge.'

'I accept them,' said Alena without hesitation. She turned to Mkeldi's signaller. 'Those are the exact words you will send to the Zookspmate. Nothing more.'

'But you haven't heard what the Zookspmate demands,' the disbelieving Sklim answered. 'Even though the terms were always going to be heavily one-sided, there are a couple of things that we should definitely dispute as absurdly unfair. He seeks your death, which is no surprise. But he is forbidding any attempt at taking action by anyone against him for your death. He is demanding that you admit you committed treason as your last act of life. You are to have no weapons while he may use whatever weapon he desires. And you are not permitted to disarm him. Others can intervene on his behalf at his command. Alena; he knows he can't possibly get away with his absurd proposals. He will negotiate. He knows he has to.'

'I accept the challenge,' Alena repeated. 'Send him that exact message. Word for word. Do what I have instructed, signaller.'

'But... Alena, do you want to die as badly as this? How can you ensure your side of the story will ever be revealed if you accept those terms? His power will be unchallenged for a long time. He is ruthless. Don't let him get away with this.'

'I have made my request twice Sklim.'

'As you wish,' the Sklim said as a whisper. 'But what shall we ask for if you win? Even if that seems impossible.'

Alena shrugged. 'Banishment and a permanent loss of his rank,' she responded casually.

'As you wish,' the Sklim replied with a sigh. He dispatched the signaller. But he had to repeat his request before the reluctant signaller took heed of his instructions.

As Blakey studied Alena's remarkably calm face, his clundrn was re-filled. She had to be desperate. After quashing off another clundrn, he followed a man carrying a large jug of the brew. Villagers kept getting in his way, wanting to hug him or tap him on the shoulder.

The Safi stepped in front of him. Her mood was solemn. 'Yes, you should celebrate, Rossblakey. But, on this your last day, is it your only wish to seek the company of those who administer alcohol?'

Blakey winced. 'Jsete, I'm despairing. This is the only way I can cope.' She sought his company. Jsete had glowed with radiance when she was dancing. That was how he wished to remember her when he drew his final breath. Not with her stricken with sorrow.

'Rossblakey, draw upon your inner strength. I know you have it in you. Take inspiration from my Spmite. She is also destined to die. In shame, but her head is held high. And her thoughts are of the world she will soon depart.'

'Yes. But she belongs here. I don't.'

The Safi bristled. 'You are mistaken, Rossblakey. Embrace elapelc. Do so and you will find that you belong anywhere you choose to linger. With... whoever... you choose to be with.'

He cringed. She was reaching out to him. He craved to scoop her in his arms. But no; he was a dead man. And no one brimmed with life more than the stunning woman standing, expectant, before him. In his darkest thoughts, he never believed that Tsalc would be so heartless.

'I won't be lingering, Jsete.'

'Those are sad words, Rossblakey.'

'It's how I feel. I'm sorry. But it is best for me if I keep drinking.'

Jsete's gaze was hard. 'You promised you would not disappoint me again.'

'I'm doing what I think will disappoint you the least.'

She blinked. 'I do not understand.'

Blakey wrenched his eyes from hers. It struck him hard just how deep his feelings for her had become. Forcing himself to walk away was tearing him apart. Bad choice of words!

Later, a tipsy Sklim approached Blakey to tearily announce how happy he was. The old man slurred his words, but Blakey guessed the Sklim was telling him that work would begin the next day on an irrigation system around the uckliablaht pen. In the meantime, the uckliablahts could wander freely. Tsalc's patience was not to be tested. Blakey gave the Sklim a smile and went in search of someone with a jug. Getting drunk proved problematic. The villagers wanted to talk to their alien hero. Damned elapelc! His clundrn was filled with mostly non-alcoholic local teas. Steaming plates of food were thrust before him.

Blakey didn't care to eat but accepted some offerings from those with sympathetic eyes. He caught glimpses of the Safi, who was a popular choice of dancing partner. She seemed cheerful. But when she looked his way, she became downcast. To see her sad cut him to the bone. Crap choice of words. Again! After eating, talking and drinking so many teas, he prised himself free. Finally, Blakey got to sit against a tree, cradling a clundrn of alcohol. He closed his eyes to signify his desire to be left alone. And he must have dozed.

Awake again, Ross Blakey was oblivious to the passing of time. He set out on a search for someone holding a jug of alcohol, brushing past well-meaning villagers. He found no jugs. Only then did he comprehend that the mood in the village had turned grave.

Saddled uckliablahts were led towards the Safi and him.

'Rossblakey,' said a pensive Jsete, 'the shadows have lengthened. It is time to face judgement. We ride now to the Zookspmate's camp.' Blakey took a deep breath. He gazed at the deepening-blue sky.

The tipsy Sklim pushed his way to them and poured Blakey a drink with a smile. It would be a final toast. *This* was the elapelc Blakey had desperately wanted. 'To my life.' He quaffed the liquid in one gulp as the Sklim swaggered away. Only it wasn't alcohol.

Blakey was devastated. 'Did the Sklim fill my clundrn with a liquid to make me sober?' Hell... he was barely tipsy.

'Of course,' the Safi whispered. 'It is for your own good. You have been given a strong dose. You surely want the villagers to see you brave and alert as you go to your execution. Being drunk would diminish your death in the eyes of those who look upon you as a hero.'

Blakey replied in his native language. But Jsete's expression was resolute.

There was no longer any festive spirit to be seen. The villagers, still crowded about him, were now deeply solemn.

Jsete grasped Blakey firmly by the arm. 'Jump on this uckliablaht. I have chosen one that will follow mine so you will not have to steer it.' Blakey hesitated. 'Many villagers are watching. Be their hero,' Jsete said softly, her eyes pleading. 'Do not go to your judgement bound and tethered. Most likely nursing an injury.'

Blakey whispered a choice Earth word. He had disappointed Jsete too many times; he would not do so again. He mounted the uckliablaht with a sigh. They both set off with the villagers walking silently beside them. He tried his damnest to look brave. Doing so involved a major distortion of his face. He'd have done it much better if only he wasn't peeved at how all vestiges of alcohol in his system were dissipating.

A short way along the path, Rystyn, Abrik, the Sklim and Brlma, also atop uckliablahts, joined them. Rystyn looked even grumpier than Rystyn usually did. Unlike Blakey, the Sklim and Abrik seemed not to have taken the same concoction he'd been given. They swayed in their saddles.

'Earshman,' the Sklim blurted as he came alongside. 'It ish time to faysh jushment.' He grasped the tether to prevent himself from unbalancing.

Blakey turned to Jsete. 'This is my chief defender?'

She shrugged. 'For you it doesn't matter. And Alena is challenging and not facing judgement. The Sklim and Abrik will soon take the antidote. Maybe a lower dose to what you had. They will be sober at the Zooksmate's camp.'

The villagers rushed from all directions to flank the path, their faces etched by sadness. 'Die well, Earthman. I will never forget you,' they repeated.

'May Tsalc smile on you, Safi.'

Ross Blakey did his best to smile in return. Plooglits scampered about as the riders rode on.

'Did you say that you expect to be banished?' Blakey asked Jsete. He preferred to gaze at her lovely face rather than contemplate his impending fate.

She sighed. 'With Mkeldi village's support, that is what I predict. Hopefully, temporary banishment. The Zookspmate will seek a harsher punishment but I am confident he won't get his way. It will be sad to leave the Three Villages. Yet I regret nothing.'

'But your punishment isn't certain.'

'No. Tsalc sometimes disappoints. Sometimes it is kind.'

Tsalc. Kind. *Crap!* Blakey looked around. 'And Kasmin?'

'She will stay in Mkeldi village. My Spmite and Abrik insist she will face no judgement, though the Zookspmate will likely disagree. Nothing that took place was a fault of hers. She is also still upset with the death of Trimff and is worried about the fate of Gentok, of whom she is especially fond. She is young. These setbacks hit young people the hardest. But she is from a village close by and has friends in Mkeldi. With their support, she will be okay in time.'

Having regained control of his uckliablaht, the Sklim rode beside Blakey. 'Earshman. We mush knowsh yer name.'

Blakey deciphered the Sklim's slurred question. 'Ross Blakey,' he responded.

The Sklim blinked. 'Rush Blashey,' he announced proudly. 'Hero of Mkelshi villash.'

'Rush Blashey,' echoed Abrik.

'Die well, Rush Blashey. May Tsalc smile on you, Safi,' echoed the villagers within earshot.

'I thang you again, Rush Blashey. Lashur you will be in too mush agony to unnershtand,' the Sklim said. 'Mkeldi villash will never forget shat name. Nevesh.'

Jsete turned to Blakey. 'Wait. He will be sober soon.' Indeed, both the old man and Abrik took a sip from a vial.

As the riders passed the empty uckliablaht pen, Blakey looked up the dusty, rock-strewn cliff and ridge before him. He sucked in a breath. He made out the apex of the perpendicular rock that had signified an all-too fleeting salvation. Only to have him condemned to an unimaginably horrible death. Blakey cringed. To the right of the perpendicular rock, wispy smoke drifted lazily into the sky. It had to be rising from the Zookspmate's camp.

In front of Blakey, Rystyn rode alongside Abrik. 'I need you to strongly present my case, Grycyryn. I admit I cut the nets that bound the Dsolcspmite-Spmite, but I had pledged my allegiance to her in the desert. Under threat of death, you must understand. I was obliged to help, wasn't I? For that reason, you need to argue strongly against me being banished. Certainly argue for temporary banishment if it comes to that. I have family in the Three Villages.'

'Thash wha' I inten' to do,' Abrik replied.

Rystyn was adamant. 'If it wasn't for the Earthman...' He shook his head. 'The Dsolcspmite-Spmite should have cut out the imbecile's tongue when we'd first come across him. He would have been useless to the aktel chasing us. Not knowing hand signals as he does. Or we could have let him go the next morning; despite the storms, cfaldi or no cfaldi.' Rystyn did not look back at Blakey.

'Speak at yer hearing,' Abrik replied in irritation.

Blakey was about to let loose with some choice Earth words but Jsete spoke first. 'Turn around, Rossblakey.' What seemed to be the entire village, including children, had gathered along its edge. Many sent hand signals. Others waved. Blakey waved back.

'The night will be spent mourning the coming death of a hero. Many tears will be shed.'

He no doubt would be shedding a great many tears as well. 'How long will the judgements take?'

'For you, not long,' said Jsete, looking sadly back at him. 'Abrik will want to inform those present of your fine deed.' She gave a brief chuckle. 'But she cannot praise you for your insult of the Zookspmate. Apart from that, the process will be over very quickly. For what good will more words do?'

He sucked a breath. 'Guess so. But where is the Dsolcspmite-Spmite? Shouldn't she be here with us?'

'I thought she would be,' Jsete answered. 'My guess is that my

Spmite is making arrangements for after her challenge. I can understand that. But she will certainly come and try to provide important testimony at the judgements of Rystyn and me. But I expect the Zookspmate will do everything in his power to prevent her.'

She sighed. 'After she dies, Mkeldi village will recognise a Spmite from the neighbouring region. By a quirk of its isolation, Mkeldi has that option. Our Zookspmate will be furious when Mkeldi rejects being placed temporarily under his Arak-zook.' She smirked.

It didn't matter to Blakey. He was fighting a losing battle against a dark foreboding. 'And who is the Arak-zook?'

'She is a former Spmite selected to represent the Zookspmate, who was a Grycyryn-da, on matters dealing with aktel.'

'Oh, right.' Blakey looked over the edge of the cliff ledge. 'As for me, don't be concerned. I'm resigned to my fate. I can't keep battling against this whole planet anymore. Everything I've done since I walked out of my compound has been a disaster.'

The Safi looked at him strangely. 'You have helped save a village, Rossblakey.'

'Yeah. That was great for everyone but me.' Though his mood was melancholy he took pride at having helped save a delightful young woman with gorgeous, laughing green eyes. Screw Rystyn! When the Safi turned to look across at Mkeldi village, he took in her enticing profile. So easy on the eyes. And he sighed. 'I hope you will remember me with a smile,' he mused as a whisper, 'when you recall how we saved Mkeldi village. And maybe that magical time when we bathed.'

His eyes were then drawn to the perpendicular rock coming increasingly into view. His thoughts, when he wasn't interrupted by a plooglit jumping on (Hmmmmmmmmmm) and off his uckliablaht, drifted to his past. His children. His past lovers. His wife during the good times. The cheering, joyful villagers. Then of Jsete at the lake. Jsete riding on the uckliablaht in front of him, looking down on the village.

With Rystyn still complaining, the group reached the perpendicular rock. Ross Blakey gasped as he passed over the line of stones that had brought him inside the sanctuary of Mkeldi territory.

11

THE ARAK-ZOOK

THERE CAME the sound of pounding hooves. Perhaps twelve armed aktel, wearing full armour, thundered into view, their beasts kicking up a cloud of dust. Three cradled dart shooters. The aktel surrounded the unarmed judgement party, halting in a spray of grit.

The Sklim stiffened as he waved the dust away. 'This ish an outrage. I expected an escort to greet us, not thish blatant display of intimidation. We ash unarmed. You knew we would be.'

He was sobering up. He needed to; Blakey felt alarm. As did the others. The Sklim and Abrik sat upright on their saddles. 'Put down yer dart shooters. Explain yewrself!'

'You are in the company of dangerous renegades.' It was the same male safi who had led the ambush. He brought his steed beside the Sklim's.

'That is no—'

'Enough! Tell me; where is the renegade Alena?'

Abrik placed a restraining hand on Brlma's thigh. Adding a surreal dimension to the confrontation, plooglits from both parties set off together to play and chase, sometimes leaping onto the laps of the riders. Hmmmmmmmmmm. The Zygols ignored them, as Zygols do.

'She was consherned for her safety,' Abrik answered. She was becoming sober. A bit. 'You have demonshtrated her reashoning to be sound.'

The male Safi hissed his disapproval.

'Should you try and harm any of us, I guarantee she will seek redress,' Brlma growled. 'As will the people from my village.'

The simmering Sklim looked across at Abrik. 'Let's all shettle down. The Dsolcspmite-Spmite—'

'She is the renegade Alena,' spat the bristling Safi.

'—will appear for the challenge. I promish. She will arrive before the judgements begin. If her shafety can be assured.'

'Her safety has been guaranteed by my Zookspmate,' snarled the male Safi. 'He will be furious that she is not with you. She must be summoned immediately. Perhaps she has fled, as she did at the Three Villages. As a true coward would. It will be dusk soon. This challenge needs to be dealt with urgently.'

'You insult a person whose courage dwarfs yours, Safi.' Jsete was fuming.

'Dze... dze... dze…' The male Safi laughed.

The Sklim signalled Brlma and Jsete to be calm. Mkeldi's Dsolcspmite looked ready to take on every armed aktel, though unarmed and hampered by a smashed foot.

'You know nothing about my Spmite,' Jsete said curtly. 'Or is it your intention to goad us to retaliate? It is strange that I have never come across you in the Three Villages. Where did you come by your rank?'

'Stay silent, renegade,' barked the male Safi. 'We will send a message to Mkeldi village demanding Alena's immediate presence.' He dispatched an aktel, who set off at speed. 'The judgements are to take place without delay. With or without Alena. My Zookspmate's patience has been stretched beyond endurance. And, oh, Safi, must I remind you that he is also *your* Zookspmate?'

'I have pledged my loyalty to *your* Spmite. Banishment has never seemed more of a reward to me, now that I have met you.'

'She is a renegade,' growled the male Safi. 'I hold no allegiance to her.'

'She will definitely want to watch me being dissected,' Ross Blakey volunteered. 'So don't be too hasty executing me.'

The belligerent Safi brought his uckliablaht so close to Blakey that their beasts touched. 'Your punishment will begin first,' was the sneering reply. 'After your intervention when we last met, I crave to witness your suffering.'

'The Earthman is unprincipled and ignorant,' Rystyn piped up. 'But he speaks the truth about our Dsolcspmite-Spmite. She will be livid if you begin his much-deserved very painful execution without her being able to inflict some injury herself.'

'The challenge will proceed after the dissection begins,' chimed in Abrik. 'That has been agreed to by your Zookspmate. Our Dsolcspmite-Spmite demands to be present.'

Rystyn butted in. 'As for me, I wish to make it known to all concerned that I have done nothing to deserve banishment. I only fulfilled a sworn duty. To claim otherwise is grossly unfair.'

Jsete sent the Zygol cook hand signals, delivered with a scowl.

'Ah yes, Rystyn.' The male Safi took on a bored expression.

Rystyn stuck out his chin.

'You can bleat all you wish at your hearing, but I don't care for it here.'

'Tell me what else could I have done in my—'

The Safi twirled his finger in the air above his head as he looked the other way. 'Dze... dze... dze...'

'How dare you—'

'Say no more! Or you will not have a tongue to plead your case.' Ross Blakey managed a smile.

Seeing the Earthman's grin, Rystyn shot him a hand signal. Blakey had a pretty good idea what he meant. His grin became wider.

By this time, the Zookspmate's aktel had begun using their uckliablahts to nudge the judgement party into motion.

'It seems the Zookspmate appoints Safis who need considerable mentoring on how to seek elapelc,' Jsete ventured.

The male Safi bristled. 'I suggest that you need to approach elapelc from more than your own, limited and naïve perspective.'

Jsete and the Safi stared vitriol at one another.

'Your ignorance shows no bounds, Safi,' chimed in Brlma. 'Never have I come across such blatant opitek.'

'Ah yes, Mkeldi village has its own Dsolcspmite,' was the smug reply. 'A remarkable achievement for a village of puny and unambitious inhabitants. A village that does not have a single Grycyryn-da.'

Abrik looked chastened.

Blakey's forlorn gaze drifted back to the line of stones that marked the border to Mkeldi territory.

After passing between the perpendicular rock and the rounded hill, the group came to a clearing within a circle of large, rounded boulders. Here lay an encampment of three large tents and a tarpaulin. Perhaps fifteen Zygols sat around a campfire. All but five were armed aktel in full battle armour. Four of the others wore common grey or brown tunics; the fifth was a black-haired female Grycyryn who looked no older than Jsete.

Three aktel guarded one of the tents. Four more aktel guarded the large tarpaulin, which adjoined two craggy hillocks.

A dry, stony creek bed ran across the far edge of the encampment. To Blakey's disappointment, there was no cliff.

When the arrivals dismounted, the aktel beside the campfire hurried over. Some greeted Jsete with hand signals that seemed friendly. Jsete returned the signals in kind. Rystyn was ignored, while some aktel viewed Blakey with a bemused curiosity.

Some less-friendly aktel pressed close, almost touching the judgement party, their hands hovering over their kraxl-das. Despite being propped against their walking canes, an angry Brlma and Sklim took a bold step towards them. Brlma's step caused her to wince in pain. The aktel took a pace or two back.

Other aktel led all the uckliablahts behind the nearest boulder, which removed the playful plooglits.

Ross Blakey had no idea what the Zookspmate looked like but, with mostly aktel and recognisable tunics in sight, he guessed the butt of Alena's hate (apart from Blakey himself) was not present.

A squat strongly built woman dressed in a crimson tunic that sported both a wide orange and blue sash strode from beneath the tarpaulin. She did not wear armour but a kraxl and a kraxl-da hung from her belt. Her shoulder-length hair showed the first signs of greying. She approached the judgement party, eyes darting, as if spoiling for a fight. This woman was not to be trifled with. She had to be the Arak-zook.

'Alena did not come with them,' explained the male Safi sourly.

'Jkilm!' The Arak-zook glared at the Sklim, who broke into a grin. 'Realise, Sklim, that she is a renegade. You were duty bound to bring her. Bound if need be.'

'We adjudged her to not be a renegade,' Abrik interjected. 'Besides, with a challenge agreed to, she no longer faces any charges.'

The Arak-zook simmered. 'Safis, double the guard around the perimeter and around the Zookspmate. There is no telling what Alena might revert to.'

Hand signals were sent and six aktel spread out; many disappearing from view. Two approached the tarpaulin from where the Arak-zook had emerged.

Brlma snarled and took a pained step towards a few aktel who had, again, crowded in on the judgement party; their hands on the hilts of their kraxl-das.

'Let us all calm down and get to business. As Sklim, I bring you greetings from Mkeldi village, Arak-zook,' the Sklim spoke through gritted teeth, 'despite the unwarranted intimidation we received... and continue to receive... from you and your aktel.' Thankfully, he seemed sober.

The Arak-zook did not reply. The glowering expression on her face was enough.

The Sklim then gruffly introduced Abrik, Brlma and the others, who nodded unsmiling greetings. In no mood for niceties, Blakey stood with his arms folded, acutely aware that this woman before him would definitely not shirk from the task of dissecting him. He tried to look calm. But he had to be failing dismally.

'I am honoured by your presence,' the stout woman said at last, her demeanour far more severe than her words. 'I am glad your village was spared. What took place was a true miracle.'

'Thank you, Arak-zook,' said the Sklim with exaggerated politeness. 'It has indeed been a memorable day for Mkeldi village. I would be rejoicing now with my fellow citizens if it were not for the judgements that are to take place.'

The Arak-zook grunted. 'We will proceed with haste. It is already late in the day and most of the aktel you see wish to return home in the early morning. But I, and some others, must remain for perhaps a few days more. Duty calls after all.' She smiled at Blakey, who took an involuntary step backwards.

'I understand your desire to proceed, Arak-zook,' Abrik replied. 'I, as head Grycyryn, will act as a judge and advocate for the Earthman, the Safi here and Rystyn. Our Sklim will be a judge for the Earthman and will oversee the challenge by the Dsolcspmite-Spmite. And Dsolcspmite Brlma here will assist me with the other judgements, as we consider the charges the other accused face to be far less serious.'

'That is acceptable to me,' replied the Arak-zook. 'But where is the other aktel?'

'Kasmin? Clearly her minor role is not deserving of a judgement.'

'We dispute this. But it is late in the day and we have more pressing matters. I will discuss her culpability when we are done here. As for now, I, and the Grycyryn behind me will act as judges for the Earthman and the renegades.' The young female Grycyryn beside the campfire approached to stand behind the Arak-zook.

Blakey whispered to Jsete, 'Is she in charge?' The interruption irked the Arak-zook.

Her reaction brought a smile to Jsete's face. 'With the offences having occurred outside Mkeldi village's territory, and my Spmite's rank in dispute, only the Zookspmate has a higher rank than his Arak-zook. She will be acting on his direct orders.'

'Are you saying that these aktel are normally answerable to a Spmite as much as they are to the Zookspmate?'

'They would be if Alena was Spmite. But, to those here, she is not.'

'Are you now satisfied, Earthman?' sneered the annoyed Arak-zook.

Her tone suggested firmly that he be satisfied. She looked at Blakey with such intensity that he took another involuntary step back. The Arak-zook curled her lips in bemusement.

'Oh yes. This is the Earthman.' She strode up to Blakey. Hands on hips, she examined him uncomfortably closely. 'A fairly impressive male specimen. But, from all reports, quite an unruly, and ignorant one. You are quite the fool, aren't you? It will give me the greatest pleasure to personally inflict punishment on you, Earthman... if the judgement goes against you, of course.' Her lips curled. Smiling definitely did not suit her. 'Grossly insulting a Zookspmate is the main charge against you... not to mention denying his orders to have Alena executed... twice. Your abhorrent behaviour demands that I inflict the greatest amount of suffering I can muster for as long as your personal constitution can bear, before death eventually sets you free. I know my Zookspmate expects nothing less from me. He looks forward to watching until your screams bore him.'

'You're cracking me up.' Blakey spoke with bravado. He grinned nervously. But only he appreciated his Earth humour.

The Arak-zook looked at Blakey with distaste. 'Let us make a judgement on the Earthman immediately, shall we? Not only do I wish to prepare him for punishment. But it may also hasten the appearance of the reluctant Alena.'

'I have no problem with that,' said the Sklim gravely,' as long as the punishment begins in accordance with Alena's wishes to be present. Only after this will the challenge take place.'

Abrik leaned her head to the right. Blakey wasn't as eager. He needed to remain as intact as possible lest Alena somehow win her challenge. Even though her victory would merely secure him a swifter death. Jsete sidled up beside him.

'Let us begin. I can summon our signaller to report what message was received from Mkeldi village. The tenor of the exchange is that the Earthman grossly insulted the Zookspmate.'

'There is no need to fetch your signaller. That fact is not disputed,' said the Sklim. Blakey was stunned. Events were happening way too fast.

'Then the charge is proven. Do you wish to ask anything?' the Arak-zook asked the Grycyryn behind her, who leaned her head to the left. 'Fine. Is there anything else that needs to be said before he is prepared for punishment, Sklim?'

'Only that Rush Blashey is a hero of Mkeldi village. He played a major part in averting the chageen attack. Accordingly, he is to be treated with utmost respect as you inflict unbearable agony on him.'

'Yes, yes,' the Arak-zook stifled a yawn. 'A hero and a fool. We shall prepare for the execution.' She sneered triumphantly at Blakey as she sent hand signals to aktel who then raced into the tarpaulin-like structure to quickly emerge with four short, stout poles with pointed ends, two mallets and various lengths of rope.

'That was quick.' Blakey crossed his arms and gazed forlornly at the Sklim. 'I thought I'd be given a chance to say something.' His voice wavered.

The Arak-zook eyed him.

'What is there left to say?' Abrik broke in. 'You have accepted guilt for your gross insult of the Zookspmate.'

'Perhaps the Earthman wishes to offer an apology before he is executed,' said the Arak-zook. 'Should he issue such an apology directly to the Zookspmate, I will make his death much less painful and ensure he dies much quicker.'

Abrik flashed a pleading glance at Blakey. A solid punch in his lower back suggested he be silent. Directly behind him, Jsete was stony faced. Other members of the judgement party pleaded silently with him. To Blakey's surprise, a few of the nearby aktel also leaned their heads ever-so-briefly to the left. Behind him, Jsete gripped the back of his thigh with her sharp fingernails.

He leaned his head to the left. 'It seems...' the fingernails dug deeper into his thigh. 'Ow! Your Zookspmate seems to me to be cruel and unworthy.' Damn it. He sighed. He would die horribly. But at least he would die a hero, rather than the fool and coward he truly was. And... should Alena win the challenge before he was damaged beyond repair, then... But that was clutching at straws. His words were greeted by looks of relief from many onlookers. Some sent subtle hand signals that he didn't understand.

Blakey considered the scene before him. It appeared that Alena, the Safi and Mkeldi village had quite a few friends.

'Enough!' spat the Arak-zook. Behind him, Jsete gave Blakey a light caress where she had punched him.

'Thanks for all your help, Abrik. And you too Sklim.' Both Abrik and the Sklim smiled, oblivious to his irony.

The Arak-zook gave withering stares at all those looking on. 'You annoy me greatly, Earthman,' she said icily.

Rystyn chuckled.

'Breaking down your vitality and having you plead for leniency before me and the Zookspmate will provide us with considerable pleasure. But no matter how pathetic your pleas will be, you will receive no mercy.' She smiled.

'Gee. I've brought so much joy to so many Zygols today,' Blakey replied. 'And I haven't finished spreading the joy yet. How glad I am that I came to your lovely planet and am standing here before you.'

'Such courage,' whispered Jsete as she returned to stand beside him. A couple of aktel who overheard her leaned their heads to the right. 'For a despicable enemy of the Zookspmate,' Jsete added hastily after the Arak-zook glared at her. But Jsete was grinning as she took a step away from Blakey, whose eyes drifted to the aktel holding the poles and rope.

'Earthman, I am told you can't interpret hand signals. Is that true?' The Arak-zook looked smug.

Blakey jolted. 'Apart from a few basic signals, that is correct. I can't.'

The Arak-zook puffed out her chest as her gaze took in those gathered. 'You demonstrate clearly to everyone here what a barbarian you are. How could an ignorant fool from an alien planet believe he has the right to insult a Zookspmate who is so vastly superior to you in every way?'

Blakey glared. 'There is one hand signal I want to show you.' He did so.

'So... you know the very basic sign to denote the number one? Do you believe this pathetic iota of knowledge will impress me? Observe, Earthman. You used the wrong finger to denote the number one. And your hand is the wrong way around.' She showed him the correct Zygol signal. The aktel who stood holding the poles and rope that would bind Blakey, chuckled. Some others issued cries of derision at a grinning Blakey.

'Prepare the restraints,' she commanded.

The aktel began hammering four poles into the ground, forming the shape of a wide rectangle. Watching on, Blakey lost much of his fake bravado. The Arak-zook was exultant as she studied the transformation of his face.

As the aktel toiled, the Sklim spoke. 'Arak-zook, give Alena more time to arrive. She has insisted on being here to witness the first cuts on the Earthman. She wishes to inflict one or two herself as punishment for him disposing of her talisman.'

'It is almost dusk. The challenge will not take place in darkness. If she doesn't come very soon, she will be hunted as a renegade. Then she will not be able to claim sanctuary in Mkeldi village. Or anywhere. And there will be no challenge.'

'What you ask is reasonable, Arak-zook,' said the Sklim gravely, as he scanned the landscape.

'Now tie this barbarian up!'

Ross Blakey turned to Jsete. She turned to him, a vision of sorrow. As the two reached for one another, four aktel tackled Blakey hard, throwing him on to his back. He let off some choice Earth words as the aktel dragged him with no ceremony to prostrate him amid the poles. The aktel bound his legs to poles as one fumbled about, confused with his shirt buttons. Somehow, Blakey yanked an arm free and undid a button before his arm was pinned again. The looming aktel leant his head to the right, undid the other buttons and pulled off his shirt. With breath-taking swiftness, Blakey was tied and spreadeagled between the four poles. He tugged with all of his strength, to no avail. A rough stone the size of an apricot dug into him. He squirmed but it wouldn't budge.

'Could one of you do me a favour?' Blakey asked. 'Please get this stone out from under my shoulder blade?' An aktel bent over.

'Leave him be!' the Arak-zook boomed.

As the aktel retreated hurriedly, she took a self-satisfied look at the squirming Earthman before she addressed the Sklim. 'Let us proceed with the other judgements. Their punishments can be decided before Alena arrives.'

'It is too early to talk of punishment, Arak-zook,' the Sklim said testily. 'Alena will be called upon to explain why she escaped judgement. We will also argue the accused are only partially responsible for Rush Blashey's unforeseen intervention.'

'Alena will not be called upon to speak,' the Arak-zook snarled. 'The charges relate only to the disobeying of the orders of a Zookspmate. Nothing more. Besides, the accused, the offenders—the terms are irrelevant. Regardless, the renegades will be sentenced to death.'

There were gasps and looks of surprise from the condemned, the Sklim, Abrik and Brlma, and some of the gathered aktel. Other aktel placed their hands over their weapons.

'You cannot believe you can get away with this abomination.'

'The ruling is absurd!' snapped Rystyn. 'It is absolutely clear...' His mouth flapped uselessly as he swallowed.

The Sklim signalled Rystyn to be silent and a bristling Brlma to calm down. 'What is the meaning of this outrage? How can you condemn these people without a hearing? Even if your allegations are proven, the punishment of death is absurdly excessive. Our judges will never agree to such a sentence.'

'Sklim, argue all you wish but the death sentences will be carried out. It is the will of my Zookspmate. Your bias against our Zookspmate is well known. For this reason, we anticipated a long and trying impasse regarding sentencing and have brought a second Grycyryn, whose name is Ajeta, from the Three Villages to act as a fifth, and deciding, member of the judgement panel.'

The judgement party were incredulous. As were some of the Zookspmate's aktel.

No one was more indignant than the Sklim. 'A fifth member?' he spluttered. 'You cannot initiate a procedural change without consultation. You affront the ideal of elapelc. Confrontation can only be contemplated as a last resort. Even if we were prepared to consider a fifth member, at the very least we need to assess this person. Your confidence in this unjust outcome suggests that this person may not be impartial. I demand that judgements be reserved until we summon our own Zookspmate. In these unprecedented and unprincipled circumstances, his presence is now vital.'

'I refuse your request. This is not your land. You will not dispute my authority and that of my Zookspmate here,' the Arak-zook said calmly. 'Only the presence of a Spmite from our region may do that. And there is no Spmite. As I see it, we are camped in a place where we are subject to searing heat and fierce dust storms. I refuse to engage in a long and unnecessary debate over punishment. You come from a village that is the laughing-stock of the region. Over countless years, your people have shown little or no ability or initiative. I am doing your village an undeserved favour by allowing you to make up two out of the five judges. Besides, selecting a fifth member does not contradict elapelc or the six elements. Rather, it is a logical step that has been overlooked by people who lack flexibility of thought. Until now. That is the end of the matter.'

'I know the six elements full well, Arak-zook. I also recognise injustice and arrogance,' spat Abrik. 'You are required to consult with us before making any decision on procedure. To think you once filled the honoured rank of Spmite. If you—'

'Enough talk,' snapped the Arak-zook. 'It is time to act.'

'Hear me out, pretender to the six elements.'

The Arak-zook flinched.

'If you proceed with your flawed process, you further insult Mkeldi village. But, more than this, you demonstrate to everyone that your Zookspmate is motivated only by a desire for power and vengeance. Tell me, are your sentences designed to provoke our Dsolcspmite-

Spmite to turn renegade? For, if she tries to rescue the condemned, you would have an excuse to kill her without the need for a challenge.'

'Dze... dze... dze... Think what you will. It matters not to me.'

'Arak-zook; you will come to regret your actions. This I promise.'

Abrik and the Sklim looked at the aktel gathered nearby. Some returned cold stares, but others appeared embarrassed.

'For someone from the backwaters,' said the prone Blakey, 'she makes a whole lot of sense to me.'

'Hold your tongue, Earthman,' the Arak-zook thundered. 'Or your suffering will be worse than I envisaged.'

'Really? You can do that?'

The Arak-zook glowered. 'Sklim, Abrik, know that the fifth judge, Ajeta, has held extensive interviews with aktel who were present during events in the desert and with those who were present during what happened across from here. Ajeta has also interviewed the other accused. He is entirely familiar with the facts.'

'What? Who is the third accused?' Abrik was puzzled.

'But,' said the Sklim, 'your fifth judge... this Ajeta... has not spoken to those who we represent, as is required for any hearing.'

'You are about to find out Grycyryn. The judgements will now begin,' decreed the Arak-zook.

'Aktel, fetch the other accused. Inform Grycyryn Ajeta that I require his services.'

An aktel ran to the tarpaulin while two others dashed inside a tent where three aktel stood guard. 'Observe.' These aktel brought out a stretcher on which a male aktel lay propped on one elbow.

'Gentok!' Jsete exclaimed as she rushed to the stretcher. 'You are alive!'

'For now,' Gentok said grim-faced. He touched Jsete's arm while cradling his side with his other hand. 'They are calling for my death for rescuing the Dsolcspmite-Spmite.'

'Not only you. The Zookspmate is also asking for my death and Rystyn's. He is a tyrant.' She looked intently at the faces of the Zookspmate's aktel.

The Sklim shook his walking stick above his head. 'We refuse to take part in this charade until the terms of the judgements are negotiated.'

'It is all the Earthman's fault,' wailed Rystyn. 'I cannot be held responsible for his actions.'

'We are well aware of the Earthman's role,' replied the Arak-zook. 'But none of you can deflect the blame. As for you, Rystyn, you cut the nets binding Alena. She should never have been allowed to escape.'

'The Dsolcspmite-Spmite sought true and independent judgement,' Abrik fumed. 'I don't regard that as escaping justice. If not for the loss of her talisman... As of the accused, the penalty of death is highly inappropriate. Your fifth judge must concede that point if he has any credibility.'

'Yes, these judgements will fester with some Zygols after the punishments are administered. But I deem the harsh punishments necessary because the will of the Zookspmate has been frustrated well beyond the limits of endurance.'

'But these events took place because Alena was accused of charges we consider are fabricated. For—'

'You raise matters that are now irrelevant,' interrupted the Arak-zook smugly. 'Whatever Alena might have told you can only be speculation and rumour.' She looked about to make sure the gathered aktel were listening.

'If Alena had faced judgement in the Three Villages, it is abundantly clear she would have been denied justice, as she surmised. You change processes to suit your purposes. Alena may have been given little opportunity to counter her charges. I see before me a farce. And the punishments of Rystyn, the Safi and this aktel, are not only acts to provoke Alena but are meant to silence those who would inform Zygols of what has transpired. You are surely implying that anyone who annoys the Zookspmate will face dire consequences.'

'Think what you will, Sklim. I have heard enough.'

'You may smile, Arak-zook,' spat Abrik, 'but your undoing is at hand. As is your Zookspmate's rule. You cannot silence everyone. You underestimate the vitality of the six elements.' As she spoke, she looked at the gathered aktel in the face, one by one.

'Then we shall find out,' said the Arak-zook, smiling. 'But you and the Sklim are advised to tread carefully. For you are insulting me and the Zookspmate.'

'I care not for your threats.'

The Arak-zook twirled her finger above her head. 'Dze... dze... dze...'

Abrik clenched her fists.

'Go get her, Abrik. This bitch so deserves it,' Blakey called out.

The Arak-zook's face turned ugly. She took up an intimidatory stance over the Earthman and drew her kraxl. Her powerful, unblinking eyes drilled into his. 'One more comment from you and I will remove your tongue. Followed by your other appendage.' She waved her kraxl around Blakey's groin. 'How will you then beg for mercy?' If her snarling comments had sought to put him back in his place, they worked superbly; Blakey shut up.

The Arak-zook backed away, her eyes fixed on Blakey, daring him to defy her.

'Arak-zook,' growled Abrik, 'the families of those judged here today and many others, friends, those who value the six elements, will seek recourse. Rest assured they will be told exactly what takes place here.'

'As you please,' the Arak-zook replied off-handed.

'We refuse to participate in the judgements as you have laid out. However, the Earthman can face his punishment as his guilt is beyond question. As agreed.'

'Oh, thank you, Sklim!' Blakey blurted.

'If you do not wish to participate further in the judgements, I hereby declare the three offenders guilty and will proceed with their punishment.'

There were gasps of surprise. 'You cannot do this! It is an outrage.'

The Arak-zook ignored the Sklim. 'Aktel, draw your dart shooters and kraxl-das in case of any resistance. Be ready in case Alena comes to their defence. You five, bind the offenders. The Zookspmate has expressed the desire to view the executions.'

Most aktel did as they were told; some reluctantly. Others held back.

'Remember me,' hissed an aktel in Jsete's ear as he roughly pulled back her arms. It was the male Safi again.

'Jkilm! Aktel,' Jsete pleaded as her hands were bound behind her back, 'I ask you to make known what injustice is meted out here by those who seek only to further their power.'

Some aktel gazed at one another, embarrassed, as the three condemned were pushed to their knees and held down by aktel who gripped their shoulders and heads. Gentok was dragged from his stretcher and treated no differently; his cries of pain ignored.

'Stop hurting him!' Jsete called out.

The male Safi twisted her arm until she yelled in pain. 'You are renegades,' he spat. 'You deserve no mercy.'

An aktel called out. 'Jsete, many of us are uneasy with the harshness of your sentences. But there is nothing we can do.'

'What do the six elements ask of you?' Many aktel looked at their feet. None moved. Jsete bowed her head.

'I have been patient enough!' decreed the Arak-zook, who glared at the aktel who had spoken. 'The executions will take place as soon as the Zookspmate is ready. I will wait no longer for Alena.'

'She will come,' said Abrik. She anxiously scanned the nearby boulders and hills. Others did the same.

The Arak-zook looked self-assured. 'I have aktel posted all around the encampment. Many hidden from view. They will alert me if Alena approaches.'

The shadows were melding with the coming of dusk and transforming the hills and boulders to an eerie orange-purple, beneath a deepening, mauve sky, and sprinkled by the first, faint, emerging stars.

The flap to the tarpaulin was shoved roughly aside.

12

THE ZOOKSPMATE

TWO ARMED ZYGOLS emerged from beneath the tarpaulin. They were flanked by four aktel wearing armour; their kraxl-das drawn. Three aktel, holding dart shooters, moved to join them.

One of the two who emerged was a tall Grycyryn with long, brown hair, aged in his early thirties. It was the first time Ross Blakey had seen an armed Grycyryn. The second Zygol was perhaps in his late thirties and wore a deep-blue tunic with a wide orange stripe. It was this male who caught Blakey's attention. Although he wore simple uckliablaht-hide sandals, as did all Zygols, he differed from every Zygol that Blakey had ever met or seen. He walked with a swaggering confidence, yet held an expression of bored indifference. To Ross Blakey, the man appeared about average height for a male Zygol, and was reasonably well built, despite showing the first signs of a paunch. He had a long, thin face and nose and a pointy chin. As like most Zygols, he had long, wavy black hair.

Jsete whispered something derogatory. The male Safi holding her down, slapped the back of her head. But a couple of other aktel, within earshot, leaned their heads slightly—but very briefly—to the right. Blakey was in no doubt—this was the infamous Zookspmate. As the man studied the faces of the gathered aktel, it was clear not everyone in the encampment was his friend.

Blakey sucked in a breath. He quivered as he gazed towards the perpendicular rock. Alena needed to arrive real quick.

The Zookspmate halted before the Arak-zook. He looked about. To Ross Blakey, it seemed the man sneered at everyone he set his eyes on, even his Arak-zook.

'Ajeta,' decreed the Arak-zook, 'as with your fellow Grycyryn, Brigala, you are not required to participate in the judgements. The villagers have deferred the verdicts to me.'

'That is not so!' exclaimed the Sklim. 'We chose not to be part of a sham. We demand a stay in proceedings!'

'Excellent,' said the tall Grycyryn. He seemed relieved.

The Zookspmate focused on the bound Blakey, looking him up and down. He stepped boldly forward, smirking. 'Ah, the Earthman! The ignorant fool who hindered me, and then dared to insult me. Me! Your impertinent words, Earthman, betray the limitless depth of your stupidity. I now know that the fence around your compound was built to keep you barbarians away from us Zygols. If only you were a person of rank, we could settle this in a challenge instead of an execution. But no… I find myself looking down upon a being that is no better than a steent, fit only for crawling in excrement.'

'Battle me then. With fists,' Blakey retorted. He was a poor fighter. At least, by standing, he would get rid of the small rock biting into his shoulder blade.

A flash of anger rippled across the Zookspmate's face before he composed himself. He examined Blakey as if to sum up his prowess, and then he smiled. 'You, Earthman, are not worthy of my energy. I will gain great satisfaction from watching your oh-so-painful execution. You have no idea what suffering you are about to be subjected to.'

He sneered as Blakey tugged against the ropes that firmly bound him. 'You dare ask me to fight you! I am a Zookspmate.' He glowered. 'Do you appreciate the incredible dedication, effort and application I have had to demonstrate to earn my rank? Yet always there are those who strive to undermine me. Pretenders who can't grasp that only a very select few possess the qualities required to become Zookspmate. And this is my *third* consecutive appointment to my rank. I have fully deserved the rewards for my endeavours. But you,' he spat, 'have demonstrated only what an imbecile you are.' His mouth twitched in irritation.

'Does being a Zookspmate give you the right to condemn good people to death on your whim?' Blakey said defiantly. Some aktel standing nearby leaned forward.

The Zookspmate bristled in anger but hastily took on an expression of bemusement. 'Good people? But of course. No doubt you have you been charmed by our delightful ex-Spmite. Oh yes. Alena can be such a charmer, can't she? And she certainly is very alluring in her completely untouchable way. But she charms people only when it suits her purposes. No one knows that better than me.'

'Well, a steent has more charm than you.'

The Zookspmate's mood darkened. 'I don't seek your approval, Earthman. You don't know Alena as I do. As soon as she was pronounced a Spmite, she sought to usurp me. Me, about to begin my third term as Zookspmate. What disappointed me most was how generous I was after her appointment. I was quite prepared to allow her to progressively take on her full duties as Spmite. But my fine gestures weren't enough for her. She was too impatient and started to meddle in my affairs. She sought to change the way matters are dealt with, casting doubt in the minds of the more feeble-minded. She acted against me. Whatever you or anybody else might have been charmed by her to believe, progress for my people will be far more forthcoming with her stripped of her rank. Only she is to blame for her fate. It was the course she chose to pursue.'

'She remains true to the six elements,' Jsete chimed in, twisting her head as the male Safi tried to cover her mouth with his hand. 'Tell me, why do you need to take full control over who rises through the ranks? Why do you seek vengeance on those who disagree with you?'

'What is this you claim, aktel?' the Zookspmate snapped. 'Would you prefer I select the likes of you who have displayed abject incompetence? It is because of you that we are gathered here. Yet you have such an inflated opinion of yourself that you believe you can make insulting accusations.'

Jsete struggled to respond but the male Safi smothered her words with his hand. Another aktel twisted her arm hard against her back, eliciting a wince of pain.

'I will hear from you no more,' the Zookspmate boomed. 'You too deserve your fate.'

Jsete unable to reply, swallowed but her eyes burned.

'Arak-zook,' he spoke with a voice that dripped arrogance, 'are you confident that Alena will not act as a barbarian without warning?'

'With her hatred for you, I cannot give such an assurance, Zookspmate. But we are prepared. She has no chance of succeeding. Alena risks only damaging her reputation even more. When the first of the executions is enacted, she will be declared a renegade if she hasn't arrived.'

He grunted. 'Fine. Alena is highly treacherous. She will very likely stop at nothing.' The Zookspmate took in the faces of those around to ensure that they were paying heed.

More aktel removed their kraxl-das and dart shooters from their belts; their eyes combing the surrounds.

'Your concern is understandable, Zookspmate.'

Satisfied, the Zookspmate stood before each of the three condemned Zygols in turn. As he did, their heads were pushed down until their noses almost touched the ground. Gentok gave a short, sharp cry of pain.

The Zookspmate swaggered to face the Mkeldi village dignitaries. 'Sklim, as outlined in my conditions for the challenge, be aware that I seek Alena's death and accept no responsibility whatsoever for her death. No members of her family and none of her friends are to take any action against me for what I am about to do.'

He looked at the gathered aktel, then at the Arak-zook and the Sklim.

'Alena agreed to those conditions,' replied the Sklim with a sigh. 'She was adamant that she wished to accept the challenge. She seemed unperturbed about your demands, against my advice.'

The Zookspmate sneered as he leaned his head to the right.

'Aktel will have their weapons drawn as the challenge begins. They can intervene at any time and disable Alena if required. But I wish it known that she is not to be killed. That act must be reserved for me alone.'

'As you specified.'

'So be it then,' he scowled. 'But where is she? Darkness approaches. I need to be able to see her. This annoying matter has to be dealt with immediately!'

He turned to the Sklim who shrugged.

'Poor Alena. Facing death, stripped of her rank. Such humiliation.' The Zookspmate broke into a smile. His smile became even broader on seeing the Sklim's sour expression.

The Zookspmate strutted about. 'Yet, with her death, I fear that Alena's misguided followers will eventually get their way. But I will resist them to the end. I must do everything possible to preserve my legacy.' He gave a shrug. 'Even when the usurpers succeed, I will not sulk. I yearn, one day, to be rid of the ceaseless demands of my responsibilities and, instead, experience a life of genuine peace.'

He turned to the smiling dark-haired young Grycyryn behind him. 'I will be able to spend more time with my beloved Brigala. I would then be content to live a simple life as a mere Grycyryn-da once more. Far away from the plotting and intrigue that blight my life.'

'Should I begin the executions, Zookspmate? Then Alena can be declared a renegade.'

Blakey angled for a delay. 'What? You're telling me you want to step away from the idolisation you crave? To have your brilliant mind given little recognition. To lose the power you enjoy dispensing. I think you're talking shit.'

The Sklim spoke hurriedly. 'The Earth word shit refers to something that is unseen and has to come out, if my memory serves me right.'

The Zookspmate bristled and drew his kraxl-da. Blakey jolted, fearing he'd kick-started his execution.

'You continue to insult me, Earthman,' he growled. 'You, a worthless low-life.'

'It is widely said that you have a low tolerance for dissent, Zookspmate,' Abrik said calmly.

The Zookspmate glowered at her but then his mood seemed to soften.

'My tolerance for opposition has limits, Grycyryn. I make no apologies for being hard on my fellow Zygols to get things done. I do not cling to a static view of the six elements. Too many of my people wallow in the rut of complacency. All Zygols who desire better lives will welcome me shoving aside those who hold them back. So, yes, I have become a hard man—and I have not the slightest desire to change.' He shrugged. 'That is how I have achieved magnificent things. However, Alena and others choose to champion the lazy and unappreciative.'

'But if you were to take into account the opinions of people who are disadvantaged by your decisions, you—'

The Zookspmate cut Abrik off. 'Why should I? It is impossible to please everyone.'

The Sklim piped up. 'But elapelc requires we should—'

'Don't preach to me about elapelc! I rose from the ranks of Grycyryn.' The Zookspmate spun on his heel to face the Arak-zook.

Blakey was surprised at the Zookspmate's equal arrogance towards the Arak-zook.

'I've wasted enough time. It is almost dark. The executions will take place as soon as I have put on my armour. You, aktel. Fetch it for me.' The aktel scurried towards the tarpaulin. 'Move faster! Faster!'

The Zookspmate sneered at everyone in turn. Then he began making practice lunges with his kraxl-da. 'I need to make some things known to all of you before the executions begin,' he pronounced. 'By accepting Alena's challenge, I do not acknowledge anyone's account of events involving her and me other than those I alone outline. There are some aspects of my accusations against her that only I am aware of. And which I reserve the right to divulge or withhold at my discretion.'

The Zookspmate turned to Blakey and broke into a broad smile as he brandished his sword. 'Observe me, Earthman as I have observed your kind in that fenced off land you reside in. You creatures who use strange tools to do your bidding, some which are almost as huge as a hill, churning up the ground.' The Zookspmate clearly got a buzz out of impressing his audience.

'We call those things machines.'

'Mach... ines? Whatever,' the Zookspmate waved dismissively. 'That is not the point I wish to make. Those tools are so massive they dominate over you who work with them.' He smiled knowingly. 'When you are using these huge tools of yours, who is the slave?' Who or which is in control? Does my logic confuse you?' He gloated at Blakey. 'If you wish to establish the answer to my question, dispose of your tools and find out how you manage without them.'

Some aktel chuckled. A few others leaned their heads to the right. The Zookspmate puffed out his chest. 'Do you now see why I am Zookspmate, Earthman?' he mocked. 'It is because I *can* grasp these issues. Issues well above your capabilities. Just as they are beyond the capabilities of many of my fellow Zygols. Now, observe a Zygol Zookspmate with *his* tools, Earthman. Perhaps to you this kraxl-da is a tool for killing. Hmm? But, on my planet, the killing of any being— animal or human—is an undesirable end. Something to avoid if possible. The use of a kraxl-da, is more of an act of artistry. Yes. A striving for discipline. Do you understand me? Do you even *begin* to understand what I am talking about?'

It was Blakey's turn to break into a smile. 'I've figured you out all right. You talk about artistry, but you enjoy condemning people to death. You don't fool me. So, stop talking shit.'

The Zookspmate scowled, aware that some aktel were glancing uneasily at one another. 'That comment is not worthy of a reply. Your presence tires me, Earthman.'

The aktel who had been dispatched to fetch his armour approached and began dressing the Zookspmate.

'Arak-zook, begin the very slow execution of the Earthman. Begin by cutting out his tongue.' His smile was triumphant.

Blakey swallowed.

As the aktel put on the Zookspmate's shoulder armour, the Arak-zook approached Blakey, twirling her kraxl. Her expression was fierce. He tugged hard against his firm bonds. Utterly futile.

'Arak-zook. You will do no such thing!'

The words echoed throughout the encampment. Many gasped. For standing atop one of the boulders beside the tarpaulin was a fully armoured Amazon of a woman, clothed in the zain and pfin of a Spmite.

It was Alena in her full glory. With not a bandage, nor an injury in sight. 'Zookspmate, what depraved cravings for vengeance made you proclaim such outrageous punishments on those who came here seeking judgement?' she boomed. 'As I am now undisputed as a Spmite, and your equal, I deem that all punishments will be reviewed after our challenge is concluded.'

The Arak-zook's eyes bulged. Aktel stared at one another in bewilderment. Blakey grasped at a glimmer of hope, if only from a long, painful death.

There was a clang. It was probably the Zookspmate's kraxl-da dropping onto a stone. Then again, by the look of sheer terror on the man's face, it might have been the Zookspmate's jaw hitting the ground.

'Wait a minute,' said an emboldened Ross Blakey to no one in particular. As he spoke, Alena leaped from the boulder, turning to cut and pierce the air mid-leap. She landed easily. Only the most observant would have noticed the barest wince as she touched the ground, and that she held the weapon with her undamaged arm.

'Now I'd call *that* display, artistry,' Blakey ventured, willing to face the consequences of the delicious pleasure of that moment.

The Zookspmate stared at Alena in disbelief without seeming to hear what Blakey said.

Some aktel took a couple of tentative steps towards her, weapons drawn; sensibly, mostly dart shooters. Immediately, those aktel were flanked and outnumbered by other aktel; their weapons also drawn. Weapons directed at those threatening Alena.

Alena glared at them. 'Desist aktel. I say so as your Spmite.'

All aktel sheathed their weapons and eyes turned towards the wide-eyed Zookspmate and the stunned Arak-zook.

'Your pathetic ploy won't work, Alena,' the Zookspmate called out, 'For you to be Spmite you need to have your talisman.'

Alena grinned. She pulled the disk from her zain and held it before her. It glinted faintly green and orange even in the early dusk. The talisman drew gasps.

The Arak-zook sheathed her kraxl and approached Alena. 'Yes, it is her talisman, Zookspmate,' she said, her voice wavering. Then she hastily backed away.

Alena covered the ground to stand beside the Sklim in seconds. 'I am ready to begin the challenge,' she said with purpose. Her eyes revealed the coldest intent.

As the Zookspmate's eyes glazed, the Arak-zook looked accusingly at the Sklim. 'I am as mystified as you are Arak-zook,' he said grinning. Brlma's beaming smile was even broader.

The Zookspmate's designated aktel sought to place his helmet on his head. He shoved her roughly aside, throwing his armour to the ground in fury. 'What manner of trickery is this? Talisman or not; what right does this traitor have to challenge me as a Spmite?'

As he spoke, Alena tucked her talisman in her zain and leaped into the air. She twisted mid-air, thrusting her kraxl-da in two directions before her feet softly touched the ground, with her weapon pointed at his chest. Her grimace may have expressed her fury. Or a stab of pain.

'Answer my question, renegade,' the Zookspmate bellowed.

'She is without question a Spmite,' countered Abrik. 'You must address her as such. All charges against her were dropped when you agreed to the challenge, Zookspmate.' Abrik covered her mouth in a vain attempt to suppress a guffaw.

'I am unsure how to proceed,' muttered a sullen Arak-zook. Others weren't so conflicted. The aktel holding down Jsete, Rystyn and Gentok let go of their prisoners and stepped swiftly away, mingling behind their fellow aktel. Three aktel came forward and hastily undid the ropes that bound Rystyn, Jsete and Gentok. The three rose to their feet, staring at Alena with awe.

'I am ready to begin the challenge. As was agreed,' Alena smirked as she took up her fighting stance.

'This is trickery at its most evil,' the affronted Zookspmate howled. 'Alena defies the terms of the challenge.'

'When you agreed to the challenge, Zookspmate, I was restored as a Spmite. Isn't that so, Brlma?'

'It is the truth, Alena. I can vouch for it.' Brlma smirked. 'When you sent your aktel to intimidate the judgement party, Zookspmate, I had to keep telling myself, "Don't react! Wait for this very moment." And the wait has proved every bit as pleasurable as I hoped it would be.'

Alena's face broke into a satisfied smile. 'Brlma searched the cave near Mkeldi village all through the night and into the morning. Her great strength of body and spirit enabled her to climb and crawl into the treacherous shaft of the chimneys. She had to drag herself through narrow submerged passages where most would have drowned. The cuts on her hands and arms, and bruises to her legs and body, bear testament to her dedication. And I can't imagine what agony she endured because of her injured foot. Incredibly, she found the talisman. Too late to get to me before the chageen were swarming. When she was told the village had been saved, she rushed over and gave it to me.'

'Tsalc was kind,' Brlma beamed. 'The talisman glinted... just a little… in the light of a fire stick. And the water level was lower than usual.'

'We knew you have spies in the village, Zookspmate,' Alena beamed. 'So no one but us two knew that the talisman had passed between us. When the challenge was accepted by me and by you, it was made with me as your equal; Spmite against Zookspmate. There can be no preconditions when a challenge involves equals, except for the choice of outcome. And so, as equals we will fight. Because of what is at stake—my life—we will fight with kraxl-das or kraxls. I am not fussed which.'

'Did you know about this, Sklim?' the furious Zookspmate demanded.

'By the six elements, I knew nothing.'

The Arak-zook and the Zookspmate exchanged urgent hand signals. The young female Grycyryn and the male Grycyryn glanced at one another.

Blakey looked quizzically at the freed Jsete. She grinned back. Things were looking good. Especially for her.

'Take up your stance, Zookspmate,' demanded the Sklim. 'The challenge will begin immediately.'

Both furious and terrified, the Zookspmate took no heed. 'Arak-zook. Sklim. I accepted her challenge believing this... traitor... to be a renegade. A Dsolcspmite at the very most. It is obvious that she deliberately deceived me. Accordingly, the challenge must be declared invalid and, instead, Alena will face judgement as before.'

'The Spmite was under no obligation to reveal her restored rank when she accepted the challenge,' Abrik said, bemused. 'Accordingly, it cannot be deemed as deception. However, I acknowledge that her actions reflect poorly on her integrity.'

'Also,' interrupted the Sklim, 'Alena gave one message and one message alone; agree to the challenge. She said nothing about agreeing to the terms. As such, there are absolutely no grounds for the challenge to be annulled. Or conducted on the Zookspmate's terms.'

'Arak-zook,' pleaded the Zookspmate. 'What do you say about this?'

As if shaken awake, the Arak-zook looked at the faces about her anxiously. 'It is as the Sklim described. Alena only agreed that the challenge be accepted. I stood beside the signaller when the message was received. She has indeed acted dishonourably. But the challenge can proceed. As equals.' There were muted cheers from some aktel, groans from others.

'Besides, Zookspmate,' said Abrik, 'you, too, have acted

dishonourably. You laid out absurdly unequal conditions for the challenge. And you selected an unprecedented fifth member to judge the accused, without consulting your fellow judges.'

'She *cannot* fight me as an equal,' the Zookspmate boomed. 'She cannot! She is a traitor. My terms *must* be upheld.'

'I say again, Zookspmate, the charges of treachery were abandoned when you accepted the challenge,' Abrik said calmly. 'Besides, it must be obvious to all who are gathered here that Alena fled, not to escape justice, but to obtain it.'

The Arak-zook sighed.

The Zookspmate was having none of it. 'I demand Alena be viewed as a Dsolcspmite. Brigala!' he pleaded with the young female Grycyryn. 'You will surely back up my claim.' When she looked at him aghast, he turned to the male Grycyryn. 'Ajeta! You need to speak.'

The uneasy Grycyryn merely gazed back at him, stony faced.

The Zookspmate spun around desperately and swallowed. 'Alena, if you have any sense of honour, you must abandon this challenge. I am prepared to drop all charges.'

'No!' Her gaze was fierce. 'I am prepared to live with doubts about my integrity, but I bow to the greater purpose of dispensing genuine justice. Not just for me. But for those you unfairly condemned to death. And for everyone else treated with disdain by you.'

Just then, an aktel yelled from beside a large boulder nearby. 'Zookspmate, Zookspmate! The renegade Alena has been spotted nearby. You need to be on your guard!' He spotted Alena. The aktel swallowed. 'Oh.' And hastily disappeared.

'I am surrounded by incompetents,' The Zookspmate moaned. He looked about pleadingly as a flood of hand signals spread as a ripple.

'Arak-zook, Grycyryn, you choose to abandon me. I, a Zookspmate.' His plea was met by icy stares and brief and sharp hand signals.

'Wait! Doesn't convention allow an Arak-zook to fight for her Zookspmate?' he asked in desperation. 'Alena would not kill you. I'm certain of it.'

'Convention does allow that. Yes,' said the Arak-zook calmly. She and the Zookspmate gazed at one another. 'Do you wish to fight with armour, Zookspmate?'

'Jkilm!' the Zookspmate snarled. A female aktel placed the body armour on the Zookspmate once more but he shrugged free. 'This cannot be. It... cannot... be.'

The Arak-zook turned to Alena. 'Alena, when you accepted the challenge you sought the punishment of banishment. That means, to achieve his surrender, you must resist administering a fatal blow. Should you do so, it will reflect very badly on your integrity, even if the fatal injury was accidental.'

The Zookspmate looked aghast, Alena considered the request. 'I will do whatever is required for him to concede. When he surrenders, yes, I will demand his immediate permanent banishment. He will forfeit his rank as Zookspmate and promise never to seek to attain that rank again. Should he break that promise, I, and my aktel, will hunt him as the worst of criminals. But, before we fight, I wish it to acknowledge that many of his achievements have been beneficial to my fellow Zygols. But, as time has passed, he has increasingly elevated his desire for power and privilege above his dedication to the six elements. I have said my piece. The challenge begins!'

The Zookspmate's eyes bulged as she stalked him, brandishing her kraxl-da. 'No. No. No.' He strode before the gathered aktel. 'All of you here are witness to this blatant act of deception. By declaring the challenge valid, the Arak-zook and Grycyryn, who owe their rank to me... to me! reveal themselves to be cowards. Cowards! This is an Arak-zook who has sworn to defend me to her death. To her death!' The aktel frowned. At him.

'Zookspmate,' the Arak-zook said calmly. 'It is to the six elements that I have sworn my greatest allegiance. The challenge continues. Immediately.'

The Zookspmate glared at her. She returned his glare. 'Useless. The lot of you,' he thundered. 'This is why I am the only one who is worthy—'

'Alena, you may proceed,' commanded the Sklim gruffly.

The Zookspmate faced Alena not with a kraxl-da, which lay at his feet, but with a smile. 'I surrender. Violence is something to be detested, as the six elements state emphatically.' Many of those gathered uttered gasps of derision. A couple whispered jkilms.

The Zookspmate grabbed a nearby aktel by the shoulders and cowered behind her. He raised his hands, his face ashen. 'Dear Alena, I freely accept all your demands. I renounce my rank of Zookspmate with immediate effect and accept banishment. Consider me a Grycyryn-da as before.'

Everyone looked at Alena.

'No. You are but a Grycyryn. I will grant you no higher status than that.' The new Grycyryn glowered. Abrik looked on, satisfied.

The Sklim's brow was furrowed. 'Alena, I urge you to take stronger action. If you think this devious man will fade away, I fear you are deluded.'

Alena paced, twiddling her kraxl-da. 'He knows his fate if he goes back on his word. Grycyryn, hand over the talisman in your possession.'

'Open your mind, Spmite,' pleaded the ex-Zookspmate. 'Think what great things you could achieve with me installed as your loyal servant, offering you all of my accumulated wisdom and experience.'

Alena's short and sharp hand signal seemed decidedly rude.

The ex-Zookspmate recoiled. He fumbled about in the pouch of his tunic and brought out a slightly glinting blue and orange disc. Snarling, he tossed it to the pensive Arak-zook.

'As I do not have a Zookspmate to serve,' said the Arak-zook, 'I am now a Dsolcspmite once more. I will see that the talisman is given to a respected male Grycyryn-da until a new Zookspmate is chosen.' Ajeta looked at his feet.

Alena smiled. 'That is so... Dsolcspmite Elevata. As I am now the sole authority in our region, I pronounce the judgements of Jsete, Rystyn and Gentok to be hereby declared invalid. They committed no offence.' Jsete, Gentok and even Rystyn clasped one another, grinning.

Blakey cleared his throat. Only the recently designated Grycyryn glanced his way. Blakey cleared his throat again. Louder.

'Although I cannot oppose your annulment of those three judgements, Spmite,' simmered the former Zookspmate, 'deeply insulting a Zookspmate cannot be pardoned under any circumstances. Not to mention disposing of a Spmite's talisman. The Earthman must be punished. I insist on it.'

Blakey groaned.

'Even if what the Earthman said about you has now been shown to be true?' Abrik queried.

The ex-Zookspmate bristled. Alena's half-raised kraxl-da kept him silent.

'Rest assured, new Grycyryn. I give you my word that the Earthman will be punished. But only for what he inflicted upon me. Indeed, I have long anticipated the pleasure of watching him suffer.'

Ross Blakey gasped.

'Spmite,' Jsete pleaded. 'Don't you think this wonderful, magical day should not end by any death or severe injury? Even for the unworthy Earthman?'

Alena grimaced, sheathed her kraxl-da, and shot out hand signals to Jsete and to the former Arak-zook, now Dsolcspmite Elevata. Jsete leaned her head to the right. 'I see your point, Spmite. Yes, his deeds must be punished. I have no objections.'

Blakey let out a strangled cry of despair. 'Jsete! Surely you won't desert me!'

The ex-Zookspmate stepped hesitantly from behind his sanctuary of the female aktel.

'The matter is settled, and the challenge is ended,' pronounced Alena. 'Disrobe and leave immediately, Grycyryn. You are never to return to the lands of the Three Villages. I will assign aktel to fetch your possessions. They will take them to Mkeldi village. Make arrangements with the Sklim to have then sent to you. If you wish to.'

The new Grycyryn scowled at the villagers from Mkeldi, but said nothing.

The Sklim sighed. 'If that is all you desire, Alena. But I add this: this former Zookspmate will not find sanctuary in the lands of Mkeldi village.'

Ajeta, the tall male Grycyryn, who stood beside the female Grycyryn, edged his way towards the tarpaulin. 'I will fetch my spare robe for him. That will have to do until he is suitably dressed in clothes that fit him.' He began hurrying away.

Alena called after him. 'Be aware, Grycyryn; your role volunteering to act as an unprecedented fifth judge to satisfy the Zookspmate's vengeance has been noted and will be addressed on your return to the Three Villages.' A smiling Abrik leaned her head to the right.

Ajeta looked chastened. 'I promised to be a judge when I had been in the Swamp for a considerable time. I accept I have brought about dishonour on myself. When I return to the Three Villages, I will thoroughly reacquaint myself with the writings of our most esteemed past Grycyryn-da.' He hastily disappeared under the tarpaulin.

'Hello? Someone,' pleaded Blakey. 'Can I say something? A truly sincere apology. I'll do or say anything.' He was ignored.

Brlma caught sight of a well-built figure cowering at the back of a group of aktel. 'You,' she commanded. A head bobbed out of view. 'You know full well I am talking to you. Come to me!' The male Safi stepped cautiously towards her, cringing. He tried to stay clear of Alena, but the Spmite joined him at his side—uncomfortably close to his side.

'Spmite,' stammered the cowering male Safi. 'I was merely obeying the orders of my Arak-zook. I freely apologise to everyone I have offended. I, too, acknowledge the need to vastly improve my understanding of the six elements and elapelc. I announce before you all that I am relinquishing my rank of Safi as of this moment. Indeed, I will change my tunic immediately.' He stripped off some of his armour. But Alena kept her firm hand on his shoulder.

'Spmite, I am thinking; this aktel takes great pleasure obeying unpleasant orders,' Brlma grunted. 'Shouldn't we foster a talent such as his? Certainly, until he is better able to apply the six elements to his decision making?'

'Hmm,' Alena mused. 'Assigned to someone who could act as his mentor perhaps. Someone such as you, Brlma.'

The aktel swallowed. 'No. No. Don't send me to Mkeldi village. Please; anything... banishment... but not that. They are all idiots there.' He hurried to divest more of his armour.

'Assigning an able-bodied aktel such as this to help with the construction works around the uckliablaht pen, and to help with your duties while you recover, sounds like a perfect assignment, Brlma. In your spare time, the two of you can have pleasant discussions on the six elements and elapelc. As he is apparently not an idiot, he should learn quickly from your... teaching. It has to be the ideal solution.'

'I accept your proposal, Alena,' Brlma said grinning. Rather wickedly.

The deposed aktel looked decidedly miserable. 'For how long?' he groaned.

Both Alena and Brlma shrugged nonchalantly.

'I will change my tunic now.' The deflated former Safi began to slink away. As he passed Jsete, she punched him hard in the stomach. He crumpled to the ground.

'I'm sure some part of the six elements allowed me to do that,' she said grinning.

Many smiled, and heads leaned to the right. The deposed Safi ran to a tent clutching his stomach.

When Ajeta emerged from the tarpaulin holding a Grycyryn's tunic, Alena sent him some curt hand signals and touched the hilt of her kraxl-da.

Ajeta halted and nervously handed the change of clothes to a nearby aktel. He warily edged towards a boulder. 'Tonight, I will sleep in the aktel guard post on the other side of Mkeldi village,' he blustered, 'so I can have a head start in the morning.' Yet he hesitated. Two aktel volunteered to escort him.

Blakey cleared his throat again. 'Doesn't anyone think *my* punishment is unfair or excessive?' he groveled. 'Even the bastard who caused all this is getting off easy.'

No one paid him any heed.

'How about a bit of elapelc, eh? Damn it! Hey, Spmite.' To his chagrin, Jsete seemed disinterested. Even smug.

The Sklim looked towards Alena and Elevata in turn. Each of their faces were expressionless.

'Dsolcspmite Elevata—the former Arak-zook—has been given her orders regarding you, Earthman,' Alena said, triumphant. 'Her skill at conducting punishments is unprecedented. The matter is settled. For what you have done, you have no grounds for complaint.'

'But...' He moaned.

The deposed Zookspmate turned to the young female Grycyryn, who'd taken a few steps away from him. He reached towards her. 'Brigala. It's just you and me now to face this whole ungrateful world that has schemed against us. Now, you and I will seek a place where my contributions and forward thinking will be appreciated.'

Brigala looked intently at the man before her. 'There is something that I have been meaning to talk to you about,' she said. 'This seems the most appropriate time to do so. I am ending our relationship.'

The deposed Zookspmate gaped. 'You too, Brigala,' he whispered.

'Ajeta,' she said. 'I will travel with you.' And, together, they, and two escorting aktel, hurried off.

In the shocked silence that followed, the ex-Zookspmate snatched his new clothes with a snarl and, after glaring at everyone, slunk under cover of the tarpaulin.

'Aktel; see that he leaves his weapons behind,' Alena commanded. 'Follow him until he leaves both the territory belonging to the Three Villages and Mkeldi.'

Three aktel ran off after the new Grycyryn.

A desperate Ross Blakey called out. 'Jsete. Surely you don't believe I deserve to be punished this way. Not after the wonderful deeds we did in the village.'

Jsete stepped beside Alena. 'Rossblakey; your punishment is fully deserved. I will not seek to change my Spmite's mind. A precedent for your despicable crimes has to be made. But I sent hand signals to Elevata to mete out your punishment more swiftly. Our Spmite has agreed to my request. Such is her generosity of spirit. Given the wonderful events that have happened this day, you do deserve a little mercy.'

Alena leaned her head to the right.

'Generosity of spirit!' boomed Blakey. 'Bullshit! The villagers have been saved. You have been set free. None of you are going to die. Just me. She is a Spmite again. The Zookspmate has been deposed. Hasn't everything turned out right? That must count for something. Surely.'

'No!' Alena and Jsete said in unison.

'After I dispense justice to the Earthman, am I to be punished for my role in the events of this day?' an anxious Elevata asked.

As Alena contemplated the question, Abrik spoke. 'I have a suggestion Spmite. With Brlma's injury, Mkeldi village is without a fit Dsolcspmite. Elevata has observed that Mkeldi village is a backwater. As such, it needs assistance for it to be lifted from its inferior status. Apart from training our aktel, there is also the urgent task of diverting water around our uckliablaht pen so we can plant shade trees. This task will involve breaking up a great deal of solid rock. I should think the strength of both Elevata and the former Safi would play a key role in this urgent work.'

Elevata sucked her breath. The Sklim and Brlma leaned their heads to the right.

'I consider your request to be reasonable, Abrik,' Alena said. 'It will provide Elevata with a fine opportunity to redeem herself. I suggest she be at your village's disposal until Brlma is fully recovered and major progress has been made on your vital project. If that proposal is not suitable to Elevata, she may prefer to face judgement instead.'

The stout woman sighed deeply. 'I accept your offer, Alena. I am grateful for your faith in me. When you first became a Safi, you were so young but, even then, I knew you were destined to become a Spmite. My only concern all along, has been your personal side. Your unwavering dedication to your ambition and to your role has meant you have made many sacrifices, at a personal level. It may yet prove to be a weakness in your make up.'

Alena nodded. 'Your comment is interesting. Perhaps my personality would have become more formed if you and the

Zookspmate hadn't treated me as if I was still a Safi after I became Spmite. I have expended needless energy asserting myself. Now that I feel able to act as a fully fledged Spmite, my true self should emerge.'

Elevata nodded. 'I apologise for my obstruction, Alena. But, before I take on my new duties in Mkeldi village, I will proceed with the punishment of the annoying Earthman. Doing so would give both you and I considerable satisfaction.'

'And me,' piped Rystyn

Blakey uttered a strangled moan.

'That is so, Elevata,' replied Alena, smirking at Blakey. 'I await his punishment with more anticipation than anyone.'

'Don't do this!' pleaded Ross Blakey as he struggled with his tight bonds. His breath came in desperate gulps. 'I'll go back to my compound. On foot. By myself. Cfaldi or no cfaldi. If I make it there, I'll return to my planet straight away. You needn't see me ever again.'

Alena smirked. 'Begin, Elevata.'

Blakey gasped. A smiling Elevata, kraxl in hand, stood poised, looking down on the helpless Earthman.

'No! Don't! Please.'

Rystyn sidled up beside Alena, who had taken a stance beside the frantically wriggling Blakey. 'I will have no more of your bravado, Spmite. Aktel, remove the Spmite's armour and fetch me a sling for her injured shoulder.' His main concern, however, seemed to be getting a clearer vantage point to view Blakey's punishment. The cook was in an unusually buoyant mood.

'I can put the sling on myself,' said the embarrassed Spmite as she pushed the Zygol cook aside.

'No, you will not,' Rystyn ordered.

Alena raised her arm to shoulder height, her eyes never leaving the prone Blakey. 'It's not so bad. See how freely I can move it.' She lifted her arm a short way above her head but winced in pain.

Rystyn gave her a look of disgust. Embarrassed, Alena allowed a grinning aktel to remove her armour.

The exchange between Alena and Rystyn meant nothing to a trembling Ross Blakey. His eyes were fixed on Elevata who twirled her kraxl with nonchalance, before dropping to her knees beside him, her face one of a frighteningly calm intent.

'Remain as you are, Earthman,' Elevata said, smiling, 'and don't complain. Never have I met someone who deserves to have their tongue cut out. And you have fully deserved what I am about to do. It is best if you don't make any sudden movements.' A smiling Alena moved across for an unhindered view, with a very pleased Rystyn and a smug-looking Jsete—the young woman with sparkling green eyes— beside her. Aktel also drifted to surround him.

'Bastards! Sadists! All of you!'

Alena broke into a wicked grin. 'My spirits are soaring, watching you tied up, waiting to be sliced into pieces, Earthman. Your punishment will end this memorable day perfectly.'

Ross Blakey snarled at her, making Alena chuckle. 'Oh, you so deserve to be punished.'

As Elevata leant over him, Blakey became more conciliatory. 'Spmite, please. There must be something in the six elements about showing mercy to someone whose crime is merely to be an ignorant fool. Nothing more.'

'Ha! There is that most certainly that provision. If only this request came from someone remotely worthy.'

Blakey cringed. 'Please...' his voice a tremor.

'Enough! I will begin.' Elevata grinned as she passed the kraxl before a gasping Blakey's eyes. Alena's gaze was fixed on his face. He pulled hard at his constraints.

An aktel handed Rystyn a sling. The Zygol cook began placing it on the Spmite, his eyes never deviating from Blakey. Elevata waited for the task to be completed. Her blade hovering in front of Blakey's face.

'You heartless bitch!' Blakey called out to Alena in his Earth language.

'I don't understand your Earth words,' Elevata said as she moved the flat of her cold kraxl against his groin. 'It is most likely an insult. But your words only serve to please us all even more.'

Distraction came again by the sound of a flap being pushed hard, as the deposed Zookspmate, dressed in an oversized Grycyryn's tunic, emerged from the tarpaulin, mightily contrite, unarmed and flanked by three aktel. He looked at no one and said nothing.

Elevata called out to him. 'I will arrange—'

'I want no help from you!' was his angry retort. 'I choose to journey by myself. I trust no one. Fools and cowards. All of you.' He slunk towards the uckliablahts.

'You have your orders,' Alena said to the aktel following him. They leaned their heads to the right. 'Keep your distance. I also ask the signaller and some of those guarding the encampment to spread the word of what has taken place here.' Five aktel headed off.

'I will personally ensure that he does not dwell in our territory for long,' added the Sklim.

Ross Blakey was close to hyperventilating. He badly needed to pee. It would be the last act of a part of him that he treasured. Still Elevata hesitated until she heard the sound of four uckliablahts being ridden away, as she kept rubbing her kraxl against Blakey's upper thigh. Then she gazed on him again, her mood brightening. 'It's time to attend to you at last, Earthman.'

'Spmite! Jsete!' Blakey's pleaded. The two women stepped closer, their smiles even broader.

Elevata leaned over, the blade of her kraxl catching a final ray of the sinking sun. 'Enough! Hero of Mkeldi.' Ross Blakey shut his eyes and clamped his jaw tight. If her first task was to cut out his tongue, she would need to prise his jaw open. By the look of her forearms, she could achieve that with ease. As for his other appendage, he was helpless.

Blakey held his breath. The blade was passed from his thigh to his groin, his stomach, then his chest, until it dwelt at his throat. The blade was removed. He let out a gasp, quivering. The kraxl returned to his groin. Then withdrew. For an indeterminable time, nothing seemed to happen. Until Blakey felt the ropes binding his legs loosen. The same happened with the ropes binding his arms. He dared to open one eye.

'I am done,' Elevata said with satisfaction as she rose.

Blakey was dumbfounded. The stout woman was truly skilled in the art of execution for he had felt no stab of pain. In fact, he had felt nothing but the loosening of his bonds, and the savage beating of his heart. He looked over his body, knowing that rivers of blood had to be pouring out from a fatal wound. But he saw no wound. He cautiously felt around his body, expecting to find his hands covered in blood. But no. Everyone in sight was smiling. Some were giggling. Alena was doubled over, laughing. As was Jsete, her arm wrapped around her Spmite's (good) shoulder.

'We must return to Mkeldi village now Alena,' the Sklim announced. 'My people will be fretting, having feared the worst.'

Alena was reluctant. 'As much as I long to keep watching the Earthman's face, I must agree.' But she hesitated, not averting her eyes from Blakey. She chuckled. 'Aktel, provide Gentok with proper medical care,' she pronounced. 'He is to remain here until he is fit for travel to Mkeldi.'

Brlma sent the deposed male Safi a hand signal, to which he leaned his head to the right. He trudged towards where the uckliablahts were tethered.

Spmite Alena took one more triumphant look at Blakey then, with a contented sigh, strode briskly towards a gap in the boulders, her slight limp noticeable once more. The Sklim, Abrik, Elevata and a limping Brlma followed her. They slapped each other's backs with glee. Only a still-beaming Jsete remained. Though Gentok also smiled faintly, he sat on the ground as two aktel rushed to aid him. As Gentok sent hand signals, he was removed on a stretcher, and ointment was applied to his re-opened wound. A satisfied Jsete turned to Ross Blakey.

Realisation at what had taken place dawned on Blakey. His puzzled then angry face made Jsete giggle.

'So, this was a prank, was it?' He got to his feet, testily freeing his hands and feet from the remnants of his bindings. 'You Zygols say that you are compassionate. But the truth is, you're very cruel.'

'We are compassionate. Oh, you should have seen the look on your face.' Jsete grinned. 'Even now it amuses me.'

'Do you realise how terrified I was?'

'Oh, most definitely.' She looked far too happy for Blakey's liking. 'I saw far less terror on the faces of villagers when we were facing the chageen.'

Blakey fumbled with the buttons on his shirt with trembling hands. 'Jsete. I have never felt so terrified. Ever. Yet, you stand there as if it was one huge joke.' To think that he had come to... like... Jsete a lot. No more! He'd seen her nasty... maybe her true... side.

'Oh yes, it was a horrible thing to subject you to, Rossblakey. Horrible. I freely acknowledge it.' She placed a hand over her mouth to suppress a chuckle. 'Look at it for what it was; the prank released much of the tension among those gathered. May it set the tone for a new joyous era for the Three Villages. Realise also that my good spirits have much to do with knowing you would live, Rossblakey. Accept that my Spmite had to punish you for your despicable deed. You had to be made to suffer. If she had deemed to inflict an injury on you... even to seek your death, no one would have decried her right to do so.'

A simmering Ross Blakey was not appeased. 'Everyone was entertained, were they? With me lying there, helpless, in utter terror.'

'Calm down. I say it again, Rossblakey; you are alive. And uncut. Is your embarrassment too great a price to pay for being spared? Your terror was brief. Appreciate how very fortunate you are. Now you will be given safe passage to your compound. As you have wished.'

'No; I don't appreciate what's happened. I've been treated like a plaything! Right from the beginning, captured for no good reason and forced into a hell-hole of a desert. I could have died out there and no one would have cared. Hell, everybody wanted me dead. Are you aware of what I've gone through? And this prank was the final...' Only he didn't know the word for straw.

'I acknowledge the considerable trials you have been put through, Rossblakey. Yet, it is clear that Tsalc takes pleasure from your company. And it was essential that our Spmite be appeased. Be calm. Rejoice knowing that your trials are now over.'

'No! I won't accept it. She has to apologise to me! For everything she's put me through. *You* need to realise something; I saved her life.' He followed in the direction Alena had gone.

Jsete grasped him by the shoulder. 'Do not do anything silly. Take our Spmite's treatment with the good humour it was intended. The consequences of doing something impulsive could yet bring about a very painful punishment. Tsalc often does not look kindly upon those who do not accept its pronouncements.'

Blakey brushed away Jsete's hand and dashed on. When he reached the small clearing where the uckliablahts were tethered, he saw Alena riding off at pace with Mkeldi village's dignitaries and Elevata close behind.

Blakey snarled as he untethered an uckliablaht. He recognised the beast as the one he had found relatively easy to ride earlier. Taking a large leaf from beside the feed lot, he wiped the beast's saddle. He would not look at Jsete; she who had basked joyful at his suffering.

'I will come with you.' Jsete was no longer grinning. 'Your uckliablaht knows to follow mine. Maybe I can yet make you see sense. Do not ruin this wonderful day.'

'Please yourself.' With a grim-faced Jsete riding beside him, Blakey set off after Alena, towards Mkeldi village. His slow and haphazard progress did nothing to improve his mood. Neither did a group of four aktel, who drew alongside him as they passed the perpendicular rock, for they turned to smirk at the Earthman. Blakey glared back at them. His anger only brought them mirth.

As try as Jsete could to persuade him otherwise, Blakey was resolute. As they neared the village's uckliablaht pen in the Zygol twilight, the Safi looked straight ahead. 'If you promise not to confront our Spmite, I will bathe with you tonight.' She averted her eyes.

'No!' he said firmly. But after a few moments thinking about it.

'Then face the consequences, Earthman!'

'Oh. I'm back to being an Earthman now, am I?'

'Yes! A stupid, ignorant Earthman,' snapped Jsete. 'To think that I was so foolish to believe that elapelc was happening within you. How could I have been so wrong?'

She rode on ahead, unable to restrain her fury.

Ross Blakey didn't care. He was simmering. After all that he had endured, with the malevolent combination of Death and Tsalc peering constantly over his shoulder, he needed to let this Alena know exactly how he felt about what he'd been put through.

13

AN EARTHMAN'S LEGACY

IT WAS ONLY when Jsete rode on that Blakey looked where he was going. He swallowed. Spread along both sides of the path that snaked through the trees of Mkeldi had to be a hundred or more visible, bobbing, small red-white lights, held by lines of villagers, jostling for positions. Many faces were illuminated by the flames. They crowded around Jsete to whisper their well-wishes or to pat her on the back and legs. Many sent her welcoming hand signals, which Jsete acknowledged by leaning over and touching the hands and shoulders of those she passed. As awkward as he was on his uckliablaht, Blakey figured he'd stay mounted; otherwise, he risked being smothered by the pressing villagers. He was greeted with the same warmth as was shown to Jsete. He took in their faces: children, old people, some expressing joy, others solemn, some in awe. Their welcome humbled him. Many whispered his name. Sort of. *"Rush Blashey; you are alive!" "Tsalc has brought our hero back to us." "Never has there been such a day as this!" "Is that his name?" "Yes, Rush Blashey; the Sklim said so."* The crowding villagers brought Blakey's uckliablaht to a halt. Despite his urgings, the uckliablaht would not budge. He was left trying to mask his annoyance in front of his well-wishers.

'You dance with Tsalc,' an old woman at the back of the crowd called out. Others murmured their agreement and many heads leaned to the right. Her words became a refrain.

An uptight Jsete rode towards him, parting the crowd. 'Throw me the tether Earthman.' Blakey did so and the Safi forged a slow, stop-start route towards the village square. She did not look at him.

Ross Blakey smiled at the crowd and touched as many upraised hands as he could. Some villagers offered him dishes of steaming food. 'I need to get to the village square,' he kept repeating. 'I will see you all afterwards. I promise.'

The villagers crowded around Jsete and Blakey. They followed them to the village square, where three small fires burned, around which groups of villagers in high spirits were having a feast. Fire sticks hung from the surrounding vegetation like lights on Christmas trees. Stern-faced, Jsete dismounted her uckliablaht, and Blakey did the same. They were mobbed by villagers who jostled to hug them and tap them on their shoulders. In the rapturous din, Blakey made out some words. *"You are alive!" "It is another miracle." "Welcome back heroes of Mkeldi village!"* Their faces were visions of unbridled joy.

Their uckliablahts were whisked away. An excited Kasmin appeared. 'I thought I'd never see Ross Blakey alive again. Our Spmite told me that Gentok lives, too. I can't believe it. Do you know when they will bring him here?'

'He will stay in the hills until he is healthy enough to journey here,' said Jsete. 'Our Spmite has demanded he receive the best of care.'

'Then I will go to him now,' Kasmin replied.

'But it is dark. You run the risk—'

Kasmin dashed away.

Jsete shrugged as she watched the young aktel disappear through the crowd. 'She shouldn't be riding unarmed in the dark by herself. But how can I stop her?' Then she smiled. Until she looked at Blakey's face.

Despite their enthusiastic reception, Ross Blakey was fuming.

Suddenly, there was Alena before him, having brushed through the throng to greet Mkeldi village's two heroes. She wore no armour but a kraxl and a kraxl-da hung from her belt. She hugged Jsete warmly with her unhurt arm. Jsete whispered in her ear. Alena grinned and turned to face Blakey, who was simmering, a mere pace away.

'You look angry, Earthman,' she chided him. 'To see you in such a mood pleases me. Not as much as seeing you lying on your back, bound by ropes, with Elevata leaning over you with her kraxl. Oh, the expression on your face as you waited to die so horribly. Your eyes were shut tight. You gritted your jaw oh-so hard. May Tsalc grant me the joy to see you bound again. From the look on your face, perhaps you desire to say something that will see my wish realised. Is there something you wish to say?' She had the most wicked smile.

'Oh yes. Right from the start you've treated me like dirt,' Blakey hissed. 'It's a miracle I'm still alive. Yet, you owe your life to me. Then, when I was tied up, helpless and terrified, there you were, laughing.'

That set her laughing. 'That is true. I did enjoy myself immensely. Yes, you make a valid point; I am alive because of you. But I also owe much to Brlma and Tsalc.'

Listening in on the conversation, the surrounding villagers fell silent. Behind Alena, an agonised Jsete leaned her head to the left and averted her eyes.

Alena's smile broadened. 'I haven't laughed like that for such a long time. I earned that pleasure, Earthman. You lost my talisman. You do not seem to comprehend the devastation your act may have caused. Not just for me but for my region. Oh how you had me craving to drive my kraxl-da through your body. To gaze into your eyes as you died before me. Me, who pledged with my entire being to protect all life. When, incredibly, you became a hero, how then could I enact your punishment? Thankfully, Tsalc came to my aid again. It whispered to me at the encampment. It was the perfect suggestion. Perhaps you don't agree?' She offered him an even more wicked grin.

Ross Blakey glanced at the anxious faces of the pressing villagers reflected in the speckled light. So many heads leaned to the right. He glanced towards Jsete. Her averted face was bowed. Then he looked at a beaming Alena. Alena who treated him with cruelty and indifference. And had laughed aloud as he shook with terror. Yet... this was the

Alena who could have deserted him and Rystyn in the desert, for they had been slowing her down. Alena who fetched their water from God knows where. Alena who risked her life so the renegades could escape to Mkeldi village. She who had stood tall and defiant before the massive swarm of chageen. Now, before him, Ross Blakey looked at, not a heartless or fearless warrior, but at a woman happy like an excited teenager. And... hanging from her belt was a kraxl and a kraxl-da. And she knew how to wield them.

Blakey thought a while and sucked a breath. 'Yes. You deserved to see me humiliated.' His admission surprised him. He stared at her, confused by what he'd said. But the words would see him taken safely to his compound. Alena sighed in disappointment.

Jsete, though, spun around, a look of sheer relief across her face. The villagers smiled and tapped him on his shoulders with the back of their hands in respect. Alena did the same.

'It has been a wonderful day, Earthman. Celebrate. But, understand, I am still wary of you. It is best that you keep your distance and return to your compound at first light.'

Blakey wasn't about to slink away quietly. 'I will. And I'll go straight back to Earth. But now, I expect some elapelc in return.'

Alena stared at him, bemused.

'From this point in time, I expect to be treated with dignity.' When Alena blinked, he became more emboldened. 'First of all; understand that Earth humans like to be addressed by our names. My name is Ross Blakey.'

'Ross Blakey,' went the murmur by the villagers crowded around them.

'Told you,' some said to others.

'No, it isn't,' insisted a couple of others. 'Ask the Sklim.'

Alena studied his face. 'I will consider your request. You are a hero of the village. For that I thank you deeply. Yet you must realise that I don't trust you.' Frowning, she signalled the end of a formal conversation and pushed through the crowd.

'Rossblakey,' squealed Jsete as she leaped into his arms. 'You have acted sensibly. I knew you were capable of it. Deep down, I knew. Yes.

Very... deep down. I will organise for you to be taken to your compound. Some aktel who need to return to the Three Villages, will travel with us. The Three Villages are a full day's ride from here. Maybe two days if you wish to ride your own uckliablaht. Do not be concerned; we won't travel through the desert. We will pass through the green hills.' She let her head rest on his shoulder as he wrapped his arms around her.

'Okay. All I have to do is keep away from... the Spmite and not do anything stupid. Can I manage that?' But, for the present, he soaked up this precious moment. Jsete felt so incredibly good in his arms; his earlier animosity towards her flung gleefully aside. Clasping her made deferring to Alena worthwhile, a hundred-fold.

Leaning back in his arms, Jsete looked radiant. Those green eyes, sparkling and alive again, as they did at the lake, gazed into his. 'Rossblakey, celebrate this incredible day. Make it clear to those who wish to share your company that they need to be tolerant of your unformed capacity for elapelc. But treat us Zygols with respect. Be alert for warning signs. Zygols almost invariably issue them before acting. Look for exaggerated hand signals. When you return to your compound, reflect on what you have learned. Teach your fellow humans about our ways.'

Ross Blakey longed only for the company of one person. He would ride slowly back to his compound with Jsete the next day. Blakey even had a wild, fanciful notion: take Jsete with him to Earth. Although... doing so would come with major risks, certainly. For starters, many powerful men on Earth would be at serious risk of losing their balls.

How would he relate to his children again? They'd at least know him when he no longer kept vomiting. But their first sight of him would be from behind the iron bars of the brig. Explaining going AWOL at the compound was going to be tricky. Best to keep his mouth shut, at least until he was back on Earth. Hopefully he'd get to throw one—or two—whiskies down before they tossed him unceremoniously in the Chute. Those whiskies would, no doubt, return to Earth independent of he who imbibed it.

He was about to whisper in Jsete's ear how he felt about her when she looked away and lowered those enticing, alive eyes. 'As for now, I have not forgotten that I promised I would bathe with you.'

He stroked her back. 'It is a promise I won't hold you to, Jsete. You owe me nothing. It is me who owes you so much.' Turning down the offer to bathe with a wonderful and beautiful young woman was a major wrench. Of course, should she insist... But she had to do so from her own free will.

Jsete stiffened. She gazed at his face strangely, then leaned her head to the right. Suddenly, she pushed away from him—roughly—then took a few hurried backward steps, stepping behind some villagers. There she glared at him.

Blakey was taken aback. He thought his gesture had been noble. Obviously not. 'Have I—?'

Jsete frowned, turned on her heels, and fled.

'Don't go, Jsete. Please!' Blakey called out. She ran faster.

'I can't believe it,' he lamented in his Earth language. 'She thinks I've...' Blakey's chest heaved. 'I didn't mean to insult you,' he called out. He went to chase after her, but murmuring villagers stood in his way. They were too preoccupied with shoving each other good naturedly, wanting to lead Blakey to a particular fire. His eyes could only peer desperately as her form disappeared into the vegetation.

Deflated, Ross Blakey cared nothing about food. He craved only to hold Jsete in his arms and set his blunder right. Clundrns and jugs of a now-familiar liquid were brought out. He asked for water; the last thing he needed was a befuddled mind.

Blakey good-naturedly ate some food offered to him. As much as Blakey appreciated the praise and smiles of the villagers, he soon told his hosts that he needed to take a walk and to rest. The villagers respected his wishes. Such is elapelc.

Blakey set off in search of Jsete. He would drop on his knees before her and plead for forgiveness.

Near the lake, he caught sight of her peering at him from behind a distant tree. He called out. 'Jsete, I have to talk to you!' She ran off. 'Stop! Please!' he begged. She sped up.

Blakey tried to give chase, but she was too nimble. All he caught were fresh doses of plooglit piss.

After an indeterminable time searching for her in the dark, Blakey succumbed to exhaustion. She had chosen her hiding spot well. He opted to rest in the hut and wait for her. If she was tardy, he would seek her even if it took all night. Flopping on his bed, Ross Blakey drifted into an aching, restless sleep. His thoughts filled only with Jsete.

SOMETIME LATER, he felt a tugging at his sleeve. Blakey opened his eyes. Jsete? But, no, it was Kasmin who squatted beside him as the ruckus sounds of celebration and laughter drifted from the village square.

'They keep asking me, "Where is Rush Blashey?" Abrik and the Sklim wish to call you by that name. I think otherwise. You need to come to the community hut. All the dignitaries are waiting for you. You can rest later.'

Blakey sat up and yawned, scratching at his new, but thankfully not overly itching, doses of plooglit piss. He nodded. 'Just keep a low profile, Ross.' Find Jsete and apologise. Maybe she was inside the hut.

'It is best that we avoid the villagers in the square,' Kasmin explained. 'As you can hear, they are in high spirits. You might find it difficult breaking free of them. They will still be there if you care to join them later.' Kasmin led Blakey along a minor path.

'How is Gentok?'

Kasmin smiled. 'He is in fine spirits, but he needs to rest. He does not want to be fussed over. It embarrasses him.'

They walked past wandering uckliablahts. Curious plooglits noisily scrambled up and down trees. Blakey moved cautiously, careful not to brush against any vegetation.

He caught sight of a man, a woman and three children huddling in the shadows off the path. Even in the near darkness, Blakey could see they were dressed in rags. He waved a cheerful greeting, but the gesture caused the five to recoil. They slunk further into the shadows.

'Shit!' Blakey whispered to himself. 'I've insulted them.'

'You have broken no protocols,' Kasmin assured him.

Not wanting any more misunderstandings, Blakey edged towards the family. The five cowered. Blakey spread his arms wide. 'I only wanted to say hello. If I've upset you, I'm very sorry. I didn't mean any offence.'

'Upset us?' spluttered the wife. 'Ross Blakey, you honour us with your presence. You dance with Tsalc, yet you seek out and greet us whose status in the village is low.' The woman was close to tears. Her husband placed a reassuring arm around her. Their children huddled around their mother, gazing at Blakey with awe.

'Why are people telling me I dance with Tsalc?' Blakey quizzed the woman.

'But you do,' she answered emphatically. 'Surely it is clear to you. And it is a glorious thing.'

It was Blakey's turn to be shocked. 'That's so—'

'Whether you approve or not,' interrupted Kasmin, 'I fear that a legend is being created.'

'But I'm a bumbling fool.' One who had upset a woman he had come to adore.

Kasmin whispered in his ear. 'Everyone who has spent time in your presence knows that full well, but—'

'Such modesty,' said the man.

'You dance with Tsalc!' said the woman emphatically. 'We are honoured that you talk to us.'

Kasmin took Blakey by the arm. 'We should not dwell.'

'I don't want to be part of a legend,' Blakey grumbled as they set off. 'How can I stop this without losing my balls?'

'Protest all you like,' Kasmin chuckled. 'It will do you no good.'

Blakey snorted. What would it matter, anyway, when he was back on Earth?

He was acutely aware that Alena was likely to be inside the hut. And she'd warned him to keep his distance. But if Jsete was there... Strictly no alcohol.

Kasmin left Blakey at the door. He took a deep breath and stepped inside. He was greeted with exclamations of joy.

Some fifteen Zygols were standing about, chatting, in the main meeting room, including the Sklim, Abrik, Brlma, Elevata and the village's other female Grycyryn. Some swayed a little on their feet. Elevata, now wearing the tunic of a Dsolcspmite, looked contrite as the Sklim spoke to her. In the centre of the meeting room, lit by the half-light of fire sticks, were steaming pots of food and drink. Bowls, ladles and clundrns lined low tables.

At first, Blakey's heart fell, thinking Jsete wasn't in the room. But he caught sight of her behind three aktel in a far corner. She had her back to him.

The room was quite large by Zygol standards but any room with Alena there was not big enough. She was, thankfully, in the far end of the room, talking to Brlma. Even though she sported no weapons, Blakey became tense.

'Rush Blashey,' Abrik exclaimed as she led him into the centre of the room. 'I am so glad you could join us. We celebrate for we have much to discuss and plan after this day's incredible events. In these days of severe drought, we need to preserve the village's fragile elapelc. Some of our uckliablahts will accompany you to the Three Villages to allow them to regain their full health.'

Blakey adopted a clear strategy; agree to everything. But not to the clundrn of alcohol offered to him. 'Great idea.' His other strategy was to manoeuvre to Jsete's side, without passing close to Alena. Managing that would be difficult; the two stood near one another. A wall blocked his other approach.

Abrik handed him his notebook and pen. 'With the challenges we face, we must act swiftly. Tomorrow we elect a new Sklim. As for you, Rush Blashey, I am honoured to be in the presence of someone who dances with Tsalc.'

The label irked Blakey. He looked furtively towards the Sklim, who smiled.

'I am proud to announce that, from this day, Rush Blashey,' Abrik continued, 'you will always be welcome, and be feted, whenever you visit Mkeldi village. Never forget that.'

'Thank you.' He kept it to himself that he'd be thrown in the Chute within hours after returning to the compound. Besides, his dancing partner, Tsalc, had huge and discordant feet.

'Your Earth colleagues will surely give you a rousing welcome when you return to your compound as a hero of our village,' the Sklim added, his chest puffed out.

As he would never pass this way again, Blakey opted to be honest. 'Actually, they will be angry with me. I shouldn't be here.'

'How can they be?' replied an indignant Abrik. 'If any of your colleagues is displeased, inform them that the Sklim and lead Grycyryn of Mkeldi village have deemed that you dance with Tsalc. Tell them this and watch how they react.'

'Oh, they will definitely react if I tell them that. For sure.'

'Good.' Abrik seemed satisfied.

Jsete had drifted so that she stood immediately behind Alena and Brlma. The Spmite glanced at Blakey for the briefest moment before, thankfully, turning to Brlma. That suited Blakey fine.

Brlma's alcohol-fuelled voice boomed through the room. 'I cannot wait for my next opportunity to thrash and humiliate you in a contest Alena. You have no idea how much pleasure I will get from it. I will desist only when you beg me for mercy.'

'Oho. Try your best,' Alena countered. 'I will remind you of those foolish and boastful words when *you* beg *me* for mercy.'

'You would be wise to stay silent.' Brlma replied. 'You only make it worse for yourself by chiding me.'

'Think what you will.' Then Alena's face softened. 'Yet, although I will cause you pain, I will do so never forgetting that I owe you so much. It is because of you that I am alive and am Spmite. Together, we deposed an unworthy Zookspmate. Things could so easily have—'

'Let us not to dwell on such matters.' The two smiled and touched each other's shoulders with the back of their hands in a show of great respect and affection.

Blakey tried to edge closer to the front door, ready for an escape if the situation threatened to go awry. Not making it easy for him; Jsete seemed intent on staying behind Alena, while remaining in the company of three aktel. To Blakey's consternation, the Sklim and Abrik kept ushering him back into the centre of the room to be thanked by more villagers.

He almost panicked when he was led by the arm towards Alena and Brlma. He averted his eyes, clamped his mouth shut and put his hands in his pockets. Jsete edged away. Brlma thanked him warmly for his heroic efforts and gave him a hug that, again, must have displaced several discs in his back. Alena whispered the briefest thank you, wished him a safe journey to his compound and gave him a formal tap on the shoulder with the back of her hand. She leaned over and whispered in his ear. 'I hope you know what you must do now.' Then she turned to Brlma once more.

Ross Blakey sucked in a breath. She had to be warning him to leave.

He became aware of a change in the atmosphere, which spread as a wave of subtle hand signals across the room, towards him. As the ruckus of the celebrations continued outside, those in the community hut now wore looks of puzzlement. Whatever the problem was, it was clear to Blakey that he was the cause. It was best that he leave. But, to Blakey's annoyance, the Sklim was yabbering in his ear about something. When the old man paused for breath, Blakey resolved to feign tiredness. Actually, he didn't have to feign. Then he would go. With Jsete intent on staying as far from him as possible, maybe his best strategy was to wait outside the hut for her. If it took all night.

The villagers began whispering. Blakey couldn't help but notice the many accusing gazes that dwelt briefly on him. None were more intimidating than Alena's glare. Jsete was becoming agitated. Now uncomfortable, he put on a show of yawning. 'I must go to my hut. I am very tired.'

The old man leaned his head to the left. 'Don't go yet. This is my last night as Sklim. It is a time for renewal in my village. Come, I will show you our grain store.' He took Blakey firmly by the arm. The Earthman cringed. Alena's glance his way made her displeasure clear.

As Blakey was practically being dragged to the storage room, he had a wild idea; could it be that he was being led to his execution? Cleaning up his blood there would cause minimal inconvenience. Heroes are known more fondly when dead. The villagers would, most likely, have already chosen a spot to mount a bone that would be torn from his body. It would, no doubt, he placed in its prominent spot with deep reverence.

When he was inside the room, Elevata stood by the door flap, blocking his escape. The square grain room looked like a grain room should: it had numerous sacks of grain stacked high, mostly around the walls. The room seemed to be a source of pride to the Sklim. 'Do you see how the roof and walls are especially reinforced to keep the produce dry?'

'A solid roof over your food stocks? Great idea,' answered Blakey with as much enthusiasm as he could fake. He tried to gently prise himself from the Sklim's grip.

'Because of you, Rush Blashey, the food in the storage room will feed us all. And not just the few of the Survival Party.' Blakey smiled and made to leave the room.

He recoiled. Alena's imposing frame now filled the doorway. She was definitely not pleased. Trapped, he drew a breath. At first, his panicked mind did not make out what the Spmite said to him.

'What?' he asked weakly.

'You *must* talk to her,' Alena demanded.

'Jsete?'

'Of course, Jsete.'

'She's upset because of me, isn't she?'

'Yes. Because of you,' Alena replied. 'You must go to her.'

Blakey nodded. He took a deep breath. Alena stepped aside and he stepped into the meeting room. His heart was thumping.

Jsete was still talking to some aktel in a corner of the room. Again, she had her back to him. When Blakey approached her, the aktel about her drifted away. Jsete's back stiffened and she folded her arms against her midriff. She knew he was close by but would not look at him.

'I have made arrangements for some aktel to take you back to your compound at dawn.'

'Won't you be coming?'

She shot a brief glance his way, then looked away. 'No! I will wait here until Gentok is ready to return to the Three Villages. I am his Safi, after all. And Kasmin will want to travel with him. I will sleep in a different hut tonight. So we will say our goodbyes here. Now.'

'It's my fault that you're like this, isn't it?'

'I never would have guessed you would do such a thing to me.'

Blakey became flustered. 'Please believe me, Jsete. I didn't intend to insult you. I would never do anything to harm you. I just keep doing the wrong thing. I care for you... very much. And I don't want to leave with you angry with me like this.'

Jsete turned to face him, perplexed. 'I am not angry with you, Rossblakey. You should not feel any blame for my affliction. Not much anyway.'

Blakey was bewildered. 'What affliction?'

Jsete glared at him. He reached out and touched her forearm. Instantly, she backed away, colliding against the hut wall. She looked at him, mortified.

'Oh,' was all Blakey could get out. His touch had been so very brief. But it had been long enough. He'd felt her goose bumps on a balmy night.

Jsete composed herself. 'Do not be concerned. What ails me will be gone in a day or two. I need only to apply my mind to it. I have done so before. The humiliation of my affliction will last longer. But I can deal with that as well. It will be far easier with you gone. You have helped save Mkeldi village, Rossblakey. I have found you... interesting. There are some... noble aspects to your personality. And, you have begun... begun... to become familiar with our ways and philosophy. But, me shivering for someone so incredibly ignorant as you is...' She shook her head and looked at her feet, close to tears. 'It defies all logic that I am afflicted this way. Me, who aspires to be a Grycyryn! A Grycyryn!'

Suppressing a sob, Jsete spun around to face the wall.

'You really want to be with me?'

'I... No. What you say is absurd. I want you gone. Now! Say goodbye and go to your hut. Leave Mkeldi at first light. That way you help me rid myself of this appalling condition.' She glanced at Blakey. It was her eyes that betrayed her.

'I'm sorry I've made you miserable, Jsete. I've come to feel... a great deal of affection for you. I will be devastated if I leave with you sad. Tell me; what can I do for you? Anything.'

Jsete clasped her arms tightly about herself. 'No! You can't do anything! I have shivered for an undeserving man before. In some ways the feeling is strangely pleasant. A celebration of being a woman. Just leave me. You *must.* If you have any desire to make me happy, do that.' She turned her back on him.

He longed to reach out and hold her but feared her reaction. 'If that's what you want, I will go. I wish you every happiness, Jsete. You deserve it. You are an incredible woman. You honour your name. I can't tell you how much I admire you and how I appreciate what you've done for me.' He so very nearly confessed his love for her. 'You will surely be a fine Grycyryn. Goodbye.'

Jsete lowered her head and whispered a faint goodbye, but she would not face him.

For a time, Ross Blakey did not move, clinging to a hope she would ask him to stay. Or say something so they could hug. He would hold her for a long time. But she did not respond. He sighed, and headed briskly for the door, brushing past those seeking his company.

Blakey avoided the celebrating villagers; their joy irritated him. A day of triumph had ended miserably for both of Mkeldi village's heroes, who craved to be with one another. He should have told her he loved her. But he would soon be back on Earth. Maybe this sad parting was for the better.

In the hut, he flopped heavily onto his bed and undressed. And stared, miserable, at the hole-ridden roof.

ROSS BLAKEY WAS JOLTED from his restless sleep by the door flap being shoved aside. A figure, head low, and draped in a neck-to-ankle heavy blanket, stood in the doorway. A hand protruded from the folds of the blanket, holding a small fire stick that lit tumbling red hair. Jsete. He drew a breath.

'I cannot sleep, Rossblakey, though I crave so badly to,' Jsete wailed, as she drew the thick blanket even tighter around her and sat on his bed. 'I cannot get warm. Can I rest here and feel your warmth? But heed me, I seek your warmth and nothing more. When I am asleep, go to the hut with the yellow fire stick on the door. It is a short way along the path to the right. Hmm?'

Before Blakey could utter a stuttered reply, Jsete stabbed out the fire stick and threw her blanket over his bed. With a shiver, she flung away her tunic and, bare-shouldered and bare-chested, snuggled beside him. He wrapped his arms around her, ecstatic to have her lying beside him.

'My, you are cold,' he said good-naturedly. Wrong thing to say. When she tried to pull away, he held her firmly. 'Please. I cannot tell you how happy I am to have you here. Now relax and go to sleep.'

Jsete sighed. 'You are so warm. Do not forget; go to the other hut when I am asleep. At sunrise, go to the village square and you will be taken to your compound. Do not wake me. I must rest. With rest, I will be better able to deal with my affliction.'

'Jsete. You feel good.' She relaxed a little. The coldness of her was not so good. He didn't care. His heart was soaring.

'I am enjoying your warmth,' she said dreamily. Blakey nuzzled his head against her hair. 'Hmm. I didn't think you would be so...'

But she let the comment go.

JSETE STIRRED, now warm and pleasant beside him. He was sweating under the thick coverings. It was a small sacrifice. He cursed the coming of the dawn, which had to be all too near. Leaving Jsete would be one hell of a wrench.

'You are still here, Rossblakey,' Jsete whispered. 'You shouldn't be.'

'I must have fallen asleep, and awoken, the same time as you.' There are no lie detectors on Zygol III.

'It is almost dawn and I have rested. I will sleep again before I become cold. You can leave now.'

'I don't want to.' He drew her tightly against him.

Jsete became annoyed. Briefly, and not much. 'Go! You will be leaving for your compound soon.'

'Perhaps I will stay here longer.'

Jsete was silent for a few seconds. 'If you stay longer, you make it harder for me to shake off my affliction. Do not do that to me, Rossblakey. Besides, any time we spend together may end badly. Anyway, our Spmite told me you will return to your home planet as soon as you arrive at your compound. Is that so?'

'I won't have a choice. They will send me back to Earth for being away from the compound for so long. Without permission.'

She turned to face him. 'They will... banish you! That surely is an overly harsh judgement. After all, you were caught up with events that were mostly no fault of yours.'

'There won't be any judgement, Jsete. They will force me to leave.'

Jsete drew herself onto her elbow, facing him. 'What? Who makes these unjust decisions?'

Blakey thought for a few seconds. 'I suppose you could call him a Sklim.'

'Is your Sklim so cruel? You must not accept being banished, Rossblakey. Surely that is more in keeping with your ways.'

'My Sklim won't care what I think. And his... aktel will see that his orders are followed.'

Jsete became indignant. 'That is both unjust and illogical. If you leave, everything you have learnt about us Zygols would come to nothing. Along with the elapelc you have begun to adopt. Doesn't that mean anything to you, and to your people?'

Ross Blakey sighed. 'I will write up my thoughts when I am on Earth and pass them to my Sklim. That's the best I can do.'

Jsete was adamant. 'That is not so. If you wish to stay on my planet, our Spmite would demand you face independent judgement. The Zygol judges would surely support your wish to stay. You helped save a Zygol village, Rossblakey. And our Spmite can be very persuasive.'

He rubbed her back. 'My Sklim won't agree to a judgement.'

'Jkilm! Should he not agree, our Spmite will issue a challenge to your Sklim's rule. He resides in territory that belongs to the Three Villages after all. He would refuse at his own peril.'

Blakey conjured up an image of his thin, balding fifties-something, head manager. Faced with the sight of Alena stalking him, brandishing a kraxl-da, he would surely piss himself. 'He definitely won't agree to a challenge.'

'Then our Spmite will confront him, nevertheless. Do not think your fence of metal is capable of keeping her out of your compound.'

Blakey took a breath. 'That I believe. But, Jsete, she wants me off this planet.'

'You are wrong, Rossblakey. You are a hero, and she is your Spmite. She will approve of you staying. Well... perhaps keep your distance for a while. She told me that she could eventually come to tolerate you. Probably. But you need to demonstrate that you are evolving.'

'She'd tolerate me?'

Jsete sighed. 'Think, Rossblakey. Your elapelc with her, which you totally destroyed in the desert hills, only truly began when you accepted her right to punish you. Before that time, she despised you. That is true. Her reaction was understandable. You cannot expect her to trust you so swiftly.'

'But you think her attitude to me is changing?'

'Well, her attitude has the potential to change more. Elapelc demands it. Just as the first signs of my affliction also began when you deferred to her. Then, when you told me I was not obliged to bathe with you, I was overcome by this affliction. I tried to resist it.' She did not sound pleased. But her tone softened. 'So, realise, Rossblakey, our Spmite's attitude towards you will evolve as you evolve.' Jsete sighed. 'Oh, I am so conflicted. If only you had argued with her. She would have gladly had you bound to poles again. And I believe I would have avoided my annoying affliction.'

'You wanted me tied up? And you say you are compassionate!'

'But, Rossblakey,' Jsete's grin was visible in the near darkness, 'you would have been bound mostly in jest. Not out of malice. It would have been a lesson for you to strive harder to achieve elapelc. Surely you wouldn't take much offence to that.'

'That is a strange way of seeking elapelc.'

'Perhaps.' Jsete smiled. 'But it would be a response to someone who is as stubborn, and who takes life too seriously, as you do.' She shrugged 'But that is irrelevant now; you chose not to defy her. You showed her true elapelc. And then you did so to me. It was my undoing. Now, here I am. Desperately wanting you gone, yet wishing you could stay.' She turned away from him.

Well, it had been elapelc with Alena, much assisted by the twin blades of a kraxl-da and a kraxl.

'Does your display of elapelc mean nothing to you?' Jsete sighed. 'Do you not believe that, in time, you can learn to live in harmony among us? In time. Perhaps a lot of time. Yes, it will require patience on your part. And ours.'

'What? You want me to live on your planet?'

She turned to face him once more. 'Why not? Much good could come from you staying. For us as well as your people. You have shown us that we must embrace Tsalc more, as fickle as it is. I believe we have shown you how to embrace elapelc more. You can improve the understanding between our two peoples.'

Her longing was open before him. 'Stay if you wish. Do you not see the benefits of staying?'

One massive benefit was gazing into Blakey's eyes.

Jsete averted her eyes. 'I only ask you to consider staying. If you do not wish to stay, then go to the other hut. Now.' She tried to draw away from him. But he was not ready to let her go.

'But a Zygol in the Three Villages wants to do me harm.'

'You can ask any number of Zygols to mediate your conflict. And think: if you stay, you can teach our aktel the art of throwing stones.' She giggled. 'Maybe aspire to becoming a Grycyryn. That sounds ridiculous. And, it is, mostly. But saving a village is a good start. And you know our language. You would become a Grycyryn to consult when nothing makes any sense.'

'But I have children back on Earth. I have to see them.'

Jsete grinned. 'You would be granted full protection of movement at all times, Rossblakey. Full. Protection.'

'You can't promise that. If I go back to Earth, they only have to refuse to allow me to come back.'

Jsete laughed. 'Our Spmite will convince them to allow you back. Of that you can be assured.'

Blakey could foresee innumerable complications. If he stayed, he would need to learn a whole lot of new dance steps with Tsalc. And Tsalc was gazing at him through laughing, green eyes. Jsete, warm and alive in his arms, made thinking clearly really hard. Her eyes, her lips were so close. Blakey swallowed. Hell, she was an alien! If his mind was functioning, he would be bidding Jsete a sad and heartfelt goodbye and run, brokenhearted, to the other hut, rest if that was possible and, at dawn, be escorted to the mining compound.

Go back to Earth. Start again. Simple? No. It wasn't simple. There would be only different major hurdles. There were good reasons why he fled to Zygol III.

'But I keep making mistakes. You know I do. What if I keep making them?'

Jsete wriggled her torso in his arms. Her feet rested against the outside of his ankles. 'That is of no consequence. I will cut off your balls and feed them to a cfaldi.' For a few seconds there was silence. Then Jsete giggled. He chuckled with her. Sort of.

'Are you trying to convince me to stay? Or get me to leave?'

'I am nice and warm, Rossblakey,' Jsete whispered as she drew him further into her arms. If he was to escape, it had to be there and then. With his free hand, Blakey stroked her smooth shoulders, then her back. He liked the feel of her. He liked the way she let him know with her body and her soft breath that she enjoyed his touch. Blakey kissed her cheek and nuzzled her neck. She sighed and ran her hands over his arms and shoulders. If only his tired body could conjure a reserve of energy.

'Curb your expectations, Jsete. Caressing you is all I can manage. I am too sore and too exhausted to do anything more.'

'You think so,' she whispered in his ear. She began stroking him with fluid, strong motions, dwelling on his strength. 'I want more of your warmth, Rossblakey.'

Jsete seemed quite warm enough. 'Listen, I am not capable of anything more.' Jsete eagerly basked in Blakey's arms. Her lips demanded he kiss her. She felt so good. Blakey nuzzled his forehead into her hair. She liked that. He no longer heard the muted sound of the villagers celebrating.

'Tell me,' she cooed in his ear, 'what is Tsalc telling you to do? It will soon be morning. You must decide.' She began stroking him once more.

Fleeing was no longer an option. 'You are very persuasive, Jsete.'

'I should warn you,' she panted. 'Some people say that I can be… can be… difficult.'

'And some people say that I have the mind of a plooglit.'

Jsete giggled. She kept stroking him. His chest. His legs. Gentle, flowing strokes that occasionally dwelt to grasp, ever-so-gently, at his muscles.

He caressed her curves.

Jsete's lips parted. He kissed her. And again. And again.

'Well, I'll be!' Blakey exclaimed as he realised he might be able to, after all.

Jsete, well aware of the change that was taking place, arched her back so that her small, but well-formed breasts filled Blakey's vision. Then she pulled him and the blanket down over her.

Two plooglits leapt onto the roof of their hut. They dashed hither and thither, climbed, then frolicked, shaking leaves and limbs, causing the fragile ceiling to quiver. Such is the way of plooglits.

ZYGOL GLOSSARY

WHILE THE AUTHOR IS, overall, content to allow readers to pronounce the following words as they see fit, one exception needs to be made. The word Zygol should be pronounced as Psi-goal and not Sea-gull, which is a seabird.

TERMS

Ahk: A water container the size of a human torso, made of uckliablaht hide.

Aktel: Defender(s) of the six elements (see later). An aktel is primarily a warrior or guard, though an aktel can also defend the first five elements by pursuing many callings in life, such as teacher, trainer or official. An aktel wears a crimson tunic.

Arak-zook: When a Zookspmate or Spmite has risen to his or her rank after being a Grycyryn-da (see later), he or she selects an Arak-zook from the rank of Dsolcspmite (preferably one who had been a Spmite or Zookspmate). When, for example, a new Spmite is chosen from the rank of Grycyryn-da, an Arak-zook is selected by her as her advisor on matters dealing with aktel and with a Zookspmate, who was a Dsolcspmite (see later). An Arak-zook has a crimson uniform that sports both a wide orange and blue or green sash.

Cfaldi: This predator, when fully grown, is taller than a man. It is strongly built and somewhat resembles a werewolf with its oversized, wolf-like head that contains long, sharp teeth. It is comfortable when walking upright on its powerful hind legs, though is just as adept when moving on all fours. It also has two, short but strong, clawed arms. Cfaldi dwell mostly in the rugged, often semi-desert, hills.

Chageen: A batlike, flying animal that eats mostly 'insects,' or vegetation. However, it has been known to become voraciously carnivorous on rare occasion.

Clundrn: Bowl-like cup.

Dsolcspmite: A man or woman selected from the ranks of Safi based on past heroic deeds and performance at the rigorous Succession Games (see later). Dsolcspmites choose to pursue the pathway of a warrior, rather than the pathway of a Grycyryn. They wear a green tunic with a crimson streak in the shape of a lightning bolt.

Elapelc: The process whereby people (and nature) evolve to discover harmony with one another. This change may be subconscious. Along with knowing the six elements, elapelc is one pathway to achieving wisdom and maturity.

Grycyryn: A rank achieved by Safis during Succession Games (see later), marking someone noted for being wise. They are often advisors, teachers or officials and act as judges. A Grycyryn may be male or female. They dress in simple orange tunics, though some specialists may wear a tunic with a design.

Grycyryn-da: A highly respected and knowledgeable Grycyryn. They also dress in simple orange tunics.

Kraxl: A dagger with a thin blade.

Kraxl-da: A short, broad sword.

Opitek: Knowledge without wisdom; considered to lead to dangerous, selfish, or rudderless thinking if not curbed.

Pfin: The emerald-green top worn by a Spmite who has been selected from the rank of Dsolcspmite. The pfin and zain (see later) are covered by a green see-through gossamer-like slitted wrap-around of the same colour.

Plooglit: An agile and moronic lemur-like animal, about the size of a small, thin dog but with stronger hind legs. It is equally adept on the ground, in trees or rocky terrain. From a young age, plooglits become periodic companions to uckliablahts. They deposit a substance referred to as plooglit piss (see following) by Earth people, on their companion uckliablahts or on vegetation uckliablahts are liable to brush against.

Plooglit Piss: This is not urine. Rather, it is the substance a plooglit generates from glands around its belly, particularly when it is on the back of uckliablahts or on vegetation that an uckliablaht is likely to brush against. The substance somehow soothes uckliablahts. While Zygols are not affected by the substance, Earth humans find it very itchy for some days.

Safi: A male or female leader of a group of aktel, selected by peers at Succession Games. A Safi can choose to pursue any aspect of the first five elements (as can any aktel). Safis sport a gold streak across their crimson uniform.

Sklim: The 'mayor' in a town or village, usually selected from the rank of Grycyryn. This person wears a brown tunic with an orange stripe.

Six Elements: These cornerstones of Zygol life, along with elapelc, are the essential philosophical tools on Zygol III associated with the seeking of guidance with life's decisions (though they are not always definitive). Briefly, the elements are: 1) justice and integrity; 2) compassion and caring; 3) learning and teaching; 4) strength and agility of mind and body; 5) courage and application. The sixth element is the mysterious Tsalc (see later).

Spmite: The foremost female rank designated to protect the six elements and promote the obtaining of wisdom. A Spmite obtains her rank through past notable deeds and the Succession Games, which are held every two years. A Spmite may be chosen either from the Grycyryn or Dsolcspmite stream. A Spmite who was a Dsolcspmite wears a green pfin and zain; if she was a Grycyryn, she wears a green tunic with an orange streak and will appoint an Arak-zook. She has joint control of aktel, along with a Zookspmate, who is her equal.

Steent: A soft-shelled, dark-brown insect, the size of a large grain of rice, that usually lives under trees and assists with the decomposing of waste. The steent breed profusely in toilets and, for example, uckliablaht pens.

Succession Games: A competition designed to select Safis, Grycyryn, Dsolcspmites, Spmites and Zookspmates. The competition covers events across the entire spectrum of the six elements and also involves the consideration of previous deeds of note. The process is designed so that when individuals with particular skills are chosen for the higher ranks, it becomes increasingly difficult for a person of the opposite sex, who has identical skills, to qualify. As such, if a Zookspmate comes from the rank of Grycyryn, it is highly likely that the Spmite will be chosen from the rank of Dsolcspmite.

Tsalc: Chance, luck or the unforeseen. It is the mysterious 'sixth' element' of Zygol philosophy and culture. Though considered to be fickle in nature, Tsalc is to be embraced in the same way as are the other five elements.

Uckliablaht: This creature is bull-sized but is longer along the back and resembles a cross between a hippopotamus, a camel, gorilla and a hyena, only that it is totally different. It walks on four limbs, with particularly strong hind legs, but also has two much thinner and shorter armlike limbs protruding from its shoulders. It is mostly vegetarian.

Zain: Emerald-coloured long shorts worn by a Spmite who was formerly a Dsolcspmite. The Spmite carries her talisman in a pouch in her zain.

Zookspmate: The foremost male rank designated to protect the six elements and encourage the obtaining of wisdom. The Zookspmate is selected by past notable deeds and by means of the Succession Games. A Zookspmate is appointed for two years. If the Zookspmate was a Dsolcspmite, he wears a blue (waist-long) pfin and zain; if he was a Grycyryn, he wears a blue uniform with a large orange streak. If he was a Grycyryn, he will select an Arak-zook to assist with his dealings with aktel and with a Spmite, who is his equal.

COMING IN 2021

Copyright © 2020 Evan Jones
By Ian Aisch

The Bird of Paradise Tree and Other Stories

An alien tree with telepathic powers that emits a spectacular light show is obstructing a major earthmoving project. Earth law protects it, as does the botanist, Ben Starkey. But he, and this planet, are a long way from Earth.

Lieutenant Louise Attley is dispatched to the desert to record and decipher the language of visitors from a distant galaxy. The authorities want access to the visitors' technology. The visitors, though, are obsessed by planet Earth's pollution.

A teenage boy wins a singing competition in his small town, allowing him to audition at the Rock and Blues Music Academy. He sits in a waiting room with kids dressed in glitz. He, like them, intends to perform that massive hit of the late 2020s, sung by the embodiment of glitz, Lorna Kiss and Jason Tell.

These stories, and more are presented in this collection of sci-fi tales that showcase Ian Aisch's imagination. Here is an excerpt from this title.

'Good morning Zally,' Starkey spoke to the tree. That he could converse with a being unable to hear, never ceased to astound him. Neither Zally nor he could explain how it could be so. Only strong winds blocked their conversation. 'Hearing is like feeling the wind,' he had told the tree, 'with that wind carrying to us words.'

'Good morning, Key to the Stars,' came the cheerful thought. 'Thank you for your gift of water.' The words were formed, distinct, inside Starkey's head, as if the tree was playing a verbal tune within his mind. At the beginning, Starkey found this somewhat disconcerting, but to the scientist and explorer he was, his overwhelming reaction was surprised exhilaration. He was actually conversing with an alien being in his own language. Such a phenomenon had to be impossible. But, somehow, it wasn't. Starkey needed to speak; it did not respond to his thoughts, even when directed at the tree, by name. That he found comforting.

'Thank you for your gift of shade. I'll be glad when the rains come again. It has barely rained since the big flood. The grass and plants need to grow to help protect the land from being washed away.' Zally understood. What the tree found odd was that Starkey did not wish to bask in the sheer joy of the energy-giving sun. Inexplicably, he had no roots.

'The rains will also raise many of my kind from the dormant state they were forced to revert to.'

'I look forward to that happening. The valley will be joyful once more.'

His mind became filled with warmth. It was Zally's equivalent of a smile. 'I tell you again; Key to the Stars, even if the water in the pond becomes far less than it is now, it will only cause us to drop a branch or two. And, if we have prolonged dryness, we can… hibernate…

because we can store water and nutrition within our roots for a long time. But your gesture of giving water is welcome.'

Starkey chuckled.

'Why do you laugh Key to the Stars?'

The botanist stroked his chin. 'I can't help it. I'll never get used to the name you've given me, no matter how many times I hear it.'

'Yes, I understand it is a name you inherited from those who gave you life. It is not supposed to have any meaning. Yet, to me, it has great meaning.'

'A key reveals something that is hidden, as you explained to me. So you are a key. You tell me about the universe that I could never discover. I find that knowledge enjoyable, even if it is not entirely necessary. As for the stars, you experience them with the senses you have. But you cannot experience the pleasure they bring to my kind. Their soft energy sweeps slowly and gently across me. I bask in them. As I do with the sun, especially, and the moon, the rain and wind.'

'I wish I could feel what you do, Zally. I can only appreciate the stars in my inadequate human way.'

'I, too, wish that you could. I can't imagine having so little feeling as you have.'

The first contact between human and tree had happened a day after the massive debris-filled torrent, tore the narrow valley apart. From the cave, Starkey had tearfully gazed down at the devastation. He'd set off to inspect the nearby pond where he often sat in the shade, composing his notes. Reading them back to himself. A crushing blow confronted him. The two largest trees had been swept away. In their place was a dump of rubble, gravel and mud that spread across the width of the cleft in the hill. This new barrier was causing the water level in the pond to rise; the lower trunks of the four remaining trees stood in water.

As Starkey lamented the loss of the two trees, he felt an unexplained sense of what had to be alarm. Then, without having any conscious intent, he'd waded into the pond and began clawing urgently at the new debris with his bare hands until the water began spilling into the valley. With his hands bruised and bloodied, and gasping for breath, he kept clawing desperately at the barrier, stopping only when the trees stood on dry land. He felt a strange ecstasy. As he panted for breath and examined the blood dripping from his torn hands, his mind became cluttered. It made him wince in discomfort. Then, his mind cleared. Distinct words formed in his head.

'What are you?' Starkey had spun around, expecting to see... he didn't know what. 'What are you?' the words formed again.

'I call myself a human. I am from a planet called Earth. Show yourself,' Starkey blurted. He backed away fearful, tripping into the pond.

'I am beside the water that we feared might engulf us,' came the hesitant reply. 'Thank you for helping us.'

Wide-eyed, Starkey swore. He had to be insane. He opted to do what only an insane man would do; he pursued a notion that was surely impossible. And he found Zalltextrophene. Zally.

ZYGOL BOOKS

To order a book from Zygol Books, please visit www.zygolbooks.com.au or ebay.com.au. It is expected that ebook versions will also become available through Amazon.

ABOUT THE AUTHOR

Ian Aisch was born in Tremadog, North Wales. His early childhood was spent in nearby Penrhyndeudraeth. A little way up the hill from his home, heritage steam trains from the Ffestiniog Railway chugged by. His father worked in the local gunpowder works. Shortly after Ian turned seven, his family took up the £10 offer to migrate to Australia, settling in Echuca. He studied sociology and politics at Monash University before becoming a public servant, first in Canberra and then Melbourne. He became an editor at Lonely Planet, on the back of his deep love of travel.

Ian is now a full-time author and lives in Victoria's Macedon Ranges.

Thanks need to go to the cafés in Woodend, and the Top of the Range Café on Mt Macedon, where many of these words were written. An especially huge thanks goes to the Woodend Library where most of the writing took place. Thanks also go to the many holiday destinations Ian visited, particularly Byron Bay, where many of the ideas for how the story would unfold came together. Another deep thank you goes to Holgate's Brewhouse, though very little writing was done there.

ACKNOWLEDGMENTS

The glitches with the layout are either the fault of the author or the limitations of the layout package. However you regard this book, it would have been a lesser work if it had not been for the help of the following; Josephine Burnell, AC Collins, Imelda Cribbin. Ebony McKenna, and Louisa West.

www.ingramcontent.com/pod-product-compliance
Lightning Source LLC
Chambersburg PA
CBHW070554120726
47909CB00007B/2342